Prologue

July 31, 1878

The young woman walked through the woods, soft summer wind caressing her face. Startled out of her daydream by a sound, she stopped for a moment, listening intently. Hearing nothing, she walked on. Her destination was the Lawrence family farm, for a rare evening of gossip with her friend Erin. Stopping in a clearing she spread her shawl on the ground to sit for a brief rest. A pair of legs, clad in dusty black pants and familiar boots appeared in her line of sight. She looked up quizzically, but the sun blocked all but a dim outline of the man's features.

When he spoke, she realized who he was. "Hello Isabelle, it's a beautiful day, isn't it?" She moved to stand, suddenly feeling small and vulnerable. He allowed her to get to her knees, then roughly pushed her back to the ground. Her terrified mind registered no surprise. She knew that she had let her guard down. He dragged a stunned Isabelle off the path and into the thicker woods, out of sight. She began to twist and kick when she saw the knife glinting in his hand. "Please, I'll do whatever you want, you don't need to force me!" He laughed at her plea. "Do you think I mean to take you by force, Isabelle? I would never do that! I'm a gentleman!" Confusion, and a small flicker of relief crossed Isabelle's face.

A moment later, she froze as cold steel touched her neck. The blade sliced through the delicate skin of her neck, and she felt warmth trickling down her chest. There was very little pain. Her eyes lifted from the man's strangely handsome face before her, as her gaze turned skyward. Storm clouds were gathering, the sun all but gone now. She could feel the tug of the blade, rending her flesh, but mercifully, she felt no pain. The first fat drops of rain hit the soil around her. Night was falling. Isabelle felt the hard ground beneath her and understood that she had been left for dead, and in fact would soon likely be. She could feel the rain on her face, falling into her open eyes. Then she felt nothing.

Present Day

Chapter 1 - Thursday

A winter storm had threatened the Portland, Maine waterfront all morning. Safe in her second-floor office and working with single-minded intensity, Jade Danner was only vaguely aware of the violent tempest building just outside her window.

At 38, Jade was one of the best antique appraisers in the business. In this historically male-dominated field, Jade's quiet expertise had earned her an excellent reputation. Her warm, engaging manner was the perfect compliment to her quirky sense of humor and her sharp mind. People had always told her how lovely she was, but it wasn't something she worked at. A little blush and eye shadow, a quick comb through her straight blonde hair, and she was good to go. In spite of her casual approach to beauty (or maybe because of it), Jade was consistently noticed by the opposite sex, but she often seemed unaware of it.

Even though she hadn't yet found her special someone, Jade was a happy person who enjoyed her life. She was thankful, every day, that she was doing something she loved to do, and making a good living at it. She believed that, if she was fated to marry, and to raise children, it would eventually be so.

Jade completed her morning's work and placed her finished appraisal report in her outbox. She peeled off her latex gloves and tossed them into the waste can beside her desk. Finally, she thought, she was ready to work on an assignment for which she had been waiting days. With a happy sigh, Jade donned a fresh pair of gloves and made a beeline to the vault at the back of her office. She emerged from the vault carrying a breadbox-sized wooden crate.

Jade always did her assignments in the order they were received, and she had been thinking about this assignment as she completed the several jobs that had been received prior to this one. Placing the wooden crate on her desk, she used a small crowbar to carefully pull the top off the box. She then pulled the sides of the box away, one by one. She stood back and looked at it. It was wooden jewelry case, with inlaid gems. The work order identified it as a Lawrence family heirloom. It was stunning! Jade's excitement grew as she realized the pictures she had seen didn't do it justice. Her task would be to authenticate the age and origin of the case, then to prepare an appraisal report. Green eyes sparkling, Jade eagerly got to work.

Several minutes later, she had determined that, not only was the case authentic, it was going to appraise very well, if she could authenticate the provenance. She took a few moments to admire the detail work, turning the case over in her hands. On the underside of the case, Jade saw the initials "WBL" carved into the wood and underlined in gold gilt. A tag, brown and stiff with age, was tied to the top hinge of the box with an ancient piece of twine.

Jade spent a few moments working out the faded writing on the tag. The case had apparently been shipped from Maine to the United Kingdom, "FOB" in 1873, then back again, later in the year. "FOB", Jade knew, meant "free on board", i.e., that the transportation fee and taxes had been paid. The gold gilding bisected, almost precisely, the bottom of the case. Curious, Jade gently traced the golden line with a latex-gloved thumbnail. To her amazement, the case parted slightly to reveal a secret compartment!

Jade pressed her thumb into the parted edges more firmly. The opening in the bottom of the box broadened and a piece of yellowed, tattered paper dropped from the opening and seesawed lazily to the floor. Jade stepped back, watched the paper land, then bent to retrieve it. As soon as her fingers touched the paper, a feeling of unreality washed over her. For just a moment, she suddenly felt as though she were someone else. A series of odd images flickered quickly through her mind. The images were so brief that she couldn't fully register them. But what she felt in that short moment caused Jade to recoil in panic, both physically and mentally. She dropped the note on her desk and, with relief, she could feel the strangeness, the "other-ness" that had possessed her a moment ago begin to recede.

Using a pair of tongs, Jade gingerly picked up the ancient document again. On one side of the note, she saw a symbol. It looked like the number eight. Jade recalled from her college studies that this symbol was called a Möbius strip. Sometimes, she remembered, they were pictured as a ring, which is considered to be one-sided. Often, however, they were depicted as a twisted ring, also one-sided, as this one was. This Möbius had a lidless eye drawn inside one of the loops and a droplet inside the other. Jade turned the note over. The other side contained three lines of very faint, hand-written text. Still using the tongs, she moved the paper closer to her face, trying, in vain, to make out the words.

Jade was suddenly consumed with a need to find out what the text said. She remembered her mother telling her, when she was very small, that she had the soul of a detective. She remembered giggling at the image of a tiny, blonde and pig-tailed Sherlock Holmes. Jade knew her mother was right, she was irresistibly drawn to mysterious things like this. That quality, among others, made her so good at what she did. Jade continued to study the note, but could not decipher it. She examined the paper itself, as well as the writing style, and quickly reviewed several of her reference volumes, but she was unable to get any useful information about the text itself.

The jewelry case sat on the desk, forgotten for the moment, as Jade continued her examination of the note. She was able to determine, from the watermark, that the paper was an ubiquitous brand used between the late 1850's and the early 1880's. An hour passed, unnoticed. Outside, the storm slowly lost momentum. The blowing snow gradually gave way to quiet gray skies, pierced by shafts of soft winter sunlight. Disappointed with her lack of progress on the note, Jade placed the sheet of yellowed paper in her desk drawer, and locked it. She resolutely turned her attention back to the small wooden jewelry case.

As she worked, however, her mind continued turning over the mystery of the note. She knew she should reference the note in her report and return it to the owner of the case. As usual, her curious nature was at odds with her sense of propriety. She knew that it was likely that the family's representative who requested the appraisal had no idea the note existed. Jade's instinctive fear once again tried to weigh in on the issue, begging that she just put the note back and leave it. She decided that, once she figured out what the note said (and she *would,* she thought firmly), any message of consequence would dutifully be relayed to the Lawrence family. Having made a decision with which her conscience could live, Jade turned back to her work in earnest.

An hour later, Jade had secured and authenticated the documentation related to the jewelry case and had completed her detailed review of the item itself. As she signed the third and final copy of her appraisal report, Jade looked up to see her boss, Malcolm Remerick, approaching her office with a smile on his broad, pleasant face. Malcolm was a large man, with uncommonly large hands. Looking at him, you'd never guess the gentle reverence with which he performed his work. Jade knew how fortunate she was to be working for an antique appraiser of his caliber. He was also the best boss she ever had. Jade was still astounded that he had hired her, a relative unknown in the business, on the word of their mutual friend, Diane Venezia.

Malcolm exuded charm and gracious style. His partner, Dominic, was also in the antique furniture business, but his specialty was furniture restoration. Dominic and Malcolm often worked together, and referrals back and forth between them were common. Jade understood and shared their love of the distant past and the ability to appreciate and cherish objects from another age.

"How are things going with the Lawrence case?" Malcolm asked, his Australian accent in endearing evidence.

Jade smiled. "I'm just finishing it up now. It's worth a small fortune! I've never seen detail work that good. The gems are also of very high quality and in excellent condition". Jade handed Malcolm two of the three appraisal copies, retaining one for her file. Malcolm quickly reviewed the last page of the report, where the final appraisal figure was listed. Jade had already done the math to determine Remerick & Company's profit for her work, and, of course, based on that, her own commission.

"Well this is a nice day's work, isn't it?" Malcolm asked with a grin.

Jade smiled at Malcolm's retreating figure. "Beats flipping burgers."

She realized that she still had the note from the jewelry case, in her desk drawer. She decided to hold on to it for awhile, to see if she could figure out the message. She tried, unsuccessfully, to tell herself that her decision to keep the note, even for the time being, was not influenced by the weird pull of the thing.

At 4:30, Jade logged out of her computer and put on her jacket. She was still thinking about the three lines of text on the note. The idea of taking the note home with her made her feel uncomfortable, which was only partly explained by the potential impropriety of doing so. She also didn't want to touch it again, she realized with dismay. She feared a repeat of that strange feeling that had come over her earlier.

Shrugging back out of her coat, Jade grabbed her ceramic tongs and used them to retrieve the yellowed note from her desk drawer. She slipped the note into a plastic sheet protector, and made two photocopies of it. She put the copies into her briefcase, and locked the original note back inside her desk drawer. Jade put her coat back on, grabbed her briefcase, and walked briskly out into the waning winter sunlight.

Chapter 2

At her front door, Jade put her key in the lock and immediately heard scrambling and whining from the other side of the door.

"Bardo!," she exclaimed playfully. She listened for a moment, smiling as the scrambling from the other side of the door became more frantic. Jade opened the door and slipped inside.

Looking down at her Jack Russell she said, "Sit!" She laughed as Bardo sat, looking at her pleadingly, his nubby little tail sweeping the floor. Jade pulled a doggie treat from the little bag in her pocket and threw it up in the air. Bardo jumped, caught it on the way down and sat, crunching happily.

Heading to the kitchen, Bardo at her heel, Jade sorted quickly through her mail. She dropped her coat and purse on a kitchen chair, and put her mail on the table to open later. Jade gave Bardo fresh food and water, then turned on the television. She always listened to the world news report while she did her evening chores. Part of the allure of her mostly solitary life, she knew, was that she could do whatever she wanted, whenever she wanted.

Jade's simple dinner consisted of a PB&J sandwich and the remaining coffee from her Thermos. While devouring her sandwich, Jade listened to the messages on her answering machine. Her mother had called to invite her to a birthday party for her brother, on Saturday. Jade made a mental note to think up a plausible excuse to get out of it. Her sister Phyllis had also left a message. In an almost comically long-suffering voice, Phyllis talked about how disappointed she was that Jade did not attend her niece's Kindergarten graduation ceremony the night before. Jade rewarded her sister's recorded diatribe with an eye roll, and made a mental note to call Phyllis back to explain why she was not able to attend. After, of course, she came up with a suitable reason. Her relationship with her family put her more in mind of "The Simpsons" than "The Waltons".

After dinner, she retrieved one of the photocopies of the jewelry box note from her briefcase. She spent a few minutes re-examining the text. It looked like English, but the writing was extremely ornate. The ink was dark and blotted in some areas, almost invisible in others. The note was written in overtly feminine longhand script, and penned many years ago as each "s" looked like a large, stylized letter "f". Jade knew that, given time, she'd likely work out most of the message.

She studied each letter of the note, in turn, to get a sense of how certain letters were written. A few of the letters were obvious, but others continued to puzzle her.

Jade looked at the clock and was shocked to realize she'd been at it for almost an hour. With several other chores to do before bedtime, she put the copy aside, resolving to pick up where she left off tomorrow. Entering the kitchen, Jade saw Bardo snuggled in his basket next to the stove. He looked up at her, a little accusingly, she thought. Usually she spent much more time with him in the evening. She knelt down in front of him and rubbed his ears. Eyes closed, Bardo smiled in his happy-doggy way and Jade knew that she was forgiven for her momentary confusion of priorities. When she started up the stairs to bed, Bardo crawled out of his kitchen basket and dutifully followed her.

Jade's Friday morning passed quickly, as she completed an appraisal on a crystal dollhouse. At a few minutes before noon, her telephone rang. The caller ID said "Diane's Treasures". Diane and Jade had been best friends since Jade finished college in Massachusetts and moved back to Maine to work in the appraising business. It was Diane who had hooked Jade up with Remerick & Company. Several years ago, Diane's parents were killed in a car accident. Since then, Jade and Diane had grown closer. Jade had given her a special nickname, "PD", which stood for "Postal Diane", in honor of her highly dramatic nature.

She picked up the phone, "Hey PD! How are you!?"

Diane's voice sounded upbeat. "Hey yourself! Got time for some lunch today?" Jade checked her desk calendar, then made arrangements to meet Diane at the Sportsman's Grill in half an hour.

When she got there, Diane was already in their favorite booth in the 3rd dining room. Jade stood in line, behind several other people, waiting to be seated. Diane hadn't spotted her yet. She watched Diane, seated several tables away, as she waited. Diane was two years younger than she, and looked younger, even, than that. Diane's piercing hazel eyes shone from her slightly-freckled pixie face, framed by long, thick dark hair. Diane hugged Jade over the table as they sat down. As usual, they both ordered lasagna. After the waitress left, Jade glanced over at Diane and found her beaming back at her.

"What's up, girlfriend? You look like the cat that ate the canary!" Diane did look about to burst.

She said, "Jade, I've met the most wonderful man!"

Jade put on a playfully skeptical look. "Oh really?"

Diane stuck her bottom lip out in an exaggerated pout. "Stop it, this time I really mean it!"

Jade relented, smiling. "Well if you're that sure, he *must* be special". Diane nodded, then launched into what was now a familiar tale.

She had met Bruce on-line, through a dating site two weeks ago. They met up at the Border's bookstore coffee shop and hit it off right away. For their second date, they went out to dinner, then saw a movie together, last weekend. Diane was now looking forward to their third date, which would be this coming weekend.

Jade, of course, had to tease Diane about what's supposed to happen on the third date. "You know, of course, that certain things will be expected of the two of you on your next date?" Diane shot Jade a confused expression.

Jade went on, "Surely you understand that dating etiquette requires that the two of you consummate the relationship on the third date?" Diane's mischievous expression told Jade that this expectation wasn't going to be a problem.

Diane explained that Bruce was going to pick her up Saturday afternoon for a trip to North Conway for some shopping. Diane planned to pack an overnight bag, just in case. Jade smiled at her friend's obvious excitement, but she also felt a slight prickle of unease.

"Diane, what do you know about this man? Where does he live?"

She rolled her eyes exaggeratedly, surprising a laugh from Jade, and answered, "He lives in Falmouth. I have the address, but I haven't been there yet. He's picked me up for our other two dates, and he's going to pick me up at 3:00 Saturday, right after I close up shop."

Her excitement over her new man was infectious, and although Jade enjoyed listening to Diane's enthusiastic chatter, it reminded her of how alone she was. After a few minutes, Diane noticed Jade's silence and her flood of words slowed. Jade tried to smile, tried to look happy for her, but she knew Diane wasn't buying it.

Diane sighed heavily, obviously deciding to take the bull by the horns. She said, "Jade, you are such an awesome lady. I just wish you would try harder to find someone to share your life. I know you aren't into on-line dating, but there are other ways to meet nice eligible men."

Jade was touched by her friend's concern. "I know you're right, Diane. I'm just so busy, and most days, my life is fine. I'm just not in the market to complicate my life right now".

Diane looked knowingly at her old friend. "How much of your reluctance is because you still equate love with eventual heartbreak?"

Jade shifted uncomfortably. Diane knew her too well, and loved her too much for Jade to evade the truth, or the question. "Most of it, I imagine".

Diane nodded. "J, you and I both know I'd walk through fire for you. I know you don't want to open old wounds but I just have to say this."

Diane took a deep breath and looked at her best friend, all the love she felt for her showing clearly in her eyes. "I can't imagine how hard it must have been for you to give up your child, twenty years ago. You and I both know you did the right thing for both you and your son. I remember your tears when you told me about it. Then, when you met Craig, I was so happy for you. Since you both had just finished college, it seemed the perfect time. Then, when you found out that Craig wasn't who you thought he was, I remember how devastated you were. I was afraid you would never recover. But you have, and you will continue to recover, if you let it happen.

"You've done fantastic things with your life since then. I just hope you will allow yourself to trust again. I know that there's an amazing man out there for you, who has the power to coax you out of your safe little world. I want your promise that you will be open enough to the idea to recognize him when you see him." Jade readily agreed, if only to stop the discussion from centering around her non-existent love life.

Back at the office, Jade decided to take a few minutes to once again look over the text of her "mystery note". She unlocked the drawer and retrieved the note, still in the clear sheet protector. Looking at the text, so dark in some places and light in others, she thought of something that may help to clarify the message. She photocopied the note again, but this time she set the copier to provide a few very dark, and also a few very light, copies. Jade resisted the urge to look at the new copies now. Duty called. She reluctantly put the handful of new copies in her briefcase, carefully re-locked the original note into her center desk drawer, and got back to work.

Checking the Remerick & Company website, Jade found several responses to inquiries she had sent out last week. The information she received allowed her to complete the research on a few pending assignments. As she worked, she thought about what Diane had said at lunch. She knew, as little as she wanted to hear it, that Diane was right, she had a lot to share and would like to someday have that opportunity. She resolved to do exactly as she promised. She *would* be open to the possibility of finding love.

At 4:30, Jade cleared her work space, logged off her computer and put on her coat. A quick look out the window confirmed that it was already getting dark. And it was snowing. Again. Winter in Maine lasted at least 6 months, it seemed, and they weren't half way through it.

Standing at her office window, needing brief respite from the dreary day, Jade's mind hit the play button on her favorite winter fantasy. She was sitting in a lawn chair, in her bikini, on a beautiful tropical island, sipping a chocolate milkshake that was being held for her by, who else? Nicholas Cage. The fantasy had many moving parts. Sometimes she was naked. Sometimes the milkshake was a mimosa. Sometimes she was being attended (in whatever way she needed at the moment) by Stephen King or Dean Koontz, or both.

With a heavy sigh, Jade reluctantly slipped back to reality. She packed three of her historic reference books into her briefcase to do some research at home. The crisp, snowy breeze blew away her fatigue, and she found herself looking forward to the weekend and the warmth and comfort of home.

Chapter 3

"Jade, darling, please just be reasonable?! Why do we always have to beg you to come to family gatherings? It would mean so much to your brother if you would be there to share his birthday!" Jade listened with barely contained impatience as her mother shamelessly wheedled. With a sigh, Jade decided to give in, to avoid World War III - the Family Version.

She waited until her mother stopped to take a breath, then flawlessly timed her interjection. "OK, mom, I'll shift some things around and I'll be there. But I can't stay very long". Bardo was laying beside her on the couch. He looked up at her, his knowing expression mocking her for her quick capitulation.

Having gotten her way, her mother's tone immediately brightened. "Excellent! It'll be nice to see you. I don't see enough of you these days, honey."

Jade smiled in spite of herself. It's always nice to feel needed. Jade asked, "Will Dad be there?"

Her mother's voice took on a slightly melancholy tone. "I hope he will. He's teaching a psychology class at the University this semester and he has a study group every Saturday night until 7:00. He said he'd be late, but he'd try to make it."

Jade could feel her mother's disappointment. "Mom, he's GOT to be almost done teaching now, I thought he was retiring after the summer semester?"

Her mother said, "Yes, that was the plan. But when the school asked for his help, he just couldn't say no. He said, 'Agatha, I'm bored silly, and I know I'm under foot. This won't take much of my time, I promise'. Jade, he looked like a kid begging his mother to let him go out to play. I just didn't have the heart to remind him about his promise to retire." Agatha was silent for a moment, lost in thought, then continued more briskly, "Anyway, I'm glad so glad you'll be there." Her mother's voice suddenly dropped in volume. "You know how much trouble Peter has had this past year. I'm sure that, if the police had found the murder weapon, Peter would probably be in jail right now, even though he had nothing to do with that poor young woman's death last winter. Thank goodness all that's over now."

Her mother's uncharacteristic candor surprised Jade, as the "incident" last winter had seemed all but buried in their already burgeoning graveyard of family secrets. Jade felt a sudden premonitory chill, and her mind was drawn back to the mysterious note she had found in the jewelry case. She had no idea why her mind would insist on connecting these two unrelated but equally disquieting things.

Jade promised to be at her parents' house at the appointed hour tomorrow, and dutifully wrote down the Saturday evening party in her day planner as soon as she hung up the phone. Now, she thought grimly, what to get Peter for a gift…Soap on a rope? Always popular for prison-bound men. No, she'd better not. There was an outside chance her mom would figure out the meaning of the gift and blow a head gasket. Jade sometimes wondered what kind of cruel God would give only one member of a family a sense of humor. She supposed she'd better get Peter some new socks, or maybe, at the absolute most mischievous, a nose-hair trimming kit.

Jade remembered how frightened her mother had been when the police came, late last winter, and had taken Peter away in handcuffs. Apparently a woman had been stabbed to death two days before, on the waterfront, and Peter had had the bad luck to be clubbing in the Old Port area, on the waterfront, that night. Someone had seen a man matching Peter's description, arguing with the woman in question.

Subsequent examination of the victim's wounds by the medical examiner indicated that the murder weapon was a knife with a very unusual double-serrated blade. The police hadn't found the murder weapon, and didn't have enough evidence to formally charge Peter, so he was released 24 hours later. It seemed to Jade that, in her parent's eyes, Peter could never do something so heinous. But Jade knew Peter in ways her parents did not, and she didn't share their seemingly unconditional confidence in his innocence.

Growing up, Jade and Peter had little in common. Jade was five years younger. What she remembered most about Peter when they were children was Peter's ability to present one face to their parents, and to be a completely different person when their parents weren't around. He was a strange and lonely child. Jade, on the other hand, had always been happy and loving. These very traits resulted in her becoming a target for Peter and his constant frustration.

Jade's most vivid childhood memory of Peter was something about which her parents still knew nothing. It happened just before Jade turned 13. Jade's birthday was a few weeks after Peter's, so birthday plans were being made for Peter, and soon after, Jade knew, her own birthday plans could begin. Jade remembered being almost unbearably excited to be becoming a teenager. Sullen and often argumentative, Peter had told his parents he didn't want a party. So they didn't give him one. Jade's mom baked a cake, there were presents for Peter, but it was a very low-key celebration. Jade remembered that Peter acted like he didn't want to be there, and he had escaped his birthday celebration as soon as he could.

Jade, on the other hand, made no secret of her desire for a party. Jade's older sister Phyllis turned 16 earlier in the summer, and there had been a big party for her. Now it was Jade's turn for birthday festivities and she was going to take full advantage of being the "birthday girl". The day before the party, Jade,

Phyllis and their mother spent hours decorating the house and patio, baking the cake, and putting together party snacks. At nightfall, a pleasantly exhausted Jade was laying in the grass, at the side of the house next to the patio, staring up at the rapidly darkening sky. She still remembered how she felt, lying there. The pang of sadness she felt for the year that was almost gone, and for the end of her pre-teen years.

Jade's thoughts were interrupted by the sound of someone walking toward the house from the woods, close by her. The footsteps crossed the backyard, toward the patio. She lifted her head slightly to see who it was. Peter. He was soaked and filthy, his eyes wild. Jade was sitting in the shadow of the house, and it was almost fully dark. Jade stayed still, hoping he would walk straight into the house through the back door, and not notice her. Instead, Peter stopped short of the patio. Jade saw him look around at the decorations that the rest of his family had so carefully put up. Jade watched his face twist in disgust. He looked like someone possessed. A sob escaped him. Then another. He reached up, hooked a loop of crepe paper and ripped it down. He then circled the entire patio, ripping down the crepe and the balloons, then finally tearing through the banner that said "Happy Birthday". The patio floor was now awash in brightly colored decorations, looking as if the party had already happened.

Jade continued to watch in horror, as Peter slipped to his knees, sobbing hoarsely into his hands. She instinctively realized that he'd be livid if he knew that she was here, witnessing his loss of control. After a time, Peter lifted his head and locked eyes with Jade. He had known she was there, probably from the moment he approached. The look in Peter's eyes branded itself on Jade's memory. They were the eyes of a child just beginning to understand what unspeakable thing awaits him, as he tumbles into the abyss. Jade saw, in that moment, something that she previously only suspected. Peter was losing his battle with the dark forces with which he had fought throughout his entire childhood.

As if he could read Jade's thoughts, he stepped toward her, into the light, and smiled at her. A smile that didn't reach his eyes. By the garish patio light, Peter's eyes reflected pure loathing. She suddenly realized that he hadn't been crying, he'd been laughing. This was the real Peter, stripped of the civilized veneer he used when dealing with others. "Don't look too closely at me, little Jade. Once you find out things you shouldn't know, you can never go back and you'll never be safe." Jade scrambled off the ground and ran around the house, toward the front door. Toward safety, toward sanity. The sound of Peter's laughter chased closely behind her.

The memory of Peter's bizarre behavior that night forever changed how she felt about him. She made sure she was never alone with him. She was careful to never say anything bad about him, as she had this strange feeling that he would know it if she did, and she would be very sorry, when all was said and done. Looking back, Jade understood that the latter part of her childhood had been colored by her fear of Peter. And, even now, the thought of being summoned by her mother to attend a birthday party for Peter filled her with uneasiness.

After dinner, Jade sat at her kitchen table with the lightened and darkened copies of her "mystery note". She turned the copies around, so the words were upside down to her, and arranged them in a line before her on the table. In a document examination class, she had been trained to do this. Turning the question document upside down helped break patterns that the reader's eye insisted on seeing, patterns that were often not helpful in discerning the message. The darkest copy provided the clearest image. Squinting, she was suddenly able to make out a handful of words: "…In the house at 118 Commercial Street, on the… there is a…" One other word was legible, near the end of the message. *Murder*. The pig-tailed Sherlock Holmes within her leapt at this information. Now she had an address. And that one tantalizing clue.

After several more minutes of study, Jade had made no further progress.

She'd try again later. She suspected, since the note was so old, the building located at that address may no longer exist anyway. The jewelry case was made locally, for a member of the Lawrence family. Jade found it amazing that no one had found the note in the intervening decades.

Jade's reference books contained photos of the Portland Waterfront, many featuring Commercial Street. Her sources also indicated that the addresses of the houses on Commercial Street had been re-numbered several times since the 1870's. This wouldn't be much of a problem. Any current source that referenced the Lawrence family would probably give an updated address for the family home, if there still was one. Jade decided to take a ride down to Commercial Street tomorrow and take some pictures of the area. She could then compare them with the pictures she had in her books from the 1870's. This would tell her whether the house that used to be at 118 Commercial Street in the 1870's still stood, even if the house numbers on the street had been changed. Feeling as though she had made some headway, Jade put her books and notes away.

Saturday dawned cold and clear. At just past 7:00 AM, Jade packed her digital camera and the reference books. Bardo stood at the door, obviously hoping to be invited wherever she was going. Jade gave Bardo a distracted pat on the head and barely noticed when Bardo plodded down the hallway to his kitchen basket, both head and tail at half-mast. Outside, snow crunched underfoot as Jade walked to her Blazer. She started the truck, scraped the ice off the windshield, and headed out toward the waterfront.

Parking in the lot next to DiMillo's floating restaurant, Jade then spent a few hours walking from one end of Commercial Street to the other, snapping pictures of the buildings. She also walked out to the end of two of the piers and snapped pictures as she looked back at the buildings, trying to reproduce the view from the bay, from which her reference book pictures had been taken. When she was satisfied, Jade walked back to her car. On impulse, she walked past the lot where her car was and went inside DiMillo's restaurant where she enjoyed a solitary seafood lunch.

At home, Jade uploaded the pictures she had taken earlier, and while they uploaded, she glanced through her reference books. In the first two books, she had found no published photos that would help her, and there was nothing listed about the Lawrence family. She had better luck with the third book. There was a complete chapter about the Lawrence family and their Commercial Street home. Pay dirt! The book also provided the name of the one known surviving member of the Lawrence clan, which matched the sources she used in researching the jewelry case. The man's name was Benjamin Robert Lawrence. The reference book indicated, and Jade knew from her research, that the very elderly Mr. Lawrence had recently been relocated to an assisted living facility in the area. The book contained pictures of the Lawrence home, first as it was in the earlier days, and then as it was just a few years ago.

Jade's heartbeat accelerated when she realized that the house referenced in the note was still standing. The address was now 178 Commercial Street. She looked at the pictures she had taken. One of the pictures included the Lawrence House. The re-numbering of the homes accounted for the difference in address, but the house was unmistakable. It seemed empty, and had a sad, neglected appearance. Jade went through all her photos and found another one which included the house at 178 Commercial Street. Using a magnifying glass, she took a closer look. Jade was shocked to realize that one picture seemed to show a shadow in a third floor window. A distinctly human-shaped shadow. The hairs on the back of her neck stood up. She placed both pictures in front of her, side by side. She knew they were taken within seconds of each other, yet the other picture showed no such figure in the third floor window. Jade could no longer deny the uneasiness she was feeling.

It wasn't the note or the jewelry case causing her disquiet now. It was the house. That figure in the window. Jade looked at both pictures again. She tried to tell her frightened mind that it was probably just a trick of the sunlight.

Jade decided to have another go at the note. The part of the message she had been able to read said that there was (or had been) something in the house. With something like dismay, she realized that she would now need to find out if the item the note referenced was still in the house. On the other hand, she didn't think it would be difficult, or even very risky, to get in to a vacant house and take a look around. After all, what could go wrong?

Chapter 4

Having unsuccessfully attempted to duck tonight's party, Jade showed her passive aggression by taking her time showering, putting on makeup and getting into her "little green dress". A freshly-coiffed Jade appeared on her parent's doorstep at exactly 7:00. Unfortunately, as she knew, she had been due at 6:00.

Her knock was answered by an elderly woman, who led her into the kitchen where several people were drinking margaritas and trying to be heard over the music. Jade put her gift certificate on the table with a stack of other gifts, then wandered into the living room and sat down on the couch.

On the other side of the room, standing against the wall, was a very attractive, 40-ish man who looked as out of place as Jade felt. Their eyes met, and Jade gave him a polite smile. He smiled back, and looked away uncomfortably. Jade had no idea who this man was, but she found his discomfort curiously appealing. She stood up and walked across to stand in front of him.

She held out her hand and said, "Hi, I'm Peter's sister, Jade".

He looked into her eyes, and seemed momentarily stunned. He quickly recovered his composure and shook hands with her. "Hi yourself, I'm Steven".

Just a name didn't really explain how he knew Peter, and Jade wasn't sure there was a polite way to ask. She started to turn away, but he gently seized her arm and said, "Don't go." She looked at his hand on her arm, then frowned uncertainly into his eyes.

He let go of her arm and smiled self-consciously. "I don't really know anyone here. I'm what you might call a 'drinking buddy' of Peter's. He called me last night to tell me he was having this party. As soon as I arrived, your mother cornered me. She wanted to know who I was, what I did for a living, and how I knew Peter. Apparently she decided I wasn't dangerous as she got me a drink and we had a nice little chat. She told me all about you, how you were single, sweet and pretty. And single, did I say that already?" Peter graced Jade with an embarrassed smile.

Jade didn't even attempt to hide her chagrin. "I'm so sorry. My mother is a dear, but she's somehow got it into her head that a woman without a man is somehow less of a woman."

Steven said, "So, you are, what you said, 'a woman without a man'?"

Jade felt herself flush and looked at the floor. She excused herself, pointedly ignoring his question, and walked away. When she was out of the living room, her polite expression slipped into one of sheer frustration. She began to search for her "dear" mother.

Jade found her mother on the patio, surrounded by friends and family. The patio flagstones were heated, and most of the guests were there, some walking around in stocking feet, enjoying the crisp evening air. Jade stood back and watched her mother for a moment. From her vantage point in the kitchen doorway, Jade could see the light coming from the kitchen, filtering beautifully through the huge blue marbled glass vase perched regally on its own custom-made stand in the kitchen, well out of the path of the back door. The blue shadow, cast over the flagstones, looked oddly human-shaped.

Jade watched her mother walk across the patio and into the blue shadow. A strange uneasiness settled into Jade's chest as the strange indigo light fell across her mother's face. For a moment, her mother seemed horribly dead, her face blue, her eyes open and staring. Her mother moved out of the blue shadow, laughing and chatting with her guests, and the horrific illusion was mercifully broken. Jade's uneasiness, however, remained.

Looking at the vase, Jade recalled as a young girl, running through the kitchen one day and accidentally knocking the huge blue vase off its stand. Miraculously, it didn't break. Jade's father came on the run. He stopped in the kitchen doorway, taking in the fallen vase and Jade's stricken expression, then he laughed. He said, "Never worry about that vase, honey. It's been in my family for generations, but only because it's so strong no one can seem to break the ugly thing. Someday, someone will actually destroy it, and probably change the course of the whole family!" Jade remembered feeling so thankful to have a father like hers. Jade smiled at the memory, and looked around again for her mother. They spotted each other at the same moment. Her mother held a hand up to her in recognition, as she finished a conversation with an older gentleman.

She worked her way over to Jade, greeting people on the way. "I'm so glad you were able to make it, Jade! Have you seen your brother yet? He was supposed to be here an hour ago."

Jade knew that she was late, but she was amazed that somehow Peter managed to be even later, and for his own party, no less. Some people never change. Jade looked at her mother. Under the sunny smile and the perfect makeup, her mother was hurt and worried; she could see it. Her previous anger with her mother evaporated. Jade took her arm and gave it a reassuring squeeze. "Let's make some calls, and see if we can find Peter". Her mother nodded, looking relieved.

Forty-five minutes later, two hours into the party, Peter still hadn't arrived, and calls to all his favorite haunts had turned up nothing. Everyone had left the party except Jade, Steven, and Jade's parents. They sat the kitchen table, talking. Jade noted that Steven wasn't particularly forthcoming, which was probably because he had only known them only two hours.

As usual, Jade's father wanted to know all about what Jade was currently working on. Everyone found the mystery of the Lawrence jewelry case fascinating. Jade didn't tell them the name of the family, but she told them that they were a prominent waterfront family, which she knew would probably be enough. They found Jade's tale of the partially unreadable note particularly interesting.

Jade and her mother cleaned up as the men took a walk through the woods behind the house. Jade watched the two of them from the kitchen window. She found it odd that, for strangers, they seemed to be standing very close together, their posture one of sharing intimate information. Jade watched a moment longer, as the men walked to the edge of the woods and disappeared, then she turned back to her sink full of dishes.

It was at least a half hour before the men came back into view, at exactly the spot they had disappeared. Jade and her mother had finished their cleaning and were sitting in chaises, enjoying a glass of wine under the cool night sky. Both men were laughing, Jade noticed. They looked comfortable with each other. Her mother also noticed, as she said, "Will you look at that? Your father has bonded with this young man!" Jade felt an explicable stab of foreboding.

As they drew closer, Jade saw that both of them had soaking wet pant legs and muddy feet. Agatha stood up to greet them. "Boys will be boys, won't they?", she called out. The "boys" looked at each other, identical sheepish expressions on their faces. Jade's mother rolled her eyes dramatically, produced a long suffering sigh, and shuffled into the house.

Steven said his goodbyes to the elder Danners, and asked Jade to walk him to his truck. Jade's parents exchanged a knowing look as Jade grabbed her jacket and followed Steven outside.

Wordlessly, Jade walked beside Steven, down the driveway to a black pickup truck parked at the curb. Steven turned to her, looking uncertain. Jade said, "Thank you for being here tonight. I apologize for my mom's matchmaking."

The silence stretched, as they stood in the dark, looking into each other's eyes. Steven opened his arms, and Jade stepped into them. As he closed his arms around her, Jade thought about how good, how solid and real, he felt. Her arms slid around his waist and a contended little murmur escaped her. After a moment, Steven drew back and studied Jade's face. He looked puzzled. He didn't explain and Jade was afraid to ask.

"Can I see you again?", he asked.

"I would like that", Jade answered. She pulled out one of her business cards and wrote her cell phone number on the back. Steven slipped the card in his wallet, then climbed into the cab of his truck, started the engine, and rolled down the window.

"Now get back in the house before you catch cold!", he said.

She grinned, then turned and walked back up the driveway, a new spring in her step. Out of the corner of her eye, she saw a kitchen curtain drop into place. Her mother, of course, watching her from the kitchen window.

Jade woke to the sound of the wind, howling under the eaves of her house. She lay quietly, enjoying the warmth of her king-sized waterbed, the softness of her micro-fleece blanket, and the dance of sunlight on the back wall of her bedroom. She thought, as she often did, about what it would be like to be sharing her life with that special (but elusive) Mr. Wonderful, instead of her wiry-haired Jack Russell. Jade knew she'd need to make some changes in her life, unless she really did want to spend the rest of it as a solitary spinster.

Her life, such that it was, didn't include much social interaction. Her habit of doing most everything alone really didn't help, she knew. She felt as though it was better to feel nothing than to even take a chance of being hurt. Still, it would be such a nice change to wake up next to Nicholas Cage, or maybe Stephen King, and have him smiling down at her, watching her sleep. It must have been meeting Steven last night that had dredged all this up, she decided. Jade resolutely shrugged off the blanket and headed for the shower.

After she was showered, dressed and had eaten a handful of chocolate covered peanuts (a Jade Main Selection dietary staple), she pulled out the photocopies of her "mystery note". She placed them on her kitchen table. She turned them sideways, then upside down again. Jade took a deep breath and looked across the table to a spot just beyond the notes. This gave her peripheral vision a chance to see the note.

A few more words leapt out at her. "In the house at 118 Commercial Street, on the 3rd fl…. there is a di…. that will prove my ….. was not kill.. by … but … murdered by …husb…'s b…… Jade's initial interpretation was that there was *something* on the third floor of the Lawrence house that would prove *someone* was not killed by *someone* but was killed by *someone else* (husband?). Exhilaration ran through her. She was finally able to read a good part of the note! Of course, her limited understanding presented more questions than answers, but it was a good start. She knew that she had done much more with far less, in her line of work.

Jade drove her Blazer slowly down the length of Commercial Street, passing number 178. This early on a Sunday morning, parking spaces were plentiful. Jade decided to leave the truck one block over from the Lawrence house, so that she wouldn't be easily associated with the breaking and entering she may need to do.

Jade grabbed the flashlight from her glove box and put it in her jacket pocket. She put on a pair of latex gloves, then she put her driving gloves on over them, so she wouldn't look suspicious. She walked down the street that ran behind the vacant Lawrence house. Heart thumping, she brazenly walked up the back steps of the house, and on to the back deck. She crossed the deck and reached the back door. She glanced quickly around. No one seemed to be watching her. She hoped she looked like someone who had the authority to be there. Jade tried the back door. It was locked, as expected.

She knew that climbing through one of the windows on the first floor (in plain sight of the neighbors) should be a last resort. Walking back down the porch stairs, she spotted a storm cellar to the left of the back door, at ground level. She tried one of the doors and it opened with a rusty squeal. She ducked into the cellar and, with another screech of protest from the door hinges, Jade pulled the door closed over herself.

_____

Chapter 5

Jade stood quietly in the dark, halfway down the stairs. She could almost sense the house not wanting her there. She listened for any movement. The wind outside suddenly picked up, a strangely forlorn sound, gone as quickly as it had come.

Jade pulled out her flashlight and turned it on. There were several pieces of ancient furniture, covered with dust. The air smelled strangely of sulfur, like a newly struck match. Jade picked her way carefully between pieces of furniture and found a winding staircase near the center of the house.

Shining her flashlight up the stairwell, she saw that the stairs continued up all three floors. The creaking of the stairs accompanied her as she climbed. She stopped at the first floor and listened. Again, she only heard the wind. The open floor plan of the house allowed her to immediately see that the first floor was empty. The walls were painted off-white, and they were tagged with graffiti. The sun shone through the windows, illuminating the floating dust particles into a sparkling fog.

She continued up the stairs to the second floor. Another empty set of white-walled rooms, with less graffiti. On the third floor, Jade panned the space with her flashlight. The room was filled with built-in bookcases, floor to ceiling. The third floor was also open space, but the space appeared smaller. The book shelves were all empty. Jade realized, looking around the room, that it was highly likely that, since no one lived here, what she sought would also likely no longer be here. If the mysterious "di…" referenced by the note *was* here, it wasn't in plain sight. There were no obvious hiding places, no bureau drawers or cupboards.

Jade walked slowly around the room, lightly trailing her fingers along the dusty shelves. On the third wall, she discovered a shelf that was slightly lower than the others. She directed the flashlight beam to that wall and saw that all the shelves on that section of bookcase were slightly lower than the shelves on the bookcases to either side.

Jade tried knocking on the back wall of the bookcase (as she had seen television detectives do, with interesting result). The bookcase didn't move. Starting at the lowest shelf, she grabbed each shelf in turn and gave a little tug. Nothing happened, until she got to the top shelf, directly at eye-level. The shelf came out, dropping into her hand. She looked into the slim horizontal space where the shelf had been and saw a tiny round wooden button.

She pushed the button, and the top panel of the bookcase slid down, leaving a rectangular hole in the wall about two feet high and three feet wide. Jade stepped up onto the lowest shelf and tried to see into the hole. She wasn't quite tall enough. Jade climbed up to the next shelf and peered into the darkness behind the bookcase. It was a small room! Now she understood why the third floor had seemed smaller to her. Jade shined her flashlight into the space. The room was about four feet wide and about ten feet long. There was a small table and two chairs, and a pile of clothing on one of the chairs.

Jade realized that, if she decided to climb into the narrow room, she could probably use one of the chairs to stand on, to hoist herself back out of the room. This idea decided her, and she spent a moment congratulating herself for her foresight. Jade stepped up to the third shelf, stepped over the wall and sat down on the bookcase wall, facing the tiny room. Legs dangling into the room, she jumped down into the three-foot space, landing with a solid thump on the floor of the hidden room.

Dust flew in all directions. Jade listened for a moment, hoping the noise hadn't attracted outside attention. She heard nothing. She used her flashlight to take a closer look at the space. Her glance was immediately drawn to the pile of clothing on the chair. She took a step toward the table and chairs, then another. As she drew nearer, she realized the pile of clothing was arranged in the shape of a person, strangely flattened, sitting at the table. Taking another step, and a closer look, Jade saw that the pile of clothing contained a body! Bones were clearly visible at the wrists and ankles. With almost detached horror, Jade realized there was no head.

Heart hammering, Jade looked wildly around the room. She spotted the skull, laying on it's side under the table. Near panic, Jade looked away, and took a deep breath, struggling for control. She sought reassurance in the knowledge that the person sitting at the table had probably been dead for decades and was certainly no threat to her.

Jade turned to look around the narrow space, careful not to turn her back on the skeleton. She saw a small black book poking out of the skeleton's apron pocket. The book was the only object she saw in the room, except the table, chairs and the skeleton itself. Fighting nausea, she snatched at the book. It hooked briefly on the side of the apron pocket. Jade gave it a yank and the book pulled free, the momentum causing Jade to involuntarily step backward. The body shifted toward her, producing the unspeakable rasp of stiff, moldering cloth sliding against bone. Jade glanced down at the book in her hand. On the cover, there was a crudely drawn Möbius symbol, with an eye in one loop and a teardrop in the other. Remembering the same symbol on the note she had found in the jewelry case, she knew that this was likely to be the item for which she was searching. She placed the book carefully in the inside pocket of her jacket.

Jade walked gingerly around the table, giving the skeleton a wide berth, and grabbed the empty chair. She dragged the chair across the room and placed it under the hole in the bookcase.

Looking over her shoulder at the long-term resident of this hidden room, it seemed almost possible to Jade that this poor forgotten creature could somehow awaken from its slumber, long-unused tendons creaking as it stood and slowly moved toward her, hands extended in supplication. Jade scrambled onto the chair and through the hole in the bookcase. She ignored the sound of something metal hitting the floor of the hidden room as she beat her hasty retreat. As her feet hit the floor of the library, the dust again flew upward and enveloped her. She reached for her flashlight, then realized she had dropped it, inside the narrow room, during her frantic exit. She heard a stealthy creaking sound from somewhere close by. Glancing around in fright, Jade felt a presence in the room with her. She suddenly recalled the pictures she had taken of this house yesterday, and the shadow she had seen at one of the third floor windows.

Without her flashlight, and with dust swirling throughout the room, Jade was almost completely blind. She stood motionless as she waited anxiously for her eyes to adjust to the darkness and for the dust to settle. She struggled to control the terror that threatened to engulf her as she anticipated the touch of some undead horror. Finally the dust began to clear. Moving only her eyes, she looked around the room. She didn't see anyone or anything that could account for the creaking sound. She walked as quietly as possible across the room. She knew the stairs would creak, and she paused at the top of the winding staircase to listen. She heard nothing. Her feet barely touching the stairs, Jade raced down all three flights, back through the basement, and out the storm cellar door.

In a dark corner of the third floor, the man struck a wooden match on his thumbnail and lit a cigarette. His gold-flecked hazel eyes watched through the window as Jade exited the house. Worry clouded his lined features. He walked over to the still-open bookcase and looked inside. On the floor next to the table, a flashlight beam illuminated the skull under the table. The man nimbly pulled himself up and through the open space, picked up the flashlight, then bounded neatly back out. "Jade Danner" was engraved in tiny letters on the barrel of the flashlight. The man turned it off and slid it into his pocket.

——

Chapter 6

As Jade drove home, she took off her gloves and stuffed them into her purse. At home, Jade washed her hands and put on a fresh pair of latex gloves. She could not believe that she had just sneaked into a stranger's house and stolen something from it. She realized that the jewelry box, the note, and now the book she had just stolen, all had some kind of power over her.

She thought about the person (or rather, the post-person remains, not to put too fine a point on it) she discovered sitting at the table in that secret room. The clothing looked to be female. She briefly thought about calling the police. Then she realized that she would have to explain why she was there. As she had no legitimate reason to be there, she decided a decades-old potential homicide wasn't a priority reporting event. As she had risked life and limb, not to mention incarceration, Jade was more determined than ever to find out what was in the stolen book and why it was apparently so important.

In the light and comfort of her own home, Jade was still convinced that someone had been in that vacant house with her. She knew that, depending on exactly who witnessed her little crime spree and whether they actually saw her take the book, she may either be in danger of being arrested, or in danger of being hurt. She needed to know why this book may have been important enough for someone to die carrying it. Jade brewed a pot of coffee and pulled out a fresh legal pad to take notes.

Opening the book to the first page, Jade realized it was a diary. That explains the "di…" part of the note, she thought with satisfaction. She began to read.

Wednesday, 21 August, 1878, 11:20 PM

Today, dear diary, another woman went missing. She was a townie named Mary, working nights at the tavern down street and taking care of her elderly mum by day. I knew her, but just to say g'day. The newspaper said that she was last seen at the tavern last night, but that she disappeared sometime during the evening. Her mum sent word to fetch the constable this morning, as her daughter still had not come home. People are so frightened that none of us women will walk anywhere outside without a male escort. There have now been 5 women taken from our midst and only two of them have turned up, and both of them turned up dead.

Saturday, 24 August, 1878, 9:00 PM

Mary still hasn't been found. Her mother is quite sure she's dead. The constable went through Mary's room and found something strange, I'm told. Apparently there was a piece of leather than Mary had been using to tie up her hair, with a strange design painted on it. It looked like a number "8", lain on it's side, with an eye painted inside one loop and a droplet painted inside the other. Even more odd, I've also heard a rumor that this symbol was found carved into a wooden dowel that had been used to brutalize one of the other women. That girl was found dead, two days after she went missing. I don't believe this bodes well for our Mary.

Friday, 30 August, 1878, 10:10 PM

I don't know what to do. Tonight, I saw Mrs. Lawrence behind the house with Tim, her husband Trevor's twin brother. (the Missus said I can call her by her given name, Marie, but only when we are alone, so I will do her the honor of calling her by her proper name here). What I saw was a decidedly ungentlemanly man forcing his attention on a woman who was too refined to firmly object. What's more, he's tried to force his attention on me also, and just last week!

I walked right out into the field, practically running straight into them, pretending I didn't see them. Tim jumped back from Mrs. Lawrence so quickly he almost fell! I can't describe the evil intention I saw in his eyes, but I was suddenly frightened to have crossed him. The look of relief in Mrs. Lawrence's eyes told me I did the right thing. I'm so glad I was there today! I've known Mrs. Lawrence since we were small children. I was a townie, and she grew up in a well-to-do family that lived just up the road from the Lawrences. I spent a great deal of time working alongside my mother, here at the Lawrence Estate. Back then, she was just "Marie". We met here, at the Lawrence house, and were fast friends from the very start. Marie's family was able to provide her with a wonderful education, and Marie, in turn, would teach me everything she could. She and I shared a thirst for knowledge, and I have her to thank for my ability to read and write and to do complex sums.

When she and Trevor started dating I was thrilled. I knew that I would soon be taking my mother's place as a servant for the Lawrences, and the new Mrs.

Lawrence used her prominent position in the family to make sure that I would be allowed to work for her and only her. I owe her so very much!

I must try harder to stay close by Mrs. Lawrence. With Mr. Lawrence away on his fishing trips for days at a time, I may be all Mrs. Lawrence has to keep her safe, since she insists on believing in only the good in everyone.

Tuesday, 3 September, 1878, 8:15 PM

It's been a busy week, dearest diary. The seasons are beginning to change. Soon it will be time to help harvest the last hay of the year and put the shutters on the windows. Workers from a neighboring farm discovered a woman's body in their lower field yesterday. The constable has identified her as Isabelle Fournier. She was the second girl to disappear, several weeks ago. She was found without most of her clothing, laying on her back, her eyes staring up into the rainy sky. Clutched in her hand, I'm told, was a gold medallion with a sideways number eight carved into it. I also heard that Isabelle was beaten and brutalized, and her parts of her body had been horribly cut or bitten. I pray every day that whatever evil has come to our quiet little town will leave us without doing further harm. But then another poor girl goes missing.

The families of the other missing girls are out of their minds with grief as they can no longer pretend their girl ran away or is being held unwilling but alive somewhere. I know Tim used to date Isabelle before she and I became friends last year. I remember how, of late, Isabelle would go out of her way to avoid running into Tim. I can understand that, he has the same effect on me. Isabelle was a great friend to me, and I feel disquieted to realize that her body was found on the path between her home and mine. She may have been on her way to see me.

The first girl to have gone missing was found two days after she vanished, washed up on the Atlantic shore, at the Promenade. She was barely *recognizable as human, having spent two days feeding the ocean creatures.*

Like later women, the constable's men found evidence that the first known murdered woman had been horribly brutalized. I didn't know her, but I know that my cousin Mark dated her for awhile, and Mark works for the Lawrences, as do I. I sometimes used to see Mark walking with this sweet, beautiful girl, in the fields around the Lawrence estate, or sometimes down at the docks. I remember seeing Tim watching from his room with narrowed eyes as Mark and his lady love walked the fields with hands joined. Tim doesn't seem to want to see anyone happy. Mr. And Mrs. Lawrence have both been looking for Tim today, to tell him about the discovery of Isabelle's body, but he was not to be found. My little sister and brother just arrived here to tell me that my mother needs me. They said she sounded upset and wanted me to hurry home at first chance.

Wednesday, 11 September, 1878, 9:00 PM

I saw Tim this morning. I heard the back door squeak as he came in while I was making breakfast. He looked like he had slept outside, his clothing was torn and filthy. I pretended to be busy at the stove so he wouldn't know that I had taken note of his appearance. He walked behind me, on his way to the stairs, and he paused when he was inches away from my back. I couldn't help shuddering. He laughed and continued on his way. He frightens me quite badly, and I know I'm not the only one. I've worked in this house since I was 13 years old, and I've always known there's something wrong about Tim, something that goes more wrong with time. I'm going to talk to Mrs. Lawrence about Tim as soon as I can. She may laugh at me, but she may also become a little more careful.

I went to visit my mother Tuesday last. I was almost stunned to disbelief with what she told me. As I already knew, my mother knows the Lawrences very well, as she worked for them years ago, long before I did. She told me that there were several disappearances and murders similar to what has been taking place currently, about 25 or 30 years ago, when she was but a teen. She said that at least 8 women had gone missing, during an approximate 10-year period. Five of the women were found dead, all bearing mute witness to the atrocities done to them. At least three women, as she recalled, went missing and were just never found at all.

At that time, my mother recalled to me, my grandmother had said something to her about it "happening again". Grandmother thought our town cursed. Of course, my mother didn't believe in curses, and she didn't pay much attention to what her mother said. My mother also told me that Tim and Trevor's father, William, was a suspect in this previous spate of killings. In fact, what she said, Dear Diary, was that it was a badly-kept secret throughout the town that William was peculiar, and everyone was all but sure it was him. There was just never any proof found. My mother was worried that the killing had now started again. She was relieved when I told her that William passed away several years ago.

She opined that maybe everyone had been wrong, back then, and that William had not been the killer, after all. Or, I reminded her, maybe the "curse" was back once again. My mother scoffed at that. She has never believed in curses and "all that rot." She may be right to conclude that the murders happening now are not related to the murders that happened in her teenage years. After all, several of the current murders involved that strange symbol, almost like a macabre calling card. I asked my mother about the symbol and she didn't recall that there was any thing like that found on any of the bodies from the prior murders, she said she'd likely have remembered something like that, I think she's probably right.

Could the Lawrence family sons have some kind of murderous legacy, passed down from generation to generation? It's all I can think about. I guess I must be superstitious, but I think my grandmother may have been right. She said there were killings, when she was younger, also. Then, there were the killings that happened when William was a young man as recalled by my own mother. Now, it's happening again. Three separate sets of killings, happening almost exactly 30 years apart. I'm convinced that the Lawrence family men are the key.

I must find out more. I'll start at the library. They have records of deaths and disappearances going back decades. If I find anything to confirm my suspicions, I'll talk to my grandmother about it. She's not well, and I know she won't be with us much longer. I'll just need to make sure I have that talk with her, if it becomes necessary, sooner rather than later.

Friday, 13 September, 1878, 7:30 PM

Mrs. Lawrence's husband has left for another fishing trip. My room is next door to theirs, and I overheard her crying and begging Mr. Lawrence not to go, late last night. I think it may be possible that Mrs. Lawrence realizes there's danger, but she putting on a brave face. Yesterday, I told Mrs. Lawrence that she shouldn't walk the grounds alone and she just said, "Erin, you leave the worrying to me, I'll be just fine." I would have been reassured, too, except for what I saw in her eyes as she spoke. She's clearly frightened of something. And I think I understand what that something is.

Every day, my disquiet grows. I want to leave this place, but I simply will not leave Mrs. Lawrence, especially now, while she's alone. If someone wanted to hurt her, or me, now, tonight, would be the perfect time. The only man in the house right now is someone I fear and distrust. I watched the sun go down tonight. It was blood red at the last of it. Today is Friday the 13th, and I feel as if something evil has watched and waited for just this night.

Chapter 7

Jade put the diary down, poured another cup of coffee and looked at the clock. She couldn't believe it had been almost an hour since she started reading. The printing was difficult to read, the letters formed differently than today's writing. She had taken notes as she was reading. So far, she understood that Erin, and probably Mrs. Lawrence, had been afraid of the killer that was apparently active there at that time. Jade also thought it obvious that something was going on inside the Lawrence home which may or may not have been related to the murders. Jade thought about the skeleton in female clothes sitting alone in the dark, in that secret room for so long. She wondered if the skeleton was Erin.

Jade spent the rest of her Sunday doing chores. As she went about her day, her mind wandered back to 1878, reliving the raw fear she felt emanating from every line of Erin's diary. By the time she was finished with her chores, it was almost 10:00 P.M. Jade didn't want to start reading the diary at this late hour, so she drew a bubble bath, made herself a chocolate milkshake and spent an hour in the bathtub, listening to jazz. Jade drowsily crawled into bed at 11:00 and was asleep almost instantly.

Jade opened her eyes to almost complete darkness. She heard the wind whistling through the trees and, strangely, felt hard ground under her back. Cold rain fell on her face, mixing with her tears. She closed her eyes. Strangely familiar images, filled with agony and terror, were flashing through her mind. She suddenly felt hopeless and lost, weakening as her life force drained from her. She felt rather than heard dead leaves crunching as head slipped to one side. She opened her eyes and tried to focus on the red blur that suddenly filled her vision.

The red blur slowly resolved into the digital display of the clock radio on her night stand. She lay quietly for a moment, trying not to think. Jade almost wept with relief when she realized that her horrible death in the woods wasn't real. She lay awake for a long time, thinking about the victims of the killer in Erin's world of 1870's Portland, Maine. She knew she couldn't let this go until she had found out all she could about what had happened back then, and what had become of Erin. She felt that the dream was sent to her as a plea to help bring each of the unfortunate victims into the safe lighted warmth of the here and now.

Monday morning's gray dawn found Jade already awake. The nightmare from the night before was still with her. Jade carefully packed the diary into her briefcase and took it to work with her, not comfortable being separated from it. She left the folder containing her notes on the kitchen table, knowing she would want to read more of the diary that night.

Jade spent her morning and most of her afternoon working diligently on the appraisal requests that had come in over the weekend. When she had time to take a break, Jade took a few minutes to review the file she had created on the Lawrence family jewelry box appraisal. She quickly located the name and address of the facility to which Mr. Lawrence had been moved. She looked up the telephone number and wrote it down. Jade was conflicted about misrepresenting her purpose, but there was information she needed and she thought Mr. Lawrence may be able to help her. Jade dialed the number. After speaking briefly with the receptionist, she was connected to Mr. Lawrence's room. Mr. Lawrence picked up the phone after the first ring.

"Good day, Mr. Lawrence, my name is Jade Danner. I'm calling from Remerick & Company."

There was a pause on the line, then Mr. Lawrence's surprisingly deep, melodious voice responded, "Well, hello, Ms. Danner. I don't care where you are calling from, I'm just happy to have someone to talk to. Especially a young lady who sounds as pretty as you do." Jade suppressed a smile. Mr. Lawrence was apparently a shameless flirt!

She went along, enjoying the banter. "Thank you so much, Mr. Lawrence, it's nice of you to say that. I'm hoping you can help me. I've been asked by a representative of your family to appraise a jewelry box that I understand has been in your family for several generations. Do you recall the jewelry box?"

Mr. Lawrence was silent for a moment, and then he responded, "Of course I do! How could I forget it? It's been handed down from and to Lawrence family women for about 150 years." There was a pause, the phlegm-laden sound of a throat clearing, then Mr. Lawrence said, "Now, who did you say you were again?" With a sinking heart, Jade realized that Mr. Lawrence may have memory issues. Which wasn't surprising, given that he was, according to her files, close to 100 years old!

Jade again recited who she was and why she was calling. Mr. Lawrence, it seemed, was just as pleased to make her acquaintance the second time around. She asked him if he had time to meet with her later in the week, to discuss an appraisal of an item he owned. He said he could certainly squeeze her in to his "busy social calendar", and they made plans to meet, at 7:00 PM on Wednesday. Jade disconnected, then called the facility number back and spoke to the charge nurse, clearing her impending visit with her.

Jade checked the Remerick & Company website and printed off her inquiry responses from last week, which had come in over the weekend. Finished with her day's work, Jade packed up her work station and headed home, looking forward to reading more of Erin's diary.

Jade parked the Blazer in her driveway, grabbed her purse and briefcase, and headed for her front door. She didn't realize that something was wrong until she was halfway up the walk. Her front door was slightly ajar, a narrow strip of the darkness inside visible. She stopped where she was and looked around at the darkening yard. Gooseflesh marbled her arms. She felt as if someone were watching her. Jade thought about calling the police, but realized that she hadn't yet seen any evidence of a crime. The door didn't appear to be broken. She realized, with everything on her mind lately, she may have left the door unlocked this morning when she left. She needed to get inside and find out if anything was missing or disturbed. She pulled a can of pepper spray from her purse and cautiously approached the front door.

She pushed the door the rest of the way open, reached a hand inside and flipped up two light switches beside the door, turning on the porch light and the inside hallway light. Nobody jumped out at her. Yet. She called Bardo, and was relieved to hear him bark, from somewhere deep inside the house. Jade slipped inside the door, pepper spray at the ready. She spent the next ten minutes walking through her house, checking every possible hiding place for unwelcome visitors. She found Bardo under her bed, shaking. She knew then that she hadn't left her door unlocked. Nothing appeared to be missing, but it seemed that a couple pieces of furniture in the living room had been slightly moved, a couple of knickknacks also not quite where they were before. Of course, that may be just her own paranoia.

She completed her tour of the house by checking all the doors and windows to make sure they were locked.

Later, Jade still felt uneasy. She threw away her mostly untouched dinner, and decided to read more of Erin's diary. She took the diary out of her briefcase and looked in the folder on the kitchen table for the notes she had taken while she read the diary the night before. The folder was there, but the notes were missing! She clearly remembered taking the diary to work with her, but leaving the notes in the folder on the table. Now they were gone. She realized the notes must have been important to someone. She was suddenly very glad she had taken the diary to work with her. On the other hand, she thought, the notes referenced the diary, so whoever took them would now know about the diary.

Jade tried to figure out who would be interested in her notes about the Lawrence family in the 1870's, and she could only think of two possibilities. One would be the elderly Mr. Lawrence, since he was the last surviving member of the family. She dismissed that possibility as it was probably beyond Mr. Lawrence's physical capacity, as he was currently living in a nursing home. She found the other possibility much more unsettling, but she had to consider it.

The only person who could know about her having something from the Lawrence family house would be the person whom she sensed was there in the abandoned house, when she had taken the diary. Jade knew that whoever took her notes would probably now badly want the diary. She'd have to be extremely careful. Jade thought it may be time to look into getting a security system installed.

Instead of reading more of Erin's diary, Jade decided to go back to the beginning of the diary and re-read it, so she could re-create her notes while they were fresh in her mind. She knew that any of the details captured in her notes could clarify something she read later, so taking notes was a necessary part of reading the diary.

Chapter 8

Jade made sure she had the diary AND her notes folder with her when she left for work the next morning. She drove to work her usual way, stopping for coffee at a local drive-through coffee shop. Jade had several interesting assignments to complete that day and she was happily thinking through her morning's work as she drove. A glance in her rear-view mirror would have revealed a black Mercedes, several cars back, following her.

As Jade parked her Blazer in the office lot, she heard her cell phone ring from inside her purse. She made a lucky grab for it and flipped it open. The caller ID read "private caller". Curious, Jade hit the connect button and said, "Hello?" Silence. Jade tried again. "Hello-ooo?".

This time the caller spoke, in a deep, gravelly voice. "Jade Danner? You have something I want. If you don't want to get yourself hurt, I suggest that you do exactly what I say. Bring the diary to the Maine Mall this afternoon. Sit at the center table at the food court, and wait for my call at 5:00. I'll tell you then where you can leave the diary, and after that, you'll never see or hear from me again."

Jade didn't like being told what to do, especially by someone who had likely broken into her home. She felt herself becoming incensed and she retorted, "I don't know why you want the diary, but I suggest you get over it. If I hear from you again, I'll contact the police." There was a stunned moment of silence on the other end, punctuated by her caller's harsh breathing.

Then he spoke again. "And tell them what? That you took a diary that didn't belong to you then had it stolen from you? I suggest you rethink your position. Be there with the diary. This will be your only warning." Furious, Jade stabbed the disconnect button without responding.

Jade worked her way through her day, one eye on the door. Her worry about the strange call this morning put a damper on the pleasure she usually got from her work. This fueled her anger. She realized that, if he was brazen enough to break into her house, then threaten her on the telephone, he would likely know where she worked. She half expected the ballsy creep to show up. It would be better for him, Jade fumed, if he didn't.

After work, Jade headed to the mall. She had the diary in her briefcase, but she had no intention of giving it up. Instead, she brought another small black book with her, as a "decoy", which she left on the vacant table at the center of the food court. By 4:00, Jade was sitting on one of the benches placed around the perimeter of the food court, watching the center table.

As she sat waited, she considered once again who he might be, and why he wanted the diary. As far as she knew, the elderly Mr. Ben Lawrence, with whom she had set up a meeting for tomorrow night, was the only living Lawrence. Jade made a mental note to ask Mr. Lawrence if he was, in fact, the last in his line.

She thought about who else it may be. She remembered the Lawrence family lawyer, Ron Corey, Jr. She had met Mr. Corey when he had dropped off the jewelry case to be appraised. He had a high, reedy voice she would recognize anywhere, so she eliminated Mr. Corey from her short list of suspects.

At twenty minutes past five, Jade realized that either the man wasn't coming, or she had somehow missed him. She picked up the unsuccessful decoy book from the table, then purposefully walked in the opposite direction from where her truck was parked. She took a roundabout, internal route to her truck, wanting to stay near people, and wanting to throw off anyone who may be following her. Twice, she ducked into stores, waited a few minutes, and left.

When she was about 20 feet away from her truck, she pushed the button on her key chain to unlock the Blazer. Nothing happened. She walked up to the Blazer and looked into the window. Her dashboard was hanging askew, ripped open and destroyed. There were wires snaking out in every direction from under the dashboard. She realized that while she had been in the mall waiting to catch a glimpse of the sneaky bastard, he was out here, breaking into her truck and trashing it.

Now Jade was scared stiff AND furious! Self-preservation suddenly kicked in, and she looked around her, wondering if he might still be nearby, maybe watching for her reaction. She didn't see anyone. But there were so many cars and people, he would likely blend in. How could he have NOT been seen doing this? Jade walked away from the Blazer, back to the mall. She thought about how much damage had been done and realized that she wouldn't be able to afford to get it fixed without filing an insurance claim. And in order to file a claim, she knew, she would need to submit a police report. Just inside the mall doors, she pulled out her cell phone and called 911. The dispatcher took the information about what happened, and where she was, and said that an officer would be there shortly.

Jade waited impatiently, pacing back and forth in front of the entrance doors. Twenty minutes after she called, an officer pulled up in front of the doors. She walked outside to meet him. At first glance, he appeared to be middle-aged. But as she got closer to him, she realized the gray hair she initially saw was misleading. The officer had youthful blue eyes and a quick smile. He introduced himself as Officer Derrick Zachary. Jade shook hands with him, immediately feeling safer. She led him across the parking lot to her Blazer.

Jade kept her distance as the officer took a look inside the driver's side window. He walked around to the back of the Blazer and wordlessly took the remote from Jade's hand. He hit the unlock button and the tailgate door swung up. He glanced into the storage compartment. There was a box of brightly-colored squeaky toys. He looked quizzically at Jade, a slight smile turning one corner of his mouth slightly upward.

She hastily explained. "I have a dog, he's like a son to me. We bring his toys for long trips and he climbs back here and plays when he gets bored."

Jade saw just a quick hint of toothy grin as Derrick picked up a yellow rubber ducky, squeezed it once, and was rewarded by a flatulent croak. He dropped the toy and shut the back of the Blazer.

He turned back to her, his demeanor sobering. He said, "Mrs. Danner, do you have any idea who would have done this?"

Jade knew that it was going to be very tough explaining the sequence of events that led to her truck being vandalized. She also knew that she had broken the law, on at least two occasions, once, when she went into the Lawrence house without permission, and once when she took the diary that didn't belong to her. She wasn't sure if it may also be a crime to not report a dead body. And then, of course, she had to consider her initial theft of the note from inside the jewelry box. While Jade had been thoroughly weighing her crimes, both real and imagined, Officer Zachary had been watching the play of emotions on her face.

He looked a bit skeptical when she replied, "It's Miss, not Missus. Actually, call me Jade. I have no idea who would do something like this to me."

Officer Zachary, having obviously noticed her long delay in responding, seemed about to say something, then apparently thought the better of it. His expression carefully neutral, he said, "I'll write up the report and mail a copy to you within 48 hours. I'll also check with Mall Security and have the surveillance videos reviewed. Besides that, there's not much more we can do. If anything else happens, please call us".

He passed her a card with his name, badge and telephone number on it. "Since I handled this call, if a related call comes in from you, I'll be assigned that one as well." As Jade took the card and thanked him for his help, she turned away quickly, blinking furiously to dispel the tears she could no longer hold back. Officer Zachary looked closely at Jade, his expression softening. "Are you going to be okay? I know this has to be upsetting. Let me help. Let's call a tow truck for your Blazer, then I'll take you home".

Jade was grateful for the officer's take-charge attitude, and she allowed herself to be helped into his blessedly warm cruiser. She fished out her driver's club card and her cell phone. She called the toll-free number on her card and made arrangements for them to pick up her Blazer. Jade made self-conscious small talk with the officer while they waited for the tow truck. Sitting heavily between them was his obvious suspicion, and Jade's certain knowledge, that she wasn't being completely forthcoming with Officer Zachary.

When the tow truck arrived, Jade gave the driver the name and address of her auto repair shop, then she walked back to the cruiser and got in. Officer Zachary took a quick look at Jade's address on the written report beside him, then pulled out into traffic and headed toward Jade's house. The trip was made in silence. The cruiser pulled up in front of Jade's house and Jade turned to get out.

"Thank you, Mr. Zachary, for your help today. You made a difficult situation easier, and I appreciate it."

Officer Zachary put a delaying hand gently on her shoulder. "Call me Derrick, please. Jade, I can see that something is going on here, something you don't want to talk about. If someone wants to hurt you, I can't protect you unless and until you level with me."

Jade spoke up, "I AM leveling with you. Some wacko just decided to damage my truck. End of story." Her voice sounded defensive, she knew.

Derrick looked at her, his disbelief clearly written on his features. "I'm not comfortable dropping you off like this when I know you may have been specifically targeted. If you'd like me to, I can go inside and have a look around, just to make sure everything is secure in there and no one is there who isn't supposed to be there".

Jade gratefully accepted his offer. She really was worried that whoever had broken in would come back, now that she was obviously not on board with his plan to get the diary away from her.

As Derrick walked through her front door, Jade noticed that he looked back at the closed door and frowned. "What's wrong?", she said.

He said, "If you aren't going to have a decent lock on your door, you at least need a security system. I'm guessing by the absence of a keypad that you don't have one."

Jade shook her head, feeling absurdly like she had somehow flunked a test. "I appreciate your advice, Officer Zachary." Her words were fine, but her tone was pure sarcasm.

Derrick smiled tightly and pulled out his wallet. When he flipped it open, Jade saw the gold badge. "Actually, it's Detective Zachary."

Jade was ashamed of her sarcastic retort. "I'm sorry. It's been a trying day. I didn't realize that they'd send a detective out on a routine property destruction call."

Derrick looked only partially mollified. "I'm a detective, but in a police force as small as ours, most of the detectives do double-duty, including the occasional patrol shift."

Derrick walked through Jade's house, room by room, with Jade bringing up the rear. Nothing seemed amiss. No monsters in the closet, nothing under the bed but a couple of dust bunnies. Jade felt reassured as she walked Derrick to the door.

He said, "I'll call you in a few days, just to make sure nothing else has happened and to make sure you got my report, for your insurance claim. If I find out anything about the damage to your truck, I'll contact you sooner. In the meantime, please be careful. Do you have a remote for your Blazer?"

Jade wasn't sure why he was asking, but confirmed that she did.

"Well, you can often trigger your vehicle alarm while inside your home. It could be useful to chase away a bad guy. After your Blazer is fixed and back in your driveway, give it a try. If it works, keep the remote next to you at all times. By the look of your truck, you've somehow managed to piss off a seriously dangerous person."

Jade promised to be careful and thanked Derrick for his help. She locked the door behind him, and then watched from the window as he got into his cruiser and drove away. She suddenly felt very alone. And being without a vehicle made her feel even more vulnerable than she already felt, given her new enemy.

Jade indulged in another moment of self-pity, then gave herself a mental kick in the ass. "First things first" as her mother liked to say. She needed a vehicle. She picked up the telephone and called her mother. After giving her a watered-down version of what happened, her mom agreed to bring over her "backup" vehicle, which Peter usually drove, when he was at home. Jade hung up the phone feeling a bit better.

A few minutes later, her mother pulled up in front of her house. Jade grabbed her purse, and her briefcase (with the diary stowed safely inside), and carefully locked up her house. She drove her mother home, only half listening to her mother's comforting chatter. Of all the information contained in her mother's random small talk, one item stood out. Peter hadn't been seen or heard from since early on the day of his party. Peter often would take off, for a day or two at a time, but it was odd that he didn't even call to apologize when he didn't make it home to his own party, a party he knew about.

After dropping her mother off, she headed to the office. Since it was 9:30 P.M., there was little traffic. Even so, she carefully drove the VW Bug aimlessly around town for several minutes, to make sure she wasn't being followed. She finally pulled in to her office's parking lot, locked up the car and took her purse and her briefcase with her into the building.

Once she was in her office, she turned on the photocopier. She took the diary out of her briefcase and began photocopying it. She started with the strange symbol on the cover, then she opened to the first page and laid it flat across the copier glass. Since the diary was fairly small, each photocopy was of two pages of the diary. The diary wasn't more than several pages long. Jade noticed that there were blank pages after the last entry. Copying completed, Jade then made a second copy, put each complete set of copies into their own plastic sleeves. After a thoughtful tour of her office, Jade taped one copy of the diary to the underside of her trash can. Since she was responsible for taking out her own trash, it would be safe there. The other copy went into her briefcase with the original diary. Jade turned off all the lights, locked up, and left the building.

At home, Jade took the remaining diary copy out to her backyard. She stood motionlessly for a moment, listening and looking. Hoping she wasn't being watched, Jade moved a small pile of wood, dug a hole, placed the other diary copy in it, filled the hole back in and replaced the wood on top of it. She felt better knowing that, if someone managed to take the diary from her, there were two copies in two different places. She went back in to the house and got ready for bed. Tiredness overtook Jade's worry, and she was asleep almost as soon as her head touched the pillow.

Chapter 9

Winter sunlight slanted through her bedroom windows as Jade sleepily rolled over and checked the time. She bolted out of bed when she realized it was past seven. She was always at work by eight. In spite of yesterday's harrowing adventures, she slept well and felt recharged this morning. She showered, dressed, fed Bardo, and left the house, diligently locking the door behind her.

The VW in the driveway brought back yesterday's events, and Jade felt her unease return. She depressed the trunk lock button on the remote and the trunk slowly opened. She hoisted her briefcase toward the opening trunk, then her eye was drawn to a flash of metal inside. She put her briefcase down on the driveway and reached into the trunk. There was a balled up towel in one corner, partly covering something metal. She recognized the towel, it was part of a set she gave her parents for Christmas the year before last. Jade reached in and unwrapped the towel. Inside, was a knife, with a double-serrated blade. And what could only be blood caking both wickedly sharp sides of the blade. Jade froze.

Several seemingly unrelated things suddenly clicked together. Peter's disappearance. The murder of the woman last summer, and the missing murder weapon, which had been described as a double-serrated blade knife, from that crime. The fact that Peter usually drove this car. Jade now suspected that these facts were all horribly linked.

Jade left the unwrapped towel, with it's grisly secret exposed, where it was in the open trunk. She picked up her briefcase and went back into the house. She knew she had two calls to make. Her parents or the police first? She knew her mother would never forgive her if she contacted the police first. With trembling fingers, Jade speed-dialed her mother's cell number.

After two rings, her mother's trilling "Hello, Jade!" filled her ears. "Mom, thank God you answered. We need to talk. I found something in the trunk of the VW. Can you please come right over?"

There was a pause, then Jade's mother responded, sounded put out. "Oh, Jade, can't it wait? I'm on my way to work and I don't want to be late."

Jade persisted, trying hard to keep her cool. "Mom, I don't want to talk about this over the phone, but you will definitely want to come over to my house, before I hang up and call the police. I found something in the car. Something I need you to see."

She heard her mother's sharp intake of breath on the line. Her mother, sounding frightened, said she'd be there in a few minutes. Jade made one more call, to Malcolm. She explained that she had a slight "situation" at home to deal with and she'd be in later. Malcolm was concerned and supportive, as Jade knew he would be. Jade sat down at her kitchen table to wait for her mother.

Within minutes, Agatha pulled up in front of Jade's house. She climbed out of her Lexus and, like a prisoner to execution, walked slowly up the driveway, her dread almost palpable. Jade crossed the kitchen, opened the door and walked outside. Agatha and Jade looked at each other as Agatha neared, neither saying a word. Awareness that things were about to change profoundly for both of them and for all time, clearly written on both their faces.

"Mom, I think Peter may have had something to do with that woman being murdered in the Old Port last year."

Agatha visibly paled, but her voice was steady and quiet, "Show me what you found." Jade put her arm around her mother and wordlessly steered her toward the car. She opened the trunk and started to pick up the crumpled towel, but her mother took one look at the bloody towel, and held a hand out to stop her.

"Jade, wait. Just tell me what is in the towel, you don't have to show me. If it's something the police would consider evidence, we don't want to handle it any more than we have to."

Jade looked into her mother's face and was shocked by her mother's paleness, but also by her seeming lack of surprise. "Of course, you're right, mom. I'm just so upset, I guess I'm not thinking clearly."

Now it was Agatha's turn to put a steadying arm around her daughter. Jade said, "Mom, it's a knife. With dried blood on it."

Agatha took a deep breath and said, "That's exactly what I was afraid of. I think we'd better go inside. There are a couple things I haven't told you, but now I think you need to know. Then we need to contact the police."

What Jade immediately felt was, oddly enough, relief. She realized now how convinced she was that her mother would try to talk her out of going to the police, in order to protect Peter. Jade shut the trunk and the women walked together into the house.

Agatha sat down in the chair in which Jade had, moments ago, been sitting. After taking a moment to gather her thoughts, Agatha said, "The first time I realized there was something wrong with Peter, you were about two years old, Peter was seven. You were outside playing in the back yard, I was hanging out laundry and watching you. Peter came outside with a wooden kitchen match in his hand. He struck it on the bottom of his shoe, you know, like your dad does.

Then he deliberately held the burning match to your dress and your dress caught fire. He did it before I could even get to you. I grabbed you, covered you with the wet towel I was holding and was able to put out the fire out before it burned your skin. I couldn't believe it had happened. You were inconsolable. Peter was your whole world, back then. I checked you all over for burns, but we were unbelievably lucky. Then I started scolding Peter. Peter stood there for a moment, then he started to laugh, and ran away into the woods. We didn't find him until almost midnight that night."

"Then, when you were ten years old and Peter was fifteen, do you remember when Peter ran away? He was gone for the better part of a whole day, and none of us could find him. When we did find him, he was almost a mile back in the woods, behind our house. What we didn't tell you then was that when we found him, he was covered with blood, and he was nearly catatonic. We took him to the hospital. The blood wasn't his, he didn't have a cut on him. It wasn't pursued at the time, but your father and I were convinced that he hurt someone or something very badly, in fact maybe killed them, then he ran away because he knew what he did was wrong and he'd be punished. Which is exactly what he had done before, when he set your dress on fire. We were afraid he had done something else, only this time, much worse.

"Peter did eventually come most of the way out of the strange state he was in, but he was never really the same. There was an almost frightening intensity to him after that. He wouldn't talk about what happened that night, or on following day, before we found him. At least he didn't talk about it to us. We got him counseling, but that didn't help.

"When Peter moved out to go to college, I cleaned out his room to make it into a study. I found a trunk in his closet that was padlocked. I was afraid of what might be in it. As you can imagine, by now, I knew something may be seriously wrong with Peter. I took a sledgehammer to the lock. Inside, I found several mismatched items of women's clothing and some jewelry. Honestly, at the time, I thought I may have discovered that Peter had a "thing" for women's clothing. That was shocking enough, so I guess I didn't allow myself to think beyond it. I also found several pieces of your father's jewelry in the chest, which I figured Peter must have stolen. I removed the jewelry, then I threw out the trunk, with all the women's clothing still in it.

"When Peter quit college and came back home to live a few months later, I asked him about that trunk. He said he had never used the closet in his room, in fact, his bureau used to be in front of it, so the trunk wasn't his. I knew he must have been lying, but with him quitting college, I was already upset enough and I, probably foolishly, just let it go.

"So, when you called me this morning, I wasn't surprised that you found something incriminating in the car. I think I've always known, in my secret heart, that it was just a question of time before something like this happened." Tears rolling down her face, Jade sat motionless.

Agatha was also fighting tears. "Jade, we still haven't seen or heard from Peter since early on the day before his party. So now there are two reasons we need to call the police. We need to report what you found and we also need to file a missing person report on Peter." Wordlessly, Jade crossed the kitchen and picked up the phone.

Jade spoke briefly on the telephone with the police, while Agatha watched her anxiously. Jade hung up the receiver and turned to Agatha. "The police said they'll send a cruiser by, in just a few minutes, to take a look at the knife in the trunk, and to also take a missing person report on Peter."

Within fifteen minutes, Jade saw a cruiser pull up in front of her house. Two policemen exited the vehicle and walked, shoulder to shoulder, up the front walk. Jade saw, with an unexpected jolt, that one of them was Derrick Zachary. The other officer was a bit shorter and older, with a fringe of gray hair surrounding his shiny pate, and a friendly, open face. Jade stood watching them approach from her open front door.

Derrick introduced the other officer as Gavin Leo, and Jade introduced her mother to the two officers. Jade then led the way down the driveway, and opened the trunk of the VW. Derrick expertly slid his hands into a pair of rubber gloves and gently moved the towel until the knife was visible within. Without picking it up or examining it further, he shut the trunk and removed his gloves. Jade then watched him as he used the radio that was clipped to his shoulder.

When Derrick crossed the driveway and rejoined the group, he said, "I've requested a CSU team to secure the car and tow it to the lab. Meanwhile, I can take your missing person report on the laptop in my cruiser. Climb into the back and we can take care of that now." Jade and Agatha followed him to the cruiser. Derrick opened a back door, and both women climbed in.

Gavin got in front, with Derrick. Derrick opened a blank form on his laptop, asked Agatha and Jade several questions about Peter, his address, his date of birth and the places he hung out. Derrick typed their responses with impressive speed.

Derrick then turned to the right, looking back at Agatha. "This is where the questions get harder. Can you tell me when the last time was that you saw Peter?"

Agatha answered, "The morning of his party, last Saturday, he left our house around 10:00 A.M. and said he'd be back in a couple of hours, but he never came back."

Derrick typed for a moment, then stopped and looked at Agatha again. "Did he seem to be acting normally at the time?"

Agatha appeared to consider this. "Yes, he seemed fine." Derrick typed for a few seconds.

Jade watched his hands and wondered what else those clever fingers of his could do. She immediately flushed at the thought. Almost as if he knew what

Jade was thinking, Derrick turned and gave Jade a considering look.

Derrick looked over at Agatha again. "Does Peter have any enemies that you know of?"

Agatha thought a moment, then answered, "I don't think my son was the most popular person, but I don't recall anyone being out to get him."

To Jade's knowing ear, her mother's voice was starting to sound just the slightest bit protective. She didn't blame her, she knew she'd be feeling exactly that way. She squeezed her mother's hand reassuringly. Jade could tell, from her mother's stricken expression, that these questions were cranking up her mother's worry.

After another moment, the silence punctuated only by the soothing sound of Derrick's typing, he said, "Well, that's it for the report. Do you have a recent picture of Peter?"

Wordlessly, Agatha got out of the car and headed for the house. A white box van with CSU written in black letters across the side backed into the driveway, blocking the VW. Jade saw Derrick give Gavin a nod, and Gavin got out of the cruiser and walked toward the van.

Derrick looked at Jade. "Have you considered that that the vandalism to your truck at the mall yesterday may be connected to the disappearance of your brother?"

Jade thought about that, surprised it hadn't occurred to her already. Things had just been so completely haywire lately; she was trying to just take it all in, not yet at the point where she could make sense of it.

Derrick watched the now-familiar play of conflicting emotions on Jade's face. He held up his hands in an attitude of surrender. "I just wanted to bring up that possibility, Jade, just in case the thought might make you act a little more cautiously than you otherwise would have done. Are you absolutely sure there isn't anything you want to tell me?"

Jade looked down at her hands, clutching each other in her lap and mumbled "no".

Derrick reached over the seat and covered Jade's clasped hands with his own large, warm hand. "Jade, I…" Before he could finish, they both spotted Agatha coming out of the house.

Agatha walked down the driveway, back to the cruiser. She stopped for a moment and watched as the VW disappeared into the white box van. Jade could see that she had been crying.

Agatha returned to the cruiser and handed Officer Zachary the wallet snapshot of Peter she carried in her purse. "This was taken almost two years ago, but he really hasn't changed much".

Gavin watched the white van drive away, then walked back to the cruiser and opened Jade's door for her. It seemed strangely chivalrous, then as she got out, she realized there were no handles on the inside of the back doors.

Officer Zachary handed Agatha a printed copy of the missing person report. "Mrs. Danner, I'll contact you tomorrow to set a time to go through Peter's room, in case there's something that will help us locate him. I also have to inform you that we will also be looking for any further evidence concerning the knife Jade found in the car this morning. Do I have your permission to conduct the search of Peter's room?" Agatha nodded grimly. Officer Zachary continued. "I'll bring a form for you to sign tomorrow before we start our search. In the meantime, I would appreciate it if you would keep everyone out of his room. Also, if you think of anything else, or if anyone contacts you with information that will help with either investigation involving your son, please let me know, right away."

Agatha nodded curtly, turning her tear-stained face away as she headed back to the house.

Derrick watched her walk away, sympathy clearly etched in his handsome face. He turned to Jade, standing next to his cruiser door. "Jade, we'll get the VW back to your mother as quickly as we can."

Jade nodded, then said, "Would it be okay if I went with you to my mother's house when you search Peter's room?" Derrick answered, "That's fine. I'll tell you what. I'll call you tomorrow and we'll set a time for me to pick you up, okay?" Jade nodded. Gavin took up his shotgun position next to Derrick in the cruiser, and Jade thanked them both for their help. She stood at the end of the driveway and watched as the cruiser pulled away. Agatha was standing on the porch, her gaze fastened on the horizon and her expression unreadable. Jade walked to her mother, and together they walked back into the house.

Agatha gathered the items from her purse which she had scattered across the table as she had looked for Peter's picture. Putting everything back in it's place seemed to calm her. She wiped her eyes and blew her nose, trying to smile at Jade through the tears that were, even now, continuing to fall.

Jade and her mother hugged for a long, silent moment, and then Agatha pulled away and gave Jade a watery smile. "Okay, little girl, let's go rent you a car. We can't have you housebound."

Agatha drove Jade to the Enterprise Car Rental in Westbrook and dropped her off. Fifteen minutes later, Jade was driving, of all things, a VW bug, out of the parking lot and toward the turnpike. Even with all that had happened yesterday and this morning, Jade found herself strangely empowered to at least have wheels under her.

Chapter 10

Back at home, Jade parked the VW in her driveway and went into the house. Now that she was home, and all that had transpired there earlier began to take hold, the good feelings she had on the drive home abandoned her. She looked around the kitchen and could still hear her mother's sobs. She looked out at the driveway and could still see the knife in the trunk of the car, still smell the sour metallic scent of the crusted blood. Feeling overwhelmed, Jade sat at her kitchen table, a shaft of winter sunlight warm at her back. She thought about all that had changed in her life just since getting up this morning. Her brother may be a psychopathic killer. Or dead. Or both. Her mother apparently had pieces of the puzzle from Peter's earliest days and had chosen to say and do nothing. Now Jade understood why she never felt comfortable around her brother. She wondered if her older sister Phyllis knew anything about Peter's "issues". She resolved that, when she called her later to tell her about Peter's apparent vanishing act, she'd ask her sister if she had ever seen anything odd or alarming in Peter's behavior.

Jade straightened up the kitchen and made her bed. The ordinariness of these tasks helped to calm her frayed nerves, and to distance her from what had happened earlier. She realized that she needed something to fully engage her mind. She needed to be working. She grabbed the VW key fob and headed out.

At work, Jade sat at her desk and reviewed the assignments that had come in that morning. It was as comforting as she knew it would be to slip into her professional persona and get to work.

Malcolm stopped by her desk, briefly, to check on her. Jade considered telling him about the events of the morning, but in the end, she just reassured him that the situation at home was under control. The rest of the day passed uneventfully and Jade worked past her usual quitting time, to make up for missing time that morning. At 6:45, she took a few minutes to freshen up, then headed out to keep her appointment with Mr. Lawrence.

The assisted living facility was located on Marginal Way, which was about two miles from her office. Jade parked in the large, mostly empty lot and entered the lobby. She was pleased to see it looked more like a hotel than a hospice. She asked the receptionist to ring Mr. Lawrence's room, and she was instructed to take the East elevator to the third floor, Room 303. In just a few moments, Jade was knocking on the door to Room 303. The man who answered the door was taller than she thought he would be; taller and younger-looking! Jade could tell by looking at him that he had always been a handsome and fit man. He reminded Jade of her own father, maybe 30 years from now. She hoped her father lived to this age!

Jade followed him into a tidy kitchenette and sat down at the table. While Mr. Lawrence busied himself preparing coffee, Jade took the opportunity to look around her. The apartment was clean, but the table at which she was sitting was strewn with papers. Curious, Jade tried to surreptitiously scan the papers. The only one that was placed right-side up and facing her was a letter, hand-written and dated this week, addressed to Mr. Ben Lawrence from Daniel Lawrence. Jade couldn't quite make out the tiny, slanted cursive writing in the body of the letter. She did notice that, at the bottom of the letter after Daniel's signature there was an ornate seal, which was branded deeply into a dribble of wax. She recognized the seal as being the Lawrence family crest; she had seen this on the appraisal request letter that accompanied the jewelry box from the Lawrences and on the note and the diary. It was the Möbius. Jade realized that she may have the answer to her question about whether Ben was the last surviving Lawrence family member.

Mr. Lawrence poured each of them a cup of coffee. He picked up a pair of glasses from the table and put them on. He smiled pleasantly across the table at Jade. "Well, young lady, what…..? His voice trailed off, and his face immediately drained of color. He looked like he had seen a ghost.

"Mr. Lawrence, are you okay?" Jade put a hand on his arm, concerned, but he snatched it back as if burned.

Eyes swimming with unshed tears, Mr. Lawrence looked at Jade. He opened his mouth to say something. Closed it again. Tried again. "You are the devil, that's who you are. Coming here to hurt me like this. You knew how I'd feel when I saw you, didn't you? And you didn't care. Well, I want you to leave. Right now. I don't ever want to see you again."

Alarmed, Jade slid out of her chair and sidled around behind Mr. Lawrence, toward the front door.

Mr. Lawrence turned in his chair, suspicion clear on his features as he marked her progress around the perimeter of his tiny kitchen. "I know Timothy sent you. Well, I told Timothy yesterday, and I'll tell you today. What I know will die with me. I will never speak of it. Not even to a Döppelganger!"

Jade put her hand on the doorknob, then turned back to take one last look at the confused and upset elderly man. Mr. Lawrence was hunched in his chair, shoulders heaving as he sobbed. Jade felt her own tears threatening. She had somehow upset him terribly. She suddenly felt very selfish. Coming here to get information under false pretenses was a mistake on her part, and now she had hurt this poor man, for no good reason at all. Jade did the only thing she could do to help him. She fled.

At the front desk, Jade had sufficiently recovered her composure to ask the receptionist if she might talk to the nurse on duty in East wing. The receptionist made a brief phone call and five minutes later Jade saw a small, neat woman of about her own age approaching. As she neared, Jade realized that the woman looked familiar. Jade searched her memory urgently, knowing she needed whatever advantage she could get in finding out more about Mr. Lawrence. Then she had it. She went to high school with her! They had several classes together early in high school. Now, Jade thought quickly, what was her name? Daisy! Her name was Daisy. The woman held out her hand, looked into Jade's eyes and obviously recognized her, too.

Jade shook her hand and said, "Hi Daisy! It's nice to see you. How have you been?" Daisy smiled.

"Hi Jade! It's been ages since I last saw you. I've been just fine. I'm a nurse now, as you can tell. I love it. So, what brings you to our humble little

Home?"

Jade grinned at Daisy's little double entendre. "Thank you for seeing me. Do you have a few minutes?"

Daisy said, "Of course." Jade said, "After I finished high school, I went away to college, then came back and started working for Remerick & Company, appraising antiques. One of my recent assignments is a jewelry case belonging to Ben Lawrence. As part of securing the provenance, I'm gathering information about the family, and specifically, about Ben Lawrence, the last surviving member of the Lawrence family. Can you tell me anything about him?" Jade held her breath, hoping that Daisy would take the bait. Jade purposefully misstated to Daisy that Ben Lawrence was the last of his line, hoping Daisy would correct her, then provide details.

Daisy frowned thoughtfully. "Let's go in one of the meeting rooms."

Standing her ground for the moment, Jade told her, "Wait, I need to tell you something. I think I just accidentally upset him. I sat down with him at his kitchen table, he took one look at me and he got very upset. He told me that he knew 'Timothy' sent me. I have no idea who that is. Do you think you could go check on him?"

Daisy was looking progressively more concerned as Jade spoke, then she said "Go ahead into conference room A, on your right. I'll be right back".

True to her word, within a few minutes she was back. "He was upset, but already beginning to calm down. He asked who you were. He was very insistent that he knew you. He said to give you his apology if he frightened or upset you." Daisy closed the conference room door and sat down opposite Jade. "First, Jade, I need you to understand that I'm telling you this in the strictest confidence. Privacy laws being what they are, it could mean my job if word gets out that I told you anything. Agreed?"

"Yes, of course", Jade answered. Daisy sat in a chair that faced the door, nervously drumming her fingers on the table between them. She looked at Jade, and seemed to be weighing how much to say.

Finally, she said, "I'm only telling you this because I'm so worried about Mr. Lawrence and you are the only visitor he's had. Except, well, I'll get into that. Fact is, I know you, and I know what a caring person you are. I'm hoping there may be something you can do to help Ben, I mean, Mr. Lawrence. He's a dear, sweet man, and I hate to see him declining the way he has been lately. Even a few weeks ago, he wasn't this bad. Part of my job is to check in with the residents every day. Mr. Lawrence is one of my favorites. Except these days, he sometimes doesn't even know who I am. He keeps saying that 'Timothy' must have sent me, too."

Daisy looked at Jade intently. "On Monday, Mr. Lawrence had a visitor. The man said his name was - you guessed it - Timothy." Jade felt gooseflesh ripple up and down her arms. Daisy continued, "'Timothy' spent about an hour with Mr. Lawrence, then he stomped down the stairs and slammed out the door. A minute later, I saw him rocket out of the parking lot, driving a black Mercedes. I immediately ran up to check on Mr. Lawrence. He was sitting in his rocker, staring out the window. His hands were shaking. I asked him if he was okay. He said the man who just left was his grandson. I didn't want to upset him but I had to ask how that could be, since I thought HE was the last Lawrence. He said he thought so, too.

"He told me to sit down, then he told me the most amazing story. He said that, when he was in his 20's, he fell in love with a beautiful young lady. Her name was Alois. She was from a very strict family and barely out of her teens. They dated for years, waiting for her family to give them their blessing to marry. As Ben Lawrence wasn't from as prominent a family as Alois was, the blessing wasn't given. Ben and Alois decided to marry anyway, forsaking their families' money and support, in order to be together. Ben had given Alois his family ring, bearing the Lawrence family crest, and with an inscription beside the crest containing a code number that indicated that it belonged to him. Before they could complete their plans to elope, Alois became pregnant. When her parents found out, they sent her away to relatives in another state. Ben didn't know about it until it was a fait accompli. Word got back to him that she had died giving birth to his child, and he was told that the child had also died. There was no sense in coming forward to claim the child as his, as the child and his beloved Alois were both dead. He made discreet inquiries, but he was never able to confirm whether his child was dead.

"Eventually, he moved on with his life. He worked much too hard, spent too much time alone. He never again found anyone to love, and there were no other children for him. Then, his whole lifetime later, just a few weeks ago, Mr. Lawrence got a letter. The letter was from his son, Daniel. He knew it could only be his son as the letter was sealed with wax, and the wax bore the imprint of the Lawrence family crest, complete with Ben Lawrence's coded number, made from the ring he had given to his one true love, all those years ago. The shock was almost too much for him. He took to his bed for days. Then, when he began to feel better, he wrote back to Daniel, telling him about the mother Daniel never knew. Daniel and Mr. Lawrence made plans to meet. Daniel came here, a little over a week ago. I met him. He's an elderly gentleman himself. It's almost eerie how much Daniel and Ben resemble each other. Both of them have those strange hazel-and-gold eyes, which, Mr. Lawrence has told me, is a common feature to the Lawrence men.

"Mr. Lawrence seemed conflicted about discovering that, not only had his son survived, but Daniel also had a son, which meant the Lawrence family *had* continued. I found that odd, that Mr. Lawrence had mixed feelings about his family line continuing. Mr. Lawrence told me that he asked Daniel to bring his son, Timothy, next time. Then, just a few days ago, as I said, Timothy showed up. Alone. Mr. Lawrence wouldn't tell me anything about his grandson's visit.

I knew it had upset him; he seemed worried, afterward. That's all I know about his family situation, I hope it helps you."

Jade took a moment to absorb the startling information. Finally she said, "Daisy, thank you so much for sharing this information with me. I can see how concerned you are about him, and I'm going to try to help Mr. Lawrence if I can. Meanwhile, this conversation never happened." Jade gave Daisy a wink.

Daisy looked relieved. "I know, as you said, you are researching something in connection with the Lawrence family. Anything you can do to help bring Mr. Lawrence peace will be so appreciated. We are all so fond of him."

Daisy led Jade out of the conference room and they walked together toward the exit. Jade pulled out her wallet and extracted one of her business cards. She wrote her cell phone number on the back and passed it to Daisy. "Would you please call me if anything else happens? I mean, specifically if Mr. Lawrence's grand son comes back? I think you may be right, Daisy, I think that Timothy may be bad news for Mr. Lawrence." Daisy nodded, and the women exchanged a quick hug.

Jade made her way back to the VW, lost in thought. She knew, in order to make sense of the things happening now with the Lawrences, she'd need to go back to the start, back to 1870's Portland, Maine. Her first step in that direction would be to finish reading Erin's diary. Even though it was already 9:30, she knew she wouldn't sleep tonight until she finished reading the diary.

Chapter 11

At home, Jade pulled all the shades in her house, and checked that her doors and windows were all locked. She took a few minutes to walk through the house, to make sure nothing had been moved. Bardo followed comfortingly along behind her. To her relief, everything looked to be exactly as she had left it. As she was already upstairs, with the VW keys and remote in her hand, she took the opportunity to do what Derrick had suggested. She hit the red panic button on her the remote. From her driveway, she could clearly hear the loud rhythmic beeping of the horn that signaled the car's alarm. Satisfied, she hit the button again to stop it. She never would have thought of this, but having this additional line of defense DID make her feel a little safer. She also knew he was right about getting a security system installed. She'd make some calls about that tomorrow.

A red blinking light caught her attention as she walked through her bedroom. Her answering machine. There were two messages. One call was from her sister Phyllis, returning her call from earlier that day. Jade had previously left Phyllis a voicemail message from work, asking if she had seen Peter recently, and telling her that he seemed to be either missing or incommunicado. Phyllis' responding voicemail message had said, sorry, but she hadn't seen him for weeks. Jade thought Phyllis' message sounded snippy, and not at all worried. More sad than unusual, Jade thought, pushing the button to erase the message and play the next one.

The other message started with loud electronic hissing. After a long moment, a deep, quiet voice said, "Please, Jade, whatever you know about the Lawrences, forget you know it. It could mean your life if you don't let it go. There are unimaginably unstable people involved. People who don't care if you live or die." Shocked, Jade played the message again, turning up the volume. It was obvious that whoever left the message didn't want to see her hurt and may even be afraid for her. The voice carried the ring of truth. Jade checked her caller ID and noted that the telephone number associated with the time stamp on this message was listed as "private caller". Of course.

Jade thought about contacting the police but realized that Derrick would likely be assigned the case. Regardless of whether it was Derrick or someone else, the idea of contacting the police at all, knowing how little they would probably be able to do to protect her, given the vagueness of the message, didn't really seem like a useful idea.

She removed her notes and the diary from her briefcase and took them to the kitchen table. A moment later, Erin's words had transported Jade back in time once more.

Friday, 13 September, 1878, 9:30 PM

I'm back, dear diary. How can so much horror happen in two short hours? I have to get this down, just in case, well....Just in case. I heard a crash earlier, when I was writing at my desk. I knew immediately that it came from the room next to mine, which is the Lawrence's suite. I ran in, without knocking first, as I was worried that Mrs. Lawrence may be hurt. I saw a man on his knees in front of Mrs. Lawrence, who was sitting in her favorite chair. The man had his head on Mrs. Lawrence's lap, his back heaving with anguished sobs. I recognized him by the clothing he wore. It was Mrs. Lawrence's husband, Trevor!

At least, that's what I first thought. Then he raised his eyes to meet mine and I saw that it was Tim, and he was wearing Trevor's clothing. And he wasn't sobbing, he was laughing! My frantically searching gaze fell on Mrs. Lawrence's face, and I was relieved to see she was sitting serenely, looking out the window. My eyes traveled downward, and I saw that her partially clad bosom was soaked with blood. One shoulder of her dress had been cut away, and the fabric had fallen to expose one breast. The skirts of her dress had been ripped down, exposing her slim waist, and even more shockingly, her most private place. There was blood between Mrs. Lawrence's thighs. I realized that Tim must have cut her there, too.

Against the pristine whiteness of her stomach I saw, cut into her very flesh, the symbol I had previously heard was found with or on some of the murdered town girls. It was a horizontal number eight, with something carved into each of the circles. I heard a prolonged and terrifying cry, eventually realizing that the strange keening noise was coming from me.

I tore my eyes from Mrs. Lawrence in time to see that Tim was now pointing the knife toward me, and was moving toward me. His eyes held no trace of whatever humanity there had been in him. He smiled, revealing blood-stained teeth. I realized then that Tim had not just cut Mrs. Lawrence.

I shook off my paralysis and, just as Tim was almost close enough to reach for me, I whirled and ran down the stairs. Looking up the stairs as I fumbled with the front door lock, I saw that Tim continued to give chase, his bloody knife held out before him. The lock on the front door finally released and I fled into the night.

I ran down the lane, past houses in which, I was dimly aware, my friends and neighbors were passing their evening with no idea of the horror unfolding mere feet away. I glanced back as I ran, and realized with relief that Tim was no longer behind me. Tim was walking away from me, back toward the house. I darted to the left, into the woods, and let myself fall to my knees. In the comparative safety of the trees, I gave vent to my anger and sorrow.

I think I must have been overcome for quite some time as when next I was aware, the moon had begun to rise and the air had cooled. Staying in the cover of the trees and keeping the road in sight, I cautiously walked back toward the Lawrence estate. Instead of walking the path to the front door, I circled the property, and waited in the woods behind the house. Several minutes later, my caution was rewarded as I heard the back door squeak open, then I saw a lone man leave the house, climb into his waiting carriage and ride away.

Knowing the only man in the house that evening was Tim, I knew the house would now be empty. After what I had seen, it was not safe for me to stay there. But before I left, I knew I needed to do one last thing for Mrs. Lawrence. I could not leave her to be found the way I had seen her. I went into the house, through the back door, and I made my way back up the stairs to Mrs. Lawrence's suite.

Inside the door to her sitting room I paused. So intently did I listen that I heard my heart, beating in my ears. The smell of blood was overwhelming. I stood in front of Mrs. Lawrence, and her sightless eyes appeared to watch me as I cried for her, for the terrible way she had to die and for the world's loss of her. I took her cold hand in mine, held it to my lips, and kissed her goodbye. I said a short prayer for her, wishing her soul Godspeed to her well-earned reward.

I heard a slight sound from the floor below, and I suddenly recalled that Tim could return at any moment. I wiped my tears away and grabbed the afghan from Mrs. Lawrence's bed, placing it over her. I tucked the top under her chin and straightened the folds so that it would completely cover her mostly naked, bloody and defiled body. Satisfied that I had done what I could for my best friend, I left the room, closing the door softly behind me. I went down the hall to my own room, grabbed my diary, my cool-weather shawl and my purse. I put my diary in my purse and my shawl around my shoulders. Just then, I heard a sound from the back of the house. Alarmed, I realized that my time had run out. Tim was back.

I stood at the top of the stairs, thinking furiously. Since Tim usually put up his carriage at the back of the house, the chances were good that he would enter the house through the back door. As the back door was in full sight of the front door, directly across two open rooms, I knew I had to get to the front door and out before Tim opened the back door to come in, or he would see me. I dashed down the stairs, grabbed the front door knob and pulled. Thankfully, when I left earlier it didn't latch. I ran through the door and threw it shut behind me. As I darted down the porch stairs, I heard the tell-tale squeak of the back door being opened. I ran on, praying that Tim didn't hear the front door closing as he *came in the back door.*

I didn't know where else to go, so I went to my mother's house. She was puzzled to see me at this hour, but seemed pleased for all that. Right now, I'm sitting in my old bedroom, writing by candle light as I used to do as a child. I know I'm not safe here, and I don't want to endanger my family by being here. In the morning, I will leave the area and I will never return. I've already told my mother that I'm leaving, but I didn't tell her where I would go, and I didn't tell her what happened tonight, although she could clearly see that something did. She'll know that soon enough. With all the tragedy unfolding around us, I know my mother will miss me, but I also know she'll be relieved to have me out of harm's way.

Friday, 13 September, 1878, 11:45 PM.

I remain at my mother's house still. It's almost midnight and the constable just left. Apparently, a neighbor of the Lawrences heard loud crashing coming from the Lawrence house, then he saw Trevor Lawrence, covered with blood, running past his house and down the lane, chasing me. The neighbor sent for the constable, and when the constable got to the Lawrence house, he found Trevor, kneeling at his dead wife's feet, covered with blood and screaming. His grief had destroyed his mind. He was arrested forthwith, and is now in jail, soon to be tried and likely executed for his wife's murder.

They have the wrong man. The man who was running away from the Lawrence house tonight was Tim, dressed as Trevor. Trevor must have come home from his trip, while Tim was out, and found his wife dead. Then the constable found Trevor, in shock and grief over his wife, and arrested him. I know that every law man in the county has been working very hard to solve the recent senseless killings. Since Mrs. Lawrence had the strange symbol on her body, I imagine Trevor will not just be accused of her murder, but of the several other murders that have happened recently. My mother told the constable that I had been here earlier. She knew this would keep me from having to tell the police what I saw. I'm grateful to her, but feeling guilty that I did not speak up in defense of my employer.

Saturday, 14 September, 1878, 8:20 AM.

After a sleepless night, I decided that I need to make one final trip to the Lawrence home. If there's ever to be a way for the descendants of the family to know the truth about what happened tonight, I will need to tell them. I know I cannot take what I know to the constable as it will be the word of a maid against the word of a member of the most powerful family in the county. And if I come forward, Tim will know where I am and he will kill me for what I know. Likewise, I cannot place my own family in jeopardy by telling them the truth about what has happened. Instead, I have thought of a way to tell the people who really need to know what happened. The next generations of Lawrence women need to know about their legacy. Trevor will likely be executed for his supposed crimes, then the killings will likely continue as Trevor is innocent. Although that is a tragedy, it is also a tragedy that these multiple killings have taken place before, with other generations of Lawrence family men, and will likely continue with future generations. Therefore, I know that I need to try to pass on a message to them. If my grandmother is right (and I believe she is), the only Lawrences who turn to murder are the men. Therefore, I will hide my diary in the 3rd floor library of the house. I have chosen there because it's a room that only the women of the family use, the men preferring to use the study on the first floor, because it has a fireplace.

I've written a note to direct the reader to the 3rd floor library, to find my diary, which will provide written testimony about the murders, and about Trevor's innocence. I'll put the note in the false bottom of Mrs. Lawrence's jewelry box. My dear Mrs. Lawrence once showed me the false bottom, and told me that a true lady always needed a safe place to put her most prized and secret possessions. Since the jewelry box has been handed down to the current Mrs. Lawrence of the house for generations, I'm hopeful that, if a future Mrs. Lawrence does not find this diary in the library, then the note I will place inside the jewelry box will direct a female Lawrence reader to my diary, and it will be found that way.

I am also hoping that, dear reader, if you are a female member of the Lawrence family, that you can finish the work I started, if I am not destined to complete it. Please, if you are reading this, find a way to stop the killing. Please also know that Mrs. Trevor Lawrence was NOT killed by her husband, Trevor. Tim Lawrence killed her, as I believe he killed several other young women. He is a monster in human skin. I beg that you make this truth known to all, to give Mrs. Lawrence whatever justice is ours to give her.

Jade finished reading this entry, then turned several blank pages, her vision blurred by tears. That was the last entry. Jade was overwhelmed by Erin's heroic selflessness. Erin could have slipped away in the night and found a safe place to live, far away from the cursed Lawrences of Portland, Maine. Instead of seeking safety, Erin risked, and ultimately gave, her life for a chance to help her friend, a chance to make things right, a chance to end a horror with which most women could not even have dealt. Jade knew she must now take up the cause for which Erin gave her life.

Jade suddenly realized the likely reason the note in the bottom of the jewelry case was not found sooner. After Mrs. Lawrence was killed, there may not have been a Mrs. Lawrence to be the lady of the house for quite some time, and no one to whom the secret of the jewelry case's false bottom could be passed. As the diary indicated that there may have been several generations of murdering Lawrence men, Jade knew that finding out more about the current Lawrence men would be her priority. She immediately began to formulate her plan. She could start at the Portland Public Library. She could cross-reference what she could find on the Lawrence family with whatever murders happened in the area, starting with current records and working backward through the last 200 years. She would look specifically for murders of young women, and give special attention to murders involving cutting or dismembering of the bodies. Jade would also confirm through public records whether Trevor Lawrence was found guilty and executed for the murder of his wife, and possibly for other murders as well. If Trevor had been unjustly executed, Jade wanted his memory vindicated.

Based on the fact that Jade had found the note in the jewelry case, but had found the diary in the skeleton's pocket, walled up behind the 3rd floor library, Jade realized that Erin had successfully planted the note in the false bottom of the jewelry box, but may have been caught as she tried to put the diary in the 3rd floor library. Caught, killed, and then her body hidden inside that secret room. As Trevor had been arrested at that point, he could not have killed Erin. And, if Jade could prove that the murders continued after Trevor was imprisoned and executed, that would be additional compelling evidence to prove Trevor didn't murder his wife, and likely never killed anyone else, either.

Jade thought it sadly apt that Erin, who's courageous sacrifice had provided the best chance for the truth to be known, had herself been consigned to sit silently and alone, for decades, faithfully concealing and protecting the most incriminating of evidence, in her apron pocket.

Chapter 12

Jade made her way, bleary-eyed and groggy, to the kitchen the next morning. It was just before 7:00 AM and she had slept less than six hours. Standing at the kitchen sink, drinking her first of coffee, Jade looked out the window and tried to make sense of everything that had happened yesterday. From finding the knife, to her mother's revelations about Peter, including his being missing. The desperate ending to Erin's diary. Everything was beginning to feel surreal, and ominously connected. Jade took a shower, got dressed and packed her lunch, moving through her morning chores on autopilot. Jade gave Bardo a cuddle then locked up the house and left for work.

At the office, Jade worked straight through until noon, grateful for the diversion of her heavy workload. She was about to break for lunch when her cell phone rang. Knowing Malcolm frowned on personal calls at work, Jade grabbed the phone and flipped it open before it could ring again. Jade's heartbeat accelerated when she saw the caller ID. It was Derrick Zachary. She was developing a serious crush on this man. Could it be his handsome face? His long muscular legs? Perhaps his caring manner? Jade knew it was all of these things, and more. Jade managed to keep the direction of her thoughts out of her voice as she told Derrick that she'd be home by 5:00, if he was free then. He said he'd be there. She made a mental note to be out of work at 4:15, so she could take a shower and change clothes before Derrick got there. She disconnected the call and started to flip her telephone closed, then she spotted the voicemail icon. She must have missed a call earlier when she stepped out of her office. She dialed in. It was Steven, the man she met at her mother's party for Peter the other night. Steven was asking to see her, perhaps this coming weekend. She kept the message in her voicemail box and flipped the cell phone closed. Between Derrick and Steven, her love life was definitely looking up. Finally something interesting to tell Diane, Jade thought wryly.

At mid-afternoon, Jade took a break to get a fresh cup of coffee from the coffee shop two doors down. When she came back, she took a few moments, as she promised herself she would, to check into getting a home security system.

She contacted the one security installation and surveillance company listed in the telephone book that she had actually heard of, and they agreed to meet her at her house at 5:00 on Monday afternoon.

That afternoon, promptly at 5:00, Jade watched from her porch stairs as Derrick pulled his cruiser into her driveway. It occurred to her that the neighbors might be a little alarmed by the police presence in and around her house lately. She knew it couldn't be helped, and that she hadn't done anything wrong. But she couldn't completely stifle the guilt she felt. She furtively looked up and down the street, but saw no nosy neighbors lining the sidewalks. But, she reasoned, they were probably frightened and were peeking through their curtains from inside their homes. Jade headed down her driveway to meet Derrick, giving her street, both up and down, a reassuring smile just in case anyone was looking.

She watched Derrick get out of the cruiser and walk toward her. Once again she felt the power of his presence. She knew she was dangerously attracted to this man. She suddenly realized that she didn't even know if Derrick was married! She looked at his hands. No rings. These days, that didn't mean much. Derrick looked over and caught her eye, smiled, and started toward her. He was such a handsome man, with his unlined skin and salt-and-pepper hair. She struggled to keep her feelings from showing on her face. He was, after all, a detective!

"Hi Jade. Ready to take a ride with me?"

Jade's heart skipped a beat. "Let me give my mother a call and make sure she's home."

Derrick put a staying hand on her arm. "I would appreciate it if you didn't do that."

Jade immediately realized why. Derrick didn't want to give her mother time to remove anything incriminating before they got there. And he may just have a point, Jade thought. They climbed into the cruiser together and pulled out into the late afternoon traffic.

Ten minutes later, Jade and Derrick pulled in to Agatha's driveway. Derrick strode up the driveway ahead of Jade. He was, she noticed, wearing gloves and carrying a form, a pen and several clear plastic bags. Derrick seemed to understand that his presence would be upsetting to Agatha, and he immediately got down to business.

"Hello Mrs. Danner. If you would just sign this Authorization form, then point me in the direction of Peter's room, I'll get out of your hair as quickly as I can." Agatha took a pen from Derrick's hand, signed the form, and passed the pen back.

The three of them walked through the house and up the stairs. In the doorway to Peter's bedroom, Derrick asked Jade and Agatha to wait downstairs, saying that he should only be a few minutes. He also told them that, if it was necessary to remove anything from the room, he would provide a receipt for it. Agatha agreed and Derrick entered the room, closing the door firmly behind him. Agatha and Jade stood in front of the closed door for a moment, then turned as one and went downstairs to wait.

Sitting at the kitchen table, Jade looked at her mother. She looked tired, and older than Jade had ever seen her look. Jade took her hand and gave her what she hoped was a comforting smile. Her mother squeezed her hand and somewhat tremulously, smiled back. They sat that way for a few moments, then Agatha disengaged their hands, stood up and walked to the end of the kitchen counter. She opened a drawer and took out a small stack of variously sized papers. She put them in front of Jade. Jade looked down at the papers, then looked questioningly up at her mother.

Agatha said, "Jade, please just take them and put them in your purse. I don't want your police officer friend to know about them. When he said yesterday that he'd need to search Peter's room, I worried about what he might find, so I had a quick look first. I didn't intend to take anything out of the room, I just wanted to know what was there, what he'd find, so I wouldn't feel blindsided."

She sat down and primly folded her hands on her lap. Looking down at her hands, Agatha went on. "These papers aren't incriminating in any way that I can see, but I wanted you to see them because there's information in there about the Lawrence family, and I know you were working on an appraisal for them recently. I don't know if there's anything there that'll be of interest to you, but, since I felt sure the police wouldn't need this stuff, you go ahead and take it. Let me know if there is anything in there that may explain where Peter is."

Stunned at her mother's temerity, and mystified about why Peter would have information about the Lawrences, Jade looked quickly through the papers. Some of them had Peter's scrawling handwriting on them. Others looked to be newspaper clippings and records of some kind. Jade realized that her mother had seen through her transparent attempt to hide the name of the family for which she had been doing the jewelry case appraisal, when she had told her parents and Steven about it, the night of Peter's party. Jade rolled up the papers and put them in her purse.

As she put her purse back on the floor next to her chair, she heard Derrick start down the stairs. He looked from one to the other of them, a little distrustfully, Jade thought. What was he, anyway, psychic? He was holding a small evidence bag, which contained a key. "Mrs. Danner, do you recognize this key?"

Agatha looked at him, then closely at the key. "No, I can't say I do. I know it doesn't go to the front or back door of the house, and it doesn't look like a car key."

Derrick gave Agatha a receipt for the key, tracing the outline of the key on the receipt, then Jade and Derrick got into the cruiser and drove away. Jade turned in her seat and looked back at her mother's house. It was the place where she grew up, the place that held many wonderful, warm memories for her. Except, now, cloaked in the shadow of oncoming night, it looked like a strange, unfriendly place jealously guarding its malevolent secrets.

Chapter 13

As Derrick drove her home, Jade studied his profile. His face looked forbidding, lit as it was from the dashboard lights below. As if he sensed her scrutiny, he glanced over. His smile indicated that whatever he saw pleased him, but he said nothing. Jade suddenly felt as though he knew far more about her, more about her secrets, than she wanted him to.

Derrick slung his arm across the back of the seat, his hand inadvertently brushing Jade's shoulder. She found herself powerfully drawn to him, the comfort and safety she knew he could give her. More than that, her body resonated with the passionate nature she instinctively knew he possessed. Giving herself a mental slap, she realized that she still didn't know if he was married, or if he was involved with someone. She suddenly felt that her attraction to Derrick was inappropriate, given the situation that had brought them together. She abruptly stopped her scrutiny of Derrick's face and looked down. She knew Derrick felt the sudden change in her manner as she saw him look questioningly over at her, then, with a heavy sigh, turn his attention back to his driving.

Derrick dropped Jade off at home, and with very little parting conversation, he drove away. Jade felt vaguely disappointed, realizing that Derrick probably didn't feel about her as she was beginning to feel about him. She thought to herself again that someone as handsome, sweet and smart as he is would more than likely have an equally attractive, sweet and smart "significant other" waiting at home for him. Knowing that he was investigating her brother's disappearance was reassuring, but knowing that he was also investigating the discovery of the knife in the car Peter often drove, made her feel like Derrick was leading the opposing team. Derrick was also investigating the vandalism of her truck at the mall, which was the last thing Jade wanted him looking in to. She would have to tread carefully with this Detective!

Jade made hot cocoa and toast, and sat down at the kitchen table. She took the bundle of loose papers her mother had given her out of her purse. The sheet on top featured Peter's handwriting. It was difficult to read, but Jade had grown up with Peter's handwriting. Across the top of the first paper was written, "Three Dollar Dewey's, January 3, 2002, 11:30 P.M." There was a list of eight names under the title. One of the names, Jade noticed, was "Timothy Lawry". She wondered at the name's similarity to Timothy Lawrence.

Jade knew that a woman was murdered in the Old Port section of Portland (near Three Dollar Dewey's tavern), in the early hours of January 4, 2002. This is the murder form which Peter had been brought in for questioning. Jade thought that this list was probably the bar patrons that Peter had been able to confirm were there that night. Taped to the back of Peter's handwritten list was a copy of the newspaper article about the murder. The woman, named Paulina Nielson, had been seen arguing with a "local man" (implying, Jade thought, that he had been identified by the police, but that they were not releasing his name to the press). Ms. Nielson was found, in the early hours of January 4, 2002, partially clad and partially dismembered, less than a block from where she and the local man had been seen arguing.

Jade turned back to the small stack of remaining papers. The next item was a newspaper clipping. The date was October 29, 2001. The clipping was about the murder of a young woman that happened on the Long Wharf pier in Portland. There were very few leads. The article said the woman, identified as Heather Demoree, had been brutally raped, stabbed and partially dismembered.

Peter had titled the next piece of paper "Murder #6". Three names appeared on the paper. One of the names had a question mark written next to it. Timothy Lawry. Immediately following this paper was another newspaper clipping. This one contained a story about a woman who was raped and killed on York Street in Portland, in the fall of 2002. York Street, Jade knew, was within a mile of the Old Port. Cathy Small, the York Street victim, had been "partly dismembered" and had been found with several items of her clothing apparently absent. This time, the police had questioned the woman's husband, as well as a next door neighbor named Timothy Lawry.

Jade wasn't sure what her mother was talking about when she said that these papers contained references to the Lawrences. Perhaps she had confused the name "Lawry" with "Lawrence".

With the next piece of paper, Jade found her answer. Another of Peter's handwritten notes, "Timothy Lawry" and "Timothy Lawrence" written about an inch apart, with a question mark between them.

Hoping the remaining papers would provide further illumination, Jade once again turned back to the dwindling stack. The next sheet had ornate borders and a raised seal. It was a birth certificate for a child named was Timothy Steven Lawrence. The date of birth was September 8, 1962. The mother's name was Lianne Lawrence, the father, Daniel Lawrence. On the back of the birth certificate was a seal that Jade had seen before. It was the Lawrence family crest.

The next page was a copy of a divorce decree, dated September 9, 1979. The divorce dissolved the marriage of Lianne Lawrence and Daniel Lawrence. Lianne and the "minor child" (presumably Timothy) were permitted to change their legal last name from "Lawrence" to "Lawry". Jade was stunned to realize that the Timothy Lawry that Peter had been investigating was likely a member of the Lawrence family.

Jade thought that Peter had probably started out trying to clear his name, when he realized the police suspected him of the murder of the woman in the Old Port. As Peter uncovered more information, he saw the name Timothy Lawry, at least twice. Knowing Peter, he would have had to pursue this unlikely coincidence.

It wasn't clear how Peter could have gotten the birth certificate and the divorce decree. Jade was uncomfortably aware that Peter could easily have found out where Timothy lived and could have just broken in. It wouldn't be the first time, Jade knew, that Peter decided to take the most direct (if not the most legal) route to something he wanted.

One of Peter's notes had said "Murder #6". She only saw information about three murders in the stack of papers she had. It was possible, maybe even likely, that this sheaf of papers was only part of the sum total of Peter's research. At the library, Jade would also see if there were other murders that fit the rape/kill/mutilate modus operandi of the "Lawrence" killings, and whether there was mention of Timothy Lawry in any of the records for the others. It was clear to Jade that Peter suspected Timothy of these murders.

Jade turned to the last piece of paper. And was completely blown away. It was a digital picture that looked like it had been printed on a less-than-picture-quality printer. The caption under the picture was "Timothy Lawry". Peter had written under that, "Timothy Steven Lawrence". The face was instantly recognizable to her. It was the man she had met at Peter's party the other night, who had introduced himself as Steven, and said he was a drinking buddy of Peter's. The background of the picture was also familiar. The picture of Steven had been taken outside Jade's own house! Jade remembered that she hadn't returned Steven's call from earlier in the day, to set up a date. She was glad now that she hadn't. Her attempting to be "open" to the idea of finding love, as Diane had suggested at lunch the other day, would not include dating a potential serial killer.

Shaking, Jade took out a packet of index cards and wrote what she knew and what she needed to know. When she was done, she sat back and looked at what she had written:

1. The note found in the jewelry case leads to Erin's diary. The diary names the real killer of Marie, not as her husband, Trevor but Tim, Trevor's brother. Erin wants the real killer known and wants the Lawrences, including Tim, to be exposed for the killers they've been (and may have continued to be).

2. The symbol on the note, the diary and on and around murder victims, the Möbius, means "infinity", but is there a reason it's being used in relation to these victims? How many other victims can be tied to the Möbius and also to the Lawrences?

3. Assumption: it's Erin's body inside the 3rd floor library wall in L. house.

4. The elderly Mr. Lawrence has a son, Daniel. Daniel has a son, Timothy. Timothy also goes by the name Steven and may be a serial killer.

5. Who was watching me inside the Lawrence house? Daniel's meeting with the elder Mr. L took place before I went to the L. house. Did Daniel know about the L. family house? Was it him? Did Timothy know about the Lawrence house? Was it him?

6. Who broke into my house and took my diary notes, called to threaten me and trashed my truck (assuming that it's the same person)? This was likely

Timothy. He obviously knows where I live.

7. Who called to warn me off the Lawrences, appearing worried about me? Elderly Ben Lawrence? His son, Daniel?

8. WAS there a Lawrence family curse which causes at least one of the men of the family to become a murderer every generation? If so, was Tim the killer in the 1870's? If there's some kind of killer gene in the family, did it continue AFTER the 1870's murders, possibly even up to today?

9. Did Trevor get executed for the murder of his wife? What about the other murders in the town at that time? Did any occur after Trevor's arrest? Was anything done about it, if so?

10. Peter has been missing since the day of his party. Does the information he uncovered about Timothy (Steven) Lawry/Lawrence have anything to do with his disappearance?

11. There was a knife hidden in a towel in the VW that Peter often used. There was a murder in the Old Port last winter, Peter was a suspect and may still be. Is the knife connected to that murder? Why is it in Peter's / Mom's car?

12. Peter has a history of strange, possibly dangerous behavior. This I know from my own experience, and mom has now corroborated with her own, previously unspoken perspective. Did his apparent proclivities toward violence and anti-social behavior get him killed?

13. Is there any correlation between the Lawrence family jewelry case being sent to me for appraisal now, and Peter's troubles? It seems coincidental that I

would be investigating the Lawrence family, because of the note, the diary and the murders, then I would happen across information that my brother Peter was also investigating the Lawrences.

Jade looked at the index cards in front of her. There were more questions than answers. But it was definitely helpful to her to have the information laid out. Jade knew it was possible that the information she had already found could get her killed. She also knew that, until she was able to get to the bottom of what happened, both back then and now, she would continue to be in danger. She couldn't back off now. The last thing she would be expected to do would be to take the offensive. Therefore, Jade decided, that is exactly what she would do.

Chapter 14

Nightmares woke Jade early on Friday morning. She lay quietly in her bed, listening to the profound silence. Outside, it was still mostly dark. Whatever she had been dreaming about, now forgotten, had left her feeling unsettled. She realized that she was getting to be a "nerve stick" these days. She knew she wouldn't get back to sleep, now that it was close to her usual wake up time, so she climbed out of bed and headed to the shower.

At work a bit early, Jade completed two interesting and lucrative assignments. One of them was much simpler than she initially thought it would be. The other came in with an appraisal that had been done previously by her firm, so the research and provenance was clearly documented in her files, she needed only update the appraisal. At lunch, Jade took a walk through the Old Port, as she often did. This time, however, she found that the calm her surroundings usually provided had completely changed. Instead of enjoying the tiny cobblestone-lined streets, she found herself thinking about what it must have been like for the three murder victims she now knew had died here in recent years.

It would have been cold, and dark. And when they realized that their lives end that night, in that place, they must have been terrified. The thought of the women, fighting so fiercely for their lives, only to be forced to submit in the end, made Jade furious. She instinctively knew that Peter was right to have connected Timothy Steven Lawrence to these murders. Worry continued to nibble at Jade's nerves as she again thought that Peter's disappearance may have been related to the information he had uncovered about the murders.

Jade recalled that Erin's diary told of how she, her mother, and her grandmother had all been young women when each had lived through the horror of watching friends and family members disappear, sometimes to be found dead weeks later, but sometimes never to be found. Part of the repulsiveness of this situation, Jade knew, was that the killings had happened in their own hometown. MY hometown, Jade thought angrily. Walking back to work, Jade felt more than ever how important it was to find out the truth about this Lawrence family "curse".

Jade's afternoon passed quickly, and, as she cleared her desk to leave for the weekend, Malcolm approached her.

"Jade, I'm glad I caught you. I took a telephone message for you while you were at lunch. Your phone rang, so I picked it up. A man by the name of Ben Lawrence called. He wanted me to ask you to call him back as soon as you could. I'm sorry I didn't give you the message sooner; I was right out straight this afternoon. Is Ben Lawrence one of the Lawrence family for whom we did the jewelry box appraisal?"

Jade thought quickly. "Yes, he is. I was following up on a couple loose ends, mostly just for my own information".

Malcolm handed her the pink telephone message slip. "Leave it to you to always go above and beyond the call of duty. He said he'd be available all afternoon and hoped you'd get a chance to return his call today."

Jade put the message slip in her coat pocket and thanked Malcolm, not quite making eye contact. Jade went back to her office and dialed the number to the assisted living facility. When she asked to speak with Ben Lawrence, the nurse on duty asked Jade if she was a relative. Jade immediately suspected that something must have happened to him.

She asked the nurse if Daisy was on duty and was informed that Daisy had been scheduled to work today, and she was there earlier, but that she had left unexpectedly a short time ago. With a guilty pang, Jade assured the nurse that she was, in fact, a member of Ben Lawrence's family. The nurse then expressed regret in having to inform her that Mr. Lawrence had passed away, about an hour ago. A stunned Jade thanked the nurse for informing her, and disconnected. Now she understood why Daisy left work unexpectedly earlier. She knew how fond Daisy had been of Mr. Lawrence.

Jade sat at her desk for a moment, thinking about what to do next. She wondered if her research into Ben Lawrence's family, and specifically her visit with him on Wednesday, had anything to do with his death. She hoped she didn't hasten an already imminently deadly medical problem by upsetting him as she had apparently done. She also wondered if someone may have done something to him. Jade knew that people of Mr. Lawrence's advanced age did sometimes die suddenly. But her instincts were telling her that poor Mr. Lawrence may have had help with his journey from this world to the next.

Chapter 15

Jade didn't feel like sitting at home alone. Instead, she decided to get her library research started. She drove her rented VW to the Portland Public Library on Congress Street, and parked in the parking garage around the corner.

Walking in to the library, she took a deep, fortifying breath. Spending time at a local library had always been one of Jade's favorite things to do. Today, she sorely needed the comforting quiet. The best resource in the library, she had always found, was the librarian. Especially *this* librarian, as she had helped Jade several times in the past. Displaying her best winning smile, Jade approached the librarian's large kiosk. The librarian rewarded Jade's smile with one of her own.

"Hi, Jade. How can I help you today?" Jade was pleased that the librarian remembered her name. Jade's glance darted furtively to the librarian's name plate on the desk.

"Hi, Helen. I'm so glad you are working tonight. I'm looking for reference information for a local family that I'm told is one that goes back at least two hundred years."

Helen gave Jade a strange look. "You wouldn't be talking about the Lawrence family, would you?".

Jade was astonished. "How could you know that?" Helen gave a ghost of her earlier smile. "There was a man in here a few days ago, reading up on the Lawrence family. He joked that he was catching up on his personal history."

Jade said, "Was he about 35 to 40 years old?"

Helen immediately said "No, he was older than that, probably 65 or so". Jade thought it was probably Daniel, Ben Lawrence's illegitimate and until recently unknown son.

Jade asked Helen to first show her the reference material she provided to the unknown man. Helen escorted Jade to the back wall of the library. The section was called "Families of Historic Maine." Helen went immediately to the second free-standing bookcase, about halfway down the aisle, and pulled out two ancient-looking books, which were side-by-side on the shelf.

"Here are the two books he looked through. He took the books over to the closest table and sat there for about an hour. He took notes as he read through the books. When he was done, he put the books back where he found them and he left."

Jade took the books from Helen and walked to the table that her predecessor had used. The first book was titled <u>Maine Royalty</u>. The book provided birth, marriage and death records for several prominent Maine families, as well as anecdotal information apparently gathered from friends and family members. The book was published in 1974 and contained information going back to the late 1860's. The data for the earlier part of that time period was sketchy. Jade knew from her previous research, for antiques provenance, that most records for the city don't go back further than the 1860's because there was a catastrophic fire in Portland, on July 4, 1866. The fire destroyed thousands of homes and also damaged or destroyed most centers for commerce and records storage. At that time, the buildings and homes of the city were made predominantly of wood. After the fire, brick structures became the norm. Later, concrete became less expensive and easier with which to work, so that became the dominant material in more modern times. Live and learn, Jade thought to herself.

Checking the chapter listing at the beginning of the book, she was pleased to see several pages of the book were devoted to the Lawrence family. She immediately turned to that section of the book and started to read.

The book contained copies of the Town Register listing the births, marriages and deaths in the community. The records for the Lawrence family would hopefully provide Jade with confirmation of things she already knew, but she also thought it may provide some important pieces of the Lawrence puzzle.

The first date listed in the Lawrence family chapter was 1850, no month or day given, recording the birth of Tim and Trevor Lawrence in Portland, Maine. The father was listed as Brandon Lawrence, but the mother wasn't listed. The record was entered in 1867, which was probably the time when the city officials were trying to re-create as many of the records lost in the great fire as possible. The next record was Trevor's marriage to Marie, in 1875. Jade was completely unprepared for the next entry. The date was December 2, 1878. It was a record of Trevor's death, by hanging, after he was found guilty of the murders of 7 young women in the community as well as guilty of the murder of his own wife. Jade felt tears gathering and struggled to control them. She had known that there was the possibility, maybe even the likelihood, that Trevor had been tried and convicted, based on Erin's diary. But to have solid confirmation that it had actually happened was a very different thing. Absently wiping her eyes, Jade forced herself to continue reading.

Jade turned the page and was once again blindsided. Tim, who Erin had named in her diary as the true killer of Marie Lawrence and possibly the other young women who had gone missing, had married and fathered a child late in his life. The next record was the birth of twins, Benjamin Robert Lawrence and Michael Duffy Lawrence, on April 18, 1905. The father was listed as Tim Lawrence, age 55. The mother was listed as Louisa Lawrence, age 19. A death notice recorded three months later indicated that Michael Duffy Lawrence had died of "crib death", on July 4, 1905. Jade realized that, had Tim not married and procreated, the Lawrence family would have ended with Trevor's execution. Maybe that would have been best, Jade thought grimly.

In 1907, Louisa's death was recorded. She was murdered in the Lawrence house. A newspaper clipping had been published in the book. Before moving on to the rest of the dated records in the book, Jade took a moment to read the story on the death of Louisa Lawrence:

> Local Lawrence Lassie Next Victim of Möbius Murderer
> At 5:30 this morning, the local constabulary was summoned to
> 152 Commercial Street by Tim Lawrence. Officials arrived and

quickly determined that Mrs. Louisa Lawrence had expired, obviously at the hands of another. Older members of our community will recall that some twenty-seven years ago, Tim Lawrence's twin brother Trevor was convicted of killing his wife. Elder residents will also recall that the Möbius symbol was found cut into Trevor Lawrence's wife's abdomen, and that several very similar killings pre-dated the murder of Mrs. Trevor (Marie) Lawrence in 1878, and, more interesting still, several murders post-dated the 1878 murder and the subsequent conviction

and execution of Trevor Lawrence. This morning's victim was reportedly found clutching a piece of paper bearing the now infamous Möbius symbol. Police are seeking possible witnesses and are questioning family members, including the victim's husband. Mrs. Lawrence is also survived by her two year old son, Ben. Services information is pending.

Jade looked at the few remaining pages of the book that featured the Lawrence family and didn't see any further references to this murder. If someone was arrested for the crime, it wasn't published here.

The records indicated that Tim Lawrence died in 1931, at the ripe old age of 80. Apparently, Tim Lawrence disappeared from his home one night, amid suspicious circumstances which included the finding of a great deal of blood in his bedroom, but no body was ever found and Tim was assumed to have been murdered. Jade thought about the timing of Tim's death. Tim would have been alive when his son, Ben, started his romance with Alois, but would have gone missing the following year, possibly around the time Ben's child was born and allegedly, at least, had died. Jade wondered if Ben, at the age of 26, had somehow found out about his father's deadly hobby, and decided to put an end to it.

There were no other births, marriages or deaths recorded in the formal registry section of the chapter, after the 1931 death of Tim Lawrence. However, there were two additional pages of information on the Lawrence family. Looking quickly at the haphazard format of the information, Jade realized it was a completely subjective accounting of incidents and events in the lives of several of the Lawrence family members.

The preface to this section of the book stated that the information had been culled from news reports, journal entries and informal interviews with the Lawrence family and friends. This section of the book indicated that the Lawrences of old were often in trouble with the law, and through the generations, several of the Lawrence men had been jailed for various offenses ranging from public drunkenness to rape. None of them had been locked up for more than several months, however. Possibly in part, Jade concluded, because of the local prominence of the Lawrence name.

An entry near the end of the book caught her eye. A woman named Anne had spoken out to the local newspapers against the Lawrences. The interview was dated January 19, 1879. Anne stated that her daughter, Erin, had previously worked for the Lawrences, but she recently disappeared under strange circumstances. Anne reported that Tim Lawrence had come to her house looking for Erin in the early morning hours after Marie Lawrence had been found murdered. Anne told Tim, on that morning the September prior, that she had not seen her daughter since late the night before.

Anne told Tim, and also subsequently told the reporter, that Erin seemed upset that night, and refused to discuss why with her mother. The worried mother told Erin that, if she didn't want to discuss it with her, perhaps she should write it all down in her diary. That would get it off her chest and would help her determine the best course of action. Anne then said that Erin told her she had already done that, but it didn't help. Erin then said she had to leave the area and would not be returning. This saddened Anne, as she loved her daughter so very much, but it was also a relief, as there had been several girls murdered in the area, just lately, and Anne wanted her daughter to be safe, even if that meant her being a great distance away. Anne said she knew that, would that she could, Erin would have sent word to her eventually that all was well. Since Anne had not heard from her cherished daughter, she knew that she must be dead, so close they were.

After the text of the interview with Anne, there was a short addendum to the story. The reporter had apparently gone back to Anne's house on February 21, 1879 to do a brief follow up and to ask a few additional questions. Unfortunately, Anne had been found dead in her home, horribly bludgeoned, less than 24 hours after the January newspaper article had been published. Friends and neighbors either didn't know what happened or suspected (or perhaps a bit more than suspected) what had happened and weren't willing to put themselves in danger as they seemed to feel that Anne might unwittingly have done.

Jade considered this new information. Apparently, Erin's mother suspected something was wrong that night, and knew for sure the next day, when she heard the news of Mrs. Lawrence's Anne had signed her own death warrant when she has unsuspectingly told the reporter about Erin confiding the events of that hellacious night in her diary. Tim must have read the article in the newspaper, then paid Anne a fatal visit. He must have been frantic when he realized there was a written account of what he had done, and that the information could surface at any time. Unfortunately for him, Jade thought with grim satisfaction, he never did find the incriminating diary.

There was one last short interview in the Lawrence family chapter. This interview was given by Erin's grandmother, who was Anne's mother, Charlotte. Charlotte was interviewed a week after her daughter Anne was found bludgeoned in her own home. Charlotte was apparently still in the throes of intense grief for her murdered child and her missing grandchild. She told the reporter that the Lawrence family was cursed, and that the area in which they lived was also cursed as the Lawrence men had been using it for their own personal killing ground for centuries. Charlotte related that there was a massive killing spree, all young, beautiful town women, when she was a teenager. Then, when her daughter Anne was young woman, it happened again. Finally, now that Erin was a young woman, it had been happening again. The reporter didn't provide further information in his article; he simply stated that Charlotte's reasoning must have been severely impaired by her grief. There was no information to indicate that the information provided by the distraught Charlotte was ever followed up on.

Jade closed the <u>Maine Royalty </u>book, then picked up the second book. It was very small, more of a hardcover pamphlet. The book looked to be at least as old as the first book. The cover was made of wood, which was pockmarked and splintered in places. There was no title on the book, but a label had been affixed to it, apparently fairly recently. The label said, "Southern Maine Homicides, 1840 to 1968".

Jade opened the book and saw only the inside of the back cover. Someone had ripped out all the pages. Jade took the vandalized book to Helen. She looked up from what she was reading, the chains on her glasses clinking softly. Without a word, Jade opened the book and showed Helen the inside. Helen's lips compressed in anger.

She held out her hands and reverently took the book from Jade and set it down in front of her. "I can't imagine who would do something like this! This book was a first edition and it's the only copy known to still exist. The only person I know of who's even looked at this book is the gentleman who came in a few days ago, you know, the one I was telling you about."

Jade nodded, thinking quickly. "Helen, do you have any idea what was in that book?"

Helen turned to her computer. After a brief volley of clacking keys, Helen smiled triumphantly and turned the screen to face Jade. "This is one of the few very old books that we converted to microfiche, then imaged into our computer files. We have a complete copy of the text stored on-line." Helen pressed a few more keys and her printer hummed to life. After a moment, Helen handed her a handful of pages. "Here you go."

Jade put the pages into her purse, thanked Helen for all her help and left the library. As she drove home, she thought about what she had learned, and how it had confirmed some of what she read in Erin's diary. Most interesting to her was the anecdotal information. Erin's suspicion that the cyclic killings in the area were the work of generations of Lawrence men seemed well-founded. Jade wondered if Ben, Daniel or Timothy Lawrence could be a murderer, or if maybe all of them were.

Chapter 16

When Jade got home, there was a police cruiser idling in front of her house. She parked the VW in the driveway and approached the cruiser, thinking about Peter. She immediately worried that his body had been found and they were here to inform her. But then, she reasoned, they would have told her mother first, and her mother would be here, or she'd have received a call on her cell phone summoning her to her mother's house. So it probably wasn't about Peter. As she neared the car, she realized it was Derrick. Her pulse immediately jumped. God, he was a beautiful man!

Derrick got out of the cruiser and came around to meet her at the end of her driveway. He gave her one of his (surely unintentional) sexy smiles. She found herself smiling back.

"Jade. How are you?" Jade looked into his face, noticing how tired he looked.

"I'm just fine, Derrick. And you?"

He made a sea-sawing gesture with his hand, still smiling and said, "The reason I'm here to ask you about Ben Lawrence. You called the assisted living facility where he lived, late this afternoon, and were informed of his death?"

Jade nodded that she had. Derrick said, "I knew it had to be the same Jade."

Derrick fell into step beside Jade as she walked toward her front door. "Mr. Lawrence called the police station at noontime today, apparently right after he tried to reach you. He mentioned you by name and said that he was worried that you may be in danger. Since your name was on our system in relation to an open case, and I'm the investigating officer, his call was immediately transferred to me."

Jade opened the front door and both of them entered; Jade promptly shut and locked the door behind them. They proceeded to the kitchen, Bardo at their heels. Sitting at the table now, facing each other, Derrick continued.

"Mr. Lawrence told me that he received a visit this morning, from his son, Daniel. Mr. Lawrence happened to mention you, Jade. He told Daniel about you coming to see him. When Ben said the name 'Jade', Daniel asked him to describe you. Ben said you looked just like someone he used to know. The description Ben gave to Daniel caused Daniel to become alarmed. Apparently Timothy had told Daniel, just the night before, of his obsession over a woman named Jade. Daniel realized the descriptions given by both Timothy and Ben matched. The "Jade" in each instance was one and the same. Daniel asked Ben to warn you not to associate with Timothy. Even though Timothy is Daniel's son, Daniel didn't want to put you in any danger, and he felt that you dating Timothy would do just that. Ben Lawrence told Daniel to warn you himself, if he felt that strongly about it."

Looking away from Derrick's intense stare, Jade felt her face grow warm.

She was pleased that she already knew enough about Timothy to stay away from him, and had found out about him before she ended up dating him, but she knew she couldn't tell Derrick about the papers from Peter's room that had put her on the path to enlightenment about Timothy. She glanced up at Derrick, then immediately away.

She said, "Did Daniel tell Ben Lawrence exactly *why* he thought I was in danger? Derrick apparently picked up on Jade's evasive attitude and looked questioningly at her. "Daniel said that his son, Timothy, has 'issues'".

Derrick went on, "Ben Lawrence told me that, at the end of his conversation with Daniel, Daniel said something that Ben found peculiar, something that worried Ben that Timothy may not be the only Lawrence family member that isn't quite right. Daniel told Ben Lawrence that he felt that Timothy had been following him recently. He also expressed concern that Timothy may also have bugged his phone. Daniel worried that Timothy may somehow find out that he had asked Ben to warn you, and that Timothy may retaliate. Ben was obviously worried that his new found son Daniel may be paranoid."

"Jade, it was clear to me that Ben Lawrence felt badly about asking you to leave the other day and he felt he owed you an apology, so he tried to call you. Apparently, your boss told Mr. Lawrence that you had just left for lunch. Mr. Lawrence then tried to contact the police. You have to give the old guy credit, he was really trying to do the right thing. I tried to call you in the afternoon. I'm assuming that you didn't check your cell phone for messages yet as I asked you to call me back." Derrick's voice sounded vaguely accusatory, Jade thought.

Jade pulled out her cell phone and saw that she actually had two messages. She made a mental note to check her messages later and put her cell phone back into her purse. Derrick had fallen silent and was studying her. Jade became uncomfortable.

"Derrick, I appreciate you coming over to warn me. I'll be sure to be a little more vigilant for awhile."

Jade started to get to her feet, as if her little speech had decided the matter. Derrick put a staying hand on her shoulder and Jade sat back down, looking expectantly at him.

"Jade, there is one more thing I need to tell you. Ben Lawrence's death wasn't natural. He was brutally murdered. He fought hard, there was blood everywhere. We know he was bludgeoned, and there was a leg missing from his table. I don't want to jump to conclusions, although it seems likely that was the murder weapon. The lab will probably be able to tell us more after the scene is processed and the autopsy is done. We didn't find the table leg, so apparently the killer took it with him."

Derrick seemed about to continue, but he was interrupted by a muffled chirp. With a groan of frustration, Derrick pulled his cell phone out of his jacket pocket and flipped it open. He listened for a moment, excused himself, and walked into the living room. Jade watched him disappear around the corner. She took a moment to collect her thoughts and try to get her mind around the fact that poor old Ben Lawrence had apparently been viciously beaten to death. It didn't seem real.

Derrick's black portfolio was on the table, police department insignia on the front. Jade glanced at the living room doorway. Derrick was nowhere in sight, but she could hear the murmur of his voice. She slid the black notebook closer to herself, then opened it. There was a police report, several pages in length, and behind that, several photographs. Jade flipped quickly through the pictures, keeping an eye out for Derrick. Suddenly, she froze. Her gorge rose involuntarily as she studied the photo. First she saw Mr. Lawrence's lifeless body propped against the back wall of his kitchen. There were black excoriated craters where his eyes should have been. Blood trailed down each cheek as if he had, in the end, cried blood. A familiar image was hastily scrawled in blood across the wall behind Ben. The Möbius symbol. There was an eye drawn inside one loop and the outline of a droplet drawn in the other loop.

If she had any doubt that Ben's death was related to the Lawrence family curse, it was gone. Her vision began to darken, first at the edges, then completely. Everything suddenly seemed distant and dreamlike. Jade felt herself beginning to fall. Derrick rounded the corner into the kitchen, and lunged for Jade, catching her neatly with one steely arm as she collapsed.

When Jade opened her eyes, she was on her living room couch, with a wet cloth on her head and a concerned Derrick sitting on the edge of the couch at her hip, looking down into her face. She could feel the comforting warmth of his body spreading through her from his contact. She tried to smile at him. Derrick's concerned expression eased into a relieved grin.

"Jade, I'm so sorry you had to see those pictures. I shouldn't have left them like that." Jade was amazed by his reaction. Shaking the remaining cobwebs from her brain she said,

"No, this was all my fault. I saw your book on the table. I thought, if there was a report in there about Ben's death, that maybe I'd be able to find out what happened. I'm sorry." She looked up at Derrick, willing him to forgive her. Her face must have shown what she was feeling.

Derrick said, "Don't worry about it, no harm, no foul. I just want to make sure you're okay. Seeing what you saw, especially when you aren't used to it, can be traumatic. It's even worse when it's someone you know."

Their conversation of a short time ago suddenly came flooding back. Jade squeezed her eyes shut. Tears rolled down her cheeks. She thought about poor Ben, and how he tried to warn her and probably died because of it. She thought of Peter and hoped he was okay, knowing he probably wasn't. She thought of someone breaking in to her house and taking her notes, the threatening telephone call, her truck being vandalized. And now, with this most persuasive confirmation that she was in danger, she suddenly felt vulnerable and frightened.

Jade took a moment to try to compose herself. Breathing in, breathing out, feeling the tension begin to loosen. Jade's clamoring nerves gradually began to give way to awareness of how close Derrick was. She could feel his body heat. His male scent brought her the rest of the way back. She opened her eyes. Derrick's eyes, now only inches from hers, watched the play of emotion on her face. What she saw in his eyes took her breath away. His eyes smoldered. He did nothing to hide his blatant wanting of her. He moved closer and watched her reaction. Her upper body moved upward a few inches, toward him, with a will of it's own. He slipped his arms around her and drew her against him. Her arms languidly snaked around his neck. Jade could feel his heartbeat thundering against her breasts.

She knew she was shaking, but wasn't sure if it was fear or wanting, or both. When her body had begun to settle, Derrick drew back from her and once again looked into her face. She saw clearly that he wanted to kiss her. And she also knew she wanted him to. She shifted closer to him, placing her lips close to his, but not touching. He turned his head slightly, brushing her lips gently with his. Every nerve in her body reacted, exquisitely tuned to that one tiny point of contact between them. She closed her eyes, and a small moan escaped her.

Suddenly, Derrick's lips covered hers and his arms tightened around her. His lips parted slightly, and his tongue touched her lips. She opened her lips greedily and met his thrusting tongue with her own. He groaned with pleasure, his hands now tentatively exploring her back. The chemistry between them was incendiary, as Jade knew it would be. She suddenly wanted him, more than she had ever wanted anyone. She needed to feel his taut, warm body wrapped around her. She wanted to watch his face as he gave and took his pleasure from her.

She cupped his face in her hands and pulled slightly back to look at him. His eyes were closed, and Jade marveled at the perfection of his face as she traced it with her hands. He opened his eyes, and Jade was hopelessly caught in the naked hunger she saw there. Derrick lowered Jade back to the couch, stretched his long body out beside her and once again took her into his arms. Jade shuddered as his hand slowly moved down her side, then slid around her to cup her buttock in one huge hand. She snuggled closer, giving him better access to her body, and she felt his need pushing against her thighs.

As his mouth boldly claimed hers, her senses reeled. She wanted this moment to last forever. Jade brazenly slid her leg around Derrick's body and pulled his hips close against her. She felt him moan against her mouth. Then, Jade felt a subtle shift in Derrick. His lips left hers, and his hands left her body. Jade opened her eyes and watched him as he sat up. His hair was mussed and his lips were red and swollen as she was sure hers were. He looked completely dumbfounded. Jade smiled to see his controlled manner had suddenly deserted him. "Jesus Christ! What the hell am I doing?!" He took a moment to compose himself, then turned to face her. She was still laying on the couch, her body suddenly chilled without his body heat.

"Jade, I'm sure you realize the effect you have on me. Stop looking at me like that, you make me crazy! I'm not going to take advantage of your vulnerability, as much as you make me want to. I hope there will come a time when we can continue this where we left off."

He stood up and adjusted himself uncomfortably. "God, I hope so", he muttered to himself as he began to pace restlessly. After a moment he sat back down, this time in the chair a much safer few feet away from the couch. He sat forward, elbows on his knees and looked intently at Jade. She was having a difficult time wiping the smile off her face. Derrick noticed her barely concealed delight at his discomfort and chose not to comment. Jade did, however, catch the slight upturn of his lips as he turned away.

He switched back into his Joe Friday mode. "Right now, we need to figure out what we are going to do to keep you safe. I'll do everything I can, and there's a lot I can do. In return, you need to tell me everything you know about what happened with your truck, why there was a knife in the trunk of your mother's car, and how you know Ben Lawrence. You also need to tell me about anything else that's happened. I do think you are in danger, and I think you need help. You need to put me fully in the picture if you want my help."

Amazed that she apparently had such an effect on this sweet, strong, beautiful man, Jade's heart soared. She desperately wanted to share her burden with him, and to accept his help and protection. On the heels of those comforting thoughts came the knowledge that, if she accepted his help, he would likely be in danger also. Still trying to deal with the knowledge that Ben Lawrence may have been brutally killed because he tried to warn her, she understood that her actions could put him or others in harm's way. She didn't want Derrick hurt. And as Jade had also realized previously, she had done things recently that were questionable at best, completely illegal at worst. She didn't want to have to tell Derrick about her part in the things that were now happening to her. Having made her decision, preparing to decline Derrick's offer of help, she resolutely turned to face him.

Something in her manner tipped him off. Before she could open her mouth to speak, he said, "Look, before you tell me to mind my own business, I want you to think about the pictures you saw. Whoever is responsible for Mr. Lawrence's murder wouldn't think twice about eliminating you or any other threat. You really are in danger, Jade. I thought so the day I met you at the mall when the wiring in your truck was trashed. Then, when I saw the knife in the trunk of the VW you borrowed from your mother, I knew there was something very dangerous going on."

He paused, appearing to consider his next words carefully. "I wasn't sure whether to tell you this or not, but for your own protection I feel that I should. Remember the key I found when I checked Peter's room? I got a partial fingerprint from the key and ran it through AFIS, our fingerprint database. We got a hit. The key belonged to a woman named Heather Demoree. She was killed a few years ago on Long Wharf. Finding something that belonged to a murder victim in the home of a man who was already a suspect in another murder paints a pretty grim picture for Peter's innocence. This is good reason why you and I probably shouldn't get involved on a personal level. Peter's your brother, and we are looking at him for at least one murder. That's a major conflict of interest. I do realize that there's more to the situation than I'm seeing so far."

"If you have any information to substantiate your brother's innocence, you need to tell me now. Based on this key, and the witness reports placing Peter at the scene of another murder, just before it took place, I may have enough evidence to get an arrest warrant for Peter. The good news is that this would add urgency to our search for him. The bad news is, these things will often take on a life of their own and anything he or anyone else close to him has done that may be considered suspicious would be closely scrutinized."

Listening to Derrick, Jade began to feel angry. And betrayed. She was annoyed with his obvious ploy to corner her into providing information for his investigation.

"Listen, Mr. Big Shot Investigator. You do what you think you have to do to further your investigation. But I won't be a source of information about my brother. I can't believe I was actually beginning to feel as if I could trust you! And all the time, you were just about finding my brother and pinning a bunch of murders on him!"

Derrick's demeanor immediately turned suspicious. "Jade, what do you mean by 'a bunch of murders'? I only told you about one, other than the one you knew Peter was suspected of. That hardly constitutes "a bunch". And you are wrong about my intentions. I do want to get to the bottom of your brother's disappearance, and yes, solving the murders would certainly be a great thing for me, personally and professionally. But right now, tonight, my concern is with you. You don't seem to have fully grasped the danger you may be in. That worries me more than anything."

Okay, now I've really stepped into it, Jade thought to herself. She filed away most of his righteous little speech for disassembly later. What she heard was the suspicion in his voice after she had said "bunch of murders". She didn't give Derrick enough credit for being observant, and she had messed up. She tried to smooth things over.

"I remember hearing about another murder that took place in this area within the past few years, and I just assumed that you'd be looking at that murder too. Why, ARE there others, too?" Jade walked to her living room window as she spoke and slid her eyes quickly to the side to look at Derrick, to see whether he appeared to be buying what she was so desperately selling.

He caught her look and, through a lips thinned in anger said, "Okay, fine, have it your way. We both know that you know more than you are saying, and I'm telling you that knowledge may get you killed. You think I'm only offering my protection in exchange for information about Peter. I think your protection, and Peter's guilt or innocence, are inextricably entwined. I can't make you tell me what you know, but I can and will keep an eye on you, to try to see that your foolishly stubborn insistence on keeping your sordid little family secrets doesn't get you killed."

Derrick stood and walked toward her front door. A moment later she heard the door slam shut and she was alone.

Jade looked out her living room window, watching Derrick fold his long, lean body into the driver's seat of his cruiser, and drive away. She did her nightly tour of the house, making sure that all the windows and doors were locked and headed to the kitchen for a late dinner. After her argument with Derrick, she found that she was no longer very hungry. After she had eaten a toasted English muffin, chased with a glass of chocolate milk, she decided to put an end to this very long day and get ready for bed.

Chapter 17

After she changed into her nightgown, Jade remembered that she had two voice mail messages on her cell phone. Barefoot, she padded down the stairs and into the kitchen. She listened to the first message, from Derrick. It had been left several hours ago. He was asking her to call him immediately, regarding Ben Lawrence. The sound of Derrick's concerned voice made her feel ashamed of her defensive behavior earlier. Maybe he really did care about her and wanted to protect her. Maybe she should tell him what she knew. She didn't want him to know about her part in putting herself in harm's way. It was she who took the note from the jewelry case. She broke into the Lawrence house. She took the diary. She went to see Mr. Lawrence and upset him, then possibly got him killed.

Then there was Peter. She knew things about Peter that may more strongly implicate him in the murders. She also knew things about Peter's own investigation into the one murder for which he was suspected, as well as the other murders he had uncovered in his research. This information was purely circumstantial, she knew, and it was likely there wasn't enough concrete information for the police to act on it. She knew Peter must have broken into Timothy's apartment to get some of the papers her mother had found. So there's another crime about which she'd need to tell Derrick, in the interest of full disclosure. Then, there's the information her mother had told her about Peter as a child, and the troubling childhood memories that she, herself, had of Peter. She just couldn't tell Derrick. Again, it was circumstantial and highly prejudicial to Peter, and probably not enough for the police to act on in any way helpful to the Danners.

For now, she needed to keep the secrets. But if things got any more dangerous for her, she promised herself, she would seriously consider leveling with Derrick and accepting the help he wanted to give her. That decided, she played the second voice mail message she had on her cell phone.

The other message had come in almost three hours ago. It began with a familiar, hissing dead-air sound. Then a voice spoke, one that she instantly recognized. "Jade, it's me again. Why didn't you call me back? I wanted to take you out. Now you don't have the old man to warn you. Watch your back, precious girl. I'm *going* to take you out. There was cold, mirthless laughter, then a loud click as he disconnected.

Jade's shaking hand dropped the cell phone. The clatter of the phone against the kitchen floor jolted her. His play on words chilled her. She thought that she probably should have realized before this moment that the person who broke into her house and took her notes, the person who threatened her just now, the guy she had met at her mother's house, and whoever trashed her vehicle were all likely the same man, Timothy Steven Lawrence. She found it most sickening to recall that she had once been inside the circle of his arms, and delighted to be there.

She retrieved her cell phone and looked for the telephone number in the caller ID listing. She knew the call was probably going to come up on the listing as "private caller", but she had to make sure. The phone number that came up on her call listing that matched the time stamp on the voicemail message was her parent's home telephone number. Disbelieving, Jade scrolled through her incoming calls listing again with the same result. Apparently, Timothy had left her this voice mail message from inside her parent's house! Heart pounding, Jade stood completely frozen for a moment. She couldn't believe that this evil man, whom she knew must have killed Ben Lawrence, had been inside her parent's house, and he had been there after the murder.

Jade frantically grabbed her land line receiver and speed-dialed her parent's house. She knew it was late, and she may wake them, but she had check on them. Her mother's sleepy voice answered and verified that yes, they were both there, and had been sleeping. Jade asked if they had heard from Peter yet and her mother said that they had not. Jade apologized for waking them up and wished them good night.

She wondered what it was that had caused Timothy to be now tipping his hand and revealing himself officially as her adversary. Jade suddenly also realized that Timothy could have planted the knife in her mother's VW, and maybe even planted the key in Peter's room. Jade also realized that she would have to move forward with the assumption that Timothy was extremely dangerous, especially to her.

Jade put her cell phone on the kitchen table and sat down, thinking about her next move. Her intention to go to bed was forgotten. Her initial reaction to Timothy's strange voice mail message was anger. Jade wasn't used to being afraid of anything or anyone. Now she was starting to realize how much her confidence and coping skills could be compromised by fear. It was a humbling realization.

Jade knew she was in danger before the call, but somehow hearing Timothy threaten her life, and the fact that he was resourceful enough to be calling from inside her parent's house, apparently (and thankfully) without their knowledge ratcheted up the pressure she was feeling. Before, it was an unknown person just wanting the diary from her. Her house was broken into as was her truck. But these were crimes against her possessions, and not against her. Now she had reason to think this man was a multiple murderer and she had unwittingly moved directly into his crosshairs.

Jade knew she had to calm down, so she could try to get some sleep. She sat down on her bed, still lost in her anxious thoughts. After a few minutes, she concluded that she had done what she could to keep herself safe for tonight.

Her house was locked up tight. She had her VW remote on the stand next to her bed in case she needed to push the panic button. She realized that she had left Erin's diary on her kitchen table instead of putting it away, but she was too tired to go back downstairs. After over an hour of restless tossing and turning, Jade finally slept.

Jolted from sleep, Jade looked over at the red numerals on her clock radio. 2:45 A.M. Something had awakened her, some sound that didn't belong in the usual night noises to which her sleeping self was accustomed. Straining to hear any sound, Jade sat up in her bed, soundlessly put her feet on the floor, walked silently to her bedroom door and opened it a crack, listening for any sound downstairs. She could hear Bardo stirring on the bed behind her. He started to growl softly and Jade shushed him. Listening intently, she at first thought she must have been hearing things, the silence seemed complete. Then she heard it again. It was the sound of metal scraping quietly against metal. And it was coming from her front door.

She slowly closed her bedroom door and reached for the telephone on her nightstand. Bardo stood on her pillow, teeth showing, growling softly. She picked him up, noting that every muscle in his body was taut and his ears were fully pricked as he also listened intently and tried to gauge the level of danger. She used her other hand to pick up the receiver on her bedside phone. She put the receiver to her ear. Her fright turned to terror when she heard nothing. Someone had cut the phone line. Her cell phone was downstairs, no help there. She went back to the bedroom door and listened.

She heard the unmistakable sound of her front door opening slowly. Quiet footsteps walked past the base of the stairway and into the kitchen. There was nothing she could do but listen as the person walked around her house. She was scared, but she was also angry. Outraged, in fact. How dare this common criminal, this thug, break into her house! Then she remembered the car remote. She grabbed it from her nightstand and pressed the alarm button. She saw headlights fill her windows with light and heard the horn alarm start to bleat. It sounded very loud in the silence. Bardo started barking uncontrollably.

Jade felt fierce satisfaction when she heard her intruder's footsteps run across the length of the first floor of her house and out the front door. She looked out her bedroom window, trying to spot the intruder running up or down her street. She saw nothing and realized he must have gone out the front door, around to the backyard and through to the next street. Jade stood in the window for another minute, listening to the alarm sounding and hoping someone was calling the police because of the noise.

Jade turned off the alarm and started down the stairs. Halfway down, a shadow filled her still open front doorway. She froze in mid-step.

A familiar voice said, "What in God's name is going on here? Why was your car alarm going off?". Jade ran down the remaining steps and threw herself into Derrick's arms. As his arms closed around her, she felt, rather than heard him say "You're safe, no one's going to hurt you."

Jade spent a moment letting herself cling to the solid comfort of him. Then she pulled away and looked up into his face.

"What were you doing outside my house? You left hours ago, I watched you drive away."

Derrick gave her a lopsided grin. "I've always been a sucker for a damsel in distress, and you are definitely that."

Jade didn't disagree, but she was still troubled about how Derrick happened to be outside her house, at this hour. Jade realized how easy it would have been for him to set up this little fright fest, just to convince her she needed his help. And of course, in order to get his help she'd have to tell him everything she knew about Peter and about Ben Lawrence. In so doing, she'd have to tell him about the jewelry case, the diary, the result of Peter's research into the local, current murders, and the result of her continuation of Peter's research (which wasn't completed yet). And, most significantly, the fact that she suspected that

Derrick could have set this frightening situation up for his own gain told her that she didn't trust him enough to tell him anything yet.

Derrick turned back to the front door, closed it, and turned the deadbolt lock. Then he took Jade with him as he walked through the house, checking everything for damage and making sure all the windows and doors were locked. In the kitchen, he noted that the overhead cupboard doors were open. He asked Jade if anything was missing. Jade picked up two bags of chocolate-covered peanuts that were sitting on the counter. One in each hand, she turned to Derrick. "Nope, he didn't get my most valuable treasures." She put the candy back in the cupboard and closed the cupboard doors. Derrick led Jade out of the kitchen, into the living room, and sat down with her on the couch. "Now tell me what just happened here." Starting to feel a little calmer, Jade quickly described what happened. When she told him that her telephone was dead, Derrick's expression suddenly changed from concern to alarm.

She described how she hit the panic button and then she heard the intruder run back through the house and out the door. He asked Jade which way the intruder went, and Jade told him how she checked out the window but didn't see him.

Derrick stood up and walked to the front door. Not ready yet to be left alone, Jade jumped up and followed him, her house keys in hand. She followed him outside, and she diligently turned the thumb lock on the door knob as she closed the door behind them. Derrick turned left, and walked the length of the house. At the corner of the house, he stopped, pulled a flashlight out of his belt and shined the beam against her house, at eye level. Jade could clearly see that there were wires trailing up the house, and that they had been cut. Derrick looked at Jade.

"I think they were after more than valuables or information, Jade. Intruders don't usually cut the phone lines *before* a crime unless they intend some serious mayhem."

Standing outside with Derrick, in only her short nightgown, Jade shivered miserably, struggling not to break down. Derrick shrugged out of his jacket and placed it gently around her. Welcome warmth coursed through her. Derrick put an arm around her shoulders and steered her back to the front door, using her key to let them back inside. He closed the door and guided her to the couch. Bardo immediately came to lay on her feet, offering his warmth and comfort, for which Jade was pathetically grateful. Derrick crossed to the front door and opened it. Using his flashlight, studied the outside of the deadbolt lock. Jade watched him pull something out of the lock. He walked back to Jade and handed her a small piece of wire. It looked like a straightened, extremely thin paperclip.

Derrick said, "That was in your deadbolt keyhole. This is a common way for criminals to pick a lock by tripping the tumblers. I'm glad your inside stairway is immediately in front of your front door. Do you have a woodpile to go with that woodstove?" He gestured to the pot bellied stove in the living room. Jade pointed to the back door. Derrick walked quickly to the back door, let himself out, and came back in within a few seconds. "Watch this", he said. He placed the thick piece of wood perpendicular to the front door, lodging it between the front door and the first riser of her staircase. He picked the wood back up and handed it to Jade. "After I leave, that's where I want you to put it. It will be impossible for anyone to open the door with it braced." Jade smiled up at Derrick. "You really are something else, you know that?"

Derrick led Jade back to the living room couch and sat down next to her. He looked more worried than she had seen him.

He took her cold, trembling hands in his. "After we talked earlier, I knew two things. One, that you are more involved than I realized in a dangerous situation that has included the death of at least one person, Ben Lawrence, and maybe the deaths of others. And two, you don't seem to be as concerned about the danger you are in as I think you need to be."

"Since I'm on the night shift tonight, I spent some time between calls just cruising your neighborhood. I was parked at the corner of your street eating my dinner in the cruiser when I heard your car alarm go off."

He motioned up the street and Jade could clearly see his cruiser parked on her street, just a couple of houses up, near the corner. That explained his appearance here so quickly after she triggered the panic button on her car remote. Jade felt silly for suspecting him. But she also felt more afraid than she had before, as the possibility that this was a set up for her benefit was put to rest and she had to deal with the fact that this was, in fact, a real break in, and possibly an aborted attempt on her life.

Jade retrieved her keys and made sure that her deadbolt lock was still working. She put her keys back in her purse and put her purse on the kitchen table. Jade glanced around the kitchen, then at the kitchen table, knowing something in the room wasn't right. Something had been moved or taken. Then she realized what it was. Erin's diary was gone. She remembered that she had left it on the kitchen table earlier, and she had thought about retrieving it just before she went to sleep. Apparently, her intruder must have taken it. Thank goodness she had copies. She was done reading it, but she knew that she would want to refer back to it periodically as she completed her research. She also knew, if she was successful in proving her theory that the Lawrence family had harbored generations of killers, the police would want to see that diary.

Derrick saw Jade's hesitation at the kitchen table, and he saw the shocked look on her face, there for just an instant before she carefully shuttered her expression. He knew that she probably wouldn't tell him anything if he asked her, but her reaction was so peculiar that he had to try.

"Jade, what is it? Is there something missing?" Jade looked at him, with her carefully neutral expression and said, "No, I don't think so. I guess my mind is just running in five different directions at once."

Derrick tried to look convinced. "I don't blame you. This day has been about three days long for you. Would you like me to take you to a motel? Wait a minute, that didn't come out right."

Jade smiled fleetingly at his discomfort. "No, I'll be okay here. I'm not letting anyone drive me out of my own home." Derrick looked skeptical, but decided not to make an issue of it.

"Why don't you go ahead upstairs and try to get some rest? You have your cell phone, right?" Jade nodded. "If anything else happens, call me and I'll get here just as soon as I can. I'll make sure I drive by a couple more times in the next few hours, just to make sure everything looks okay. I'll call you tomorrow afternoon, to see if you are ready to talk about all this yet. At the very least, you'll need to file a police report about the break in."

Jade thanked him for his help, once again. They hugged awkwardly, both aware of the strength of the attraction they felt, but both knowing the time wasn't right to give in to it.

Jade whistled for Bardo, who came on the run. She didn't want to leave Bardo downstairs alone. Not tonight. As the first frosty fingers of dawn touched the world outside their window, Jade and Bardo settled into bed for a few hours of sorely needed sleep.

Chapter 18

The next morning, Jade didn't get up until after 9:00 AM. Thankfully, it was Saturday. Bardo was gone. Jade realized he must have used his doggy door at the bottom of her bedroom door to go downstairs earlier. Jade climbed out of bed, took a shower, and then dressed in warm, comfortable weekend clothes. Downstairs, she put on a pot of coffee, fed Bardo, and looked out the window to see if, in the light of day, everything looked okay. She felt reassured when nothing (and no one) jumped out at her. It's a start, she thought.

Jade opened the back door and let Bardo out to run around in the back yard. She put on her boots and walked out into the back yard. At her woodpile, Jade moved a few pieces of firewood then grabbed the plastic bag containing the duplicate copy of the diary. She moved the wood back into place, and headed back to the house. The welcoming smell of freshly-brewed coffee greeted her at the door.

Jade used her cell phone to call the telephone company's line repair number and was relieved to be told that they would be able to send someone out later in the day. Feeling particularly industrious, Jade then called Kurt, her mechanic. He answered on the second ring, sounding pleased to hear from her. She knew that he liked her, and was interested in dating her, the vibe was painfully obvious, and she also knew that she used his feelings, whether intentionally or not, to get her truck repairs taken care of better and faster. He informed her, in his preening voice, that her truck was ready, and he would be happy to drop it off at her house later. She immediately nixed that plan. "How about I drop by and pick up the truck in a couple hours? There's no reason for you to have to interrupt your day." He started to protest and she cut in smoothly, "No, really, you've done enough for me and I appreciate it." He finally, reluctantly agreed to let Jade come to pick up her truck later. Relieved that she'd soon have her truck back, Jade hung up the phone.

Sitting at the table with her first cup of coffee, she remembered the second book that Helen had found for her in the library. She retrieved the printed pages from her purse. The book was untitled, but the printed copy had captured the note that was affixed to the cover that read, "Southern Maine Homicides, 1840 to 1968". There was no author or copyright information on the first couple of pages.

The first page provided a rough index. The listing was organized by year of death. Across each row was listed the sex of the deceased, the age (if known), the name and last known street address (when available) and finally, the manner of death. There seemed to be three known categories for manner of death, suicide, homicide and accidental, and a fourth category, "unknown". Jade immediately noted something significant. There were four very obvious clusters of homicide deaths of young women. The first seemed to be going on at the time the book was compiled, but the records were not complete, probably, Jade guessed, due to the 1866 fire. The first recorded wave of homicides seemed to start in 1850 but stopped around 1852, then another cluster happened between 1880 and 1889, another between 1917 and 1930 and, it seemed, another cluster had begun around 1959, and seemed to be still ongoing when the records stopped in 1968.

Jade dropped the pages on the table and sat back, stunned. Her blood was pounding in her ears as the significance of her discovery sank in. If, as she was beginning to believe, the majority of these murders were the work of the generations of "cursed" Lawrence men, there were close to 100 murders. This didn't take into account the number of women that were never found. Jade paged through the rest of the document, looking for more information that would help her determine who may have committed any of the homicides, at least something that would include or exclude Lawrence family members as suspects. The book contained some information on several of the homicides, and very little information on the suicides and accidental deaths.

Looking at the homicides one at a time, Jade saw that the place of death and the deceased's next of kin, if that was known, were listed. In addition, if the perpetrator was subsequently brought to justice, that information was provided. If the killing went unsolved that was also noted. Jade noticed that over 75% of the killings that occurred outside her identified "clusters" had been solved and prosecuted. However, the homicides that occurred during the higher-activity cluster periods were solved less than 25% of the time, and, Jade noted, the

Lawrence name was never identified as a perpetrator.

What Jade didn't understand was why someone, somewhere, didn't see this obvious, horrific pattern. After five minutes, Jade had immediately spotted it! Looking at just the homicide deaths of women age 14 to 35, the number of murders rises from 7 for the 25 years starting in 1890, to 17 during the following 25 years, a 250% increase. This pattern was repeated during each of the subsequent active killing periods.

Then something else caught Jade's eye. The number of homicides during each of the active killing periods had progressively increased, even as the number of homicides during the less active killing periods stayed level. More ominous still, Jade noticed that the active killing periods had grown progressively longer, and in some, cases, the periods between the active phases grew shorter. Whatever was happening, it was obviously accelerating.

Jade needed to find whatever additional corroborating records there may be, as what she had seen so far was indicative, but certainly not conclusive. Using the back of the handful of printed pages Helen had provided, Jade jotted a list of possible sources of more specific information. First, she needed to check current city records to see if there had been another rash of homicides after 1968. It would also be helpful to find out what kind of criminal records members of the Lawrence family had. Jade wondered if she could get information on charges that may have been leveled against members of the Lawrence family then subsequently dismissed. She felt sure that somewhere, someone must have known, or at least suspected, what the Lawrence family men were up to. Taking her logic a reluctant step further, Jade realized that there may have been others, like her, who had stumbled on to this terrible family secret, and the others may not have lived long enough to tell anyone.

She could also get names and next-of-kin information on any current murders of young women, if it turned out that there was a suspicious number of them. Jade wanted to talk to close family members of any more recent murder victims to find out if there was any connection to the Lawrence family. Jade knew of at least three of the victims from the 1870's murders that had a connection to Tim Lawrence. One was Isabelle, Erin's best friend, who had once dated Tim. Then there was the girlfriend of Erin's cousin Mark, who also went missing, later to be found murdered. There was also Trevor's wife, Marie. Erin's diary indicates that Erin actually saw Tim in the room with Marie's corpse, bloody knife in hand, moments after the murder occurred.

Jade paged through the remainder of the Southern Maine Homicides booklet, jotting down information about the last set of unsolved killings that were covered, from 1965 to 1968. As the victims were all local people, she'd start with a low-tech approach: the telephone book. Jade reviewed her list of 11 murder victims. Of the 11, five of them had last names that were unusual enough to try looking for surviving next-of-kin in the telephone book. Three of them, she noted in passing, had the exact same last name and were killed just months apart. She wondered if a Lawrence man had somehow worked his way through the women in that family. Then she wondered how on Earth that could have happened, without him being caught.

In the local telephone book, Jade found listings for all five of the next-of-kin with unusual last names. There were actually a total of three listings, as three of the victims shared one last name. Jade noted the first and last name, partial address and telephone number for each of them, on note cards:

Andress Langolier, 509 Tyng St, Portland, 555-5207
first name match with next of kin

Dana Jane Pelletieri, 98 Tate St., Portland 555-6711
first name matches next of kin, three victims with this last name.

Tina Augerbois, 728 Park St., Portland 555-8112
first name match with next of kin

No time like the present, she thought, picking up the telephone receiver. Instead of hearing a dial tone, she heard nothing. Then she remembered the telephone company hadn't yet arrived to fix her telephone lines. With a sigh, she put the receiver back down.

Jade swept up her notes and put them in her purse. Grabbing her jacket and keys, she left the house. She drove to her office, glancing in her rear view mirror often, hoping to spot a tail if there was one. She didn't see anyone. Of course, she suddenly thought, someone could have easily attached a tracking device to her vehicle. As that seemed an uncomfortably real possibility, Jade decided she would check over the outside and undercarriage of the car as soon as possible. The old saying was right, she thought: You aren't paranoid if they really are out to get to you.

At her office, Jade cleared off her desk and laid out her notes. She started with the list of five young female murder victims with unusual last names. She dialed the first telephone number for the next-of-kin. It rang through, then a recording stated that the telephone number had been disconnected.

She pulled her telephone directory from a desk drawer and looked up the last name. There were no other entries for that last name. She also contacted Directory Assistance but there were no new listings. As a last resort, Jade did a quick on-line search, but apparently Andress Langolier was either unlisted or had left the area.

She made a note for herself, then went on to the next telephone number. This time, it rang through and a cheery female voice answered.

Jade had exactly enough time to wish she had devised a plausible cover story, then said, "Good afternoon, ma'am, I'm looking into homicides that took place in Portland, back in 1968. The victims' last names were the same as yours, which is the reason I'm calling you. Were you any relation to Verna Pelletieri? Or Terry and Tammy Pelletieri? Her speech was met with shocked silence.

Then, her cheeriness now sounding a bit forced, the woman asked, "Why bring up the past? It's been 35 years, let sleeping dogs lie, I always say".

Jade knew then that she had, in fact, reached a relative of the three Pelletieri girls. Using her most persuasive tone, she said, "I understand that this situation may be painful for you. If this wasn't vitally important, I wouldn't be calling you."

The woman was quiet for a moment, then she said, "Alright, then. Tell me what you need, and I'll see if I can help you. But first, please tell me who you are."

Jade thought about how she wasn't completely honest with Ben Lawrence, and about what happened to him. She knew she couldn't misrepresent herself or her purpose again, even if it meant that the person to whom she was speaking would decide not to help her.

Jade took a chance on the truth, albeit a carefully edited version. "Mrs. Pelletieri, my name is Jade Danner. I'm an antique appraiser here in Portland. I recently appraised a jewelry case for the Lawrence family."

Mrs. Pelletieri interrupted, "Ms. Danner, I'm sorry, I just can't talk about this over the telephone. I don't really want to talk about it at all, to be completely honest with you."

Jade tried one last time. "I completely understand. Would you be willing to meet with me in person, for just a short conversation? Before you answer, let me tell me the rest of what I need you to know. The jewelry case I appraised contained a note, which referred to the Lawrence house on Commercial Street. I went there, and I found a diary that was written by a maid of the Lawrences named Erin, in the late 1870's. Two of her close friends were killed, and she felt that the perpetrator of both murders was someone connected with the Lawrence family. She also mentioned that there had been several recent murders and disappearances of young women in the area. She also said that her mother and grandmother had told her about a series of killings when each of them were young women."

Jade crossed her fingers, sent up a short prayer and continued. "Several of the murdered women had a Möbius symbol on or near them. Do you know what that is?"

There was a sharp intake of breath on the other end of the line, then Mrs. Pelletieri said, "Yes, I know what that is. I'm listening, please continue."

Jade felt a rush of adrenaline at Mrs. Pelletieri's reaction to her mention of the Möbius.

"After I read the diary, I checked the death records at the library. My research isn't complete yet, but I did find an abrupt increase in the number of unsolved homicide deaths, about every thirty years or so, from the mid-1800's to the late 1960's. That last known wave of killings involved the three woman who share your last name. After reading Erin's diary, and doing some further research, I know that something is very wrong. What I need from you, Mrs. Pelletieri, is anything that you can tell me about the deaths of these three women who shared your name. I'm willing to come to your house to talk, or, if you'd rather, we can meet somewhere public."

Having given her best pitch, Jade waited while Mrs. Pelletieri thought it over. Finally, Mrs. Pelletieri spoke. Jade could hear from the hoarseness in her voice that Mrs. Pelletieri was close to tears, and she felt a stab of guilt.

"Meet me at the McDonald's on St. John Street in one hour. I'll be wearing a red jacket and red boots". Jade started to thank her, but the woman had already hung up.

Jade was grateful for Mrs. Pelletieri's willingness to try to help. She knew what it must have cost her to agree to discuss with Jade what was obviously still so painful for her. Jade took a moment to fix herself a pot of coffee and, steaming mug in hand, she headed back to the table where her notes were laid out. Jade set the alarm timer on her cell phone for 45 minutes, then went back to work. There was one more listing to call. Tina Augerbois. She picked up the still-warm telephone receiver and dialed the number.

An elderly gentleman answered the telephone with a hearty "Hello!"

Jade smiled and responded, "Hello, to you sir! My name is Jade Danner. I'm trying to reach Tina Augerbois, do I have the correct number?"

There was a rustling sound, then a woman's voice. "Hi, I'm Tina. What can I do for you?" She sounded younger than Jade was, so Jade wondered if the Tina Augerbois listed in the next-of-kin index of the homicide book was maybe a completely different Tina Augerbois. But really, how many Tina Augerbois can there be?, Jade thought inanely.

Jade realized the silence was stretching out, so she rushed to fill it. "I was actually expecting you to be much older."

Ms. Augerbois laughed, "I'm almost 50, but I know I sound about 20, I get that all the time. You were probably looking for my mother, her name was also Tina."

Was, Jade thought with a sinking feeling. She was probably dead. Jade kept the disappointment out of her voice. "Yes, I guess I'm looking for the elder Tina. I'm looking into several homicides that took place in this area in the late 1960's, and one of the victims had the same last name as your family. Do you know if you are related to that Augerbois?"

Jade heard the woman cup the phone and speak in urgent, hushed tones with the man, then the man responded in a gruff voice. Ms. Augerbois came back on the line and answered, "My mother passed away many years ago. But yes, it was my older sister who was murdered in 1967. I was 14 years old at the time, she was 19. They never found who did it, but I'm pretty sure I know."

Jade's heart skipped a beat. "Would you be willing to talk with me about it?

I'm looking into several deaths, all young women, all around that time period and all within two miles of where you live."

The man said something else, in a muffled but obviously agitated tone, then there was another rustle as the phone was passed, and the man was back on the line. "Please don't stir up any more trouble for us, ma'am."

Jade quickly said, "I'm only trying to get to the truth. Please help me find out what happened to your daughter, and to those other innocent young girls. I have reason to believe that the killer has started killing again. If you know something that will help stop him, please tell me."

Sounding furious now, the man said, "My little girl was slaughtered by some sick bastard. Are you going to bring her back? Forcing me to relive one of the worst days of my life can serve no useful purpose. I say 'one of' because my *wife* was also murdered, about 18 months after my daughter was, and most likely by the same monster. Do you really feel the need to relive this damned nightmare for you, a complete stranger?"

Jade knew his reaction was entirely appropriate, given what he'd been through. She also knew that she needed to find a way past his defenses so she could get the information she needed. Lives may depend on her ability to be persuasive, and she knew she would only get this one chance.

"Mr. Augerbois, I can't tell you how sorry I am about the tragedies you have suffered. And I won't tell you that I understand your pain. What I will tell you is that I'm looking into several killings that happened in the late 1960's, including your daughter's murder. This may be your only chance to help bring the killer to justice and avenge the deaths of your family members. The information you provide could also help save other lives. Listen, we can do this now, right over the phone if you want. Do you have a few minutes, Mr. Augerbois, and are you willing to help me try to find your daughter's killer?"

Still sounding upset, Mr. Augerbois said, "Fine, let's get this over with. There's very little I can tell you. Louise was 19 years old, a freshman at the

University. She worked part time at the Norge Village laundrymat at Union Station. When she didn't show up for work one afternoon, her boss called us. We called all her friends and we searched for her into the night, but there was no sign of her. Then we called the police. Her body was found the next day, at the Eastern Promenade at the top of Munjoy Hill. She had been brutally violated and her throat was slashed. After she was dead, the fucking monster cut her up. The police never found the killer. Is that what you needed to hear?"

Jade quietly responded, "I'm so very sorry about your loss, Mr. Augerbois. I understand that this is difficult for you and I appreciate your help more than you will ever know. I have one question for you, about your daughter's death. Did the police find any strange marking or symbol on or near your daughter's body?"

Mr. Augerbois immediately said, "No, but my little girl was cut up so badly that I'm not sure the police would have seen anything even if there was something. But I think I know what you are after, and frankly, it's scaring the living shit out of me." Mr. Augerbois no longer sounded angry. The new intensity in his voice told Jade that she had asked exactly the right question.

He continued. "My wife Tina didn't just 'die', she was also murdered. Back in 1969. She just wasn't getting over what happened to our daughter, even after a year had passed. I thought she was dealing with it, but when she was diagnosed with breast cancer, within a year after our daughter was killed, something inside her just came loose. The cancer was caught very early and was completely treatable, but the diagnosis seemed to get her thinking about how, while she would probably get a chance to play through, her child's future had been stolen. I think it was the cancer that pushed Tina over the edge and led to her death.

"She started looking into Louise's death. Immediately, she found that our daughter's death was only one of several that happened around that time. A few days before my wife was killed, she told me that she had made an important discovery, but she needed more proof before she could tell me. I didn't approve of her investigating our daughter's death on her own, but I understood her need to make sense of it. It was giving her a purpose, which I knew she sorely needed. I didn't think then that her curiosity would get her killed.

"The day after she told me about her mysterious 'discovery', she told me that she thought someone was following her. That evening, she told me she was meeting with some kind of shrink, a teacher from over to the University. This was someone, my wife said, who may be able to help make some sense of our daughter's murder. I thought it was possible that she had finally decided to get some counseling, and I didn't push her for details as I was afraid she'd decide not to go. She said she'd be back in an hour or so. That was the last time I saw her alive.

"At midnight, when she had been gone over three hours, I called the police. They said they couldn't help until she had been missing for 24 hours. The next morning, my wife's body was found in the cemetery on the Western Promenade. She must have somehow crossed the killer's path on her way to meet with the counselor. She had been butchered. And someone had drawn something strange on the bottom of her shoe, in her blood. There was a number eight, with an eye drawn inside one loop and a droplet in the other. The police had no idea what to make of it. Is this the symbol you were talking about? Does it mean something?"

Jade explained to him how that symbol connected several deaths during that time.

Mr. Augerbois noisily blew his nose. His voice came back on the line. "Ms. Danner, there was one more strange thing that happened. Two days after my Tina was found, someone broke in to our house. They didn't take anything except my wife's journal, and her research notes about our daughter's murder. At first, the police had said they thought my wife was probably killed by some random psycho. When the burglary happened, they didn't seem to be in a hurry to change their assumption. But dead is dead. Figuring out who did it won't bring them back, but it could get me or someone else I love killed." Jade certainly couldn't argue with the man's logic.

Jade thanked Mr. Augerbois for his help. She wrote up a brief synopsis of their telephone conversation for her file. Her cell phone alarm went off. It was time to keep her appointment with Mrs. Pelletieri. Jade gathered up her papers and put them in her purse. Before she got into the VW, she spent a few minutes looking over the undercarriage and the interior of the VW, checking for a tracking device. She had no idea what one would look like, but hoped she'd recognize it if she spotted it. Finding nothing, she slid into the driver's seat and drove away.

Chapter 19

When she got to McDonald's, Jade parked the VW in the back of the parking lot and went inside. The smell of burgers and fries immediately got her stomach rumbling. She realized she hadn't eaten in several hours. She looked around the fast food restaurant but she didn't see anyone with a red coat and red boots. She stepped to the counter and ordered a burger and fries. Within two minutes, she was sitting in a booth that allowed a view of both entrances, devouring her lunch.

Five minutes after she had finished her food, she spotted an older woman getting out of an older model "K" car, which she had, strangely enough managed to park right next to Jade's VW. She came inside, and looked at her as the woman looked around. She was tall, and very thin. She had soft white hair that was bobbed attractively. She looked to be in her early sixties to the casual glance, but Jade looked more closely and realized she was likely a very well kept mid-70's. Mrs. Pelletieri stepped up to the counter, then coffee in hand, she turned and caught Jade's eye. Jade waved her over.

In front of Jade's table, she said, "Are you Jade?" Jade confirmed that she was, and the woman sat down across from her. They took a moment to look at one another, the silence stretching out between them.

Jade was first to speak. "Mrs. Pelletieri, thank you for agreeing to meet with me. I'm assuming, from your reaction on the telephone earlier, that you are related to the murder victims who share your name." The older woman, who had been looking down at her lap, lifted her head and locked eyes with Jade.

"Please, call me Dana. I only agreed to talk with you because of what you said about the Möbius. But I'll get to that. The victims were my three daughters. Verna was 19, Terry and Tammy were twins and were 17. At the time of the murders, they were my only children, I was almost 40 then. It was 1968. First, Verna went missing. She was living on campus at the University, so I didn't see her every day. I didn't worry about it, at first. When three days had passed and I hadn't heard from her, I began to worry.

"Finally, on the fourth day, they found her body, at the Bath Iron Works dock, here in Portland. My husband, Arthur, went down to identify the body, I just couldn't do it. She had been cut up something awful, apparently. Parts of her were missing. She had been raped and her throat had been slashed so badly she was almost decapitated. I was always thankful that I was not the one who had to see her that way, that I was left with my memories of her intact." Dana stopped for a moment and wiped her eyes, looking out the window. Her haunted reflection looked back at them both, and Jade caught a glimpse of the depth of her loss. She turned back to Jade.

"I became obsessed with finding out who killed my daughter. One of the detectives investigating Verna's death mentioned that there had been several other victims killed in the same area, and in a similar way. All the victims were young women, and they were all stabbed, assaulted and dismembered. I asked the detective if he would provide me with information on the other murders, but he wouldn't. He encouraged me to let go of my need to find the killer and get on with my life. Something my husband, of course, had already been telling me.

"Well, I wasn't ready to let it go yet. I went to the library and looked through the newspapers. Back in those days, they were just beginning to convert the papers to microfiche, it was quite a job, but like I said, I was obsessed. The detective was right. There were seven other cases. They were spread out over a three year period, so the news media didn't seem to have realized there was a multiple murderer on the loose. I would give my life to go back to that time, erase all the digging I did and instead just do what everyone was telling me to do, let it go. But I didn't. Instead of grieving, and possibly learning to deal, I devoted all my emotional energy to searching for Verna's killer. I was dreaming about it, talking about it all the time, to the point that my husband threatened to leave me.

"I had copies of the newspaper accounts of the other murdered girls, and the one about my Verna. I dissected every word in every article, looking for clues. I even took a magnifying glass to the newspaper photos. And I got copies of the taped footage of the television news accounts. That's when I saw it. At first, I doubted my own eyes. Then I decided it had to be a coincidence. Jade, I saw the same man, standing in the background, in *three* of the newspaper photos. He was also in the crowd on one of the recorded television news accounts." Jade watched Mrs. Pelletieri, trying to keep her outward expression impassive while her insides churned excitedly.

Mrs. Pelletieri continued, "I immediately took my information to the police. They said they wouldn't pursue the matter, they said it's a small town, and these murders happened in a very small area of the city, and he could conceivably live nearby and having seen a crowd gathering, could gone to check things out. But I knew I was on to something. I asked several of Verna's friends if they had any idea who the man in the crowd was. One of Verna's friends told me that it looked a bit like a homeless guy that was living in the Deering Oaks park. He was a mentally handicapped, middle-aged man. Some students made fun of him, others gave him money and food. Since this was the only lead I'd found in my weeks of asking around, I jumped on it."

Dana shifted forward in her seat, her eyes intent. Jade sensed that she was about to tell her the part of her strange and tragic story that she would most need to know. Dana continued, "I drove to the University area, and saw the park, right where Verna's friend said it would be. I left my car in a public parking area and starting walking around the park on foot, closely examining every face I saw. Judging by some of the looks I got back, I must have frightened some of them. But I didn't see anyone who resembled the guy I saw in the news pictures. Then I started asking people who looked like they might be homeless, if they knew Mike. It didn't take long before someone did."

"The only problem was, Mike was dead. He had died of exposure, during the previous winter. Since my daughter had been killed after Mike had died, I knew it couldn't have been him. I didn't realize how much I hoped this would be the answer, until I had to deal with being back to square one. I went back to my car and just sat in it, thinking about what else I could do to get this guy. I wasn't sure what I was going to do with him, but I wasn't thinking that far ahead. I guess I probably wasn't thinking at all. This was my way to not have to think.

"I started to back out of the parking space, looking back over my shoulder. Then I spotted him. The man I had been searching for was standing just a few feet behind my car. In the peculiar dusk light, with my red brake lights shining in his eyes, he stood behind my car and locked eyes with me. The moment went on and on, and he just stood there, looking at me. He smiled, obviously enjoying my fear, and then he started to walk around my side of the car. Since the rear of my car was now clear, I stomped on the gas, backed out of the parking spot and headed for the exit.

126

"I looked in my rear-view mirror and saw him getting in to a light-colored or white Cadillac that had been parked on the other side of the parking lot, directly across from my car. I remembered the car because it was the only other car in the lot when I got there. I had walked past the Cadillac on my way to the foot path into the park. There was a University faculty parking permit that said Department of Psychology on it. I knew I'd have to find out more about this man. I knew this was the guy. And he knew that I knew.

"I went home and told Arthur what had happened. He was upset with me for going alone, and he thought I was probably mistaken about the man who stared at me so malevolently as I was trying to leave the park. We argued about my continuing to 'indulge myself', his words, not mine, in this fantasy of finding Verna's killer myself.

"But in the end, I couldn't stop looking, and he couldn't convince me to stop. Two days later, there was a note in my mailbox. There was no postage stamp on it, so I knew it was hand-delivered. It said, 'Life is too short to spend it chasing ghosts. If you don't want to be one, back off.' I reported the note to the police and they came over. They used gloves to put the note in a clear plastic bag, and they had it fingerprinted, and they had a handwriting expert check the writing style, the ink and the paper. The only thing they could tell me was that the note was apparently written by a man. Big surprise there.

"Later that day, I took a drive to the University and drove through their faculty parking lot. Sure enough, I spotted the Cadillac. And the man. He was just getting out of his car. As he walked from his car into the building, he spotted me. His eyes narrowed, and his face transformed for just a moment into something so evil I can't even describe it. I remember suddenly feeling colder than I've ever felt. Then he turned his back on me and walked in to the building. Now I had confirmation that he was associated with the University.

"But I still didn't know who he was. I thought about trying to get a look inside his car, maybe there would be an invoice or a registration form or something showing his name. In the end, I was so frightened that I couldn't do it. I went home. I didn't tell my husband about it, we had enough to deal with already. I wish now that I had brought a gun with me that day and that I had just blown his head off right then. Life in prison would have been better than the hell he put me in.

"I couldn't tell the police. What would I say? 'I saw this man at the park, who works at the University, and who was photographed in crowds at several places where dead bodies had been found.' I still didn't have any more evidence that pointed to him. I just had my instincts, which were screaming at me that he was the one.

"The next day, my daughter Tammy told me that she thought she had been followed home from school. She was with her friends, and one of them pointed out a car that was trailing them. Tammy didn't get the license plate number, I don't think she was close enough to see that, but she told me that it was 'one those snooty cars, maybe a Cadillac'. As soon as I heard that, I panicked. The killer was sending me a clear message. I broke down and told my husband about how I had cruised the Faculty lot at the University and spotted the man's car there. I also told Arthur about how Tammy thought she had been followed home from school. He thought that was a bit too coincidental, and he did seem pretty concerned.

"Arthur and I then sat the girls down and explained to them that they may be in danger, and it was related to what happened to their older sister. We didn't want to scare them, but needed to try to keep them safe. In the end, they might as well have already been dead."

Dana again broke down, sobbing softly in to her hands. Jade made a silent pact with herself that Dana's having to relive this hell again would not be in vain. In a few moments, Dana had recovered enough to continue.

"Of course, time went on and, in a couple months, we gradually began to relax the restrictions. I did keep reminding the girls periodically that they weren't safe just because the killer had gone underground. They still needed to be aware of their surroundings and try to stay with other people. They were careful, I know they were. Both of them had always been good girls. Then came the awful day that they didn't come home from school. I didn't immediately conclude that they had been kidnapped, since they were both missing.

"When the girls were more than two hours late getting home, I started calling their friends. No one had seen the girls after school. They all said they saw them in school, but that they left school to walk home together, at the usual time. I called Arthur at work and asked him to come home. When he arrived, the girls were more than two and a half hours late. I walked the route they usually took from school, in reverse, arriving at the school without having found a clue to where they had gone. Then I checked out a couple of other routes they may have taken. By this time I was becoming frantic. I went back home and my husband told me that no one had called. By this time, it was after 6:00, and getting dark. We called the police.

"I found it strange that, when I called to report that my daughters were missing, the police immediately asked my husband and I to come down to the station. I was hoping that meant that they were taking us seriously and wanted to take our statement there, and coordinate the search immediately, from the police station. Heaven forgive me, I thought at the time that it was a good sign. I left a note on the door in case the girls came home while we were gone.

"When we got to the police station, there was an officer waiting outside for us. He told us that two young women were found dead in the cemetery behind the Western Promenade. They bore a striking resemblance to each other, and the police thought that they may be twins. The bodies had been found at 3:00 that afternoon. They were both naked and had been raped, then repeatedly stabbed. I felt my legs gave way. Arthur grabbed me before I could hit the ground. I felt darkness closing in, then I didn't feel anything but blessed oblivion for a little while.

"I remember regaining consciousness on the steps of the police station, with my husband's face close to mine, tear-stained and concerned. I remember wanting to go back to that black place where I could feel nothing. The pain was just too much to bear. Mercifully, I fainted again. This time I woke in a hospital room. There was bright sunshine outside my room, so I knew I must have been unconscious for several hours. Then reality crashed over me in a wave. Arthur was sitting in a chair beside my bed. I turned to beg him to tell me that it had been a bad dream, but the look on his face stopped me cold. That look told me what I so desperately did not want to know.

"The pain was enormous, crushing. I heard screaming, and didn't care that it was coming from me. I couldn't stop. The nurse rushed in and sedated me. Arthur pulled me into his arms and we both cried, long and hard, like two hurt and abandoned children. Arthur took me home later that day. Three days later, we buried our two remaining children.

"When I was able to feel again, I was consumed with guilt. I felt sure that Tammy and Terry were killed by the same person who had killed Verna. I also felt sure that Tammy and Terry would not have died had I not continued to chase down Verna's killer. Since I had no children left to lose, I decided to continue pursuing the sick bastard. The first thing I did was the hardest. I had the police provide me with a copy of the investigation into the deaths of all three of my children. The files included their autopsy reports, which had I refused to read up until then. I looked through each of the files, trying to find something that would give the killer's identity away. There wasn't much there. This man was very, very good at what he did.

"There was only one thing that seemed significant. An obvious message from the killer to me. On both Tammy and Terry, he had left a page from a coloring book depicting a ghost. The message was clearly intended as a reference to the note he sent me earlier that said I needed to stop chasing ghosts or I would become one. The other thing was a symbol, a Möbius, the police called it, drawn in black magic marker on back of the ghost pictures. I was furious, I knew that the killer was taunting me. The Möbius symbols didn't mean anything to me. I asked the police about the Möbius and I was told that two other victims had been found with this symbol on or near them. That's why, Jade, when you mentioned that, I knew that the murders of my daughters, and obviously others from the same time period, had to be connected to the murders you are researching.

"Anyway, by then Arthur didn't seem to care about anything at all. He went to work, came home, ate dinner, watched TV, and went to bed. He was like a man in a trance. Within days after I had decided to pursue the girls' killer, I discovered that I was pregnant. My periods had always been irregular, so not having had a period in a few months, given the emotional upheaval of my life at the time, didn't register. Now that I was about to turn 40, I was going to be a new mother again. I remember feeling conflicted at first. Then I realized it was a clear message from God that I should leave the past in the past. He was giving me another chance, a reason to go forward with my life. I took this pregnancy as reassurance that it wasn't I who had failed my children. Why else would I have been given another chance?" The intensity of Dana's stare was a challenge to find fault with her logic. Jade knew she would never do that. Dana had found peace and purpose in her life, finally.

Jade reached out a hand and clutched Dana's forearm. "You've been through everything terrible I think a mother could have gone through. Did you have the child you were pregnant with? Was it a girl or a boy?" Dana smiled, and Jade saw the young beauty she had been. "It was a boy. And I was so glad it was a boy. I'm sure you know why. If not for him, I think Arthur and I would both have just given up.

"My son is a police officer. He lives in Australia with his wife. Last year, I became a grandmother for the first time. That was something I found so hard to accept, during those dark days, that I was never going to hold my grandbabies. I miss my girls every day, but I'm so glad I'm alive. I'm also glad I didn't pursue the girls' killer. If I had continued pursuing him, I'm sure he would have someday killed me or someone else I love."

Dana and Jade both stood, threw away their empty containers and walked out the door together. At their vehicles, Dana turned to Jade, concern in her eyes. "Jade, for your own safety, please let go of this. Enough people have died. Maybe the killer is dead. Maybe he just got old and stopped. Either way, you seem like such a nice girl, I don't want anything to happen to you. I don't think my family is in danger any longer, or I wouldn't be talking to you. My son is thousands of miles away, and I have no reason to think the killer ever even knew about him. For years, I kept track of the news, trying to find out if there were any other similar murders. But I didn't find any, and eventually I stopped looking."

Jade thought about the murders that she had uncovered in Peter's papers, that were happening much more recently. She decided not to mention them. Dana gave Jade a quick hug and admonished her once again to take care. They both got into their cars and drove away, in opposite directions.

Chapter 20

While she was driving, Jade thought through the new information from Dana. It was clear to her that Dana's girls had all been killed by someone who worked at the University. And if that were the case, and if he had used the Möbius symbol, then it was either one hell of a coincidence, or these three killings were also connected to the murders she had already connected to the Lawrence family. And Tina Augerbois also had the Möbius drawn on the bottom of one of her shoes. There didn't seem to be any doubt that the murders *had* continued.

If the rash of killings from the 1960's stopped about 1970, then the next wave had been due to start around 2000 or so, if the slightly quickening timeframe also continued. The information she found in Peter's paperwork indicated murders in 2001 and 2002. Jade felt sure she'd find others, possibly just prior to that date. She'd need to determine if any of the newer murders were associated with the Möbius. And, as important, she'd take a closer look at each of the murder sprees, to see if there was anything that helped identify the perpetrator. If there was any evidence of these murderous binges before 1850, she'd find out about them, as well.

Jade found herself more determined than ever to find the truth. Her house had been broken into (twice, she reminded herself grimly), she had been followed, threatened more than once, and had her truck vandalized. She knew she was in danger, and she also knew that it couldn't deter her. For Erin's sake, for Peter's sake, and for Dana's sake, now, she needed answers. Information was her weapon. She knew that exposing the current serial killer was the only way she could ultimately secure her own safety, even if it did, for the moment, put her in more danger.

Jade used her cell phone to call a taxi, instructing it to meet her at Enterprise. She dropped off the VW car, paid the bill and got into the waiting taxi. At the truck repair shop, she picked up her Blazer and drove home.

At home, Jade was relieved to find that the telephone company had already been there. Having her land line working made her feel safer. And her security system would be installed by Monday. Jade hit the rewind button on her answering machine. Derrick had left her a message. "I just called your home number to make sure your line got fixed. I feel better knowing you have your home phone up and working. Take care, okay? I can't imagine anything happening… well, you know. I know you don't need my help. I get it. But I'm here if you need me, and I wish you'd call." Smiling, Jade saved his message. She looked at the clock and realized it was too late to call him back. She would try him tomorrow. Maybe. Grabbing a handful of chocolate covered peanuts and a glass of milk, she called Bardo and headed up to bed.

Jade awoke Sunday morning to sunshine streaming through her windows. Today, she felt like she needed a break from the Lawrence family. Besides, she thought, giving herself a little time would also give her perspective. That usually helps all the way around, right? Right!

After a long, hot shower, Jade put on her favorite comfortable jeans, a button-down cotton shirt and warm sweater. A mug of steaming coffee in one hand, Jade used the other hand to reach for the telephone. It rang under her hand, startling her. Fast reflexes kept her coffee in the cup as she answered the phone. Her smile broadened when she realized that, just as she was getting ready to call her friend Diane, Diane must have been dialing her.

"Hey Jade, what's up?" Diane didn't sound like her usual self.

"Diane, you won't believe this, I was just about to call you!"

Diane ignored her comment. "Do you have time to get together today? I really need to talk to you."

Jade was instantly worried. "Of course I do, honey. Do you want me to come over there, or do you want to meet somewhere?"

Diane thought for a moment. "Why don't we meet at the Miss Portland?" The Miss Portland was a train-car diner that had been part of Portland's proud history for more years than Jade could remember.

"Perfect. See you in 30.", Jade said.

Jade finished her coffee, rinsed out her coffee mug, made a quick bathroom stop and hit the road. When she got to the Miss Portland Diner, Diane's car was already in the lot and Diane was waiting for her in the last booth. When she sat down across from Diane, her suspicion that something was wrong was confirmed. Diane had obviously been crying. When Diane caught sight of her, she gave Jade a watery grin.

"Hi Jade, I'm so glad to see you. Sometimes I just need some face time with my best girlfriend, you know?" Jade remembered the last time they had been together, last week at the Sportsman's Grill. She remembered that Diane had been happily filling her in on the new man in her life. Oh-oh, she thought. Trouble in paradise?

She looked intently at Diane as she slid into the booth opposite her. "Okay girl, spill."

Diane looked up at her, opened her mouth to speak, and promptly dissolved into tears. Jade got up from her seat and moved over to Diane's side of the table, so she could put her arms around her. Jade was glad to see that the backs of each of the booths were high enough to protect them from prying eyes.

She spoke softly. "Diane, whatever it is, you need to tell me so I can help you." When the sobs dried up to inelegant little hiccups, Diane finally found her voice again.

"Remember me telling you about Bruce?" Jade nodded encouragingly. "Well, we did have our third date, it was wonderful! The next day, he sent flowers to my shop. I couldn't wait to hear from him, so I called him on his cell. He answered, but he sounded, I don't know, funny."

Jade, beginning to understand where this may be going, said "Funny how? Clown funny? Whacked in the head funny?"

She shot Jade an exasperated look. "See, that's exactly what I'm saying. I couldn't put my finger on it. He sounded distant. I asked him to call me back later, when he was free, he said he would do that. Then he called me 'Chuck'. Being a single girl for as long as I have been, I know what that means. He was with another woman. Probably even - his wife!" Diane collapsed into tears again as Jade passed her another handful of napkins. She was upset for Diane, and would cheerfully throttle the idiot who hurt her, if given the chance. Diane was getting herself under control, but Jade could see that there was something else coming, so she remained silent, waiting for Diane to speak.

Diane took another swipe at her eyes, then looked at Jade. "When Bruce called me later, I asked him why he seemed so distant when I called him earlier. He managed to work up a little self-righteous indignation and said it was none of my business what he did when we weren't together. I asked him if that meant we were not to assume the relationship was exclusive. He said that would be best. I told him I wasn't really looking for that kind of relationship, I was really looking for more of a long-term, committed arrangement. That's when he laughed at me! He told me I was being an immature child. Real men, in the real world, needed to be free to do whatever they wanted, whenever they wanted. I told him that I was glad we found out that we weren't compatible now, instead of later, when things may have gotten a little more involved between us."

"But Jade, the truth is, I was already more than half in love with him. Then he dropped the bombshell. He's married. Of course. His wife 'doesn't understand him', they've 'grown apart', How could I have been so stupid!?" Diane looked so devastated, Jade could feel the pain coming off her in waves.

"Diane, listen, if someone wants to keep something from you badly enough, they'll find a way to do it. It doesn't have anything to do with you, he's just a complete asshole. It was your bad luck to run across someone who turned out to be too good to be true. You deserve so much better than that."

Diane nodded sadly. "I know. But it feels good to hear it coming out of someone else's mouth. I'm so angry at him, I want to do something to ruin his nice little racket, you know?"

Jade DID know. And she had an idea. She gave Diane a sly smile. "You know where he lives, right?" Diane said, "Yes, he gave me his address and his cell phone number on our first date. I hadn't been to his house yet. Why, what are you thinking?" Jade said, "I don't think you should go there, but I don't see any problem with getting in touch with Bruce's wife, just to make sure she knows what he's up to. My guess is that she doesn't have clue one."

For the first time with Jade that day, Diane smiled. Jade continued, "There are a couple different things you could do, depending on how confrontational you want to be. You could use the address to find Bruce's wife's name on the internet, or just try the telephone directory first, then send a letter to Bruce's wife. If you address it to her and make it look professional, and for God's sake, don't put your name or your return address on it, the odds are good that the letter will get to her."

"Or, if you are really brazen, you could look up Bruce's land line telephone number, if he has a land line, and give her a call. You know Bruce works during the day, so I'd try calling during the day. If you aren't able to catch her, try calling in the evening. Just make sure that you call from a phone number that Bruce won't associate with you, maybe the pay phones at the mall. Once you reach her, you could explain to her that her husband isn't just cheating on her, he's actually advertising on-line for partners. You wouldn't be doing anything wrong, although your message probably won't be very well received. But, if you were Bruce's wife, wouldn't you want to know?"

Diane considered this. "You know, I think you're right. I'm going to tell her." Having decided that, Diane's mood began to improve. "Jade, let's go shopping. That's where I would be right now, with you-know-who, if what happened, hadn't. I was really looking forward to the shopping."

Jade, warming to the idea, said, "Let's go to Freeport, we can check out the outlet stores and go to L.L. Bean's."

Jade paid for their coffee, and they left the diner. Outside, they decided to drop Jade's Blazer off at her house and take Diane's car. At Jade's house, they stopped in so Diane could wash her face. Jade waited in Diane's car as she approached, with a familiar-looking bag in her hand.

As she slipped into the driver's seat, she said, "I hope you don't mind, I raided your candy stash. I'm feeling self-indulgent."

Jade laughed at her friend's audacity. "Don't even think twice, girl. Chocolate-covered peanuts would be my drug of choice for a broken heart. Besides, I have at least three more bags in the freezer."

Diane opened the bag, offered Jade first dibs, which Jade refused, then popped a handful of candy into her mouth. "God! I forgot how good these are!", Diane groaned. By the time they were headed up the ramp to Interstate 295, they were both laughing, and thoughts of morally bankrupt men were forgotten, at least for the moment.

Chapter 21

Jade got a late start Monday morning. Her outing with Diane yesterday was exactly what she needed. But she got home later than she wanted to, and still had shopping and laundry to do. By the time she got to bed, it had been after midnight. Then she had lain in bed, sleepless. She worried about Peter most. No one had heard anything from him in more than a week now. Even for Peter, a week without contacting anyone in the family was unusual Unless there was some reason he took off without a word, Jade knew that the chances were good that Peter was dead.

Being an equal opportunity worrier, Jade then turned to the situation with Derrick. Were they going to get a chance, as a couple? Would Derrick want her after he found out about the things she had done? Jade hoped so. She didn't know if the time would come for her to level with Derrick. Realistically, she knew that things weren't going to get resolved or go forward with Derrick until she was able to work through the Lawrence family mystery.

At work, for a few precious hours she forgot about everything that was happening and concentrated on what she did best. She worked through her lunch hour, eating at her desk while she checked the Remerick & Co. website and slogged through some paperwork. Jade was amazed at how much work she could get done when she was trying to run away from her problems. At 3:15, Jade left work to meet the security system installer at her house.

When she got there, the security van was in her driveway. She parked in front of her house and met the installer at her front door. Before he got to work, he provided Jade with information about the three different security packages he offered. They varied by the complexity and completeness of coverage for her home, and by, of course, the cost. Jade chose the middle-of-the-road coverage plan. This plan provided a keypad for both upstairs and downstairs. The system would trigger if anyone opened a window or a door, anywhere in the house, and didn't enter the four-digit code within 30 seconds. For increased overnight protection, she could program the system to arm the motion sensors for just the upstairs, just the downstairs, or both.

The installer ("Doug" was embroidered on his uniform shirt pocket), explained that she may want to have the freedom to wander around the upstairs at night, including the upstairs bathroom, without worrying about setting off the motion sensor, so they are wired separately for upstairs and downstairs. Some people only find it necessary to arm the downstairs motion sensors at night. They reasoned that, if someone wanted to break in, unless they climbed up to the second floor and staged a blitz attack through a window, they'd have to get in the house through the first floor, setting off the alarm.

By 5:00, her system was installed. Doug went through the arming and disarming process with her a couple times, and had her choose a "safe" word to give the alarm company, should she set the alarm off by accident.

An intriguing concept, Jade thought. That her alarm would go off, the security company would call within seconds, and if it was a mistake, she could provide the "safe" word and they would stand down. If the safe word wasn't given, or if they couldn't reach Jade, they would instantly contact the local police. Doug then showed Jade how to change the alarm code from the factory default code numbers.

Jade was surprised to find out how inexpensive peace of mind was, and she gratefully wrote Doug a check. After the security company van vacated her driveway, she moved her Blazer to it's accustomed place. On her way back in to the house, she retrieved her mail from the box. Inside the house, Jade activated her new security system and noted with satisfaction that she did feel safer.

While cooking dinner, Jade went through her mail. A couple of bills, and a large manila envelope with her name and address hand-written on it and no postage. It had apparently been dropped off in her mailbox. She opened the envelope gingerly, hoping that there wasn't anything deadly in it. Inside she found three 8 x 10-inch photographs. The first one was of she and Diane, while they were shopping yesterday. They were putting bags in to the trunk of Diane's car. Jade was smiling at something Diane said, and appeared to be looking almost directly into the lens of the camera. She remembered the moment. Diane was joking that, unless they found themselves a couple of Sugar Daddies, these shopping sprees would be few and far between. She thought back to yesterday afternoon, trying to think of whether she saw anyone around with a camera. She didn't recall. But obviously, whoever it was had followed them up from Portland. The idea made Jade feel sick. If this person had had a gun instead of a camera, she could be dead right now.

The second photograph was of Ben Lawrence, obviously taken just after he had been killed, but before the police had arrived to place the yellow evidence markers around. She realized that the wall behind Ben Lawrence's body was clean; there was nothing on it yet. The picture she saw from Derrick's notebook, taken by the police, had the Möbius symbol written in blood, on the back wall. This picture was likely taken by the killer, before he had painted the back wall with blood, but after he killed Ben.

The last picture was of the inside of the back compartment of her Blazer, behind the back seat. She recognized the orange first aid kit and flashlight she kept in there. What she didn't recognize was white plastic bag leaning against her spare tire compartment. The picture showed clearly that there was something sticking out over the top of the bag, something with dark smudges on it. Jade immediately realized what this picture was trying to tell her. While she was with Diane in Freeport yesterday, someone had put something in her Blazer. She hadn't had a reason to open the tailgate, so she hadn't yet found it.

Grabbing her keys, she ran to the front door and threw it open. The alarm immediately started a warning series of beeps. Jade entered her code to shut off the alarm, then ran outside to her Blazer. She used her remote to open the tailgate. Looking inside, she saw the white bag. Right where it had been in the picture. Damn it! She reached out and carefully pinched the sides of the bag, spreading them gingerly. Inside the bag was an ornate table leg. It was a light wood color, and stained with what would certainly have to be blood, by the copper odor coming from the bag.

Jade let go of the bag and backed away from the back of the truck. She knew that she should contact the police, right now, before she touched anything else and maybe destroyed evidence. On the heels of that thought, her common sense weighed in. How stupid would she have to be to call the police? She could hear the conversation now. "Hello, Police? This is Jade Danner. I found a bloody table leg in the back of my truck. Yes, I'll hold…." As she held the line, she was sure she'd hear police cruisers in the distance, screaming toward her house. She understood how reasonable their logic would be in arresting her, too. Unfortunately.

Deciding discretion was the better part of valor, she grabbed the white bag, brought it into the house, and threw it into her wood stove. She then lit the stove and watched while the white bag melted and the table leg caught fire. Jade then picked up the photos she had received in the mail and looked again at the first one. The table with a leg missing, at Ben Lawrence's murder scene, was in this picture, and the table leg she just burned was an exact match.

The three photos told a story, when taken together, Jade thought. The first one said, "I know where you are and what you do." The second one said, "I killed Ben Lawrence." The third one said, "Back off or I'll take you down, one way or another." Maybe the new security system was making her cocky, but Jade knew this latest tactic was just that, and it would do nothing to stop her from continuing her quest. Now she was more resolved than ever. The stupid bastard would be sorry for ever messing with her. This was war!

Still feeling angry and outraged, Jade settled on the couch, a steaming mug of green tea in one hand and Bardo snuggled up next to her. She thought about turning on the television but didn't want to get up to get the remote, and thought she probably had enough entertainment going on in her head right now anyway. Jade was lost in thought and jumped halfway off the couch when the telephone rang on the stand next to her. She grabbed the receiver, then realized she didn't check the caller ID first. Cautiously, she said hello.

Her mother's voice responded, sounding upset. "Jade, I'm glad I caught you at home. I'm so worried about your brother. No one's heard from him. The police haven't turned up anything. I wondered if you had a chance to look at the papers I gave you from Peter's room." The nakedly hopeful tone in her mother's voice broke Jade's heart.

Jade said, "I just can't imagine what may have happened to Peter. Going this long without getting in touch isn't like him. I'm worried too! I went through the papers, but didn't find anything that would explain where he may be. I think those papers were part of the documentation of an investigation he had been conducting into the murder that the police questioned him about last year. Maybe he was trying to clear his name." Jade suddenly realized that she was talking about her brother in the past tense, she hoped her mother hadn't noticed. She hurriedly continued, "The person he seemed to think may have been guilty is a guy named Tim Lawry, who used to be Tim Lawrence but changed his name. I'm not sure if that had anything to do with his disappearance."

Jade's mother was unconvinced. "But remember how we found that knife in the trunk of the VW? Peter went missing just a day or two before we found that. I find that extremely suspicious."

Jade tried to soothe her mother's fears. "I think, before we connect that knife to Peter's disappearance, we need to find out if that knife was involved in any way with Peter. If we can't determine that, I don't think we should jump to that conclusion." Jade marveled that her voice sounded so reasonable. She realized simultaneously that she wasn't buying a bit of what she was telling her mother. She just didn't want her mother to worry, or, even worse, put herself in danger by finding out too much about what was really happening.

"Mom, I'm as puzzled about Peter's disappearance as you are. There's just not much we can do right now except to wait, and try not to be any more concerned than we absolutely have to be, at least until we find out what happened. I can't accept that we just may never know what happened and Peter may never come back to us, but I do know it's a possibility."

Her mother said, "Yes, that's exactly what your father says. He says we need to just get on with our lives, as best we can, since we have no idea when or even if Peter will come back."

Jade heard her mom stifle a sob, say a weak goodbye, then abruptly disconnect. Jade realized that her mother hadn't mentioned Phyllis during their conversation. She wondered whether Phyllis was worrying about Peter, and she decided probably not, overly. Phyllis and Peter were never close. For that matter, Phyllis wasn't close to anyone in the family.

Jade realized that she hadn't told her mother about her discovery that the man she had met at Peter's party, Steven, was actually the same man, Timothy, that Peter was apparently investigating for the murder of which he had been accused. She decided there was probably no benefit to telling her mother about the Steven/Timothy connection, at least yet. Since he was present at Peter's party, and seemed as bewildered by Peter's absence as everyone else, he probably didn't have anything to do with his disappearance. She decided to let it go for now, and if anything else threatening happened, to either her or her parents, she would tell them.

Jade realized that she had neglected to re-set the security system when she came back in from checking her Blazer. She set the alarm, headed up the stairs, then pointed her remote control unit downstairs on her way up, to set the first floor motion sensors. Jade got ready for bed, finding comfort in the routine. Bardo headed downstairs. Doug had assured her that small animals like Bardo weren't big enough to set off the motion sensor, so he could roam the house at will. Jade crawled into bed, wondering idly if she may still be in danger from an attack by a rogue dwarf, then decided she could probably handle one. Smiling slightly, Jade drifted into sleep.

Chapter 22

Jade was on the road by 7:00 AM on Tuesday morning. Armed with coffee from her favorite drive-thru shop, Jade was at her desk by 7:30 AM. When Malcolm came in, a few minutes after 8:00, Jade was already up to her elbows, literally, inspecting a child's cradle. Malcolm told her how natural she looked, with a baby's cradle on her lap. Malcolm was rewarded with a patented Jade eye roll. Malcolm gave Jade a speculative look. "Jade, how would you like to double-date sometime with Dom and I?" Jade thought the idea was wonderful, but of course, finding a date would probably be an issue. Malcolm watched Jade grin, then watched as her face fell.

He immediately figured out the issue. "Jade, I want you to meet my younger brother. He's almost 40. Before you ask, yes, he's straight. He's a nice-looking man who works too hard and never has time for fun."

Jade thought immediately of Derrick, and their tentative, possible, future relationship. That was one too many maybes for her, and she told Malcolm she'd love to double with him. They set up a tentative weekend date. She realized she must sound really desperate, since she didn't even know what her date's name is! As Malcolm walked away, Jade called out, "Hey Malcolm? What's your brother's name?"

"Mickey", Malcolm threw over his shoulder on the way out. Jade almost giggled. Malcolm and Mickey? How cute is that?

Jade's new assignments kept her busy through the morning. As lunchtime neared, Jade was sitting cross-legged on the floor, screwdriver in hand, looking into the underside of a 1940's lamp, fashioned to look like a doll carriage. The wiring inside the lamp was original, but was completely shot. She sat back against her desk, keyboard on her lap and looked up at her computer screen, typing her recommendation that the wiring inside the lamp be replaced before anyone tried to actually use it. She heard the bell over the front door ring, and she looked up in time to see a man, on the young side of middle-age, approach her desk. "Can I help you?" Jade stood up and tried to brush some of the dirt off her clothes.

The man's grin was decidedly impish. Jade smiled back, almost against her will. Why is it, she wondered, whenever a nice-looking man comes calling, I always manage to be looking homeless and insane? Probably because I usually look like that, she shot back at herself, instantly silencing her inner trollop who, she suspected, just wanted to get laid anyway. The man reached out and gently plucked a piece of wire from her hair. "I'm Mickey. Is my brother here?"

Malcolm saved her from further humiliation by appearing behind them. "Well, hello, Mickey!" The brothers hugged briefly, then turned as one to face Jade. "I see you've met Jade", Malcolm said. Mickey looked at Jade again. This time, his eyebrows shot up and he manufactured an exaggerated leer.

"THIS is Jade? You aren't serious? This gorgeous creature is actually going to go out with ME?" He clutched his heart and staggered theatrically. Jade laughed delightedly. She liked him already! After they were properly introduced, Malcolm and Mickey left for lunch. Jade finished the lamp, cleaned up, and went out for a quick bite to eat.

When she got back from her lunch break, Malcolm was already back and working in his office. Jade went back to her desk and looked up her next assignment. It was a child's rocking chair. Jade sighed. What was up with all the kid furniture today anyway? The afternoon passed quickly. Jade took a few minutes during the afternoon to type up a list of information for her library trip later. She printed off her list and put it into her purse. Jade finished her last assignment of the day, and she was out the door by 5:00.

There was snow in the air, the temperature in the single digits. Jade walked quickly to her Blazer, snow and ice crunching companionably underfoot. The Blazer started right up, as it always did. Jade was thankful. There had been times in her life when she couldn't afford a dependable vehicle and all too often, on cold days like this, she had been stranded somewhere, in the dark and cold, trying to figure out how she was going to get home. She appreciated this improvement in her lifestyle.

Sitting in her Blazer, shivering while she waited for the truck to warm up, Jade remembered a time very similar to this moment, but also very different. She was eighteen years old and it was winter. Ricky was sitting behind the wheel of his Ford Escort. She was sitting in the front passenger seat. Their breath misted the air as they sat waiting for the car to heat up. Together yet so very alone. That morning, Jade's whole life had changed when she took a pregnancy test and got the grim news. She was pregnant. And now, still trying vainly to grasp her situation, she was trying to explain it to Ricky.

"What the fuck were you thinking, Jade? Did you get knocked up on purpose so I'd have to marry you? Well fuck that shit. Your brother told me that you were on the pill! This isn't my problem. I hope you don't think I'm sticking around, just because of this. I'll get the money together for you to take care of the problem." Ricky's cold eyes raked Jade's distraught face. "Oh Christ, don't start friggin' bawling!"

Ricky reached for Jade, and she instinctively recoiled from his touch. Ricky and Jade had known each other casually for years, as Ricky was one of Peter's best friends. Ricky and Jade had only been intimate one time. But Jade had enough to worry about, at this moment, without thinking about how she ended up having sex with this awful excuse for a human being.

Jade moved as far away from Ricky as the tiny car would allow. Ricky saw her draw back and his face twisted in anger. "Well fuck you, then. You can get the hell out and walk, if you want to be a bitch about it. I was trying to help you out, but hey, I can take a hint." Jade opened her door and got out of the car. Before she could shut the door, the car squealed away, the passenger door swinging shut as the car accelerated.

Jade stood on the curb, her hand still extended, tears starting to freeze on her face. She remembers thinking what a terrible idea it was to agree to go somewhere with Ricky alone, to discuss her pregnancy. She realized now that he could have just killed her and dumped her somewhere. She was thankful that he apparently had at least a small amount of decency. She watched the Escort's tail lights grow smaller, then disappear. The new silence soothed her, even as the falling snow isolated her. For the first time since that morning, her frenzied mind quieted. She still had to tell her parents. That would be the next thing to do. Jade turned in the direction of home and started walking.

The warmth of the blowing air inside the Blazer brought Jade back from her unhappy reflections. She knew, with profound satisfaction, that she had done the very best she could do and things turned out for her the way they were supposed to.

At home, Jade threw together a simple dinner of canned soup and bagged salad, then took a shower. Feeling energetic, Jade headed out to the library, to get some important questions answered. Within fifteen minutes, Jade was pushing thru the impressive, ornate library doors. The young man behind the center desk glanced up quickly then back down at what he was doing. He mumbled distractedly, "Can I help you?" As Jade finished her walk down the long book-lined corridor, he looked up again. As often happened, the young man took a close up look at Jade and was instantly transfixed. And as happened almost equally often, Jade was oblivious to his abrupt bout of self-consciousness.

"Is Helen working tonight?", Jade asked. The man looked almost comically crestfallen.

"No, she doesn't work on Tuesday nights. I'm Ian, and I'd be happy to help you with whatever you need."

Jade passed Ian a sheet of paper listing the information she needed:

- A list of unsolved homicides of women, aged 14 to 35, involving stabbing, slashing and/or dismembering, rape and/or genital mutilation, from 1995 to current, in or near Portland, Maine
- A copy of any police records that are available on these homicides
- A list of the recorded next-of-kin for these homicides
- Public records for any criminal matters involving the Lawrence family, for as far back as records go.

Ian glanced down through the items, looked up at Jade and asked, "Are you writing a book or something?"

Jade's smile was guarded. "Yes, 'or something'".

Intuiting that Jade didn't want to discuss her reasons for needing this information, Ian turned to his computer. After several short, staccato bursts of

148

typing Ian turned to the printer just as a page dropped into the tray. He passed the typewritten list to Jade. "Most of what you need is on recordak film downstairs. We keep the film in a climate-controlled area for now, but soon we'll be imaging everything for on-line access. I provided you with the bin, volume and tape numbers for each of the records you want. Do you need help setting up and using the recordak machine?"

Jade told him she was familiar with how the microfiche machine worked and just needed him to point the way downstairs for her.

Five minutes later, Jade had pulled several tape boxes from the wall rack and had loaded the first one into the machine. Jade gave the machine's side knob a twist and images started to zoom by her on the screen. It was a summary page for the death records on file for Southern Maine for 1995. Jade paged through the death summaries, noting that the headings on each page provided the name, address, date of death, whether it was a suicide, homicide, accident or unknown, and a short summary of how the victim was killed. The summary also indicated, if it was determined, whether the death was at the hands of another. The dates of birth for the victims were not provided on the summaries. Jade was frustrated to find that she'd need to look up the dates of birth for all the female homicide victims, in order to include or exclude them.

She sat back in her chair, looking around while she tried to figure out what to do next. A red telephone with no buttons or dial caught her eye. There was a label taped to the telephone that said, "For librarian assistance". Jade picked up the phone. She heard a telephone ringing distantly and Ian's voice came over the line. Jade explained that she needed to know the age of each of the female homicide victims from 1995 forward. Ian explained that the information she needed was easily accessible in an on-line database. There was a computer at the workstation behind her. Ian walked her through logging in and told her where to find what she needed. Thanking him for his help, Jade hung up the red phone and got down to business. This was more like it!

Turning back and forth between the microfiche reader and the computer, Jade was able to compile the information she needed for 1995. When she had finished working through 1995, she look a look at what she had. There were several unsolved homicides of young women for the year, three of them were women between the ages of 14 and 35. Of them, only one death involved cutting. Jade knew that, if the previous pattern held true, she would first find a small number of deaths per year, but not many more than could be attributable to chance. Then, the next year, she would find that the number of those particular deaths would spike. Jade moved on to 1996. Again, she found that there were several unsolved homicides of women, two of them in her particular age range, and neither of their deaths involved cutting. If there was another rash of Lawrence family murders, they had to have started after 1996.

On to 1997. And pay dirt. There were 11 female victim unsolved homicides that year. Six of them were in the target age range and all of them involved some form of mutilation. Jade knew she had likely found another killing spree, and this time, it may still be going on. Jade knew that next she'd need to find out whether each of the homicides more specifically matched the Lawrence killing M.O.

She continued her search, in the 1998 records. There were 13 murders that fit her narrow profile in 1998. When she was finished, she had found 62 homicides which matched her criteria for the period from 1997 to 2002. Jade was guessing that at least half of them were likely the work of the current Lawrence family killer.

Dear God. A wave of unreality washed over her as she struggled to deal with what she now knew, without much doubt, was happening here. She wished that she had someone to share this information with. She felt alone and overwhelmed. Jade couldn't imagine why the police weren't actively conducting a major investigation. Maybe they were, she thought. Maybe they were trying to avoid creating public hysteria. Jade understood the fine line the police in every city have to walk, every day, while they protect the public safety but try not to create unnecessary fear. She know, however, that these statistics, by themselves, would not be enough to start an investigation if the police weren't already on to this.

Jade picked up the red telephone again and Ian immediately answered. "Ian, is there an easy way to find out whether a homicide was solved after it was added to the yearly death summaries?" Ian told her there was and explained how it was done. Jade used the computer to look up each of the police file numbers and she was provided updated information on whether the case had been solved as of current date or not. Less than half an hour later, Jade had what she needed. 26 names had been crossed off her list, leaving 36 homicides that could potentially be the work of the Lawrence family. She knew it was also possible that a few of the 26 murders that she had now excluded may have been Lawrence murders that were attributed to someone else. She didn't see that there was any way to address that possibility so she decided to concentrate on the 36 unsolveds. Using the on-line sources she used before, Jade looked up each of the remaining homicides on her list, writing down any additional or updated information regarding next-of-kin.

When she was finished, Jade felt that she had made real progress. But she also knew hard work remained. Now she'd need to contact each of these families and find out if there was any connection between the victim and the Lawrence family. She hoped that, once she was able to prove that a Lawrence man was connected to a significant number of these murders, she could then take her information to the police. Apprehending the current Lawrence killer would stop the killing cycle and complete Erin's work.

Jade then turned her attention to finding out if any of the Lawrence men had criminal records. Once more, Jade picked up the red receiver, and Ian picked up his end, sighing almost comically. "Yes, what is it?"

Jade asked him about criminal records and his response was less helpful than she had hoped. "Criminal records are stored on several databases, including Lexus-Nexus, the police department on-line files and criminal court dockets. However, the easiest thing to do if you want information on someone would be have an internet background search done. It usually costs about $30.00 to $50.00. The problem is that records only go back to the 1950's and the further back you go, the more spotty the information becomes."

Jade thought about her options for a moment, then said, "I'm looking for criminal convictions for members of a certain family."

"Yes, I know", Ian interrupted, "The Lawrence family." There was silence on the line for a moment, and Jade held the red phone receiver tightly to her ear as she waited, knowing Ian may considering providing further help.

She pressed her potential advantage. "Ian, I can't tell you much about what I'm doing, but what I can tell you is that several lives may depend on my ability to get this information."

That seemed to decide him. He said, "I have a hacker friend who can probably help you. Let me make a call." Jade told him she would pack up and see him upstairs in a few minutes.

Jade put away the recordak films and logged off the computer. Upstairs, she stopped at the front desk. Ian was just hanging up the telephone as she approached.

"My friend said he'd email me several files later. We looked up the family and found three generations of Lawrence family still alive and on record. All three generations consist of just one person for each generation. Ben Lawrence, Daniel Lawrence and Timothy Lawrence Lawry. As I told you, on-line criminal records only go back to about the 1950's, but I'm sure I can get a nice, thorough background check on these boys, at least back to that point, for you." Ian beamed down at Jade from his lofty kiosk.

Jade gave him her brightest smile. "You have been so much help, I don't even know how to thank you." Ian blushed as he apparently thought of at least one.

He recovered his composure and remembered something else he wanted to tell Jade. "There are also ways to get in to court records to find out if someone was charged with a crime but not convicted. Those records are much harder to hack, because they are sealed." This was something Jade hadn't considered. Ian went on, "But, like everything else, the records ARE out there and CAN be hacked. My friend can likely get them. If you stop by here tomorrow night, I should have something for you."

Jade offered to pay Ian for his help, but he would not accept it, and, in fact, seemed a bit put off by the offer. Jade once more thanked Ian for his help. Ian tried once more, somewhat transparently, to get more information from Jade about her "top secret research project". Jade played into his sketch by telling him that it was so very secret that, if she told him, she'd have to kill him and for his own protection, she could tell him nothing. He laughed delightedly and, as Jade hoped he would, stopped probing.

Chapter 23

Jade got home just before 8:00 PM. Mail stuffed under her arm, she unlocked the front door and immediately reset the security system. She noticed her answering machine light was blinking furiously. She hit the play button. The automated voice stated self-importantly that she had four new messages. The first message was left at 2:00 A.M. With all that was happening lately, that fact alone was enough to cause Jade to feel apprehensive. The voice was familiar, the message cryptic.

Steven sounded exactly as he had the last time he left a message for her, on her cell phone. Arrogant. The smile Jade could hear in his voice chilled her.

"Jade, I'm sure you know who this is. You should check on the lady you spoke with at McDonalds recently. I told you to leave things be, but you ignored my advice." There was a moment of silence, then a click. Jade backed away from the machine in horror.

Before Jade listened to any of the other messages, she looked up the phone number for Mrs. Pelletieri. Her shaking fingers misdialed the number three times before she finally managed to punch in the right sequence of numbers.

Mrs. Pelletieri answered the phone herself. Relieved, Jade said, "Mrs. Pelletieri, I'm so glad you are okay!"

Suspicious, Mrs. Pelletieri said, "Who is this?"

Jade explained who she was and why she had called while Mrs. Pelletieri listened without comment.

When Jade finished, Mrs. Pelletieri spoke. Jade noted that there was a new angry edge to her voice. "Jade, I helped you as much as I could help you, even though it brought up all manner of terrible memories. Now I'm struggling to get that particular genie back in to it's bottle and you are telling me I may be in danger because I tried to help you? Have I got that right?"

Jade had no defense. She asked Mrs. Pelletieri to please be careful for awhile, and she apologized for possibly, albeit inadvertently, putting her in harm's way. There was a click on the line as Mrs. Pelletieri disconnected without another word.

Still feeling upset, Jade went back to the answering machine and listened to the second message. The time stamp said 5:30 PM. It was Derrick. "I just wanted to check in and make sure you are okay. I know we left things badly last time, and I wanted to let you know that I'm not angry with you and I hope you are not angry with me. We both understand each other's position, but your refusal to accept my help doesn't change how I feel about you. Let's talk soon?" Not knowing how she felt about the message, Jade went on to the third message.

The next message was left just after Derrick had called. It was Diane. "Hi J! Well I did it. I called Bruce's wife. I called from the payphone kiosk at the Maine Mall, just like you suggested. At first, she was upset. Then we got to talking and she told me that she has suspected for awhile that something like this was going on. I explained how I met Bruce, through the internet dating service, and how he told me he had been doing it for more than two years. She was hurt, but I could tell that she wasn't really surprised. I gave her the website where he 'trolls', and I gave her his screen name. She said she was going to log on and print off his profile and confront him. I think I may have broken up their marriage! I told her that I felt terrible and she said she didn't blame me, and she could hear in my voice how badly I felt. I started out doing it to get back at Bruce, but in the end, I'm glad now because hey, if I were her, I'd certainly want to know. Thanks for giving me sound advice and a caring shoulder to cry on. Love you."

The last message had been left about fifteen minutes before she got home. It was her mother. "Jade, honey, there's news about Peter. I'm afraid it isn't good. Please call me as soon as you get in, I don't care how late it is, I need to talk to you." Jade put her jacket back on and hit the road again.

At her mother's house, Jade parked behind her mother's Lexus and ran to the front door. Her mother pulled the door open just as Jade reached it. It was obvious that she had been crying. Jade held out her arms and her mother collapsed into them. Jade immediately realized that Peter must be dead. When her mother's sobs began to subside, Jade led her to the living room couch. Jade's father came in to the room and sat down on the other side of Agatha. He took her in to his arms and held her while he looked across at Jade. Jade had never seen her father look so bereft. Jade's eyes asked the crucial question and her father nodded once, grimly. Jade felt her eyes burn, then her tears fell. She looked across the room at the family pictures on the mantle. At the smiling and

155

happy boy Peter had been as a young child. Jade knew that, even then, there were forces at work within him that would shape the darkly strange man he would later become. It was inconceivable to Jade that Peter wouldn't ever be coming home again.

When Agatha's tears had, for the moment, run their course, she turned to Jade. "I'm so glad you are here. The police found Peter's body."

Jade's father tried to keep Agatha quiet, mumbling words of comfort as he rubbed her back. Jade had the strange idea that he didn't want Agatha to tell her what happened.

Agatha turned angrily to him. "Now Brandon, don't start! Jade's a big girl, and she deserves to know the truth." Agatha turned back to Jade. "They are saying that it's likely he's been dead since the first day he disappeared." Jade didn't want to upset her mother, so she didn't ask the questions she wanted to ask about how Peter had died and if there was any indication how he had died.

Instead of asking about Peter, Jade said, "Have you told Phyllis yet?"

Her father spoke up, "Phyllis was here this afternoon, but I sent her home a few minutes ago, to be with her own family."

As she sat there, in her parents' house, she realized that she wasn't very surprised about Peter's death. She had instinctively kept her fear of Peter hidden from her parents, and more importantly, from Peter himself. As an adult, Jade's fear of Peter had changed into an aversion. Jade spoke to Peter as little as possible, which had also seemed fine with Peter. Now that Peter was apparently dead, and out of their lives forever, Jade felt two very different emotions. She felt regret for the close relationship she should have had with Peter and now never would, and she felt profound relief that the vague, continuous unease she felt toward Peter had now ended. Three, she admitted to herself grimly. She felt three emotions. The third one was guilt.

As if sensing the direction of her thoughts, Agatha took Jade's hand and said, "Honey, they found Peter's body in a shallow grave in the scrub on the northern corner of the Western Promenade this morning. Your father had to go to the police station to identify him because, apparently, he had been mutilated, and his body had extensively decomposed." Agatha swallowed audibly and Jade could see her struggling to stave off panic.

Agatha opened her mouth to speak again, and Jade shushed her. "It's okay, mom, I don't need to know all the particulars. Peter's gone now, and hearing all the awful details right now won't bring him back." Agatha nodded gratefully.

Jade spent a few more minutes with her mother, then gave both her parents a hug and said her goodbyes. As she turned back to close the door behind her, she saw her mother and father, sitting together on the couch, not touching. Both had their faces buried in their hands, and both were slightly turned away from the other. Needing but not finding solace in the company of the other. Jade knew that image would always be with her, when she thought back to this night.

On the drive home, Jade pulled out her cell phone and dialed Derrick's cell. He answered on the second ring. "Hi Jade! I wasn't sure you would call. I'm glad to hear from you."

Jade realized that Derrick may think that she was calling to patch up their friendship, or whatever the hell it was they had. Jade said, "Derrick, thank you for leaving that message for me earlier. Did you hear about Peter?"

There was a moment of silence, then Derrick said, "Yes, I know about that. As the officer who filed the missing person report, I was notified, after your family was notified, earlier this evening. I wish it had been me who found him, Jade, so I could have been the one to tell you and your parents. It's not a very pleasant task, but I felt a responsibility to you and your family. Is there anything I can do to help?"

Jade answered, "I'd like to see a copy of the report that was filed when his body was found. And also a copy of the autopsy report when that has been finalized."

Derrick said, "Jade, I can only release parts of the report as this is an ongoing criminal investigation. There is information in the report that, if it fell into the wrong hands, would seriously compromise the investigation. What I can do is sit down with you and give you some of the basic information about where Peter was found, and in what condition, if that would help you. I can also get you a copy of the autopsy report when it is published. It is the family's right to have that, and I'll make sure you get it. Will that suffice?"

Jade thought Derrick sounded distant, possibly still upset about where the two of them had left things. She realized that she needed to stay on his good side as much as reasonably possible, as he was her only "in" on the investigation of Peter's death. Her mind stuttered on the words "Peter's death". Somehow, putting those two words together began to make it seem more real. So begins the process of healing, she thought.

She said, "Definitely that'll be a good start. I'll be in touch to set up a time. Meanwhile, are you finished going over my mother's VW?"

Derrick answered, "We should be by tomorrow. I'll bring it back to your mother as soon as it's released."

Jade thanked him, trying to keep the coolness she felt toward him from showing in her voice.

Derrick added, still sounding detached. "I also need to tell you that we have excluded no one from our investigation, which means that we need to get some information from you, and also, within the next few days, from your parents and sister, as well. If you don't call me within a few days, I'll call you to get something set up."

Jade realized that Derrick was telling her that she could be a potential suspect in her brother's death. One minute, she's trying to get Derrick to give her information, the next minute she's a suspect in need of questioning. Shit!

Taking care to keep the alarm she felt from showing in her voice, Jade responded, "That'll be fine. Thank you."

Jade replaced the receiver with a shaking hand. She realized that Derrick must have received the news about the discovery of Peter's body after he had left his message on her answering machine at 5:30, since he sounded cool and cautious on the telephone just now, which was a far cry from the gentle, supportive voice she heard in his earlier message. He was such a confusing man! Jade found herself caring very much about whether Derrick considered her a viable suspect or not.

Like something Jade forgot to put away, her mind kept tripping over the fact of Peter's death. She knew it would take time to sink in. Once it did, she probably wouldn't feel the grief that she should be feeling as his sister. He deserved to be mourned, missed and remembered. Jade's mind turned back to her childhood with Peter, since they hadn't seen each other very often during their adult lives. Jade could not recall even one time that Peter had shown compassion or caring toward her. In later childhood, she was happiest when Peter was busy with other things and ignoring her. Then there were times when he was bored, or angry, and would go out of his way to upset her. Some of the things he did were overtly hateful and dangerous; some were just annoying.

One of Jade's last childhood memories of Peter happened when she was 17. She was a popular, pretty girl and never lacked for male attention. But Peter saw her as a "goody two shoes". Peter had one of his friends, Ricky, ask her out. Just to shock Peter, Jade thought now in hindsight, she accepted. Ricky took Jade to a party, but was disappointed that Jade wouldn't drink the beer he gave her. She grabbed a can of soda instead. She found out later that Ricky had spiked her soda with some kind of drug when she left her soda unattended.

After she had finished the soda, Ricky took her out to his car, to "talk". Jade, who had begun to feel progressively more odd in the last several minutes, was barely conscious by then. She remembered all the other guys high-fiving Ricky on the way out the door, but it all seemed disjointed and unreal. On the way to the car, she asked him if he would drive her home. He said he would, in just a little while. Ricky told Jade that she didn't look good, and he was going to help her into the back seat of his car so she could lay down. Jade's last conscious memory up to that point in the evening was of being thankful to Ricky for his kindness.

Swimming up from unconsciousness several minutes later, Jade slowly became aware that she was naked from the waist down and splayed on her back, in the back seat of Ricky's car. Ricky was on top of her, his hips pumping wildly against her. She was pinned against the seat. She tried to move and could not. She felt an explosion of pain from the very center of her being, every time he plunged deeply into her. By degrees, her drugged brain slowly began to understand what was happening. She opened her eyes and saw that Ricky's face was a mask of concentration and pleasure. He stopped moving for a moment, and a gasp escaped him as he emptied himself into her. Crying now, Jade's hands weakly tried to push him off her. He laughed at her efforts, then finally roughly pulled out of her, climbed off and backed out of the door. He stood outside and unashamedly pulled his pants up and fastened them, whistling contentedly.

Jade eventually became aware of the cool breeze blowing across the naked lower half of her body. With effort, she pulled her skirt down to cover herself. Jade turned on to her side, pain shooting through her torn insides. Ricky picked up Jade's panties from the back seat floor and threw them at her. "Get dressed. Cut out the crying shit. Your brother told me you like it rough. You didn't like it? Too fuckin' bad." He got into the driver's seat and started the car. Jade remembered crying so hysterically that night that Ricky realized he couldn't bring her home like that. He took her up Munjoy Hill to the Eastern Promenade and parked the car.

Now that the alcohol was wearing off Ricky, and the drugs were wearing off Jade, they were both upset with Peter. Jade's body felt battered, her mind numb. She remembered telling Ricky over and over to take her home. She knew that Ricky might be afraid that she would report the rape, and that he'd go to jail. As this alarming thought occurred to her, Ricky spoke. "Jade, I apologize for what I did to you. I'm drunk, but not so drunk now as I was an hour ago. I was way out of line. Peter gave me the drugs to put in your soda and he told me to go ahead and do whatever I wanted to you, that you like men to just take what they want from you.

"Unfortunately, now I'm guilty of rape. If you tell anyone about this, I'll go to jail for a fuck of a long time. I don't want to have to hurt you, but honestly, if you are thinking of telling anyone what happened tonight, I'll be forced to do something I really don't want to do." This speech was delivered in a chillingly soft, almost compassionate voice. Jade realized that, like Peter, there was something badly broken inside Ricky. The low-key delivery of his threat of bodily harm convinced her, and she gave him her word that she would tell no one. And tell no one she did. Until she found out she was pregnant, almost three months later.

After what Peter had done to her, she couldn't summon more than a passing sense of sadness. Feeling another little pang of guilt, Jade decided to use Peter's death as an opportunity to get more of her research done. She left Malcolm a voice message stating that her brother's body had been found, and that she was taking a few days off. She knew Malcolm would be concerned about her, and she made a mental note to call him during the day tomorrow to have a real conversation with him so he'd know she was okay.

Chapter 24

Jade was up at her usual time Wednesday morning. Considering that she had been awake for a good portion of the night, she felt pretty good. She remembered that she wasn't working for the rest of the week. At least, she wasn't going "to work". Instead, she'd start her search for family and friends of the most recent homicide victims that fit the Lawrence killer profile.

Pouring herself a second cup of coffee, Jade sat down at the kitchen table and spread out her library notes. Her notes listed the homicide victim names and next of kin information, covering all the unsolved homicides of young women between 1997 and 2002 in greater Portland. Jade thought she may have better luck sooner if she started with the more recent homicides. Information would be fresher in people's minds. Jade knew that, with as many victims as she had found, the chances were very good that she would find something incriminating, and maybe even something definitive, among all the deaths.

Knowing how much work was ahead of her, she wished she could ask Derrick for help. If he could get her any part of any of these homicide files, it would greatly expedite her work. But, she reasoned, she just couldn't ask. Not without full disclosure on her part.

She knew she was tough, and she could take care of this herself. But suddenly, she didn't want to. She didn't feel equal to it, and the fear threatened to overwhelm her. She pushed those thoughts away, resolving to not let fear stop her from doing what she knew must be done. Jade also knew that anyone she allowed into her investigation would likely be in danger, as she knew that she herself was. Newly resolved to go this alone, Jade grabbed her notes and the telephone directory and got started.

After she had done her initial canvassing for both 2001 and 2002, she had chosen two homicides from 2001 and four homicides from 2002. All of them roughly matched the Lawrence family M.O., and all had next-of-kin listed in the records who were also currently listed in the telephone book by name. Jade decided that six homicides were a good start, and may provide her with enough information for her to at least know, conclusively, that the Lawrence family curse was active again. She knew that, with confirmation of the current involvement of the Lawrence family, the police would have to be informed. She hoped she could inform them anonymously. Jade reasoned that, if the police were provided a clear and convincing case, they would check it out no matter who supplied the information. Jade realized that Derrick may eventually realize that the anonymous tip had come from her, and with a bit of legwork, he could probably prove it. That was a chance she would have to take, and would be dealt with in it's own time.

For 2001, the victims she chose were Heather Demoree (murdered 10/29/01), and DeLayne McInerny (4/11/01). She remembered the first name from Peter's research papers, the second name was new to her.

For 2002, the four names included two she had seen before, also in Peter's notes, Paulina Nielson (1-4-02) and Cathy Small (10/20/02) The other two were Sylvia Parker (9-18-02) and Tracy McGarrett (12-12-02).

Jade picked up the telephone and dialed the number she had found for Daren McGarrett, Tracy McGarrett's husband. After three rings, an answering machine picked up. Jade waited for the beep, then said, "Hello, my name is Jade Danner. I'm researching several area homicides, including that of Tracy McGarrett. If I have reached the correct number, Mr. McGarrett, please call me back at 555-6123." Jade disconnected and dialed the second number on her list, the next-of-kin for Sylvia Parker. Again, she got an answering machine. With a sigh, Jade again left a message asking for a return call.

She called the third number, mentally prepared to leave another message and was shocked when a real person answered. A very deep voice with a southern accent said, "This is Nate Small." Jade immediately launched in to her story, afraid she would again be disappointed. Mr. Small waited for her to finish her explanation and he said, "You are probably not going to believe this. I'm looking in to those deaths myself!" Jade, who was pacing off her kitchen while she was talking, stopped dead. "Are you serious?" "Deadly", he drawled.

Jade said, "Mr. Small, it's extremely urgent that I get whatever information you may have about this series, and specifically the death of your wife. When would you have time to talk with me?" Mr. Small's voice suddenly cooled several degrees. "Well, you see, that may be a bit of a problem. I'm a freelance reporter. Once I got over the initial shock and grief of losing my wife, I got to thinking, then I got to digging. Before I knew it, I was knee deep in a shit-load of murders that were very similar to my wife's murder. I couldn't believe it. I contacted the police, several months after my wife died, trying to tell them what I had found out since her death, about the other murders, but they didn't feel that the murders were related.

"So now I'm putting together a story. It would be a shame for me to share that information with you, only to have you scoop me with your story." Jade rushed to reassure him. "Look, Mr. Small, I'm not a reporter, or a writer. I appraise antique furniture, actually. I don't want to scoop you. If you want to write up an agreement before you talk to me, saying that I won't use any of the information you provide to me for personal gain in any way, I'll be glad to sign it."

Mr. Small considered that for a moment, then he said, "Please, call me Nate. I'll talk to you, on the condition that we *share* information, and that you allow me to use any new information I get from you to continue my hunt for my wife's killer, and of course, for my story." Clever dude, Jade thought. She didn't care what he used her information for, she just wanted to find out what he knew. She didn't want this thing blown wide open, driving the killer underground, before she had a chance to finish her own investigation. So she'd just have to make sure, when they met, that she came across to Nate Small as not knowing all that much. Jade countered, "Only if you agree to not publish anything about these murders for at least three months." Mr. Small agreed, on the condition that this promise applied to both of them. They set up a meeting for 5:30 PM Saturday afternoon.

Jade then called the number she found in the telephone book for Paulina Nielson's next-of-kin, which was Paulina's mother. Again, Jade was able to connect with a real person. She verified that it was Mrs. Nielson and launched in to her spiel. Mrs. Nielson interrupted her and said, in a loud voice, Hold up, little missy. I can't understand anything you just said. Why do people have mumble? And talk so fast!". Slowing down and increasing the volume of her voice, Jade again went through her spiel. Mrs. Nielson listened carefully, then said, "I can't help you. I know about Paulina, but she's not a relation of mine I'm sorry." Jade found herself holding a dead phone. So much for that. Jade suspected that Mrs. Nielson and Paulina Nielson *were* family, but she knew she couldn't force anyone to talk to her.

Jade took a break from her research to call Malcolm. He answered on the first ring. "Jade, how are you? Is everything okay? I was so sorry to hear about Peter."

The unexpected concern in Malcolm's voice instantly made Jade feel guilty, about her lack of feelings for Peter's death and for missing work under somewhat false pretenses. Jade uneasily cleared her throat and replied, "Everything's fine. Or it will be. Thank you Malcolm."

Malcolm said, "I told Mickey that we'd need to postpone our double-date for awhile, I hope that's okay. He was disappointed, he's quite taken with you. Just let me know when you are ready and we'll set it up."

Jade smiled at Malcolm's attempt to cheer her up. She said, "Instead of next weekend, what about the weekend after?" Jade heard the sound of pages being turned. "The weekend after next will be fabulous. Let's plan on it. If it gets to mid-week next week and you aren't feeling up to it, though, just give me a ring." Jade agreed, they said their goodbyes, and Jade went back to the telephone directory.

With a solid lead, and two more names still on her list, Jade was beginning to feel as if she could be getting somewhere. However, her optimism took a downturn a few minutes later when she realized there was no listing in the telephone book for Heather Demoree's next-of-kin, a stepfather named Brian.

Jade decided to check the internet. Eureka! There was a listing for Brian. He had moved out of the area in mid-2002. He now lived in Lincoln, Maine. Jade called the telephone number she found on the internet, listened as it began to ring, and waited for a machine to answer. Instead, a quiet male voice answered.

Jade greeted him, and asked him if he was the Brian Demoree who's stepdaughter had been killed two years ago. After a momentary pause, the line went dead. Not to be deterred, Jade immediately dialed the number again. The man cautiously said hello. Jade jumped right in, "Please, don't hang up! I'm not trying to sell you anything and I'm not trying to take advantage of you. I don't want to capitalize on your grief. My name is Jade Danner. I'm investigating the murder of your stepdaughter as one in a series of murders that have taken place in this area in recent years. If you don't want to talk to me, that's fine. I just wanted you to be fully informed before you refuse my help."

Jade held her breath for a moment.

Brian Demoree's voice responded, sounding resigned and touchingly vulnerable. "Lady, if you could help my family figure this thing out, I'd give you everything I have."

Jade answered, "I don't want anything at all from you or your family, Mr. Demoree. I only want a little of your time. Would you be willing to meet with me and tell me what you know about your stepdaughter's murder?"

Brian said, "I can and I will. If you've got a line on the person who killed Heather, I'll help you in any way I can. The police haven't been able to get anywhere, but not from lack of trying. I do have information, but I haven't been able to make heads or tails of it. Maybe, if you put what I have with what you have, we'll get somewhere. Your number came up on my caller ID. You are calling from southern Maine, right?" Jade confirmed that she was. "Okay, let's meet in Bangor on Saturday. I have some business there anyway." Excited, Jade instantly agreed. Brian continued, "There's a coffee shop behind the City

Hall building, across the street from the municipal parking garage. Why don't you meet me at that coffee shop at 11:00 AM, this Saturday. I'll be wearing a red baseball cap that has a New York Yankee's logo on it."

Jade knew that the NY Yankees hat would set Brian Demoree apart, here in BoSox country, but far be it from her to censure a gift horse. "I'll be there. If your plans change, please call me at this number and let me know so I won't waste a trip." He agreed, and they disconnected.

There was just one person left on her list to contact. Jade checked the telephone book for a listing for Kevin McInerny, the husband of DeLayne McInerny. The newspaper had published a picture of DeLayne, which was taken from a distance and somewhat grainy. Jade noted that, interestingly, this was the only African-American woman she had yet discovered to possibly be the victim of a Lawrence killer. This fact alone made her think it was less likely that her murder would be related to the other possible Lawrence killings. But, since the M.O. was so similar, the victim fell in to the correct age range, and she was killed in the murder's comfort zone, it was possible enough that her death was related to the others that Jade felt the need to check it out.

Jade found a listing in the North Deering section of Portland for a Kevin McInerny. She called the telephone number and got a disconnect recording. Luckily, the recorded message provided the new telephone number. Jade crossed out the disconnected telephone number on her notes and listed the new number above it. She called the new telephone number and a very young child answered the phone. "Hello, who do you want?"

Immediately charmed, Jade smiled. "I'm looking for your daddy. Is he at home?" The telephone clattered noisily on to a hard surface, then Jade heard the sound of little feet running away from the phone.

A moment later, Jade heard, "Daddy, some lady is on the phone for you." A minute later, Jade heard the phone being picked up.

A male voice answered, "Hello?" Jade told him who she was and why she was calling. Although less than enthused with the idea of bringing up the painful memories of his wife's death, Mr. McInerny seemed to feel that he owed it to his wife to do whatever he could to get justice for her. In the interest of full disclosure, Jade mentioned that, for his protection and the protection of his family, she would prefer to meet with him somewhere other than his home, as her research had put her in conflict with some dangerous people. He agreed to meet with Jade on Sunday, at 5:00, at his best friend's house. Jade said she'd be there. Jade put his name, the address of their meeting place and his telephone number in her day planner and thanked him effusively for agreeing to speak with her.

Jade spent the rest of her day organizing her notes about "the Lawrence case", as she had come to think of it. Jade knew she was obsessing about the Lawrence killings instead of thinking about her brother. She wasn't ready to face her complex feelings about Peter's death.

Late in the afternoon, Agatha stopped by to talk about arrangements for Peter's funeral. The shattered look in her mother's eyes made Jade feel like an impostor. Jade agreed with her mother that the funeral should be small and intimate. Her mother had called the funeral home and booked a room for the specific date and time, but the specifics still needed to be worked out with the funeral director.

Together, they sat at Jade's kitchen table, amid Jade's notes about the Lawrence family, and they wrote two lists. One, of people who needed to be informed about Peter's death and two, people from that list who would be invited to the funeral. They divided the lists and agreed to each make their several telephone calls that evening. Jade and Agatha made plans to get together in the morning, to take a trip to the funeral home to make the rest of the arrangements.

Jade took an hour in the evening and made her calls. She then called her mother to see if she needed help with her list. Her mother had done a few of the calls, Jade's father told her, then she had to lie down, and her father had taken over and finished the calls.

Jade then called Ian at the Portland Public Library, to see what he and his hacker friend had been able to find out about the Lawrence family's criminal history.

"Jade, you are going to love this." Jade realized Ian must have found something good. He immediately launched into an altogether-too-complex explanation of what he and his friend had done to uncover the information they now had for Jade.

"Ian, I'm sure your undercover work was wonderful, and I appreciate the hoops you apparently had to jump through in order to get the information I need. Unfortunately the technical information sails right over my head. Please just let me know what you found out."

Ian, sounding a little deflated, said "Okay, I'm sorry. I'm just so into this stuff! What I found out is that the only members of your Lawrence family who ever got into any trouble were the men." This information was entirely expected. She hoped that Ian had something better.

Ian continued breathlessly, "Abuse charges were filed against them by their wives or significant others with alarming frequency. Strangely enough, we found at least eight reports of spousal or partner abuse in the police records, from the mid-1950's right up to several years ago. One of the records I found, from 1958, indicated a possible murder attempt by poison." Ian was silent for a moment, letting this information sink in.

Jade realized a reaction was expected, so she said, "What a bunch of freaks these people are!"

Ian continued, "Yeah, exactly! The woman, apparently an acquaintance, accused one of the Lawrence men of Thallium poisoning. But there were no subsequent conviction records for any of them. There were also records pertaining to several crimes of which Lawrence men were suspected, everything from rape to murder, but unfortunately, there was not sufficient evidence to bring them to trial so none of them were ever actually indicted for anything."

Amazed, Jade said, "So what you are telling me is that all three of the living Lawrence family men have pristine police records?"

Jade heard the distant click of computer keys, then Ian answered. "Yes, that's exactly what I'm telling you. Except, get this, my records indicate that there is a fourth Lawrence family member, who's likely to be still alive."

Chapter 25

Ian mistook Jade's stunned silence for disappointment. "Hey, just because these men weren't convicted of anything doesn't mean they didn't do anything, you know."

Jade spoke up, "You said there's a fourth Lawrence family member? Do you know his name, how old he is, anything at all about him?"

More keyboarding sounds. "There's really very little about him here. He would be around 65 years old, give or take. I only stumbled over the information about him because there was an incident report filed which referred to a Dillon Lawrence, in the late 1950's. Daniel, and who Daniel reported as his twin brother, Dillon, had a violent physical altercation, at the cemetery in the Western Promenade. Dillon, the report states, denied any relationship to Daniel, and filed assault charges against him.

"The officer who filed the report noted that the two men were almost identical, and so he found it strange that Dillon would deny that Daniel was related to him when he so obviously was. The officer and his partner separated the men and took reports. The record also stated that both men gave dates of birth within three days of each other, and completely out of earshot from the other. The whole thing was dropped a month later when Dillon didn't show up in court to press charges."

This was completely new information to Jade and she considered the impact of it on her investigation. Ben Lawrence didn't know, until recently, that he did, in fact, father a child with Alois, and that the child did survive. Jade wondered if Daniel told Ben that he had actually fathered twins. Her instinct told her no, not if Daniel and Dillon had this apparently contentious relationship. Of course both men would have been fairly young then and a lot of things could have happened in the intervening years.

Ian abruptly derailed Jade's train of thought. "Hey, Earth to Jade, come in Jade!" Jade realized with a start that Ian had probably been trying to get her attention for a while.

"Oh, sorry Ian, I was woolgathering."

Jade could hear the smile in Ian's voice, "Well at least you weren't sitting there idly thinking or anything." Jade thanked Ian for the information he found for her and they disconnected.

Jade took a few minutes to write up notes on the conversation she just had with Ian, while it was still fresh in her mind.

In bed later, she lay awake for a time, envisioning hotheaded Daniel and Dillon fighting among the tombstones. She knew that Daniel was likely fighting to be recognized by someone who may have meant a great deal to him, since Dillon was his twin brother. Dillon, she suspected, may have been fighting to keep Daniel out of his life. Jade welcomed the blessed oblivion of sleep, when she felt it finally coming for her.

The next morning, Jade and Agatha got an early start, arriving at the funeral home together by 10:00 A.M. Just inside the front door, Jade looked down the plush corridor and saw a small sign sitting on a tripod in front of a set of double doors. The door was open and the room beyond looked empty. The sign said, "Lawrence Family and Friends - Service at 12:00, Internment at 1:30, Forest

Lawn Cemetery". Jade realized that Ben Lawrence's funeral must be scheduled today, here. It seemed a rather odd coincidence, until she realized that this is Maine, and there aren't many funeral homes.

At first, Agatha seemed to be bearing up. But as the minutes wore on, and discussion turned from caskets to flowers to the family burial plot, Jade realized her mother wasn't up for this. Jade asked the funeral director if they could take a short break, then she gently guided her mother to the Blazer and handed her in. She went back inside alone, finished making the arrangements and wrote a check to cover the total expenses.

As she left the funeral home and walked toward her Blazer, Jade looked across the parking lot at the cab of her truck. Cold fear shot through her when she realized her mother wasn't there. Jade quickly scanned the parking lot, but her mother was gone. Jade turned and walked out to State Street. Walking up and down the street, Jade frantically scanned the faces of passersby, then started calling out for her mother. She spotted a flash of red, her mother's coat! Agatha was standing on the curb, three buildings away, staring vacuously across the street. She turned her head and looked in Jade's direction, locking eyes with her. Jade saw a strange expression cross her mother's strained features. Jade immediately recognized the expression, but she didn't understand what it meant, out of place with the situation as it was. While Jade stood, puzzled, Agatha calmly stepped off the curb and walked directly into oncoming traffic.

Jade saw the car that would hit her mother, a split second before it did. The images of the next few seconds roared through her mind, at fast-forward speed. The horrified face of the driver as she tried to brake, her mother's red coat flying open in the breeze. The unspeakable sound of the car slamming into her mother's defenseless frame. Her mother's broken body, airborne, hitting the hood of the car then sliding to the ground. Now so very still. Jade ran to her mother, fell to her knees and pulled her mother's limp upper body onto her lap.

Cradling her mother's head she began to sob. Her mother's face and neck were quickly turning blue, and the bloody road-rash across her mother's cheeks looked surreal against the blue backdrop of her mother's darkening cyanotic skin. Jade suddenly recalled the night of Peter's party, when the blue vase cast the strange blue shadow across her mother's face. She remembered how it made her mother look dead, and she shivered involuntarily. She looked into her mother's face and saw her eyelids flicker. A tiny sign of life, but there, nonetheless.

Jade screamed to the gathering crowd, "Somebody call 911, my mother's been hit by a car!" She took her jacket off and put it over her mother. Agatha moaned softly and tried to speak.

Jade said, "Shhh, now, it's going to be okay. Hang in there, mom, we need you. It's not your time."

Agatha opened her eyes, fixed Jade with an anguished and pain-laden look, then unbelievably, she tried to smile. Agatha said, "Jade, don't blame Peter, nothing he did is his fault. It's my fault. Mine and your dad's. Ask your dad about the vase." None of this made any sense to Jade, but she knew her mother's strange words, uttered *in extremis* as they were, would haunt her forever if her mother did not survive.

Part II

Chapter 26

The ambulance arrived moments later. In a flurry of activity and reassurances from concerned onlookers, Jade found herself riding in the ambulance with her mother to Mercy Hospital, just a few blocks away. Her mother was clinging to life, and the attendants were working to keep her airway open as she gasped for breath. A short while later, Jade found herself sitting alone in the Emergency Room. She fished her cell phone out of her purse and called her father's cell. He didn't answer, so Jade left a message for him, trying hard not to let her voice betray her frantic worry. Jade also called her parent's home, in case her father was there, with his cell phone off. She left another message for him there. Jade then called Phyllis' number and left a voicemail message for her.

Jade sat impatiently waiting for word while her mother was being assessed. Everything during the last hour was a blur. Jade sat forward, her head in her hands, too exhausted and shocked to cry. The silence was broken by the ring of her cell phone. Jade grabbed the phone and checked the Caller ID. It was her father. Her fingers shook as she answered the call. She explained what happened, her voice breaking as she finished. Her father seemed to immediately realize how serious it probably was. A new urgency in his tone, he promised to be there shortly. Jade suddenly felt like a child again, with her father racing in to rescue her. Only this time, it wasn't her that needed rescuing, it was her mother.

As she said goodbye to her father, she heard a beeping sound on the line. She connected the second call and heard her sister's worried voice. "Jade, what happened? Where are you?" Jade again explained the situation. Phyllis said she'd find someone to watch the kids and she'd be there as soon as she could.

As Jade continued to wait, she thought about what her mother had said, as she lay hideously broken and bleeding in the street. Would those words be her last? Jade didn't want to think about that. Jade curled into her chair, hugging her knees. Through a haze of pain, Jade became aware of someone entering the waiting room. The sound of footsteps crossing the room. Someone sitting down beside her. She looked over at the man now sitting next to her. He gave her an encouraging smile and that's all she needed. Derrick! She threw herself into his arms. Finally, safe in Derricks arms, the tears fell. He pulled her on to his lap and held her closer as she cried.

Some time later, Jade pulled away and looked sheepishly up into Derrick's face, ashamed of how she had lost control. But, she had to admit, she did feel better. He smiled down at her and carefully lifted her off his lap and put her back in her chair. Wordlessly, he took her hand and leaned back in his chair, closing his eyes. Jade knew he would stay with her until her mother's condition was known.

A few minutes later, her father walked in to the waiting room, which of course, started a new bout of tears for her. His face was white and pinched with worry. Jade rushed to him and hugged him. Jade suddenly noticed how old her father was starting to look.

He left the room for a few minutes, then came back in. "Jade, I just checked with the desk, they don't have any word on your mother yet, but they promised to tell us as soon as they know anything at all." Jade nodded. Derrick stood up and introduced himself to Jade's father. They shook hands, then all three of them sat back down to wait.

Phyllis arrived within the hour. She walked in and sat down next to her father. Jade introduced Derrick, and updated Phyllis on what had happened. Phyllis immediately pulled out her cell phone and called her husband, updating him on what they knew so far. She flipped the cell phone closed and looked at her father, her concern obvious.

Jade couldn't shake a very bad feeling about this. Try as she would, she just couldn't banish the memory of her mother laying in the street, her precious blood pooling under her head. Having her father, Phyllis and Derrick here, all together in the same room, was also contributing to her unease. Jade couldn't remember the last time she, her sister and their parents were together in one place. Sadly, they were not a close family and it took something like this to pull them together.

Just over an hour later, the doctor hurried in, looking grim. Jade immediately stood and met him halfway across the room. He approached Jade and held out his hand. "I'm Doctor Issacs. Are you the Danners?" He looked at Jade, and at her father, sister, and at Derrick, seated at the back of the room. Jade nodded, not trusting herself to speak.

Doctor Isaacs put a comforting hand on Jade's shoulder and gave them all a compassionate look. "Your mother is resting comfortably right now. She has several broken bones, which have been set. Her windpipe was crushed, which temporarily impeded her air flow. More crucially, she has a subdural hematoma, and her brain was compressed by the bleeding and the swelling. We did a craniotomy, which is the creation of an opening in her skull, to allow her brain additional space to swell without further insult to the area. We've also, temporarily, put your mother into a therapeutic coma, to allow her body to focus entirely on healing. This is often standard procedure with injuries such as the ones your mother sustained."

Jade sat back down, between Derrick and her father. She was so very grateful that her mother was alive. "Is my mother going to be okay?"

The doctor's slight smile transformed his face. "We certainly hope so, and we think she will be. The next 48 hours will be crucial to her recovery. After that, we'll assess her, and if she's progressing adequately, we'll waken her. That will be important, sooner rather than later, as it's possible that, between her brain swelling and her disrupted air supply, that she has suffered brain damage." The doctor's statement about possible brain damage tempered Jade's relief with new concern.

Jade's father cleared his throat, obviously struggling to control his emotions. He said, "Thank you, Doctor. When can we see her?" The doctor said, "Give us a few minutes. I'll send a nurse to escort you. Remember, she has a lot of wires and tubes in her and she's pretty banged up."

Derrick took this as his signal to leave them to their family reunion. He said his goodbyes and

Jade walked him to the elevator. "Derrick, I'm so glad you were here. How did you know what happened?"

Derrick said, "I was on duty and heard there was an accident on State Street. I was close by, so I responded. When I got there, witness statements were being taken. One of the pedestrians who saw the accident said she saw a young blonde woman come out of the funeral home, look around, then witness the older woman being hit by the car. She said you were hysterical. I went to speak with the funeral home director, he verified that you and Agatha had just been there. Then I found your Blazer in the parking lot. I knew it had to be your mother who was hit, so I came straight here."

Jade nodded, thankful for his support. He hugged Jade and stepped into the elevator. Jade watched the doors close, then thoughtfully strolled back to the waiting room.

As promised, in a few minutes, a nurse arrived to escort them to see Agatha. Jade was the first to enter her mother's hospital room. Since she had seen her mother right after the accident, her mother actually looked better than she did earlier.

Jade rushed to her mother's bedside and took her hand. Her father moved to the other side of the bed and took his wife's other hand. Phyllis stood next to her father, and looked anxiously down at her mother. There was an oxygen mask covering her face, and both of her eyes were blackening.

Phyllis said, "Do you think she can hear us?"

Jade answered, "Probably on some level she can, but since she's in a coma, she may not remember anything we say to her now."

After a few minutes, the nurse came in and told them politely that Agatha needed her rest, and they should go now. Reluctantly, they left Agatha's room. With a minimum of desultory conversation, they all walked through the hospital and out the door together. Jade's father gave her a ride back to the funeral home, where her Blazer was. He said he was going home to take care of a few things, then would be back, and would stay until they again kicked him out. Jade told him that she'd check with him later to see how her mother was doing, and she'd come back to the hospital tomorrow.

At the funeral home, Jade went back inside to speak with the funeral director. She explained that her mother had been hit by a car, just down the street, as they had left earlier. The funeral director knew about the accident, as Derrick had been there just after it happened. The man was very solicitous. Jade told him that her mother would likely recover, but would probably not be out of the hospital in time to attend Peter's funeral if it were held on Monday, the date they had initially reserved. Jade had him change the funeral to next Thursday, at the same time, 1:00 PM.

In her Blazer, Jade sat quietly, hand on her key in the ignition. She was emotionally exhausted. She had started the day helping to plan Peter's funeral. Then her mother's accident, which she strongly suspected may have been a suicide attempt. It was all too much for one day, on top of the shock of Peter's death and her ongoing and unwilling participation in a strange game of cat-and-mouse with a deranged stalker.

Hunger pangs gradually intruded on Jade's thoughts. That was something, thankfully, that she could actually fix. She pulled out the baggie of chocolate covered peanuts she kept in her purse and ate a few. She wanted to go to the hospital and sit at her mother's bedside, but she knew that her father had that covered, at least for tonight. Jade knew that the best way to get through a trying time in your own life is to do something for someone else. With new purpose, Jade pulled out of the funeral home parking lot. She made a quick stop at Harmon-Barton's Flower shop, and headed out to the Forest Lawn Cemetery.

At the cemetery, Jade parked her Blazer, took the flowers from the back seat, and stepped through the gates. She knew that cemeteries usually have an unofficial closing time of dusk, and it was almost dusk. She realized that she didn't have any idea exactly where Ben Lawrence's grave would be. She wandered down the aisles, hoping to catch a glimpse of a new headstone, or maybe just recently turned earth. She spotted a couple, standing close together, near what appeared to be a newly dug and filled grave. Jade headed in their direction. They didn't see her at first, and she took a moment, as she walked, to study them.

The woman was unfamiliar, but there was something curiously familiar about the man. When Jade was about thirty feet away from them she stopped. They hadn't yet taken notice of her. The man was looking down at the gravestone, and his lips were moving, as if he were talking to the person who was buried there. Jade couldn't hear what he was saying. That odd feeling of familiarity washed over her again. In the slanting last rays of the sun, his face was in shadow. Jade took another step in the couple's direction, to see if the grave was Ben Lawrence's.

As one, both of the mourners glanced in her direction. The woman gazed disinterestedly, and Jade could see the shine of tears on her face, washed orange by the setting sun. The man's gaze was much sharper, he was obviously startled by Jade's presence. Their eyes locked. Suddenly, Jade understood why this man looked so familiar to her. It was her father! He turned away from her, snaking his arm familiarly around the woman, and they strode quickly away.

Jade was so stunned that, at first, she stood her ground, watching their backs as they receded. She walked forward to the grave and looked at the headstone. She was right, this *was* Ben Lawrence's grave. But what would her father have been doing here? And who in God's name was that woman he was with? Thinking quickly, she pulled out her cell phone and dialed her parents' home number. There was no answer. So it was possible he could have been here.

Shaking her head in confusion, Jade put the flowers on Ben Lawrence's grave and walked out of the cemetery. She reasoned that, during the most stressful times, both her parents were a welcome and loving presence for her. Now that her mother was in the hospital (and she may never be the same person again, a frightened voice inside her whispered), her father was more important to her than ever. He had a way of making her feel secure and loved. Maybe, since she was under so much stress right now, she was projecting that need on to a stranger who only slightly resembled him.

At home, Jade sat down at the kitchen table, pulled out her day planner and put the date and time of Peter's funeral in it. She then called her parents' house, and got the answering machine again. She left a message that she had pushed Peter's funeral date ahead to next Thursday. Jade also asked her father to call her back so that they could plan a time to get together tomorrow, to contact the several people they had invited to the funeral to provide the new date, and to let family members know what happened to Agatha.

Sitting at the table, staring at the telephone, Jade realized how grateful she was that she didn't have to make funeral arrangements for her mother, and that her mother was probably going to be okay. She recalled what the doctor said about possible brain damage. No, she thought fiercely, on the heels of Peter's death, Fate couldn't be cruel enough to deal another devastating blow to her family. She felt that, having spared her mother's life, whomever was at the cosmic controls may not be willing to concede anything further. But still she asked. Prayed, actually, not to put too fine a point on it.

Chapter 27

The next morning, Jade's first thought on awakening was of her mother. She picked up her bedside telephone and called her father.

Jade smiled to hear his strong, steady voice say, "Hello Darlin', how are you?"

Jade said, "Hi Daddy. I'm just fine, how's Mom?"

"She's fine. She was sleeping when they finally booted me out last night. I just got off the phone with the hospital this morning. She had a quiet, restful night. If she continues to progress, they'll bring her around tomorrow. Then we'll be able to see if she's really okay."

Jade thought about the prayers she offered up the night before. She said, "I'm going to take a quick shower, then head over to the hospital. After that, do you want to get together? I can come over there, after I check in on Mom." Jade's father agreed, and they started to say their goodbyes.

Jade suddenly remembered seeing that man at the cemetery yesterday. The man who looked so much like her father. She said, "Daddy, wait. There is one more thing. There was a silence, and Jade thought that her father may have already disconnected.

Then his voice came back over the line, sounding strangely cautious. "What is it, honey?" Jade thought for a moment of asking him something else instead, of avoiding her true question completely.

Shaking off the strange impulse, Jade asked him, "Were you at Forest Lawn Cemetery yesterday afternoon?"

Her father gave a short laugh, "Why would you ask that? Of course I wasn't. I went home after I dropped you off at your Blazer, and there I stayed."

Jade remembered that she had called him at home, from the cemetery, at least a half hour after he had dropped her off, and he hadn't picked up. She told him about it, and he told her that he was probably in the shower, or out on the patio when she called. Since she didn't leave a message, he didn't realize she had called. Later, she had left a message, but by then he was in bed. It sounded reasonable, but Jade still felt a slight tug of uneasiness. She had no idea whether her father knew Ben Lawrence, but she still felt uncomfortably sure that she had seen him yesterday at the cemetery, and she couldn't imagine why he'd lie to her. Then she thought about the woman who was with him. Maybe *that's* why he would lie. At this point, there wasn't much she could do, so she decided to make a conscious effort to believe him.

After her strange conversation with her father, Jade called Malcolm and told him about her mother's "mishap", leaving out her misgivings about whether it had been an accident. Malcolm was comfortingly supportive, but when he suggested she take at least part of next week off, Jade balked. She knew that work was her escape, and she sorely needed that, and soon. Malcolm extracted a promise from her that she'd think about it over the weekend, and if she needed any additional time off, she would take it.

Jade took a shower and was on the road within the hour. She parked her Blazer in the parking lot across from the hospital and hurried through the weak morning sunlight. When she entered her mother's room, she was amazed at the difference in her mother's condition. She was still unconscious, but there was color in her cheeks, and she was now wearing one of her own nightgowns. Her bruises stood out in even sharper relief today, but there was a peaceful look on her mother's face. Jade sat in the chair beside the bed and took her mother's hand. She sat that way for a long time, thinking.

She couldn't convince herself that she had imagined the look of determined purpose on her mother's face, a moment before her mother stepped out from between parked cars, into the rush of oncoming traffic. It would be so much easier if she could just delude herself into thinking that look meant anything else but what she knew it meant. Her mother tried to commit suicide. And she chose to do it in front of Jade. Jade could not imagine that her mother's grief over the loss of her son would be so unbearable that she would choose a moment when another of her children may be watching, and then deliberately try to end her life.

Jade wondered if perhaps her mother was dealing with something else, possibly precipitated by Peter's death. Jade knew she'd have to tell her father, and they may want talk to the doctor about it as well. Whatever needed to be done, and whoever needed to be told, the important thing was to make sure her mother was prevented from doing anything else like this, at least until she was able to deal with whatever was causing her so much pain. Jade remembered her mom's very strange words, as she lay bleeding in the road, cradled in Jade's lap. She told Jade to ask her father about the vase. She knew she'd have to ask her father about it later, when she saw him. The only vase she could think of that would have any meaning for either of her parents was her father's big blue floor vase. She recalled once again how, as a child, she knocked it over and thought she may have broken it, and of how her father reassured her that it would never break, it was much too strong. Like she thought her mother was. It's possible that her mother had been trying to tell her something about why she felt the impulse to kill herself.

Sitting there in the hospital, holding her mother's limp, cool hand, Jade felt terror. She was afraid that her mother would leave her, abandon her. Her mother was the most important stabilizing influence in her life. Without her, Jade knew, she would have to make her way in the world alone. Her father was also very important to her, and her mother always joked that she would always be Daddy's Little Girl. But her mother was the one who was there to comfort her when her tender young heart was broken for the first time, and her mother had never stopped being there for her.

Her father was a calming and rational influence in her life, but her mother understood the purely emotional part of being a woman. Jade knew that she was desperately afraid that she would lose that connection with her mother, if her mother woke up and wasn't the same woman she was yesterday. Of course, she would still love her mother just as much, and would do what she could to help her recover and be happy again, but she was afraid that the dynamic between them would be forever changed.

If she was going to help her mother stay safe and recover, she was going to need to call on that emotional bond they had always shared. Jade squeezed her mother's hand. There was no responding squeeze from her mother, as she knew there probably would not be. Jade gently disentangled her fingers from her mother's, and laid her mother's smooth hand across her torso. Sweeping loose tendrils of her mother's hair back from her face, Jade kissed her mother's forehead, whispered "I love you", and quietly left the room. Jade had driven half the distance to her parent's house before she realized her cheeks were wet with tears.

Jade knew the last thing her father needed to see was evidence of her emotional turmoil. She pulled over, wiped her face and blew her nose. Her father was sitting on the front stoop when she pulled in to the driveway. She got out of her Blazer as he stood up, they hugged, then walked into the house together. Jade poured herself a cup of coffee, then sat down at the kitchen table across from her father.

"How are you, Dad?" Her father was looking at the table, then he looked up at her. His eyes glistened with unshed tears; Jade felt her own tears once again threaten.

"I'm okay, Jade. Hearing that your mother will probably be okay, at least physically, went a long way toward making me feel better. The question I keep coming back to is 'why'?"

"Why did she walk out into traffic like that? You said you saw her do it, right?" Jade nodded. "Did she say or do anything just before that? Did she seem confused?" Jade thought about it, and realized this was her opportunity to tell her dad what was on her mind.

"Dad, I know this is going to sound really strange, but I know what I saw. Before I say another word, promise me that you'll listen to what I'm about to tell you with an open mind". Jade saw a strange expression cross her father's face for the very briefest of moments. It looked almost like fear. Like he may know what she was going to say. The thought unsettled her. Later, she knew, she would need to replay this conversation and reality-check it, without the emotion she was feeling right now. She swept aside her disquiet and told her dad what her mother had said, there in the street, when both she and her mother thought her mother may be dying.

Her father looked at her, clearly puzzled. He said, "I have no idea what she might have meant by that. Are you sure that's what she said? Could she have been saying 'face'?"

Jade thought about it. "No, I'm positive she was saying that I should ask you about the vase."

Her father got up from the table, put his coffee cup in the sink and turned back to face Jade, leaning thoughtfully against the counter. "Okay, Jade, if that's what you heard, I believe you. But I really don't understand what it means."

Jade decided to go ahead and tell him the rest. "Daddy, I saw mom walk out into the road. I was several car lengths down the street, in front of the funeral home, looking around for mom, because she wasn't sitting in my Blazer where I left her. I saw her at the same moment she saw me. What I saw on her face the moment before she stepped off the curb was regret. I'm convinced she knew what she was doing, and she was choosing to do it."

Jade's father looked incredulous, and not a little angry. "What the hell are you saying, Jade? Are you trying to tell me that your mother tried to kill herself?" Jade calmly replied, "That's exactly what I'm trying to tell you."

Pacing the kitchen now, visibly upset, her father stopped before her and pierced her with his hazel eyes. "I don't want to hear any talk like that from you again. I thought of all people you would know better. Your mother would never try to kill herself. She loves me, you, Phyllis and, well, all of us." Jade's heart broke a little when she realized her father was going to include Peter.

Jade wanted so badly to believe her father, but her father's comforting words couldn't erase what she knew she saw. Since her father wasn't going to be any help in keeping her mother safe, she realized she would need to confront her mother directly, and try to get whatever was bothering her out in the open. It was high time her mother depended on *her* for something, Jade thought. Jade's father watched her face, then, seeming satisfied with what he saw there, he excused himself and went upstairs to take a shower. Jade sat at the table alone, sipping her rapidly cooling coffee. She realized that she never did get a chance to talk to her father about the change in Peter's funeral date, and the calls that would need to be made. She'd have to call him later. The bright winter sunlight streamed through the window, fracturing into marbled blue gems as it touched the floor vase next to the patio slider. The vase! Jade suddenly remembered her intention to check out the vase.

She went to the bottom of the stairs and listened. She could hear the shower running. Jade walked back to the kitchen and squatted down beside the vase. It was almost three feet tall and she knew from experience that it was very heavy. She rocked the vase up on to one side and turned it slowly, looking at the pebbled blue pattern that covered the sides. She saw nothing extraordinary about it. In fact, she felt a little silly. But then she remembered her mother's words. This had to be the vase she meant.

She wondered if her mother may have meant that she should ask her father because it wasn't the vase itself, it was something to do with the history of the vase. She thought that was probably it, because her mother would probably have said, "look at the vase" or "check the vase" and not "ask your father about the vase", if there was something on the vase itself that her mother wished her to know about. Even so, Jade decided to take this opportunity to finish looking over the vase, just in case. She carefully pulled the vase over onto it's side and looked at the bottom.

At first glance, the underside looked smoothly nondescript. She drew the tips of her fingers across the thick, reinforced glass that covered the bottom of the vase. She felt a subtle change in texture, a very slight indenting, in a definite pattern. With a great deal of effort, she carefully turned the vase completely upside down, and began to drag the inverted vase toward the center of the kitchen, into the light.

A voice from the top of the stairs startled her, and she almost let go of the vase. Jade's father quickly descended the stairs and appeared in the kitchen doorway. "Jade, what in God's name are you doing? You're going to hurt yourself!" Her father rushed into the kitchen and moved Jade to one side as he grabbed the vase, which was tottering on the brink of falling over. He righted the vase and put it back in the corner of the kitchen. Jade stood back and watched him, curiously. He was still fully dressed, his face was an alarming shade of red, and he was sweating profusely. She couldn't imagine what had caused the strength of her father's reaction.

She realized that her father was probably under a great deal of stress, with his son recently discovered dead and now his wife in the hospital with a questionable prognosis. Now, Jade herself had provided additional stress by calling what her father thought was just an accident a suicide attempt. It's no wonder he's so freaked, Jade thought. I guess I would be, too. She decided to let the situation alone. She kissed her father on the cheek, gave him a hug, grabbed her keys and purse and headed out.

On the way home, she thought again about her mother's strange words, just after the car hit her. Then she replayed her father's reaction earlier when he saw her turning the vase over and dragging it in to the light. What bothered her most, she realized was that, while her father's words said he was worried she'd hurt herself, his expression had clearly said something else. What she saw on his face was a mixture of guilt and alarm. The alarm she thought she understood. The guilt puzzled her. He didn't look her in the eye then, and he avoided her gaze after that. Was there something he didn't want her to see? She supposed something could have been inside the vase. Then she remembered the pattern in the glass, on the bottom of the vase. What was it? She decided that she'd have to get back over there and check it out, maybe when her father wasn't home. She knew it would bother her until she was able to find out.

Chapter 28

At home, Jade took a few minutes to take care of Bardo, who had been getting short shrift lately, she knew. Later, as she sat watching T.V., her cell phone rang. Jade's body immediately tensed. It was probably either the hospital or her dad, telling her that her mother had "taken a turn", or her stalker, reporting his latest mayhem, perhaps. She shook off this uncharacteristic pessimism and flipped open her cell phone.

The caller ID said "Arthur Pelletieri". She answered, "Mrs. Pelletieri, what can I do for you?"

Before she finished speaking, Mr. Pelletieri's urgent voice said, "Have you seen my wife? After she spoke with you the other day, she seemed upset, then, when you called the other day to check on her, she suddenly got really scared. A few hours after you called, on Tuesday night, she got a call at about 11:00 P.M. Then she told me that she had to go out for a little while."

"I knew she was going through some kind of emotional relapse about our daughters, which of course you brought on. She would often leave home in the middle of the night to take a drive alone, and think, when she couldn't sleep, so I didn't think too much of her taking off at that hour. But I did recall the look on her face when she got that late telephone call, so I asked her if I could come along with her. She gave me a hug and told me she'd be home very soon, not to worry.

"When she wasn't home by 5:00 A.M., I started calling around for her. I checked the caller ID on our phone, to see who it was who had called her earlier, and it said 'private caller'. At that point, I called the police. Ms. Danner, if you have any idea where my wife could have gone, please tell me." As Mr. Pelletieri spoke, a frightened clamor had set up shop in Jade's mind.

She told Mr. Pelletieri, "Your wife and I talked about the deaths of your daughters, that day we met. I'm researching a series of deaths that are happening currently and which may be related to what happened to your family all those years ago." Jade realized that, if she was going to help Mrs. Pelletier (if help was even possible, her alarmed mind added), she'd need to tell this worried husband everything she could that may help.

Jade cleared her throat and resolutely continued, "Mr. Pelletieri, the day I called your wife to check on her, last Tuesday, I think, I had received a call from someone I believe is involved in the current series of murders. He told me that your wife may have met with an unfortunate accident. I was worried, so I called to check on her. But she was fine, and I realized that the man had to be just playing games with me."

Mr. Pelletieri's heavy sigh hitched into a sob, then he completely broke down. Jade waited while he tried to collect himself. Then she said, "Do you want me to come over? Should I at least contact the police and tell them what I know? I want to help, if I can."

Mr. Pelletieri's voice was hoarse with emotion. "You know what, lady? I think you've done enough already. You could call the police, and let them know how you probably got my wife killed! Don't contact me or my family ever again." Jade cringed as Mr. Pelletieri slammed the phone down in her ear.

She closed her cell phone with shaking hands. She knew that Mrs. Pelletieri was probably dead, and all because she tried to help Jade. Jade felt sad, guilty and very, very angry. Whoever this person was, he was obviously trying to isolate her from anyone who could help her, trying to break her by triggering fear and guilt. And it was working. She wasn't sure if she was going to be able to live with the guilt she felt, knowing that something she did may have gotten two people killed. And she had yet to stop the killer. Shutting down a serial killer wouldn't make up for the lives that had already been lost, but it would go a ways toward balancing her unintentional endangering of others.

Her cell phone suddenly rang again, and Jade felt the now-familiar surge of fear. She decided not to answer it. After the phone had quieted, she picked it up and checked the caller ID for the last incoming call. "Private Caller". It was him. Furious, she pounded the keys to dial in to voicemail. He had left a message. "Hi Jade, it's me. You looked so cute earlier, playing with your dog in the living room. Thank you so much for calling Mrs. P. the other night. I have to admit, it was a bit of a ruse on my end, when I called you to say that something had happened to Mrs. P. You see, I followed you the day you went to McDonald's to pow-wow with her.

"Unfortunately, I was called away and couldn't watch you two leave. I wanted to follow her, to find out who she was and why you were talking to her. But I did the next best thing. I got you to call her, and simply watched you dial her telephone number as soon as you got off the telephone with me. The rest, as they say, is history. You performed your part admirably, Jade. By the way, kudos to you for the way you disposed of the table leg from Mr. Lawrence's room at the Home. Now, no one else will ever know it was you who killed him. But, as they say, a picture truly is worth a thousand words. Even if it is a copy.

"I also know that you have been doing a little research, and maybe talking to some people. I must strongly suggest that you stop pursuing what is a private family matter, Jade. If you were getting ready to talk to anyone else, reconsider. Understand my message, and the sacrifice that's already been made. Leave things alone, like the good little girl we know you are. Ta-ta, darling." The sound of hearty laughter, then a click as he disconnected.

Jade threw her cell phone across the room, where it smashed satisfyingly against the wall. She needed to DO something. Now. The killer had brazenly left his message on her cell phone, but had, cleverly, added the false information about her killing Mr. Lawrence, and had made a not-so-subtle reference to him having another copy of the incriminating picture of the bloody table leg sitting in the back of her Blazer. So she couldn't share this message with the police. If her stalker did take Mrs. Pelletieri, she was almost certainly already dead.

At a little past 3:00, restlessness won out and Jade set her security alarm and hit the road. First, she went to the cell phone store and got a replacement for her cell phone. This one had something her other one did not. A built-in camera. She didn't know if she'd need it, but she felt better having it. She explained to the sales clerk that she had inadvertently dropped the cell phone on her driveway, then had driven over it by accident. The sales clerk listened disinterestedly and Jade realized she had probably heard just about every story under the sun by now, some perhaps even true. She just verified that Jade had purchased the extended warranty protection, transferred Jade's telephone number to the new cell phone, and handed it over. Jade got a crash course in taking pictures, and headed out with her new camera phone.

On the way through the parking lot to her Blazer, she practiced taking pictures. When she got in the Blazer, she checked out her new pictures. The first two were blurry. The next one showed her Blazer, and a man, standing behind her truck. His face was blurry, but the rest of the picture was fairly clear. She realized that he must have spotted her coming toward him and taking pictures, and he was in the process of averting his face from her. Jade hit the button to lock all the doors and looked frantically around. He was gone. She wondered if she was just getting paranoid, or if she had somehow managed to catch her stalker "on film". She looked through the other pictures she had taken, and she looked at the parking lot around her. Her pictures showed one car in the back of the parking lot that was now, three minutes later, gone.

The other cars she had managed to catch in her pictures were all still there, and there were a few other cars that had probably arrived after she took her pictures. The one missing car was a Cadillac. She didn't catch the license plate in her picture, there were several other cars parked between hers and the Cadillac, but she did have a clear shot of the windshield. There were several stickers on the windshield, but she couldn't make them out. She decided to download the pictures from her camera phone to her computer tonight and see if she could make out any other details of either the mystery man or his potential ride.

She next stopped in at the hospital to check on her mother. Her mother looked better, even, than she did earlier in the day, and Jade found comfort in the idea that her mother's body was mending. She only hoped that what was on her mother's mind, that may have caused her to try to escape her own life, could also be fixed. She paged the doctor and got an update. Tomorrow at noontime, they would withdraw the sedation drugs, and as she regained consciousness they'd be able to determine the extent of any cognitive impairment. The conversation with the doctor made Jade feel uneasy again. She found it sad that a seemingly innocuous term like "cognitive impairment" had the ability to take her mother away from her.

As she was leaving, her father arrived. Jade told him briefly what the doctor had said, and he told her that Phyllis would be coming in later this evening. Jade felt better knowing that her mother probably wouldn't be alone today or this evening, and tomorrow, they would know if her mind was intact. Jade left the hospital and headed over to see Malcolm at work.

It was fully dark when she arrived at Remerick & Company. As she suspected, Malcolm was busy at work, sitting at his desk, clicking away at his computer, "Für Elise" playing quietly in the background. He jumped up and met Jade halfway across the room, throwing his arms around her. She hugged him back fiercely.

He pulled back and looked her over with a critical eye. "Jade, what you need is a good meal, a long soak, a good night's sleep, and a good man."

Jade laughed at his frankness. She said, "Malcolm, don't ever change. I just stopped by to see if there was anything you needed me to do, and to make sure you aren't overwhelmed with work. I feel guilty leaving you to fend for yourself so suddenly and for so long."

Malcolm gently steered Jade to the lounge and sat her down. "I can't believe you're worried about work at a time like this. You are truly a one-in-a-million, girl! Things here are a little slow lately anyway. We got in several pieces that are due to be auctioned by Christie's in a couple of months, so there's no rush on those. But there are some very interesting pieces, and I'm saving them for you to do when you get back because I know you are going to love them. Other than that, I'm handling the priority work that's coming in with no problems."

Malcolm's pleasant face turned serious. He took Jade's hand. "I'd like for you to take more time off, Jade, at least until your brother's funeral is over. Would you do that?" He knew that Jade wanted to get back to work as soon as possible.

She counter-offered. "How about I work half-days next week, then come back to full-time the following week?"

Malcolm tentatively agreed, but told her that she had the option to take more time off, when and if she decided she needed it. That settled, they said their goodbyes and Jade left. Knowing that she would be working again, come Monday, Jade suddenly felt more connected to her normal life. She made a mental list of things that would need to be done this weekend, to get ready to go back to work Monday. Malcolm would make sure she left at noontime, as they agreed, but she was always there before he was, so he wouldn't realize it if she came in at, say, 5:00 A.M.

At home, she took a few minutes to check out her new cell phone. She programmed in all of her previous speed dial entries. Then she uploaded the pictures she had taken earlier. She enlarged the pictures on her computer screen and again saw the white Cadillac in one of them. Another picture showed the shadow of the man she had spotted before, behind her Blazer. His face, as she had noticed before, was blurry. Jade used her computer's photo editing software to try to bring better focus to the face, but she was unable to make out any of the facial features.

She had better luck with the Cadillac. She was able to further enlarge the picture, then clear the blur that resulted from the enlargement. The stickers on the sides of the huge relic's windshield were faculty parking permits, for several previous years, for the University of Maine Department of Psychology. Jade recalled, in her conversation with Mrs. Pelletieri, last week, that she had mentioned that she had also spotted a light-colored Cadillac with a University faculty parking permit, when Mrs. Pelletieri's search for her eldest daughter's killer took her to the Deering Oaks park, years ago. A car matching that description was also reportedly following Mrs. Pelletieri's twin teenage girls as they walked home from school, shortly before they had disappeared. Jade also recalled that Daisy, the nurse at Mr. Lawrence's nursing home, had also seen the man who Ben Lawrence called his grandson, driving out of the home's parking lot in a big, fancy 1960's-type car. Could that also have been this car? Jade didn't believe in coincidences like that. This was, she suspected, more evidence that it was Timothy Lawrence, also known as Steven Lawry, who was stalking her.

Jade didn't believe for a minute that she was still alive simply because Timothy couldn't get to her. She knew that he had had several opportunities to kill her, but he had instead chosen to taunt and terrorize her by killing other people and threatening her. She didn't know for sure what was keeping him from killing her, she only knew that, given the circumstances, it was apparent that something was. She also wasn't sure whether circumstances would suddenly change, and killing her would suddenly become an option. In order to keep herself safe, she needed to get inside Timothy's head. One thing that would help her do this was to speak to the two family members of recent murder victims with whom she had already set up time this weekend.

Jade sat on the couch, purposely looking nervous, in case she was being watched again. Behind her fearful façade, Jade's mind worked furiously. Finally she came to a decision. She needed help and there was only one person she trusted enough to help her. She stood up, grabbed her purse and keys, and headed out the door. She drove her Blazer to the Maine Mall and made her way to the Food Court. She sat in a plastic chair and waited a few minutes, then she pulled out her cell phone and shot a few pictures of the area around her. She would scrutinize them later to see if her stalker had followed her there and was lurking in the throng of people surrounding her.

Jade then hit her speed dial number for Diane.

Diane answered on the second ring, sounding half-asleep. Jade said, "Hey PD! I hope I didn't wake you up. It's 7:30 on a Friday night. If you aren't careful, I'll start thinking you don't have a life!" Jade grinned at Diane's profane reply. "Yeah, okay, didn't think so. Listen, I could use your help with something tomorrow, if you aren't busy." Like Jade, Diane definitely had an adventurous side. Jade knew Diane well enough to know that Diane would find this whole situation intriguing. Before she brought Diane on board, she knew she needed to be completely honest about the potential danger first. "Before you agree to help me, I need you to know that someone's after me. He's killed at least one person that I know of for sure, and, I strongly suspect, several others. He's been stalking me for weeks. He's a few years older than I am, tall, good-looking, may drive a white late-1960's Cadillac. His name is Timothy, although he sometimes goes by his middle name, Steven. His last name is either Lawrence or Lawry."

Jade stopped to catch her breath, waiting for Diane's reaction.

Diane didn't make her wait long. "Jade!!? Did you say killed??!! As in dead? What the hell have you gotten yourself into? I just knew, when I saw you last weekend, that something was going on. I'm assuming you've called the police, right?" Before Jade could respond, Diane plowed forward, "You need to tell me everything, right now." Diane's characteristically manic reaction was both amusing and comforting.

Jade didn't want to go into any more detail over the phone, and she didn't want to put Diane in further danger by leading Timothy to her house. Jade agreed to meet Diane tomorrow morning at 7:00 A.M., at the Dunstan School Restaurant in Scarborough. Diane was clearly frustrated that she wasn't going to get more information now. With a guilty pang, Jade realized that it may actually be crueler to involve Diane in this dangerous situation. She had the night to think about it, and if she decided to go ahead and tell Diane everything, she needed to plan every step of her involvement, in order to stay one step ahead of Timothy and to try to keep Diane safe.

Jade left the mall and drove toward home, watching for any sign of being followed. She didn't see anyone. But she knew that Timothy knew where she lived and didn't need to follow her to catch up with her. She had to go home sometime, and Timothy would probably be there, waiting for her, when she did. She hoped he hadn't followed her to the Mall. She knew she was getting closer to the truth, and she knew that would make Timothy more dangerous.

She resolved to think more carefully about everything she did from this point on, to keep herself, her family and her friends from unnecessary danger. Giving up on her quest to bring the Lawrence family killer down was not an option. She knew that she, and everyone associated with her, would be in danger until she was able to get this murderer off the street. She had come too far and she knew too much. And Timothy may, at any time, decide that her ever-increasing knowledge had finally outweighed whatever was keeping him from killing her. Backing down was definitely not an option. And Jade wasn't the type to ever back down.

At home, Jade called to Bardo as she came in the front door. Bardo didn't come. Puzzled, she walked through the kitchen and called again. She heard a distant sound and stopped to listen carefully. It was Bardo. He was upstairs, whimpering pitifully. Concerned, Jade took the stairs on the run. At the second floor landing she stopped to listen again. He was in the bathroom. She opened the bathroom door and Bardo ran at her. She hunkered down and caught him up in her arms. He appeared to be okay, but he was shaking with fright. She felt a small piece of paper hanging from Bardo's collar. She brought him in to the light of the bathroom and ripped the paper from Bardo's collar. The familiar image of the Möbius was drawn crudely on the paper.

She wondered how Timothy had gotten into her house. Then she remembered that he knew the people she called by watching the series of buttons she pushed on the telephone. What if he could also see her entering the alarm code, and he knew the code? She shuddered to think how long he may have had her security system code, how many times he may have sneaked into her house. The thought made her feel violated, and distinctly nauseous.

Jade raced down the stairs and directly to the security system key pad. Hooding the buttons from sight with one hand, she depressed the sequence of keys to allow her to change her security code. She knew that Timothy may be able to pick the lock on her door, but without the new security code, he would still set off the alarm trying to break in. Feeling a little calmer, she remembered the pictures she had taken at the mall. She booted up her computer and uploaded the pictures. After reviewing every inch of every picture, she was satisfied that Timothy wasn't in them.

Jade went to bed, but tossed and turned, thinking about whether she could, in good conscience, really bring Diane into the nightmare that had become her life. She knew that, for Diane's own protection, she would have to put Diane fully in the picture. She knew that she just didn't want to go it alone any more, but she didn't want that to be the primary reason to bring Diane into this. She knew that Diane could help. Diane was extremely intelligent, and more resourceful than any one else Jade knew, including herself. Diane was also bold and creative.

Two things that Jade instinctively knew could be helpful right now. There was only one Timothy, and with Diane's help, they would now be two, working against him.

In order to meet Mr. Demoree in Bangor at 11:00 A.M. tomorrow, she wouldn't be able to be at the hospital tomorrow when they took her mother off sedation. She recalled that the doctor had told them that it would take several hours for the medication to fully wear off, and that Agatha would be brought up out of her coma slowly, in stages, so as not to shock her system. Jade knew that her father would be there from noontime on, until all was said and done. Jade would go to Bangor to meet Mr. Demoree, then try to visit her mother in the afternoon, between appointments, then she would meet Nate Small at 5:30, in Portland. After meeting with Nate, she would go back to the hospital to check on her mother. Having figured out her game plan for the next day, Jade descended into troubled sleep.

Chapter 29

Jade's alarm clock went off at 5:30 A.M., that sunny Saturday morning. Forty minutes later, she was on the road. Jade drove to her office building, left her Blazer in the parking lot, and walked into her building. She left the lights inside the building off, and looked out the window of her office. Just as she suspected, the black Mercedes that she had noticed on the interstate a few minutes ago had taken the same exit as she did, and was now idling at the curb down the block from her office, in sight of her Blazer.

Jade made a call from Malcolm's office line, in case her line was tapped, then she went downstairs and changed into the black leather jacket Malcolm always kept on a hook by the back door. She left her jacket on the hook. Then she locked up, and left the building by the back door. She followed several catwalks along the backs of neighboring buildings, and came out, a couple blocks away, across from the Deering Lumber building. Huddling in the unfamiliar jacket, Jade looked up the street, toward her office building. Nothing moved. Jade crossed the street and stood at the far side of the Deering Lumber building, shielded from the view of anyone on the street. Jade felt the loss of sleep from the night before as she waited, shivering, a headache throbbing distantly at her right temple. Several minutes later, as the first cold rays of morning light shone above the buildings, Jade saw a Hyundai Santa Fe driving slowly the length of Commercial Street. She almost cheered as it pulled up in front of Deering Lumber.

Jade walked out from beside the building and waved to the driver. He got out of the truck, handed Jade in to the driver's seat and walked around to get in on the passenger side. Jade drove away, in the opposite direction from her office and from the black Mercedes. She turned to the man who had driven the truck to her. He was an older man, with a careworn, appealing face.

She returned his smile. "Thank you for coming to get me. Your advertisement was right, you really do pick people up. I'll only need the rental for today, and I'll drop it off to you before 8:00 P.M."

The man nodded. "Not a problem, it's what we do. If you need the truck longer, there's no penalty as long as you call us before 8:00 P.M. to let us know."

Jade dropped him off at the rental car company and headed out to meet Diane.

The Dunstan School Restaurant, Jade was told, used to be an actual schoolhouse, several decades ago. She didn't know about that, but she knew the food was good, parking was easy, and it wasn't a place she usually went so she was not likely to be recognized there. Jade parked the Santa Fe in the back of the parking lot and looked around for Diane's car. She spotted Diane's car driving into the lot. She jumped out of the truck and walked toward Diane. Diane parked her car a few spaces away from the truck, and together they walked to the restaurant doors.

Diane looked back toward Jade's black Santa Fe. "Hey, you're really serious about this whole 'stalker' thing, aren't you? What did you do, rent that?"

Jade grimaced. "I had to. I've been followed several times lately. Remember that day that you and I went to Freeport shopping? The guy who's been following me sent me a picture of you and I, walking around outside L.L. Bean's that day." Jade pulled out the picture of she and Diane. Diane took the picture from her, frowned down at it, and passed it back. Jade could see the beginnings of fear bloom behind Diane's expression and she knew exactly how she felt.

Jade thought again about the wisdom of involving Diane in this dangerous situation, and decided that she'd lay things out, and get Diane's input, and let her decide for herself whether she wanted in. That was the whole reason for the human shell game she was playing with the killer this morning. She didn't want him to know she had met with Diane. Jade also knew that putting Diane in the picture would at least give her a clue, if something were to happen to Jade. Just the thought gave her a blue-ribbon case of the heebie-jeebies.

Jade and Diane got settled at a table as far away from the rest of the morning crowd as possible. Diane immediately leaned forward, catching Jade's eye and looking at her critically. "Girlfriend, you look like someone rode you hard and put you up wet. And NOT in a good way." Jade smiled at Diane's crude attempt at humor. She was suddenly glad she had decided to tell Diane what was happening. She knew Diane could and would help her. What else were best friends for?

The waitress came over, pad in hand, to take their order. Jade ordered a cup of coffee and a cheese danish. Diane wanted a cup of coffee and a go at the buffet. Of course. Diane always ate anything and everything she wanted, and she still had the body of a model. Jade smiled ruefully and watched Diane's exaggerated butt-swagger on the way to the buffet table. Diane looked back over her shoulder to see if Jade was watching, and Jade graced her with an eye roll. Within five minutes, the coffee and Jade's danish had arrived, and Diane was back from the buffet, mounded, steaming plate in hand. She sat down, glanced up at Jade and said, "Okay, all systems go. Shoot."

Jade took a calming breath, quickly organized her thoughts, and began. "Diane, you remember when I told you that I did an appraisal for a jewelry case for the Lawrence family, a few weeks ago?" Diane nodded, a piece of bacon disappearing into her mouth. "Well, what I didn't tell you was that I found a note hidden inside the case. The note, I found out later, was written by a servant in the Lawrence house, back in the 1870's. Her name was Erin. The note referred to a diary, which I found in the pocket of a skeleton which was buried behind a wall on the third floor of the Lawrence house on Commercial Street." Diane's mouth froze in mid-chew and she turned widened eyes up to Jade.

"Yeah, tell me about it. The diary was Erin's. I took it home and read it. It talked about three sets of murders, which took place about 30 years apart, in this area, back then. Erin had figured out that progressive generations of Lawrence family men were committing the murders. The diary abruptly ended, I think because Erin was killed.

"Erin thought that the Lawrence family men had some kind of twisted killing gene, passed from father to son. She felt that, if someone didn't stop them, the killing would keep happening, every generation, for as long as Lawrence men still lived. Diane, I had to at least check this out.

"As soon as I started looking in to this, things started happening to me. I spoke to the last surviving Lawrence man, Ben Lawrence, at an assisted living facility where he was living. He freaked when he saw me and didn't want to talk to me for some reason, but his nurse, Daisy, told me a man had visited him who claimed to be Ben Lawrence's son, and another, younger man, who claimed to be Ben Lawrence's grandson. So then I knew that there were more Lawrence men alive. A couple days after my visit to Ben Lawrence, he was violently murdered in his room.

"The week I met Ben Lawrence, my house got broken into. They didn't take anything except the notes I wrote while I was reading the diary. The diary, which I think they were after, was with me. I got a telephone call the next day telling me to meet this man at the mall and give him the diary. Of course I refused. I went to the mall, but only to see if I could spot him. No luck there, but when I left the mall and went back to my truck, someone had torn the dashboard off and completely trashed the wiring. I know a warning when I see one."

Diane was listening intently, and slowing down on her progress through the plate of food. Jade signaled the waitress and asked her to bring the pot of coffee and leave it. When the coffee cups were refilled and a fresh pot was sitting on a cozy at their table, Jade continued.

"I borrowed my mother's VW while my truck was being fixed. You remember that car? Peter used to use it whenever he was staying with my parents. I found a knife in the trunk, wrapped in one of my parents' towels. It was a double-serrated blade knife, just like the one the police said was the murder weapon in that Old Port murder last year. I was frantic, thinking that Peter must have actually committed the crime. I told my mom and we called the police. They took the knife, and the VW itself, to process it for evidence. We also gave them a missing person report as Peter had been missing since a couple days before that, when he didn't come to his own birthday party. None of this seems to have anything to do with the Lawrence family murders, right? Wrong! I met a man named Steven, at the birthday party for Peter. He said he knew Peter. I gave him my cell number and he said he'd call me."

At this point, Diane raised her hand for a high-five. Jade complied, but said, "Don't get too excited, listen to rest of this." Diane, looking intrigued, gestured with her fork for Jade to continue.

"For the missing person investigation, the police said they would need to search Peter's room, at my parents'. My mom went through Peter's room first, and she found some papers which she gave to me. Diane, the papers were all about a member of the Lawrence family. Specifically, the grandson who went to visit Ben Lawrence at the home, in the days before I went to see him. The information in those notes showed that a man named Steven Timothy Lawry used to be Steven Timothy Lawrence, before his mother changed their names when he was 17. Peter had gathered that information, as well as information related to several other recent local murders, including the one of which Peter was suspected.

"I think Peter was trying to exonerate himself, but he ended up uncovering other murders, and, more alarming, a common thread between them, in the form of this Lawrence descendent. Diane, something horrible occurred to me then."

Diane, who had long since dropped her fork and focused her attention entirely on Jade, immediately understood what Jade was about to say. "You were wondering if the killing sprees Erin talked about in her diary could somehow still be taking place here and now, 130 years later. Jesus, Jade, that's creepy as hell. This is friggin' Stephen King shit. I love it! Go on, I gotta hear this!"

Jade couldn't help but smile, thankful for Diane's single-minded focus and her quick mind. Jade knew she had done the right thing by talking to Diane about all this. She only hoped that Diane would be willing to help after she finished telling her about the increasing danger in which she now found herself.

"Okay, where was I? Oh yeah. Several times in recent days, the stalker has done things to intimidate me. Things like breaking in to my house, again, and taking Erin's diary this time. But I had a copy. He put a note on Bardo's collar for me, then he left me a couple of extremely creepy voicemail messages. He's not shooting at me yet, or anything, but I think he's getting more desperate to get me off his trail, and I'm afraid it may very well come to that."

Jade took a moment to gauge Diane's reaction. She was pleased that Diane was obviously paying close attention, and that her expression was a mixture of concern and anger. This was exactly what she was hoping for.

Encouraged, Jade continued. "I checked out the local library, and found some interesting trends. There were several other series of unsolved murders of young women in this area, between the 1870's and now. The number of these deaths spiked about every 25 to 35 years or so. And, more alarming, the deaths are becoming more numerous and the number of years between the spikes is decreasing. The most recent two series of killings started in the early to mid-1960's and late in the 1990's, respectively.

"I've found two next-of-kin that I was able to speak with from the 1960's murders, one of them having had all three of her daughters murdered. Diane, after she spoke to me, I found out yesterday that she went missing a couple days later. I got a phone call from the guy who's been stalking me, telling me in effect that I got the woman killed. I also think I may have gotten Ben Lawrence killed. So you can see why I didn't want to get you involved in this." Diane gave Jade a "go on with you" wave of her hand, and Jade continued.

"There's something else. I don't know what it means, but it keeps turning up. Have you heard of a Möbius strip?" Diane indicated that she had, and she drew one in the air between them. Jade nodded. "This symbol seems to be the calling card of the Lawrence family murderers. The reason I say that is that I've now seen it in several places. First, I saw it on Erin's note, then on the diary's cover. The text of the diary also talks about it being on or near more than one of the murder victims. I also found a record of this symbol being either drawn on victims or found on them somewhere, in several of the deaths that happened from the 1870's, and also on more than one of the murder victims from the

1960's. The Möbius symbol is being drawn with an eye in one loop and a droplet in the other. It was also found drawn on the wall behind Ben Lawrence's dead body, in his blood. I haven't found any evidence that the Möbius was on any of the current victims yet, but I'll bet I will."

Jade sat back and looked at Diane. "That's the basic story. There are details that I've left out, and I'll fill you in on those later if you want. I know this is a lot to absorb at one time. Do you have any questions for me?"

Diane spoke up thoughtfully. "Actually, something did occur to me. It may not be my place to ask, but I'm curious about it. You obviously feel that you are in danger. Why not call the police? It seems to me that our little stalker dude has messed up several times, and maybe the police can get him off your back while you finish screwing him to the wall."

Jade knew this would be hard to explain, but she gave it a try. "A good part of the reason has to do with the cop who was checking in to Peter's disappearance and who is likely still checking into Peter's possible connection to at least one recent homicide. The cop's name is Derrick Zachary. The truth is, he and I have this weird little chemistry thing going."

Diane immediately perked up, Jade noticed wryly. "I like him and I don't want to see him hurt. I think, if I involve him, because he is a cop, he'll be in danger. I also know he's been looking at Peter for at least one murder, and I'm not thinking that'll change just because Peter is dead. And I know things that I haven't told Derrick. Things which, on the surface, make Peter look more likely to be the guy. But I know he's not. The reason I know that is also another reason I can't involve the police. I have those papers that my mother took from Peter's room before the police searched it. Tampering with evidence is a federal offense."

"Also, my clever stalker planted the table leg that was used to kill Ben Lawrence in my Blazer, and I didn't call the police. Instead, I burned it. But the stalker has a picture of that table leg as it sat in my truck. I also stole the note out of the jewelry case, at the start of all this, and I also broke in to the Lawrence house, left evidence of my presence, and I took the diary, from a rotted corpse no less, none of which I've reported to the police. So, as you can see, I'm in this up to my eyeballs, and I can't imagine that any help or protection the police could provide would be worth the risk of hoping my explanations keep me out of jail." Diane followed Jade's rationale closely and, thankfully, agreed that she didn't have much choice, at least for now, but to leave the police out of it.

Having told Diane the most frightening part of the situation, Jade immediately felt better. Diane took her hand and looked at her earnestly. "There is no way I'm going to let you go another day on your own in this mess. We are a team, and I will always, always have your back." Pure relief swept through Jade.

She wiped her eyes and tried to smile at Diane through her tears. "Why is it that one of us always seems to end up crying when we are together?"

Diane gave her hand a reassuring squeeze and let go. "Okay, crybaby, you done blubbering yet?" Jade's negative head shake got Diane laughing. "When you've got your snot factory over there under control, why don't you tell me what I can do to help, except the obvious task of keeping your ass alive." Jade told Diane about the appointments she had set up for today, as they paid their check and were leaving. Diane moved her car to the back of the parking lot, got into Jade's rented Santa Fe, and the two of them headed north on I-95, through lightly falling snow.

Chapter 30

As they passed the Bangor city line, Jade called Brian Demoree to let him know she was almost there. He was waiting outside the restaurant when Diane and Jade pulled up. True to his word, he was wearing a New York Yankee's baseball cap.

Diane took note of the cap and said, "Now there's a ballsy guy."

Jade nodded, and said, "That's the guy we're here to see, Mr. New York Yankees."

They parked in the small lot beside the restaurant, got out and started toward where Brian was waiting. As they approached, Jade caught Brian's look of discomfort.

Jade took the lead. "Hi, Brian Demoree? I'm Jade Danner." Brian nodded, then shook hands with her. Jade said, "This is my friend Diane Venezia. Brian's expressed cleared slightly, and he managed a slight smile as he offered his hand to Diane, who smiled reassuringly and shook hands with him.

With Jade in the lead, they made their way through the crowded café. In front of the last booth, Jade stopped, they all removed their jackets and placed them on the hooks on the back wall and sat down. Brian was on one side of the booth, and Jade and Diane on the other, facing him. The waitress took an order for coffee all around. Brian pulled a napkin from the dispenser, took off his eyeglasses, and began to wipe the melting snow from them. Jade took the opportunity to study Brian.

Without his glasses, he looked curiously vulnerable. The pain he had experienced was clearly written on this features, and in his troubled blue eyes. Jade suddenly wanted to be far away from here and not asking this man for help. Adding to Jade's misgiving was the knowledge that Mrs. Pelletieri was missing and possibly dead, because she tried to help Jade. Jade hoped that her efforts to disguise her trip today would help to keep Brian safe. However, Jade felt compelled to be straightforward with Brian about what she wanted from him, and the danger he could potentially be in for trying to help her.

The waitress placed their coffees in front of them, along with a bowl of creamers and a container of sugar. After they had assured her that they needed nothing further at the moment, she hurried away. Jade caught Brian's eye.

"Mr. Demoree, please let me first express my condolence for your loss. Second, I want to warn you that you could be in danger if you help me. I've been in contact with other families, requesting information about the death of their loved one. One of the people who tried to help me is now missing, and I have reason to believe it's because she tried to help me. I've also been threatened, my house has been broken in to, and my truck was vandalized. I want to be clear about the potential danger to you. As I mentioned on the telephone, I'm researching several very similar homicides that happened in the Southern Maine area, between 1999 and 2002. Heather's name came up in the course of my investigation. Were you aware that there were other deaths, possibly linked to your daughter's?"

Brian sipped his coffee, then put the cup noisily back in the saucer. His face was composed, but there was a nervous tic at his jaw, and his hands were shaking. When he locked eyes with Jade, she saw the pain she had seen before, but she also saw grim determination.

"Call me Brian, please. I did know about the other, similar deaths. I read about a couple of them, after Heather was, well, after she died. I called the police, to see if there was any relationship there. They said that they were also checking into this angle, but that often, while the deaths seemed similar, they would likely turn out to be unconnected.

"Jade, I think the problem was that the police suspected me, almost from day one. They checked out my alibi, they had me take a lie detector test, which I passed. Heather's mother, Lily, was completely destroyed by the death of her only child. We tried to keep things together after, but as I understand many couples do, we drifted apart and eventually divorced, almost a year ago. Two days after the divorce was final, Lily was found dead, of an overdose, laying over Heather's grave. She didn't leave a suicide note. She didn't have to. This bastard has ruined three lives in my family. If there's even a chance that I can make him pay for what he's done, I don't care what kind of danger's involved, I'm in."

Jade felt better for having warned Brian up front. But she still worried about putting him in jeopardy. Brian seemed to see the hesitancy on her face. "This is something you have to let me try to help you with. I owe it to my family to do everything I can. Please don't take away what may be my only opportunity to find some kind of peace."

Jade watched Brian for a moment, then gathered her resolve. She took a small wire-bound notebook out of her purse, and turned to a blank page. Pen poised, she said, "Okay, Brian, I need you to tell me anything and everything you remember about Heather's death."

Brian started to stand up, and Jade, alarmed, stood also. "Jade, I've got something that may help you. Since the day Heather was found, I've been putting together a file, with every detail of the case in it. I'm not sure why I was keeping it, I guess I just wanted to feel like I was doing something constructive. I guess it was silly. But I think it helped, you know, at the time. It's in my truck, I'll just go and get it."

Brian left the diner, and Jade and Diane ordered more coffee while he was gone. After several minutes, Brian still hadn't come back in. Jade worried that he had reconsidered helping her. Then, a more worrisome thought occurred to her. What if she had been followed, and if someone had intercepted Brian in the parking lot? What if he was in danger, or hurt, maybe even dead, only 50 feet away outside? Jade shook off the thought. But, after another few minutes, worry once again gnawed it's way back in. "Diane, let's go and see what's keeping Brian. I've got a bad feeling."

Diane had obviously been thinking the same thing. "Yeah, me too. It shouldn't be taking this long. Something must have happened." Both women got up, Jade put several dollar bills on the table and they walked outside. Diane reached into her purse and pulled out a small, silver gun.

Jade's shock was clearly written on her face. "Diane, I didn't even know you owned a gun. Do you know how to shoot that thing?" Diane grinned at her. "What the hell do *you* think, girlfriend?" Diane gently pushed Jade behind her and they walked single-file, back to the parking lot.

There was no sign of movement across the lot. Jade saw several cars and four SUVs. One SUV was theirs. One had a woman and small child just getting out of it. There were two others, both in the back of the lot. Diane crossed the length of the walkway beside the parking lot, with Jade close behind. The first pickup truck was empty. When they got to the second pickup truck, they knew it was Brian's because Brian was in it, slumped against the window.

Both Diane and Jade looked around frantically, making sure that whoever had hurt Brian wasn't still here. Jade went to the passenger side of the truck and opened the door. Brian stirred, and Jade almost swooned with relief that he wasn't dead.

Brian picked up his head, looked at Jade and whispered, "I didn't even see him coming. He hit me with a metal rod of some kind. A crowbar? …got to me before I got to the file, it's behind my seat. You aren't safe, take it and go. Make sure I get it back. It's all I have left of them." Jade realized that, sitting in the truck beside him, she may be exposing him to further danger. Obviously, she had been followed here, in spite of her efforts. On the heels of that thought, Jade realized that her efforts to protect Diane had also failed, as their stalker would now know that Jade had taken someone into her confidence. Shit!

Jade felt around behind the seat and came up with a manila envelope, "Heather" was written across it in pencil. Before she got out of Brian's truck, under cover of the dashboard, she slipped the file up inside her shirt and secured it in the waistband of her pants. She and Diane scrambled back to their Santa Fe, warily keeping watch, and looked carefully around their truck, both inside and outside, before they unlocked it, got in, and drove away.

Once they were on the turnpike, Jade called 911 and reported that there was a badly injured man in a pick up truck in the parking lot of the diner behind the town hall. As they drove south, the clouds broke up and shafts of lemon-yellow sunlight slanted across the afternoon sky. It seemed inconceivable that she had a twisted killer stalking her, and likely stalking Diane, now, too. Jade couldn't figure out how the stalker (she refused to give him the benefit of an actual name, even in her thoughts) had followed her this morning. She knew she'd have to be even more careful than she'd already been, to try to keep Diane safe. Jade looked around as she drove, trying to determine whether they were being followed. Diane saw what she was doing and wordlessly started keeping a sharp eye on the traffic flowing around them.

Jade checked the time and realized with a start that it was almost 1:30. She called the hospital to check on her mother. Her father was there, with Phyllis. He said that the doctor began to withdraw the sedative from her mother's IV at noon. The step-down process would take about three hours to complete. There was no sign of Agatha waking up yet, but the doctor said it would probably begin to happen soon. Jade told her father that she'd be there shortly. Jade put the hammer down, as both Jade and Diane kept an eye on the traffic flowing around them, watching out for, oddly enough, both cops AND criminals.

Back in Portland, Jade drove Diane back to her car. They agreed that it wouldn't do any harm to try to spend more time together, it would probably be safer for both of them. They also agreed to vary their routines for the next several days, to confuse the stalker. Both of them would stay in places where there were people. Jade showed Diane the picture she had of Timothy Steven Lawrence, the one she had found in her brother's papers. Diane looked carefully at the picture, memorizing the face. Jade told Diane she'd contact her after she had been to the hospital to see her mother. They parted with a promise to meet at Nate Small's house at 5:30 for Jade's appointment with him.

Jade made it to the hospital by 3:15. On the way, she drove past Nate

Small's house, just to confirm to herself that she knew where it was, then she parked in the hospital visitor lot. She didn't dare to leave Brian's file in the truck, so she took it out from under the seat, folded it in half and stashed it in her inside coat pocket.

Jade walked off the elevator and made her way to her mother's room. Outside the door, she glanced across the hall and saw Phyllis, sitting in the waiting room. Jade pushed the door to her mother's room open slowly, and saw her father sitting on the bed, his back to her, and her mother laying in the bed, propped up with pillows but with her eyes closed and with no sign of consciousness. Jade turned from her mother's room and walked over to the waiting room instead. Jade and Phyllis looked at each other silently, as Jade took a seat, one chair separating them. Phyllis had obviously been crying. Her puffy face twisted in the parody of a smile and Jade suddenly realized that her sister was furious.

Phyllis's voice dripped sarcasm. "So glad you could join us, Jade." Jade recoiled as if slapped.

"Okay, Phyl, what's the problem?" Phyllis sighed heavily and dragged her gaze from the ceiling to Jade's face.

"Where have you been? Dad and I have been sitting here, waiting for mom to wake up for hours. I was so afraid that, if mom woke up and her mind was intact, she'd ask for you." It occurred to Jade that, not having told her family anything about her stalker problem, they wouldn't realize how anything could, or should, keep Jade away from her mother's side on this most important of days. Jade thought briefly about telling Phyllis what was happening. She didn't want her family to think she was being insensitive. But to tell them anything about what was happening could potentially put them in danger. So she elected to take the heat and say nothing. Jade looked down at her hands, entwined nervously in her lap.

"Phyllis, I'm sorry I wasn't here sooner. I'm glad mom didn't wake up enough to miss me yet, I lucked out."

Only partially mollified, Phyllis sniffled and turned away from Jade to watch their father leaving their mother's room and walk toward them.

Worry creased his features. "Your mother is starting to wake up. She's not happy about it, which the doctor did say may happen. She's still groggy, and she's started crying. She's trying to speak but not making any sense yet. Hopefully that doesn't mean the brain damage is severe. I wasn't as worried about her before as I am now."

He took the empty seat between his daughters, and turned to look at first one sister, then the other. "What's up with you two? Everything okay?" Both girls immediately reassured him that everything was fine. Jade offered to go in and keep their mother company for a while, so Phyllis and their father could get something to eat, and stretch their legs. They gratefully accepted and a moment later Jade was alone. She stood up, walked to her mother's hospital room door and opened it. The antiseptic smell of bedding and gauze assailed her.

Her mother was huddled in her bed, sobbing quietly. Jade crossed the room and sat down on the side of her mother's bed. Almost childishly, Agatha opened her arms and weakly reached up for Jade. Jade put her arms around her mother and held her. Gradually, her mother's sobs began to taper, then stopped. Jade pulled back and looked at her. Agatha looked back at Jade, nearly expressionless. Jade saw no recognition on her mother's face. Not wanting to push, Jade said nothing. The doctor already warned them that Agatha's memory may not come back all at once when she awoke, but instead, it may come back in pieces, over a period of hours, days, months or even years. And there may be permanent memory loss as well. Jade tried on a reassuring smile and was rewarded with a return smile from her mother. They sat that way for what felt to Jade like a very long time, just looking at each other and saying nothing.

Finally, Jade could stand it no longer. She spoke to her mother, softly and slowly, and watched her mother's face for a reaction. "Mom, can you hear me? You are going to be all right. Can you speak? If you can't, just blink your eyes twice so I know that you understand me." Jade watched her mother's eyes, and saw her blink, quite deliberately, twice in rapid succession. A tear rolled down her mother's face, and her mother's beautiful, expressive eyes held her own for a moment, seeming to plead desperately.

Then her mother's eyes shifted, looking past her to the door. Jade saw her mother's facial expression abruptly change. Where there had been intense emotion, now there was vacuity. Jade turned around to follow her mother's gaze and saw her father standing outside the door, looking in at them. He pushed the door open and walked to Agatha's side.

Jade suddenly suspected that her mother understood more than she was letting on. And her mother's oblivious behavior was intentional, she was sure of it. Jade's father sat down on the other side of the bed, across from Jade. Jade started to remove her hand from her mother's, and felt her mother's reflexive grip bear down on her hand, obviously not wanting her to let go.

She leaned down, gave her mother a gentle kiss on the forehead and said, "I'll be back in a few minutes, Mom."

Jade went off in search of one of her mother's doctors. Predictably enough, she didn't find one, so she went to the cafeteria, bought a cup of coffee and sat down at a round table near the window. The snow was falling again, lightly. It was beginning to get dark, and the snow sparkled in the sodium arc lights that lined the parking lot. Nights like this put Jade in mind of another time, seemingly, at this moment, another whole life, when the softly falling snow cleansed her world and all things still seemed possible. Sitting in the cold, drafty cafeteria alone, drinking tepid coffee, Jade thought about her brother's death, her mother's accident (her brain refusing, even now, to consider it anything else), the dismal state of her own solitary existence, Jade felt somehow less tethered to the living and to this life. It was frightening to discover how little there was to keep her wanting to see what tomorrow would bring.

Unsettled by the direction of her thoughts, Jade got up and got moving again. Still hoping to find a medical professional who could discuss her mother's condition knowledgeably with her, she headed to the nurses station on her mother's floor. She found a smiling, pretty nurse who said she had been spending quite a bit of time with Agatha. She and Jade took a stroll down the hallway as Jade outlined what she had observed a short time ago in her mother's room.

She asked the nurse if her mother's apparent feigning of incomprehension was normal, or if it could be evidence of paranoia, or maybe even cognitive impairment. The nurse said she didn't believe it necessarily meant anything, and it was possible that Agatha's cognition may be quickly cycling through higher and lower functioning levels, as her mind reached for a more fully alert state.

Accepting the explanation gratefully, Jade went back to her mother's bedside. As she entered her mother's room, she saw that Phyllis and their dad were both in the room, Phyllis in the chair next to the bed, their dad standing next to her. Both were watching Agatha intently. Agatha was half sitting up, looking comfortable and composed, with no evidence of the tears from just a short time ago.

Jade approached her mother and broke the silence. "Hi Mom, are you feeling better?" Agatha didn't answer, instead she just looked at Jade, then slowly turned a puzzled look to her husband. Jade watched the interaction between her parents with a sinking heart. Her mother was, at least at this moment, definitely impaired, for now or for good wasn't yet clear.

Jade's father held his hand out for Jade's and led her out of the room. "Honey, I don't think your mother recognizes you yet. I think she's beginning to recognize me, or else she's just getting used to seeing me in there. The doctor said it was possible she'd have retrograde amnesia, but that it would likely resolve in hours, or perhaps a few days. Try not to worry about it, though, okay?" Jade nodded numbly. "The good news is, she can speak, and she's making sense. She asked for some water, and she asked what happened. The doctor said she should be lightly sedated again, just to make sure all the upset from her awakening today doesn't keep her awake tonight. She really needs to get all the sleep she can. Tomorrow, I think things are going to be much better."

Jade went back in to say goodbye to her mother, and told all of them that she would be back this evening after her meeting, just to check in, and that she'd come back in the morning to visit again. Jade paused just outside her mother's room and looked back through the partially open door at the mute, frozen tableau of mother, father and daughter.

Chapter 31

Leaving the hospital, Jade first checked to make sure she still had Brian's file safely tucked into her inside jacket pocket, then she pulled out her cell phone, shielded the buttons from view and dialed Diane.

Diane answered on the first ring. "Where have you been? It's after 5:00 already! Are we going to meet with Mr. Small tonight or what?"

Jade confirmed that they would, and they agreed to meet at the parking garage at Gilman Street, which was less than a block away from Nate Small's house.

Jade then called Nate Small. He told her that he would be waiting for her. Jade took the opportunity to let him know that she would have a friend with her, someone whom she had taken into her confidence and who was assisting in her investigation. Nate asked for, and received, Jade's confirmation that the same non-disclosure agreement Jade and Nate had would extend to Diane.

Jade and Diane met as agreed and approached Nate's house together. Jade told Diane about the promise not to publish any information provided to her as a result of this interview for three months. Diane rolled her eyes, clearly not thinking much of this caveat, but she said nothing. The ornate front door opened as Jade raised a fist to knock. The man who appeared in the doorway looked artfully disheveled, and was almost shockingly attractive. Jade and Diane both took a stunned moment to complete their perusal while he looked on, amused and apparently used to their reaction. Introductions were made, and Nate invited them inside.

He closed the door behind them and ushered them into the living room. He sat down in a wooden rocker and the women sat down, as one, on the couch. Nate said, "Jade, I understand from our telephone conversation the other day that you are looking into a series of murders which apparently included my wife's death. As I told you, after my wife was killed, I started trying to find the killer. Since my wife didn't work outside the home, and since I'm a reporter, I thought there may be a good chance that her death had something to do with me, and what I do. I felt guilty about her death, and knew I wouldn't be at peace unless I could determine why she was killed." Nate looked at both women, with eyes swimming with unshed tears.

Diane spoke up, "Mr. Small, um, Nate, would it trouble you too much to describe what you know about the actual murder?" Jade explained, "Knowing exactly how and where it happened could either tie it in to the other murders we know about or exclude it."

Nate nodded sadly. "I understand. My wife, Cathy, was found dead, the morning of November 17, 2002. The police said she had been raped, bludgeoned, partially dismembered, and left in Lincoln Park. The police determined that Cathy wasn't killed in the park, so they looked for, and eventually found, the primary murder scene, which was in an alley on one of the wharves on the waterfront. They found, well, pieces of her, and a great deal of her blood. They questioned several of our neighbors and eventually narrowed their focus to two suspects. One of them was me, one of them was a neighbor named Timothy Lawry."

Jade felt a jolt when she heard the name, then she remembered that newspaper account she found in Peter's papers said that Timothy Lawry had been questioned in Cathy Small's death.

Nate continued, "Tim Lawry was definitely a ladies' man." Apparently, though, the police could find no definite link between Tim Lawry and the death of my wife. The police spent a great deal of time and effort checking me out, also. My alibi was weak; I was at home that night, alone, waiting for my wife to return from a shopping trip. Of course, had I known that my wife would pick that night to get herself killed, I certainly would have done a better job making sure I was accounted for."

Jade was shocked by Nate's apparent callousness. Jade slid a sideways glance at Diane and caught her fleeting expression of distaste.

Nate noticed their reaction, and was quick to explain. "I'm sorry, I didn't mean to sound insensitive. Comedic irony has always been my way of dealing with stress." Nate looked from Diane to Jade and back again, as if gauging their reaction. Jade nodded and gave Nate what she hoped was an encouraging smile.

Nate continued, "Where was I? Oh yes, the police didn't exactly clear me, it's more like they realized that they weren't going to be able to build a decent case against me. Likewise for Tim Lawry, probably. In the end, no arrests have been made. I call the police station every week and every week I'm told that they have nothing new to report. I still worry that I'll somehow be arrested for this. That's also partly why I want to find the murderer, to clear my own name.

"For my own investigation, I first got a copy of the police report, the crime scene photos and the autopsy report. Looking at that information was extremely hard. The police report that was filed the day after my wife's body was found indicated that there had been other similar murders, and that the murder of my wife might be connected. I was floored! I hadn't heard anything about any other killings in the area. But my subsequent research did uncover several deaths that seemed similar to my wife's murder. Now I'm convinced she *was* one of several victims of this same perpetrator." Nate's intense stare pierced Jade. "I found six other victims in the past three years that I couldn't exclude from the series. Jade, how many have you found?"

Jade felt excitement well within her. He may have information she could use! "I found two others, besides your wife, that fit the pattern. I have three others that still need to be looked into. But I wasn't finished looking yet, so sharing information will definitely help me."

Nate looked disappointed but said nothing. Jade pressed on. "Tell me specifically, Nate, what parallels have you been able to draw between your wife's death and the others'?"

Nate ticked points off on his slender fingers as he spoke. "First, my wife was in the age range of the other victims. Second, she was both killed and left in areas where previous murders had taken place. Third, she was raped, killed and partially dismembered, which was what happened to most of the other victims. Fourth, all of the murders happened at night, and all the murder scenes and dump scenes, when they differed, were in places that were sheltered from casual foot traffic." Nate's face took on a puzzled expression. "What I found odd was that there were also differences between a few of the victims. One of them was black, which was either a singularity or at least very unusual for our killer. One of them had a strange symbol drawn across her back, in her own blood."

Jade suddenly felt that all the oxygen had left the room. She looked down at her lap, thinking furiously. Nate didn't appear to notice her reaction. Jade asked, in a quiet voice, "Did you find out what the symbol was, or what it meant? And was it found on or near any of the other women?"

Nate answered with a negative shake of his head. "Since the police don't allow anyone access to open case files, the information I had was what I managed to glean from the public records. There was nothing else in the news reports about a symbol found on or near any of the other victims. The symbol, I'm told, was a Möbius." He looked at both women questioningly. Both women nodded to indicate their familiarity with the symbol. Jade was still reeling about the discovery of yet another Möbius, and this time on a current murder victim! Nate sat back, a smug expression on his face. His body language said, "There, top that!".

Jade decided to share her information first, hoping that Nate would then tell her the names of the victims he had uncovered in his research. "The three victims on my list that I know fit the pattern are named Paulina Nielson, Heather Demoree and, of course, Cathy Small." Nate picked up a notebook on a stand next to his chair and flipped through it briefly. "I had both of those other victims on my list." Nate closed the notebook and stood up. "Well, I appreciate your coming over. There isn't much new that you can tell me, apparently."

Diane and Jade looked at each other, then Diane stood up and stepped closer to Nate. "I seem to recall, Mr. Small, that the agreement was that you and Jade would *share* information. I'm sure you understand that we want what you want, to find out who is behind this. Having us provide you with the names on our list, without providing us with the rest of the names on *your* list, just isn't going to cut it." Diane put her hands on her hips and glared defiantly at Nate.

Nate allowed a patronizing smile. "You are NOT in a position to judge what's going to 'cut it'. You are in my home. If you are going to be rude, the door is right down that hallway."

Diane and Nate stared at each other, hostility apparent in both expressions. Jade stood up and moved between them.

"Nate, if you aren't going to keep your side of our verbal agreement, there's nothing I can do to force you. You are doing the memory of your dead wife a disservice by not giving us the additional names you have. I'm sure you realize that those names could be crucial to our investigation."

The look on Nate's face told Jade that he didn't care about anything that didn't directly affected him. Jade decided to try a different tactic. "You haven't been able to make any headway toward the identity of the murderer, have you? Well, we ARE making headway, and we know more than just a couple of the other victim's names. We can't force you to keep your promise but we can refuse to provide you with the rest of the information we have."

Jade strode confidently toward the front door, Diane close behind. Jade looked back at Nate, and saw a flash of naked fury in Nate's eyes. Naked fury, and something darker. Jade was suddenly very glad she had brought Diane with her tonight. They both slipped quickly out into the cold night. They didn't immediately speak, but instead devoted their energy to putting as much distance as possible between themselves and Nate Small.

Diane followed Jade to the hospital and they both parked in the hospital visitor's lot. Jade left Diane in the waiting room across from her mother's room while she went in and checked on her mother. The doctor had apparently sedated her for an early night. Phyllis was gone, and her father was half asleep in the chair next to Agatha's bed. Jade kissed her mother's cheek, then kissed her father's shiny bald pate, and tiptoed out of the room.

Chapter 32

Diane left her car in the hospital visitor's lot and rode shotgun with Jade in the Santa Fe, in search of dinner and a quiet place to talk. At a red light, Jade pulled out her cell phone and handed it to Diane.

"PD, do me a favor. Find Brian's cell number and give him a call? I just want to make sure he's okay." Diane pushed several buttons then held the phone to her ear. Jade heard her side of the conversation.

"Hi, Brian, it's Diane. You okay?" There was a pause, during which Diane was nodding. Jade grinned, knowing she, herself, always did that too when on the phone.

Diane finally spoke again, "Well that's good, then. We were worried about you. Jade wanted me to tell you that we didn't mean to bring you trouble. We have your file and we'll keep it safe until we can get it back to you. We are getting ready to look it over now. We'll copy what we need and send the whole file back to you by the first of the week." (another maddeningly long pause) "Got it. Stay safe, okay?…Okay, good. Bye."

Diane looked at Jade, smiling hugely. Under the circumstances, Jade found it a bit odd and told her so.

Diane said, "I think he may be interested in one of us, but I can't tell which one. He's fine by the way, he says hi. He went to the emergency room, they did an x-ray of his head and there wasn't any fracture. They stitched him up and let him go." Relief flooded Jade, as she realized that she hadn't (yet) gotten anyone else killed. "Diane, why do you think he is interested in one of us?" Diane said, "He said he'd be glad to come down here and collect his file. He said he didn't want it mailed. But I think he just wanted to see us again, or maybe just *one* of us."

Jade rolled her eyes. "So how did you leave it with him?" Diane said, "He asked me to call back on Monday, after we were done with the file, and we could work out how the file would get back to him."

Both women were ravenous. They picked up steak-and-cheese sandwiches and took them to Jade's office where they could talk freely.

Outside the office building, Jade looked carefully around, then pushed Diane through the door, slipping inside right behind her. Diane reached for the light switch just inside the door. Jade reached over to still Diane's hand halfway to the switch.

"Diane, don't turn the light on. I know you think I'm paranoid, but I've been followed, threatened and had my space violated enough lately to justify it. Walk straight ahead, past one door on each side of the corridor, there is a small lunchroom on the left. I'll hold this door open for a few seconds so you can see your way. Go there, don't turn on the light, just stand inside the doorway and wait for me."

The weak hallway light cut diagonally across Diane's frightened face as she stared at Jade for a moment. Jade let Diane work through things. After a moment, Diane turned away and started down the corridor, the brown paper sandwich bag in her hands crackling with each step. At the lunchroom door, Diane looked back at Jade, and then ducked inside.

Jade was relieved to see that Diane did exactly as she asked, she didn't turn on the light, she stood just inside the doorway, waiting. Jade let the door from the outside hallway close, she used her key to lock the door, then made her way in the pitch darkness to the office across from the lunchroom. She slipped into the office, turned on the photocopier, and slipped out, pulled the door to the copy room mostly closed, so the light from the machine wouldn't be seen from the hallway. She crossed the inky black corridor to Diane. Once there, she gently herded Diane into the room a few more feet, then closed the door behind them. Once the door was shut, she took off her sweater and pushed it against the crack at the bottom of the door, then turned on the light. Diane looked around, noticing there were no windows.

She laughed nervously and whispered, "I feel like a criminal!" They sat down at the table and immediately attacked their sandwiches.

After they finished eating, they cleaned up the wrappers and brewed a pot of coffee. Jade produced Brian Demoree's file folder from the inside pocket of her jacket. The file was dog-eared and stained, and Jade could see that Brian had spent hours going through this information, adding precious scraps to his file and trying to make sense of the senseless.

Jade turned out the lunchroom light, slipped out of the lunchroom, file in hand, and went back across the hall to the copy room. Within a few minutes, she was back. She closed the door, replaced the sweater at the bottom of the door, and turned the light back on. She carefully put Brian's original file into a plastic bag, then placed it back in her jacket pocket. Jade spread out the photocopies of Brian's file on the table. Diane scooted her chair closer to Jade so they could see everything together, at the same time.

There were at least 20 pieces of paper, several of them were clippings, unevenly ripped from newspapers. Jade started at the beginning. The first item was a police report, labeled as a "DD5". The crime was listed as "homicide". The body was found in Lincoln Park. The person who notified the police was listed as Tim Lawry. There was a period of silence while both women absorbed the enormity of this fact. Jade was the first to speak. "His name, in one or the other of it's incarnations, just keeps coming up. I know he has to be the one responsible for the current series of murders. We need to try to figure out the extent of what he's done. We also need to find some evidence that links him to the murders in more than just a circumstantial way. The police will HAVE to pay attention to us if we bring them hard evidence, from more than one murder."

With renewed purpose, Jade and Diane went back to the police report from Brian's file. There was yet one more surprise for them. The reverse of the form listed a complete inventory of the deceased's personal effects found at the scene. The form also stated that pictures of the personal effects were taken and were part of the file. Jade understood that the police would have immediately gone through the deceased's clothing and pockets, to determine her identity. In Heather's pocket, the police found several items, including a key chain. Jade looked behind the report and found that the next sheet contained several miniaturized pictures, including the key chain. The key chain held a vehicle ignition key and a car door key as well as what was probably a house key.

What captured Jade's attention was the key fob itself. It was made of silver, and it was a tiny, perfect Möbius.

"That's just friggin' weird", Diane said, folding her arms across her chest. Jade realized that this was now the second time she had seen the Möbius associated with the current killing spree. She also recalled that Nate Small had discovered a reference in a police report, to a Möbius being scrawled across the naked back of one of the victims. Jade also remembered her conversation with Tina Augerbois's father, about Tina's 1967 murder, he said the Möbius had been painted on the bottom of one of Tina's sneakers.

Mrs. Pelletieri also said that the Möbius had been drawn on the back of coloring book ghost pictures that were found with the bodies of her twin daughters, in 1968. As Timothy would only have been about five years old in the late 1960's, Jade realized that her research now included the work of two generations of Lawrence killers. She wondered if the 1960's serial killer was Ben or Daniel. Or perhaps it was the newly-discovered member of the clan, Dillon.

The Möbius was also found to be associated with more than one death back in the 1870's. It was becoming more important than ever that she find out about every death she could that was related to the Lawrence family, and find as many references to the Möbius as possible. It suddenly occurred to Jade that there may actually have been Möbius images at many of the crime scenes, they just may not have been discovered, or the investigators may have not realized their importance and may not have noted them specifically.

Turning haunted eyes to Diane, Jade realized by Diane's stricken expression that she, too, was grasping the enormity of what they had found. The realization that there was something concrete linking so many deaths brought the reality home to both of them. This wasn't just a mystery to be solved. They both now realized that their very lives depended on their ability to outwit their stalker and unmask him before he became threatened enough to eliminate them.

225

As if their fear could call him to them, both Jade and Diane suddenly heard a sound at the front door of the building, downstairs. Jade soundlessly slipped out of her chair and moved to the door. She flipped the light switch off, then slowly opened the door and looked down the hallway. The noises coming from the front door became louder. Someone was trying to get in.

Jade thought about ways they could get out of the building without being seen from the front door. The back door was only accessible by taking the hallway toward the front door, then turning right at the landing. Jade knew that whoever was trying to get in would be able to see them through the door's glass side panels. There was a chance that whoever was at the door didn't know they were there. Since they couldn't get out without being seen, they had no choice except to hide somewhere and wait for them to hopefully just take whatever they want and leave. Of course, if they knew she and Diane were there, they would be sitting ducks.

As quietly as possible, Jade moved back inside the lunchroom and made her way to the drawers against the back wall. Jade carefully opened a drawer and extracted two large knives, handing one to Diane. Both women moved to stand behind the door. Diane's free hand groped for Jade's and held on tight. They both clearly heard the sound of the front door opening downstairs. A heavy tread, obviously trying to be quiet, followed. The sounds grew louder as the intruder neared.

At the top of the stairs, all sound stopped. Jade imagined the intruder standing at the second floor landing, looking straight ahead to the corridor that led to where they were hiding, then looking down to the left, to the corridor that led to the back of the building. Jade and Diane stood silently, breathing shallowly, waiting for the intruder to decide where next to go.

After a moment, the heavy footsteps moved in their direction. Damn! Jade silently raised the hand that held the butcher knife, hearing the tendons in her arm creak as she did so. The intruder now stood almost outside the room where

Jade and Diane were hiding, separated from them by less than a foot of space but also, thankfully, by a wall. The hallway light cast the intruder's shadow into the little room. Jade decided he was probably male, wearing a long coat. And holding a pistol. Diane appeared to notice the intruder's deadly weapon at the same time Jade did; Jade felt Diane's body stiffen with fear.

The stranger walked a half-step into the room and looked quickly around. He acted as though he knew what he was looking for, and didn't appear to realize that Jade and Diane were there, behind the door. He retreated back to the hallway and continued to the next door. Jade's office. Jade could see him, through the crack in the door behind which she was hiding, but she knew he would not be able to see her. She stepped back slightly, Diane moving with her, just to put herself further into darkness.

****

The man crossed Jade's office and picked up her name plate. He ran his fingers over it, almost lovingly, and Jade was instantly shocked and repelled by the intimacy of the gesture. The intruder put down her name plate and moved around her desk. Jade watched as the man used some kind of tool to jimmy open the locked center desk drawer. He picked through her belongings. Then he pushed several items from the center of the drawer out to the sides. Jade felt a sense of violation, as well as a welcome sense of anger. That bastard!

Jade concentrated hard on his face, trying to discern his features in the dim light, under the hat he was wearing. She could see very little about him. She thought about Steven, and how he had looked at her brother's party the one time she had met him. She couldn't rule out that this man may be Steven. Leaving the drawer open before him, the man reached in to his coat pocket and pulled out a box, about the size of a personal packet of tissues. He placed the box in the center of the open drawer with exaggerated care. He closed the drawer most of the way, then he peeled something off the top of the box, replacing the strip with his hand. Still holding his hand on the top of the box, the man began to slowly shut the drawer, removing his hand only when the box had passed from sight and was fully inside the drawer. To Jade, it looked as though he had set up some kind of spring-loaded device, which would release when the drawer was opened. Great, he had set some kind of trap for her.

Having apparently completed his appointed task, the man stood up, walked around the desk, and left Jade's office. Once in the hallway, the man paused, head cocked in a posture of intense listening. Jade and Diane both instinctively held their breath. The man walked the length of the hallway, down the stairs and out the front door, closing it carefully behind him. Jade and Diane listened as the sound of his footsteps, crunching in the snow, faded down the street.

The women waited several moments before they walked out from behind the door. Diane started toward Jade's office, but Jade grabbed her wrist, staying her.

"If he just put what I think he put in my desk drawer, you do NOT want to go anywhere near it." Diane nodded silently and followed Jade as she headed for the front door. Jade looked through the glass door panels and verified that there was no sign of their visitor. She looked at both sides of the front door carefully, and was amazed that there was no visible sign, either inside or outside, that the door lock had been picked. Jade went back up the stairs to her office.

Diane spoke up, alarmed. "I thought you said we shouldn't go anywhere near your desk?" Without touching her desk or anything else on it, she picked up the telephone receiver and dialed 911. Diane saw what she was doing and nodded, relieved. Jade asked the dispatcher who answered her call if Derrick Zachary was on duty. After a silence punctuated by the clacking of computer keys, the dispatcher told Jade that he was. She told the dispatcher who she was and where she was calling from, and asked if she could please have Officer Zachary return her call as soon as possible. The dispatcher promised to relay the message.

Jade hung up the telephone receiver, then brought the telephone with her to the hallway where she sat down on the floor to wait. Diane sat down beside her, leaning against the wall.

"Jade, was that the guy you told me about, the cop that you didn't think you could trust with everything that's been happening?" Jade nodded.

"Well why did you call him if you don't trust him?", Diane asked.

Jade said, "Because I'm pretty sure that the man who was just here planted some kind of explosive device in my desk, that's why."

Diane's expression clearly showed her disbelief. "I'll tell you what I think. I think that guy knew we were here the whole time, he must have followed us here or something. He staged this whole thing to scare us. There's nothing dangerous in your desk, I think it was a big prank, just to scare the shit out of us."

Worried now, Jade continued looking earnestly at Diane. "That kind of thinking could get you killed. Think, Diane. Are you prepared to bet your life that you are right?"

Diane thought about that for a moment. "No. I *do* think it was some kind of sick joke, but I'm not sure enough about that to go over there and yank that drawer open."

Jade took a small measure of relief in that. She said, "That's why I called Derrick. I think our stalker just crossed the line between being sorely vexed at our interference and realizing how dangerous the knowledge we already have may be. Diane, I think he's ready to kill us. We just happened to be here tonight, and we just happened to see the trap get set. If we hadn't been here tonight, it's possible that what's in that drawer could have taken me completely out of the equation, come tomorrow." Diane shivered involuntarily, her gaze traveling back to Jade's office.

When the phone rang on the floor between them, they both started violently.

Jade reached for it. "Hello", she knew her voice sounded thin and frightened. Derrick's voice was deep and reassuringly worried. "Jade, are you okay? I just got a message from Dispatch to call you."

Taking a deep breath, Jade told him about her and Diane eating dinner at the office, and about the man who picked the lock on the front door and left a nice little surprise for her, likely set to go off if she opened her desk drawer. Jade resisted the urge to tell him everything, to just keep babbling on until Diane wrestled the sweaty phone receiver from her clutching hand. After she told him what happened, her audibly shaking voice just trailed off.

The silence stretched uncomfortably as Jade waited for Derrick to respond. Finally, he spoke, in measured tones which did little to conceal his anger. "Damn it, Jade, this is EXACTLY what I was trying to help protect you from! NOW do you get it? This friggin' lunatic has you squarely on his radar and he's not gonna stop until either you or he is dead. I'll have the bomb squad there within a half hour. Meanwhile, get out of there, get in your vehicle and drive down the street. Wait for me there."

Jade sat there, holding the receiver, fighting tears. Wordlessly, she passed the phone to Diane. Diane raised the receiver to her ear. Hi Derrick, it's Diane. Yeah, good to meet you too. Sort of. Jade's having herself a bit of a meltdown. I heard what you said. Do all men talk loud on the phone or just every man I've ever known? …Yes, I'll get Jade out of here." There was a long pause, during which Diane listened intently. "Will do. We're driving a Santa Fe. Yep, long story. Okay, we'll park down the street, lock our doors, yada yada. See you soon."

Diane hung up the phone and turned to Jade. "He sounds yummy! You've totally been holding out on me, girl! Did you hear how mad he was when he was yelling at you?" Jade's blotchy face produced a tiny little smile. Diane sized her up critically. "Let's get your face washed up. He didn't say we couldn't take a little detour before we leave. We should both use the facilities.

God knows how long it'll be before we can again." Diane hustled Jade off the floor and down the hall to the bathroom, pushed her inside and shut the door. "Now hurry up, I need to use it too!"

Jade blew her nose, then wet a paper towel and cleaned her face. Thinking about Derrick being on his way made her feel safer, and in all honesty, just a tiny bit thrilled to have him coming to her when she needed him. That wasn't something she was used to. Now, if the box the man put in her desk drawer turned out to be nothing dangerous, she was going to feel like a complete idiot. But in her heart, Jade knew the bomb was as real as it was deadly.

A pounding fist on the door startled Jade out of her worried musing. "C'mon, kiddo, get your ass out here. They'll be here any minute! If I don't get in there soon I'm going to explode! Oh – geez – sorry, I didn't mean to…well…you know".

Jade rolled her wet eyes as she heard Diane trail off self-consciously. She opened the bathroom door and Diane flew past her, throwing the door shut the second she was over the threshold.

Jade walked down the hallway and stood at the landing at the top of the stairs. After a few minutes, Diane came out, looking amazing, as she always did. Every hair in place. They went down the stairs and outside together. Jade turned back and locked the door. They hurried to the truck, looking everywhere at once, Jade unlocked it with the remote and they both jumped in. Jade pressed the button to lock all the doors, started the engine and turned on the heater. Then she pulled out her cell phone and dialed Malcolm. Dominick answered and Jade asked for Malcolm.

Malcolm came on the line, immediately sensing that something wasn't right. "What's up, Jade?" Jade explained what happened, and told him what she thought may be in her desk drawer. Malcolm, concerned, wanted to come right down. Hesitant to involve him any more than absolutely necessary, Jade told him it would be better if he stayed put and let the bomb squad assess the situation. She promised to call him shortly with an update. He reluctantly agreed to stay put, at least until he heard from her.

With a sigh of relief, Jade flipped the phone shut and put it back in her purse. Diane gave her an assessing look. "Malcolm doesn't know about any of this, does he?" Jade suddenly felt defensive.

"No, he doesn't. I didn't feel like becoming a problem child to him and losing my job over it."

Diane put her hands up, palms out in a warding-off gesture. "Okay, okay, take a chill. He'd have probably fired your ass at the first sign of any trouble. You *know* how shallow the guy is!"

Jade had to hand it to her, she had a way with sarcasm. "It's not necessary to bludgeon me with your subtlety, Diane. I know that Malcolm cares about me and if something was threatening my welfare, he'd want to know about it. In fact, he may be hurt that I didn't tell him earlier, once he knows the extent of it. But, honestly, most of why I haven't said anything is that just knowing some of the things we know may make him a target too."

Diane nodded and squeezed Jade's shoulder. It wasn't resolved, but it was shared and just lately, she had come to appreciate how much that helped.

A few minutes later, Jade spotted Derrick driving toward her office building. He passed her, then executed a perfectly illegal U-turn and pulled up behind the Santa Fe. He got out of the cruiser and walked toward Jade.

Diane's eyes widened in pleased surprise and she elbowed Jade, "Jesus, how could you *not* just jump on that sexy hunk of man-flesh?"

Jade blushed in the dark and gave her a return elbow, much harder. "Down girl!", she hissed. Derrick knocked on the window and Jade pushed the button to roll down the window, but instead the door locks all released.

Derrick opened the door, scooped Jade out of the truck and hugged her hard against him. His voice was muffled by her coat, his breath warm on her neck. "What am I going to do with you? Do you have any idea how angry I'm going to be if you go and get yourself killed?" Jade luxuriated in the safe warm feel of him, saying nothing. He pulled away, leaving a proprietary hand on Jade's back. Diane had jumped out of the truck and made her way around to Jade and Derrick. Jade introduced them and Diane, for a change, didn't say or do anything inappropriate.

The three of them walked toward Jade's office building, crunching the snow and ice in the street as they went.

Derrick stopped and turned to both women. "If we are able to take the device out of the drawer whole and examine it, we may get some trace evidence from it. Fingerprints, DNA, maybe some clue about how it's made."

Derrick turned and started walking toward the building again. Thinking out loud, he ran a restless hand through his thick hair and continued. "Sometimes these bombs can be triggered remotely as well, usually only from closer than a few hundred feet away. If the guy who planted it happens to drive by and see all the police activity around this building, and if he has a remote detonator, he may decide to set it off prematurely, simply to obscure any evidence."

At the sound of a large engine coming toward then, all three turned to look, identical expressions of panic on the faces of both women.

An unmarked box van pulled up a few buildings down from Jade's office. A powerfully built young black man threw the driver's side door open and jumped out. He strode purposefully toward the trio, extending his hand to Derrick. "Hey, DZ, what's up?"

Derrick introduced the women. His name was Al, the bomb squad commander. After the introductions, Derrick and Al walked to the front door of the building and both looked impatiently back at the ladies. Jade realized they needed her key in order to get in. She rushed over and unlocked the door for them.

Al posted a guard outside the building, and verified the radio frequency they would be using to make sure they were in constant communication. Jade realized that the guard's job would be to watch the area around the building and report any suspicious activity to Al so they could get out quickly if necessary. She cautioned them to be careful and walked back to where Diane was waiting and together they walked back to the Santa Fe. Jade was braced for the sound of an explosion.

After several minutes without incident, Jade gradually began to relax. She idly watched the road, marveling at how quiet and empty the streets were at this hour, it was barely 8:00! Then, she realized that she was late bringing the Santa Fe back. She pulled out her cell phone and redialed the car rental company. As she listened to the Prozac-ed version of "Stairway to Heaven", she noticed a black Mercedes driving on the opposite side of the road, toward them. She instinctively knew that it was the stalker, remembering the black Mercedes. She looked frantically at the guard standing in front of the building, and was relieved to see him tracking the Mercedes with his eyes as he spoke urgently into his handheld radio.

Jade looked back at the Mercedes. The driver's side window was heavily tinted and reflecting the streetlights, so Jade wasn't able to see inside. Suddenly the reflected streetlights disappeared from the window and Jade realized the window had been powered down. A gloved hand holding a small square object shot out, then Jade watched in dawning horror as the gloved thumb hovered over the object, obviously poised to press a button. Jade grabbed Diane's shoulder and Diane followed Jade's terrified glance. Diane instantly grasped the situation, grabbed Jade by the back of her neck and pulled her down behind the dashboard. A split second later, an explosion rocked the truck.

Chapter 33

Fiery chunks of mangled metal and burning wood fell on the sidewalk, the street, and onto the roof of the truck. The sound of breaking glass was muffled and strangely distant and Jade realized that her hearing had been impacted by the blast. The windshield of the truck was cracked in a thousand zigzagging lines. When the blazing rain of debris stopped, Jade and Diane crawled out of the truck and dazedly started to walk toward Jade's office building. Jade felt icy fingers of dread close on her heart. Derrick may not have escaped the explosion.

Jade's shuffling, confused gait gave way to a panicked sprint as she covered the short distance from the truck to the building. She dimly registered that the building was on fire. She dove through the front door of the building, her gasping sobs clearly audible, and straight into Derrick's arms! At first, Jade struggled to get free, not realizing this was the man she sought.

Derrick grabbed Jade's face and turned it up to his. "Jade! It's me, I'm okay!" Her sobs were stifled as his lips crushed hers. Jade clung to him as his lips provided her with the reassurance she so desperately needed.

Derrick brought Jade back outside, grabbed Diane's arm, and walked both women back to the Santa Fe. He turned the key in the ignition, making sure it would start, and instructed them to take the truck two blocks down, park behind the buildings there and wait for him. Jade understood what he wasn't saying. He needed to get back in to the building and search for Al, and he didn't want to have to worry about them, too.

Sitting a safer distance down the street, Jade heard the siren of the approaching fire truck. At least help was on the way, she thought. And her hearing appeared to be coming back. Jade heard a tinny musical sound coming from the floor of the truck. Looking down, she spotted her cell phone. She picked it up and placed it to her ear. She was still on hold with the car rental company! After a few moments, a recorded voice came on telling her to press 1 if she would like to leave a message, and Jade did. As she waited for the beep, she thought that this would be about the strangest message she had ever left for anyone.

"Hi, this is Jade Danner. I had a little mishap with the Santa Fe I rented from you. I'm glad I bought the extra insurance protection. There was an explosion at my office building on Commercial Street, and the truck was parked in front of it, so it sustained some pretty extensive damage. I need the truck to get home tonight, and it's running okay. I'll call you in the morning from home. I'm so sorry I damaged your truck." Jade flipped the cell phone shut and started to put it back in her purse. Then she realized she needed to call Malcolm.

She speed-dialed him. "Hi Malcolm, it's Jade. The bomb that was inside my desk exploded. There was a police officer in the building when it happened, but he's okay. There was also a member of the bomb squad in there, and the police and several fire fighters have gone back in to find him. There's a small fire in my office that looks to have been already contained. I can see inside through a hole in the outside wall." Jade listened for a moment, nodding, then said, "Okay, I may still be here or may not, but I'll talk to you tomorrow. I'm so sorry about all this." There was a pause, then Jade said, "Malcolm, I have no idea what I would do without you." Another pause. "Yes, I agree, thank God for insurance!" Jade looked over at Diane as she flipped the cell phone closed. "Malcolm is on his way."

Jade opened the driver's side door and got out of the truck. She walked toward the still-burning building. Diane jumped out of the passenger side of the truck and ran after Jade. "Where are you going? Derrick told us to stay put!" Jade looked back at Diane, then ahead again at her building, watching the smoke pour out of the broken windows on the second floor. Jade was relieved to see that there were no more flames, visible from the ground anyway. Several fire fighters came out of the front door, carrying a stretcher. The bloody and blanketed man had to be Al. He saw the women standing in the street and gave them both a weak thumbs-up sign. Al was trundled into a waiting ambulance, which immediately roared away, amid lights and sirens.

Suddenly chilled, Jade hugged herself as she looked back at the building. Derrick chose that moment to emerge from the doors. He immediately spotted Jade and met her halfway. "I saw them take Al out. Is he going to be okay?" Derrick searched Jade's dirty, tear-stained face, then put his arms gently around her. Jade felt his course jacket and smelled smoke on him. She put her arms around him, hugging him to her fiercely, reveling in the warmth and comfort. "I think he'll be fine. He had a couple minor burns and he took in a little smoke. Jade, no one was seriously hurt in that explosion, and I don't want you to feel like any of this was your fault, okay?"

Jade smiled tremulously against Derrick's chest, amazed by his ability to read her. "Derrick, I DO feel like this is my fault. It was me who apparently lured this sick man into my life and put everyone around me in danger." Jade struggled not to sob, but Derrick saw the fresh tears coursing down her cheeks. "Jade, we really need to talk about this, and you need to be completely honest about this whole situation. No, don't even try to deny anything, I see that look on your face. You are getting ready to push me out again. You aren't going to do it.

"We aren't going to discuss this right now. I'm off shift..." Derrick checked his watch and continued, "...ten minutes ago. We are taking Diane home, then I'm taking you home. I'll check your house to make sure everything's shipshape, then I'll tuck you in. Judging by the Samsonites under your eyes, you need some major sleep. And I'm appointing myself your personal sandman, got it?" Derrick looked at Jade, almost challengingly Jade thought, waiting for her response.

Jade was of two minds. First and foremost, of course, she wanted to "rip him a new one". Why did men insist on running her life and telling *her* what she needed? Independent Jade was unceremoniously body checked as Needy Jade emerged. Derrick wanted to take care of her! He was worried about her. It wasn't like she didn't need the help. *She* called *him*. And look at those gorgeous eyes, looking at her so tenderly! If she refused his help now, she knew, she would likely alienate him completely. So, Needy Jade reasoned, accepting his help was a political directive, in order to continue enjoying his help and protection. Right? Right?? Okay, not really. Independent Jade continued her token resistance, but the battle was over.

Jade tried on a smile, and surprisingly, found that it fit. "Obviously, trying to go this thing alone has landed me in a, well, difficult situation." Derrick worked to hid the grin that threatened, not quite pulling it off. "Yes, I know, I've been totally wrong not to trust you and ask for your help. You are, after all, a police officer, sworn to uphold the law and all that. So, with a small adjustment to your plan, I'll accept your help." Derrick's eyes narrowed suspiciously. "'Small adjustment' as in what?" Grinning, Jade said, "We need to take Diane back to her car at the hospital parking lot, that's where we left it this evening." Derrick took Jade's hand, and Jade linked arms with Diane as the three of them headed back to the Santa Fe.

Seeing through the windshield wasn't easy, but Jade took it slow and followed Derrick in his cruiser to the hospital. The parking lot was dark and mostly empty when they arrived. Jade delivered Diane to her car and kept her headlights on Diane as she unlocked her car, got in, and started it up. Derrick led Jade out of the parking lot, after watching Diane drive safely away.

At Jade's house, Derrick pulled in behind Jade, both cars fitting comfortably in the driveway. Derrick left his vehicle, walked to the Santa Fe and opened her door for her. Jade stepped out of the Santa Fe and Derrick slipped an arm around her and pushed the truck door shut behind her. Together, they walked to the front door and Jade let them in. Jade carefully unarmed the security system, then re-set it.

After Bardo was seen to, and both Jade and Derrick were settled on the couch, drink in hand, Derrick spoke. "Jade, I think you know how much I'm starting to care about you. Tonight should never have happened. If I seriously thought that you were in as much danger as you apparently are, I would have insisted on doing more to protect you. Now that I realize the seriousness of your situation, I need two things from you. First, I need you to tell me exactly what the fuck is going on. Soup to nuts, Jade, all of it. I've got all night. He took a sip of his drink, and then continued. "The second thing I need from you, is your promise that you'll listen to me and let me do whatever I feel is necessary to keep you safe. Can you do those things for me?"

Jade took a moment to think about what, and how much, she could say, then she spoke. "When I called you tonight, I knew then that I needed to tell you what's happening, that's why I called you. Okay, *partly* why I called. I was also freaked and needed you." Everything came crashing back, and Jade struggled not to break down. "I do need your help, Derrick. I can't do this alone. I'm going to end up dead if I keep trying. And now that I've confided in Diane, she could end up dead as well. I haven't been treating this as a game, exactly, but I haven't faced the fact that the person, or people I'm dealing with are playing for keeps. Derrick, I appreciate your offer of help. I'll accept it and tell you everything I can. My only caveat is that you don't act in your capacity as a police officer, on any of the information I tell you. I'm not sure how much of what I've done and what others have done is legal, and I don't want to go to jail."

Jade glanced quickly at Derrick's face as she took another sip of her drink. When she had started to speak, his face was open and inviting. Now, it was closed and dark. "Jade, how can you expect me to step in and out of my role as a police officer to suit your needs? I am what I am, and if any major infraction of the law has been committed, it's my responsibility to make sure the guilty party is held accountable." "Even if the guilty party is me?" Jade couldn't keep the hurt out of her voice. "Yes, even if the guilty party is you. But I have to tell you, I can't imagine that you've done anything that would be serious enough to be arrested for it. But then again, since you are so hesitant to share anything about you and what you've done, I really can't say for sure." Jade heard the hurt in his voice, too and she instinctively bristled.

Taking a moment to quell her rising defensiveness, Jade decided that perhaps a modified confession may be best. She decided that she could only tell Derrick what she felt was necessary in order for him to keep her and Diane safe. Derrick meanwhile, had apparently been thinking through his position, and his options for getting Jade to come clean. He took her hand and looked into her face. She fought the intensely hypnotic effect she felt whenever she looked into his eyes.

"Jade, there's an investigative tactic that we use when we know that someone is guilty of some offense, either large or small, but we may be willing to overlook it in order to get at the bigger truth. What we do is have the person we are questioning frame their 'confession' in hypothetical terms. In other words, they tell us what *may* have happened, if in fact, it did happen. We get a lot of good information, but we can't act on it to arrest the person because they didn't confess to anything, they just indicated that, had this situation occurred, it may have occurred in this particular way. Do you see what I'm saying?"

Jade nodded, although she wasn't completely convinced that this hypothetical confession would keep her out of the reach of the law. Derrick saw her indecision and pressed his advantage. "Also, Jade, remember that I can't use anything you tell me against you unless I read you your rights, which I will not do." Jade's expression remained unconvinced. "You are just going to have to trust me. As I've been right down the line, and as I will always be, I'm being completely honest with you." Jade took a moment to think things over, then nodded.

"Okay, I'm going to tell you a story. Let me preface it by saying that everything I am about to tell you is completely hypothetical." Jade looked at Derrick and felt encouraged by his curt nod. "Let's say I got a jewelry case to appraise for the Lawrence family…" Jade took her time and walked Derrick through finding the diary, her meeting with Ben Lawrence, and the killing sprees that have been happening for as far back as she had been able to research. Jade mentioned the Möbius , and how it kept turning up at murder scenes, both back in the 1870's and now. She saw Derrick's shocked expression and remembered that the Möbius was painted, in Ben Lawrence's blood, behind his dead body on the wall in his room.

Jade didn't tell Derrick any of what she knew about Peter, and his possible place in things. She didn't feel that it was essential, and she knew she could fill him in later, if she was able to fully trust that he was indeed completely on her side. Derrick asked very few questions, and listened carefully throughout. When Jade was finished, Derrick took their glasses out to the kitchen and made substantially stronger drinks for both of them. He came back to the living room and with a clink of ice cubes, passed Jade's drink to her.

After a few minutes of thoughtful silence, Derrick said, "So, basically this Timothy/Steven person is possibly the last in a long line of male serial killers in the Lawrence family. He knows you're on to him, he played cat-and-mouse with you for awhile and when he realized that you weren't going to back down, he decided he needed to do something about you. What I can't understand is why this guy didn't just take you out." Derrick watched Jade's face blanch, and he said, "What I mean is, we think this guy has killed several times. Why would he stick at killing you, when you aren't just a victim pursued for his own personal gratification, he obviously sees you as a threat. As an investigator, that feels like a clue. Maybe you know this guy, or maybe there's some kind of relationship between you that you don't know about? Is that possible?" Derrick watched Jade's face as she thought about it. Jade started to shake her head no, thought further, then finally, she shrugged.

"Jade, I didn't hear anything in what you just told me that would be an obviously prosecutable offense. Even if there *was* something, I think "mitigating circumstances" more than adequately covers your transgressions." Jade didn't realize, until that moment, how much she needed to share this information with him. The relief was immediate and intense. And the strong drink didn't hurt either. Derrick moved closer to her on the couch and put an arm around her. She leaned into the crook of his arm, feeling comfortable, warm and safe for the first time in a very long while.

Chapter 34

They finished their drink in silence, each lost in thought. Jade took their glasses back into the kitchen and rinsed them out. As she stood at the sink, warm, strong arms snaked around her gently from behind. She smiled and leaned back contentedly. After a moment, Derrick turned Jade around to face him. The question in his eyes was answered by the passion he saw rising in her beautiful green eyes. He effortlessly scooped Jade into his arms and carried her out of the kitchen, up the stairs and into her bedroom.

Once inside, he kicked the door shut and placed Jade gently on the bed, stretching his lean length beside her. Jade's eyes were closed, and Derrick watched the play of emotion on her face. In a moment, she opened her eyes to find Derrick's face above her, his eyes watching her face intently. Jade smiled at his awestruck and uncertain expression. "You are so beautiful. I'm almost afraid to touch you." Jade's smile widened. "Almost?" Derrick chuckled, "Yeah, almost."

He lowered his lips to cover hers. A shiver went though her as the kiss deepened. Jade arched her body into Derrick's and he groaned with pleasure, pulling her tighter to him. Jade felt Derrick's body shiver. She sought his eyes, and was surprised to see tears in them, more surprised, even, to feel answering tears well in her own eyes. She heard Derrick's wordless message and, in that moment, she understood how much he wanted and needed her. How he was afraid for her and wanted to keep her safe. How he was trying, unsuccessfully not to fall in love with her. She felt all that he could not say, in his lips and his touch, and her heart took flight.

The next few hours were a blur of delight and discovery. Both Jade and Derrick were amazed by their hunger for the other, and their determination to satisfy that hunger. Derrick was an instinctive and inventive lover, and their night was marked by as much laughter as there were cries of passion. There was no thought about time or about the outside world as the lovers gave and took their pleasure from one another and finally, spent, drifted into blissful oblivion, wrapped securely in each other's arms.

At 3:35 A.M., Jade awoke to the sound of rain falling outside. She could hear Derrick softly snoring beside her, one arm draped proprietarily over her, one hand lightly cupping a nude breast. She smiled contentedly and snuggled closer to his warmth, enjoying the male scent of him, and the mingled scent of their lovemaking. This moment, Jade realized, was even more precious because of all the terrifying things that had happened, and all she feared may soon happen. Jade knew that, if she survived the events of the present, she would always remember this night as the night at which the past and future divided, and she would think in terms of "before" and "after" this night with Derrick.

Jade turned carefully, not wanting to awaken Derrick. He snuggled his nakedness against her back and she realized he was already awake, or at least part of him was! She snuggled her bottom against him and suddenly going back to sleep was delightfully out of the question.

Much later, after a long, shared shower, Jade and Derrick sat at the kitchen table drinking coffee. The Winter sunlight turned Derrick's silver hair to sparkling fire as Jade sat quietly, watching Derrick over the rim of her coffee cup. Across from her, wearing a pair of Jade's outsized unisex pajama bottoms, Derrick immediately began mapping out steps to take charge of her safety. This was fine with Jade, since she knew she wouldn't win any safety badges of late. Derrick leaned forward in his chair and reached a hand to stroke Jade's cheek. Jade could see the concern in his eyes. And something more. Something she knew he could see in her eyes, too. The beginnings of love. She knew he wanted more than anything to protect her from harm, but he knew enough not to even ask her to give up her current course of action. Derrick ticked off his points on his fingers as he spoke. "Jade, I want you to program in my cell number on your speed dial list for your home, work and cell phones. I want your promise that you will keep your security system on at all times, whether you are at home or not." Jade nodded, agreeing with the need for this level of caution.

Derrick continued, "I don't want you going outside alone, except to get into your vehicle. And when you do that, I want you to use your remote to unlock your vehicle from the doorway, and go straight to you vehicle. This is the time when you will be the most vulnerable so keep your eyes and ears open. Your driveway is blocked from neighbor's view by the fence, so anything could happen to you here and no one may see a thing. At work, don't go outside and walk around at lunch or on breaks. If you get any strange calls or letters, tell me right away. Don't erase the call if it's on your voicemail. I have a telephone call recorder for you in my cruiser, I want you to use it to record all your calls for now on. We never know when we'll get lucky and this guy will tip his hand." Jade felt a thrill of gratitude when Derrick said "we".
*****

"Jade, since you know exactly who this is and where he lives, I'll be watching his house, unofficially of course. By the way, did you report the break-in you had the other night?" Jade looked at the floor, realizing that she forgot all about that. "That's okay, I'll file the report for you, since I was basically the responding officer." It's important to have the report on file, even though there was no evidence, except the piece of metal I found in your lock, just in case something turns up missing later.

"What occurs to me, given the information I have about Peter's death, is that this stalker of yours is almost certainly responsible for Peter's death. The information you just shared with me almost makes me think you've come to that conclusion, too. But I'm not sure what else you may know, and are not telling me, that led you there."

Jade thought about it. She knew that Peter was found, buried in a shallow grave in the Eastern Promenade park, but she had not yet made time to sit down with Derrick for an interview, as he had requested, so the details of Peter's death were still not known to her. Dread clutched her heart as she realized that Derrick knew something about Peter's death, something that would tie him to the Möbius killings. On the heels of that realization was the knowledge that Derrick knew *she* had already tied Peter's death to the other deaths, and that she was keeping information from him.

Jade had purposely left out the information about Peter's past disturbing behavior, and about the clippings and notes Agatha had found in his room. Derrick knew about Steven/Timothy, but not about Peter stalking him in an effort to find evidence to exonerate himself of the Old Port Murders. Jade knew that, eventually, she may need to tell Derrick, and that he may feel hurt that she had kept it from him. Jade also knew that Derrick would, at least one some level, understand Jade's need to protect her brother, or at least, his memory. She decided, at least for the moment, to keep the rest of the information about Peter to herself.

The newly minted couple sat in the warm kitchen, Bardo between their feet under the table, and enjoyed the last of the coffee, content in each other's company. As always occurs, the real world eventually interjected itself, and Derrick's cell phone began to ring insistently from the living room, inside

Derrick's jacket pocket. Derrick went to answer it and came back a few moments later, looking disappointed. Jade almost laughed to see how much like a little boy Derrick looked in that moment. He told Jade he had work to do, and that he would be tied up, off and on, for the next few days as another case he was working on was heating up. He said he'd call later, maybe set something up for the following weekend if not before. Jade sent Derrick home with a kiss and a hug.

Jade watched Derrick drive away, then immediately immersed herself in her Sunday chores. At noon, she called the hospital to check on her mother. She was told that her mother had spent a comfortable night, and that her father was there now. Jade asked the nurse to tell her father that she'd check in later. Jade then pulled out her Lawrence family research folder. She knew that careful planning could help keep her safer. Before she started reviewing her notes, she decided to take care of a couple of things. First, she called Diane to make sure she was okay. She used her cell phone and speed dialed Diane, in case anyone was watching her. Diane answered on the second ring.

"Hey Jade, how are you? Did you take that sexy Derrick home with you last night? I'll bet you did. I would have!" Jade blushed, even though she knew Diane couldn't see her. Her silence was apparently enough. Diane was off and running. "Oh my God! You did, didn't you??! I'm jealous! And I'm going to want deets, girl!" Jade grinned, knowing Diane would never get the "deets" on this particular tryst.

Jade then called Malcolm. He and Dominick were just sitting down to breakfast and had apparently been up most of the night. In the light of day, Malcolm reported, the damage to their office building wasn't extreme. There was a three-foot oval hole blown through Jade's office, through the outside wall. Jade's desk and everything in or around it was a total loss. The police were still gathering evidence but would release the office later in the day so repairs could start. Malcolm had already been in touch with his insurance company and they were sending someone down later today to inspect the damage. Jade suddenly felt much better, knowing things at the office would soon be back to normal. She realized, with a pang of regret, that the note Erin had written and placed in the jewelry case had been destroyed in the explosion. Thank goodness she had taken the copies! Once again, she had somehow managed to stay one step ahead of her stalker. Later, she promised herself, she'd drive down to the office and take a closer look at the damage.

Jade sat at the kitchen table and looked through her Lawrence file, looking for a logical next step. Her research included no less than ten murders involving the Möbius. Murders that were committed several decades apart. Jade knew that she'd need to find more about the murder sprees that occurred between the 1870's and the 1960's, to see if she could discover more references to the Möbius. Whatever there was for evidence, even circumstantial, she knew she'd probably need it, in order to convince the police when the time came.

She also knew she needed to try to locate Dillon Lawrence, if he was still alive. She didn't intend to approach him directly, in case he was also an active serial killer, but she wanted to try to find him, and, if possible, find out whether he inherited the Lawrence killing gene.

Jade packed up her file and headed out. She knew the library would be closed, because it was Sunday. Instead, she headed to her office to use Malcolm's computer to do some internet sleuthing. She had several programs linked to her work computer that she didn't have on her dial-up internet access laptop at home. And of course, Malcolm's work computer was much faster. On the way, she watched her rear review mirror and didn't spot any obvious tails. She parked behind the building and walked out to the front, letting herself in with her key.

Upstairs, she went directly to her office to take a look at the damage. There was yellow caution tape across the open doorway to her office, and the far side of the room was in shambles. Her desk was mostly gone, her computer and all the other items on her desk were also gone. There was hole in the back wall, and Jade could clearly see down into the street through the hole. Plastic sheeting had been taped up, and it crackled gently in the cold breeze. Jade ducked under the yellow tape and took two careful steps into the room. She picked up the trash can beside her desk, which had also been partially burned, and noted that the photocopy of Erin's diary which she had taped on the underside of the trashcan was still there, but the plastic bag containing it was partly melted. Jade ripped the copy off the underside of the trashcan and put it in her purse. Feeling uneasy, Jade left her office, closing the warped door part way and walking down the hall to Malcolm's office.

She booted up Malcolm's computer and logged in using her own login ID and password. She immediately found several references to other clusters of homicides that seemed to start abruptly in 1850, then again in the early 1900's, the 1930's and the 1960's. Nothing else came up about the murders from the 1870's, at least on her initial search. Inspiration struck, and she decided to cross-reference her results thus far with the word "Möbius". Jade was amazed to see several hits.

In 1929, a woman was murdered outside a night club on the Portland waterfront, the news accounts listed her as another victim of the "Möbius Murderer". Jade remembered that Louisa Lawrence, wife of Tim Lawrence, had been killed in

1907, and the media, at that time, had already taken to calling the killer "The Möbius Murderer". Apparently, this killing in 1929 must have involved the Möbius in some form, although the scant documentation she found had no direct reference to it.

There was another Möbius reference, dated 1967. An aging journalist had apparently posted journal entries on-line, back in the middle 1990's, before the proliferation of "blogging". Sam Krieger, a self-proclaimed "seeker of truth and light" spent decades studying the meaning and genesis of hundreds of family crests, from several different countries. Sam's research spanned the 1940's through the 1960's and his website included pictures of family crests, some of which Jade recognized from her own work with antiques. Jade was thankful for the inquisitive minds of people like Sam Krieger.

Unbelievably, Jade found several family crests which involved the Möbius, or some variation of it. Scrolling through them, she spotted the exact symbol she sought. The Möbius had an eye in one loop and a droplet in the other. Jade clicked on the hyperlink embedded in the symbol and a new page opened. As the page loaded, Jade saw that the website sponsor was a world-wide family crest registry. The symbol she now associated with the Lawrence family murders was registered as the family crest for the Lawrence family, late of Edinburg Village, England and more recently of Falmouth, Maine. The registration year was given as 1861. She suddenly recalled that the jewelry case which started her Lawrence family mystery had stickers and stamps on it indicating that it had spent time in England. Now, she could see why. The Lawrence family was apparently originally from there.

Fascinated, Jade read through the information provided on the website. One of the other links took her to a detailed genealogical chart of all known branches of the Lawrence family. There were branches of the Lawrence family in several countries, including the United States! The names on one branch of the family tree started with William Lawrence, who, if he was the same William whom Jade recalled from Erin's diary, lived in New England in the first half of the 1800's.

William's branch continued on to smaller branches, several of which ended with no names on them. Jade thought this may mean that additional family members may have existed, but were not confirmed or names could not be identified. Trevor and Tim Lawrence were listed, below William. Trevor's branch ended, but Tim's branch continued, and the name "Ben" was listed! After Ben, Jade was amazed to find that both Daniel and Dillon had somehow made their way on to the family tree. Jade knew that Daniel and Dillon were Ben's twins, born to Alois. Jade realized that Alois, or perhaps one of the twins themselves, must have traced their roots and made their existence known to the rest of the Lawrence family. There were no other names listed on the website, after Dillon and Daniel.

Jade recalled that the papers found in Peter's room documented that Daniel's son's name had been changed from Timothy to Steven, and even his last name had been changed from Lawrence to Lawry. Jade wondered if Daniel had known about the family "curse", possibly even first hand, and tried (likely in vain) to keep his son from being part of it.

Jade printed off the genealogical chart and the home page, complete with the website address and added the information to her folder. She then used the website provided by her new friend Ian, at the library, to run a background check. She entered the name "Dillon Lawrence" and used her credit card to pay the fee. Several sources of information came up. There was a credit history, a very outdated job history, and a scant but interesting police record. Jade noted that there was no record of this man after 1958.

Jade packed up her research materials and headed out to the hospital. Once there, she went directly to her mother's room, only to find her mother asleep, and her father sitting in a chair beside her bed, typing busily on a laptop. Jade's father seemed pleased to see Jade. "Your mother seems to be using sleep as an escape. The doctor said there isn't any reason that she should be sleeping this much. The doctor did say that everyone deals with trauma differently.
Jade thought that made sense. But her mother may be using sleep as a substitute for the more permanent oblivion she had unsuccessfully sought. She looked up to see her father watching her, probably knowing what she was thinking by the look on her face, as he had always been able to do. He reached over and gave her shoulder a reassuring squeeze. Jade put her hand over her dad's hand and held it there, for a moment. She stayed for a few more minutes, but her mother didn't stir. Jade gave her father a quick hug and left the hospital.

When she arrived home, Jade took a few moments to freshen up and to feed Bardo, then she left to keep her 5:00 appointment with Mr. McInerny. Jade drove around the city for awhile, in an effort to make sure she wasn't followed. She knew she had the address Kevin McInerny had given her, to his best friend's house, in her purse, but a quick look at the seat next to her confirmed that she left her purse at home. She thought a moment, then headed to the address culled from memory.

It was a small cape on Caldwell Street. She parked on the other end of Fellows Street, grabbed a small notebook from her glove box, and walked the two blocks on foot, once again to discourage anyone who may have followed her. There were children's snow toys scattered across the driveway. Jade smiled as she recalled the child who had answered her call to the McInerny home.

Jade walked up the porch stairs and rang the doorbell. A dog immediately started barking, and a child's voice could be heard on the other side of the door. "Daddy, someone's at the door! Do you want me to get it? Silence, punctuated by the barking of the dog, then a man's voice, "This isn't our house, you should wait for Jeremy or Debbie to answer the door. "I know, Daddy, but I can open it." The curtain whisked aside for a moment, then Jade heard the lock being disengaged. The door opened and a very tall, handsome black man and a small, exquisitely beautiful child appeared in the doorway. Jade introduced herself, and they stood aside and invited her in.

In the kitchen, Jade sat down with Mr. McInerny and briefly explained exactly why she thought Kevin's wife may have been one of several victims of the same killer. She told Kevin that she had uncovered several homicides that were strikingly similar, in method and in victim profile, to his wife's homicide.

Jade also shared her insight about how unusual it may have been for the killer to target an African American woman, as none of the victims she had so far tentatively traced to him were African American. Mr. McInerny thought for a moment, then pulled out his wallet. After flipping through his photographs, he pulled out one and handed it to Jade. "This is a picture of my wife, about two months before she was killed." Jade looked down at the picture and immediately knew why Mr. McInerny showed it to her. The smiling woman staring up at her was a fairly light-skinned woman of color. Jade could even see how she may be mistaken for Caucasian. Jade looked at Mr. McInerny and understanding passed between then as Jade handed the photo back.

Mr. McInerny walked over to the bottom of the stairs and looked up, listening.

Satisfied that his daughter was busy and out of earshot, he came back and sat down at the table again. "Ms. Danner", he began. Jade interrupted with a smile, "Please, call me Jade". He answered her smile with a sad smile of his own. "Okay, call me Kevin." Jade nodded, and Kevin continued. "I guess what I need to know from you, that you haven't told me, is what your interest is in this."

Jade said, "I work for Remerick and Company, furniture appraisers. I was recently asked to appraise a jewelry case. I examined the case and found a note inside it. The note led me to a document that eventually led me to a string of several homicides that took place in the past. When I researched those homicides, I found more that matched the M.O. Unfortunately, as I said before, my research has attracted the wrong sort of attention. I've been threatened, and worse. That's why I took care to make sure my visit with you wasn't observed." Jade looked at Kevin's face, trying to gauge how crazy he might think she was. Instead, he looked concerned, not disbelieving. Relieved, Jade continued. "Please, Kevin, tell me anything you know about your wife's death that may help me include or exclude her."

Kevin nodded. "DeLayne and I tried for eight years to have a child. Finally, in 1999, Nikki was born. DeLayne was over the moon, and we felt that our lives were complete. When Nikki was almost 2, just before Dee's 30th birthday, we found out we were having another baby.

It had been so difficult getting pregnant for Nikki, we just assumed she was all we were going to have, and we were both more than satisfied with that. But the new baby would be more than welcome. Two weeks later, DeLayne, and the baby she carried were both dead." Kevin's eyes filled with tears. "It took me months to get to the point where I could care for Nikki the way I should. Thank

God for my parents." Jade reached a hand out to Kevin and lightly brushed his shoulder. Kevin nodded his thanks absently.

Jade tried to choose her words carefully, loathe to hurt him any more than was necessary. "Kevin, was there anything specifically about DeLayne's death that seemed unusual? I know the whole situation was unusual, but was there something that maybe didn't make sense or add up, at the time?" Kevin said, "I don't remember much about that time, it's sort of a blur. I do remember that they found an indentation on her cheek that they thought may have been from a ring. They said they tried to make a cast of it, but ended up with something that resembled a snake, or a number eight. They said this may have given them an important clue to the identity of the killer." Jade instinctively knew that the imprint on DeLayne's cheek was a Möbius. As she considered mentioning the possibility, Kevin continued.

"For awhile, the police thought that her murder may have had something to do with what my wife did for a living. You see, my wife was a criminal justice professor at the University of Maine. Sometimes, she and her students would help the police with unsolved homicides. How could anyone have guessed that she, herself, would become an unsolved homicide." Distant warning bells began to clamor in Jade's mind. The harder she tried to catch hold of the thought, the more elusive it became. She thought about the possibility that DeLayne may have gotten too close to a Lawrence family murderer, who was actively at work in the area, and she knew that was part of what had set off warning bells, but she also realized that there was something more, stubbornly eluding her. She used her small wire-bound notebook to briefly capture the conversation with Kevin.

"Kevin, I appreciate your help. I know it can't be easy to relive this. I'm not sure what may turn out to be helpful to me, and I may not know until all my research is done and I put everything together. Would I be okay if I called you, if I have any other questions?" Kevin said, "That would be fine. I'll be glad to do anything I can. It's hard to relive what happened, but I enjoy the chance to talk about my wife." Jade stood, shook hands with Kevin and thanked him again. She left the house, walked down the porch stairs, and looked carefully up and down the street. There were no pedestrians and no cars in motion. Jade walked the opposite way from where her Blazer was parked, went two blocks, then took a circuitous route back to her truck. She saw no one, but surprisingly, didn't feel silly. Her days of feeling silly about taking precautions were over.

On her way home, Jade pulled her cell phone from her pocket and dialed Brian Demoree's number. He answered on the second ring. At first, his voice sounded a bit gruff, then he apparently realized who she was. "Hello? Jade, how are you?" Jade was heartened to hear that Brian's voice was sounding much stronger. "I'm great, thanks. I just wanted to let you know that I'm done with your file, and ready to get it back to you. I took a copy of everything in it, so if the original happens to get lost in transit or anything, I've got a backup that I can reproduce for you." Brian thought about it, then said, "So, is Diane with you?"

Jade suddenly realized which one of them it was that Brian may be sweet on, and it wasn't her. Jade answered, a teasing note in her voice. "No, she's at home, I would imagine." Brian tried to sound nonchalant. "Oh, well that's good then. Listen, Jade, do you know if she's dating anyone?" Jade grinned. "I happen to know for a fact that Diane is, at the moment, completely unattached." Brian's voice immediately brightened. "Well, would you mind playing cupid and telling Diane that I'd like to take her out sometime, that is, if she'd like to go? You can have her call me back, if she's interested, and if I don't hear from her I'll know she wasn't."

She told Brian that she'd be happy to call Diane as soon as she got off the phone. Now that he didn't need to use his file for an excuse to see Diane again, and since Jade had a backup copy, he consented to have Jade put the file in the mail back to him. Jade disconnected, leaving Brian considerably happier than she had found him today. Jade stopped at the Post Office and sent Brian's file on it's way back to him.

As promised, as soon as she got back into her Blazer, she speed-dialed Diane at home. Jade got her voicemail and started to leave a message. "Hi Diane, it's Jade. I've got a message for you from a secret admirer. If you're there, pick up!" After a few seconds, a breathless Diane picked up the phone. "Hey Jade! I was just getting out of the shower." Jade laughed, it was a running joke that they both seemed to have a knack for catching the other at inopportune times.

"Diane, guess who I spoke to today?" Diane was silent for a moment, then said, "Well, I'm not thinking you'd sound this mischievous if it was our stalker dude…. And since you said it was a message for ME, I'm guessing it was Brian! Please, please, please tell me it was Brian?!" Diane's excitement was infectious. "Yes! That's EXACTLY who it was! Diane, he was so cute on the phone! I called him to talk about how he wanted us to return his file. Since I took a photocopy of it, he let me put it in the mail back to him, which I did. Geez, I hope he gets it okay. If he doesn't, I'll have to make a copy of my copy and send THAT to him." Diane, barely holding her patience, finally exclaimed, "Yeah, whatever, get to the part where he talked about me!" Jade said, "He wants you to call him. But only if you are interested in going out with him." Diane took down Brian's number, then unceremoniously ditched Jade so she could call Brian back.

Chapter 35

At home, Jade found herself pacing and bored. Since it was not quite 7:00 P.M., she called the hospital to check on her mother. The floor nurse asked if Jade was a relative. Jade suddenly flashed back to her call to Ben Lawrence's nursing home, when she was asked if she was a relative, and had been told that he was dead. Frightened, Jade told the nurse that, yes, she was family. The nurse's voice immediately turned solicitous, increasing Jade's anxiety. She informed Jade that her mother had just coded, and was taken to the CCU. Alarmed, Jade asked if her father was there. The nurse said he was there a few minutes ago, but they hadn't been able to find him now. They were calling him on his cell phone, the nurse explained, as she was answering Jade's call. As the nurse started to say something else, Jade heard her cell phone ringing from inside her purse. She dumped the contents of her purse on the table, grabbed her phone and saw that it was her father calling from his cell phone. She told the nurse she'd be right there and disconnected.

She flipped open her cell phone as she grabbed her keys and headed out the door. Her father's voice sounded frantic. "Jade, they just took your mother into an operating room. I don't know what's going on." Jade took a deep breath and tried not to let her voice betray the panic she felt. "I know, Daddy, I just called the hospital to check on mom and they told me she coded. I'm on my way; I'll be there in less than ten minutes. You hang in here, they are working on mom and there's nothing you can do for her right now except exactly what you are doing. Call Phyllis, okay?" Jade's father agreed to call Phyllis and Jade disconnected, channeling all her nervous energy into her right foot on the gas pedal.

At the hospital, she went straight to her mother's floor and spoke to the charge nurse. She was sent to a waiting room several doors down. Her father was sitting in a chair with his head in his hands. Jade walked over to him and sat down. Unreality washed over her as her father looked up into her eyes, the worst possible news written clearly on his tear-stained face. "She's gone, Jade. She's just gone." Jade put her arms around her father and held him for a moment.

Jade heard the sound of footsteps approaching and looked up to see Phyllis coming through the doorway. She looked beseechingly from one to the other of them, then dreadful comprehension dawned as she read the misery on their faces. Phyllis collapsed to the floor in front of them. Jade reached down for her sister and let herself be pulled from her chair onto the floor, to fully hold her. Phyllis' voice, so like their mother's kept repeating the word "no", until Jade whispered to her, "Shhhh, she's gone. We can't help her. But we can help Daddy. Let's try to be strong for him, he's really going to need us now. Jade felt Phyllis' head nodding her agreement as Phyllis' voice fell silent. Jade's father sat above his two daughters and watched them try to console each other. So began their sad new journey together, one that would no longer include Agatha.

The next few days were a blur, as Jade helped her father and Phyllis begin, once again, the machinery of death. They decided to have a funeral for both Peter and Agatha together, as they all agreed that they would have wanted it that way. The funeral home director was shocked to hear of Agatha's passing. Jade remembered feeling that the funeral director was perfect for his job, as he had just the right amount of deferential sadness and dignified sympathy. Jade hoped, after the funeral, she would never have to lay eyes on him again, unless she was looking up out of a box herself.

After the initial sharing of their anguish, Jade, Phyllis and their father each retreated into themselves to deal with their crushing grief alone. Jade knew that Phyllis had her own family, and hoped that they would help her cope. Her father had no one. Then she remembered the woman she thought she saw with her father at Ben Lawrence's grave several days ago. She pushed the thought away angrily. She had to have been wrong about that. Jade, herself, didn't want help with her grief. Not yet.

When Jade got home from the hospital, the night her mother died, there was a call on her answering machine from Derrick, just checking in to find out how she was and to see if she'd like to get together. Jade thought about where she was just 24 hours ago, and she thought, with bitterness, how quickly everything can change. Jade decided not to return Derrick's call yet. She called Diane, instead. She explained what happened and asked Diane to wait until tomorrow morning and call Malcolm for her, since Diane and Malcolm were old friends. Diane understood that this telephone call was painful, and that her calling Malcolm for Jade will keep Jade from having to make another, equally painful telephone call. Of course, Diane wanted to come right over, but Jade told her not to. Half hour later, predictably enough, Diane was at her door. Jade let her in, Diane made sure Jade was okay, then, in a rare show of insightful understanding, left Jade alone.

The next day, Jade learned from the doctor who coordinated Agatha's resuscitation team that she had likely died of a heart attack, that the stress of the accident, with the stress she had already been under, may have been too much. She may have also had an underlying, and up to now undiagnosed, heart condition. An autopsy would be performed and the results would be available within 10 days. The toxicology report would take several weeks.

Wednesday, the day of the funeral, dawned sunny and unseasonably warm. Everywhere was the soft dripping sound of melting ice. It seemed wrong, somehow, to be given a hint of the wonder of Spring to come, on the day the Danners were to bury two of their loved ones. But things happen as they must and the day needed to be gotten through. And get through it they did. In a blur of crying relatives in somber clothes. The smell of lemon furniture polish on the walls of the funeral room. The squeak of the floor as they filed out. The smell of newly-turned, partially frozen earth at the gravesite. The cold, smooth feel of the casket against Jade's forehead as she said a final goodbye to her mother. Peter's casket sat poised over a hole, immediately beside Agatha's, all but forgotten.

After the gathering at Jade's parent's house, Jade was grateful to make her escape. Her warm, comforting home immediately enveloped her. Jade spent a good long time curled up on the couch, thinking. She was frightened by the idea that she didn't know if she could get through this.

Friday

By Friday afternoon, Jade, who had been dodging Derrick's calls for days, realized it was time to call him. God only knew what he'd been thinking. When he answered his cell phone on the second ring, he sounded both worried and relieved. "Jade, are you okay?' Jade's voice sounded foreign to her. "Derrick, I'm sorry I didn't call sooner. My mother passed away last Sunday night." There was a stunned silence, then, "I'm coming over." Jade started to protest, but found herself speaking to a dial tone.

Twenty minutes later, Derrick was at her door. She opened it and he shot in and grabbed Jade up into his arms, kicking the door shut behind him. Two things occurred to Jade almost simultaneously. One, she should have called him days ago, isolating herself in her grief wasn't fair to him, or to her. And two, she loved this man and he obviously loved her. Derrick pulled back and looked into Jade's eyes. The concern on his face almost undid her. She led him into the living room. They sat down on the couch and Derrick turned to face Jade. "I'm so sorry about your mother, Jade. I don't think anyone expected her to suddenly take a turn like that. It must be very hard." Jade nodded, not trusting herself to speak. Jade shivered involuntarily and Derrick immediately pulled her close. For the first time in days, Jade felt a measure of peace.

"Jade, wake up." Jade opened her eyes and looked around her living room, feeling as if she had never seen it before. She realized that she must have fallen asleep, in the warmth of Derrick's arms. As full awareness returned, she wondered how long she had been asleep. As if reading her thoughts, Derrick said "You've been asleep almost 2 hours. You were so peaceful, and you had such dark circles under your eyes that I just didn't want to wake you." Jade sleepily crawled out of Derrick's warm arms and padded to the bathroom, Derrick watching her anxiously.

A few minutes later she emerged, looking more awake but not much more rested. Derrick watched her as he finished up a cell phone call. When he flipped the phone closed, he told Jade, "I have absolutely nothing else to do except take care of you until tomorrow afternoon. How would you like a little company tonight?" Jade found herself pleased by the idea. She was usually a loner, and she knew she had needed some time alone right after her mother died. But now, she needed this caring man. She gave Derrick a slight smile. "I'd love some company tonight, thank you for being pushy and knowing what I need better than I know myself." Derrick smiled back, pleased to see even the small smile on her face. "Pushy? You call that pushy? You don't know from pushy, little miss."

She appreciated Derrick's attempt to cheer her up. Distraction was probably exactly what she needed. "Derrick, what do you say we go out tonight? I'd love to go somewhere outside this house, somewhere that the cooking is done for me, and I get served by someone, then maybe a movie or something?" Derrick was only too happy to indulge her. "Excellent idea, I'd love an actual 'date' with you. Why don't you take a shower, and do whatever it is you women do to get ready for a date." Jade gave him a playful punch on the arm. "So what you are saying is that I'm stinky AND vain?" Derrick, who recognized a no-win situation when he saw one, reached over and kissed Jade soundly, in lieu of an answer. The kiss turned serious, and the lovers decided a long hot shower was just the ticket, for the both of them.

On the road later, Jade watched the scenery go by and marveled at how much better she felt. Riding along in Derrick's truck, going out to eat with him and then to see a movie. Derrick took them down several smaller and smaller streets, and stopped in the driveway of a huge Tudor-style home at the end of a dead-end street. Jade looked over at Derrick quizzically . He jumped out of the truck, came around to her side and handed her out.

They walked to the front door together. Derrick pulled out a key and inserted it. "Derrick, who's house is this? We can't just let ourselves in!" Derrick looked at her, mock-sternly and said, in his best British accent, "Of course we can, you silly slip of a girl. This is MY house." Derrick took her hand and led her inside. Astonished, Jade wordlessly followed, looking everywhere at once. Finally, curiously overcame her astonishment and she had to ask. "How can you afford to live in a mansion in Falmouth Foreside, on a cop's salary?" Derrick's smile broadened. "Well, it seems we have a lady who speaks her mind. I like that. Always do that. This is the house in which I was born and raised. I was an only child, and when my parents passed away in 1987, their estate, which included this house, came to me. I was stunned when I found out how much my parents were worth. We had this big house, but lived rather simply. I don't know, it just seems like when you're a kid, you don't think about things like whether your parents are rich or not. At least I didn't."

"So, when you said you wanted to go somewhere outside your house, a place where the cooking is done for you and you get served, naturally I thought of taking you here, and cooking for you myself." Jade loved the idea, and parked herself on a stool in the gourmet kitchen while Derrick got busy. First, a glass of red wine for each of them, and some Gregorian Chant music (Derrick's personal favorite, as he told Jade). Then, Derrick fired up the grill and prepared steaks. Salad, already made and chilling in the refrigerator, completed their simple and delicious meal. After dinner, Jade sat back and patted her full belly. "I could get used to this." Derrick's face went still as he looked at her. For a moment, Jade was afraid she had committed a faux pas. Then Derrick said "I was hoping you'd feel that way. I could get used to YOU getting used to this."

After dinner, they checked the local theaters for a movie, but neither of them saw anything that looked worth seeing. Or, Jade thought, maybe they would both rather spend time alone together. They settled on renting a DVD, which they took back to Derrick's house as Jade didn't have a DVD player. After the movie, which neither of them actually paid much attention to, Jade started getting ready to leave. Derrick tackled her and, laughing, they decided it would be safer for Jade if she stayed. Making love, then spending the night in

Derrick's bed, was just what Jade needed. In the morning, she awoke amazed that she had slept almost 10 hours. Luxuriating in the circle of Derrick's arms, Jade thought about how much her mother was going to like Derrick. Then it hit her, again, that her mother was dead. She wondered how long it would be before she would stop feeling blindsided. Resolutely, she pushed her sadness away and looked around her, seeing Derrick's bedroom in the light for the first time. Nice room. Masculine and minimalist, like the man himself.

Derrick's side of the bed was empty, but she could smell bacon and coffee wafting up the stairs. A quick bathroom stop, then Jade followed her nose down to the kitchen. Derrick was wearing a terrycloth apron, and not much more. When he turned back-to, Jade could see his boxers, with the "big dog" print, saggy seat and all, and she laughed at his silliness. Derrick looked back over his shoulder, putting on a long-suffering expression. "Breakfast, madam?" Jade sat down, Derrick placed a heaping plate in front of her, and she dug in.

After breakfast, they returned the rented DVD, then Derrick took Jade home. Parked in front of Jade's house, Derrick kissed Jade goodbye. He said, "I'm working the night shift tonight, but I'll check in with you later." Jade felt sudden disappointment, which must have showed on her face, as Derrick chuckled delightedly. "I wouldn't play too much poker if I were you. That's some pout you've got there." Jade punched him on the arm, and he howled in ersatz pain. Several more kisses goodbye later, Jade got out of the truck and Derrick drove away.

In the house, Jade immediately let Bardo outside in the backyard, watching him carefully until he was safely back in he house.

Jade took a long, hot shower, then decided to give her father a call to see how he was. She thought again how, even though she still felt so sad about her mother's death, she felt much better than she did yesterday. She wondered if maybe things were going to be okay, after all. She flipped her cell phone open and discovered she had a voice mail message waiting. It was her father. His message was very short. "Jade, if you aren't busy, would you please meet me at the house, at 7:30 tonight?" Jade thought he sounded odd, distant and stressed. She checked the time and date of the message and realized it had been left late yesterday afternoon. Which meant she had missed the meeting with him. She dialed her parents' home number, hoping to catch him at home, and hoping he wouldn't be upset with her for not getting his message until now.

Her father didn't answer her call, and Jade left a voicemail message for him to return her call. She then called Phyllis, to see if Phyllis had heard from their dad and if he had seemed okay. Phyllis said she hadn't seen him since the day after the funeral, last Thursday. She had tried to call him yesterday morning, she reported, and she left a message for him. But he hadn't called her back. She thought again about how odd his voice sounded, in his voice message. She wondered what he wanted to see her about.

Jade thought about one more obligation she had. A telephone call she'd rather not make for a couple different reasons. Never one for cowardly behavior, she grabbed the phone and speed-dialed Malcolm. He answered, breathlessly, on the third ring. "Hi Jade, whew! Wait a sec while I catch my breath! I saw that it was you and didn't want it to go to the machine. How are you? So very sorry to hear about your mum. Tell me, is there anything I can do? And don't tell me to let you come back to work. You are taking at least a week off, and that's that."

Jade said, "We're going to have to negotiate my return to work date as there's

266

no way I'm taking another week off. And I'm fine, thank you for asking. It gets just a little better each day and I think I may just get through it." Malcolm responded, "I'll tell you what, you come in for lunch with me Friday, and we'll talk about when you can come back." Jade considered this, and realized he was trying to make sure she would, at the least, be taking the rest of this week off. Jade knew he meant well, but she needed to work, and SOON! She countered, "How about I come in Wednesday for lunch, and discuss actually coming in to work by the end of the week." Malcolm knew he had been outmaneuvered, and conceded graciously. "That sounds good, twelve noon Wednesday. I'll see you then, honey, take care!"

He started to disconnect when Jade said, "Wait, there's one more thing I need to tell you. I've recently started dating a man, and I think, well, I think it could become serious. Can you give Mickey my regrets?" Malcolm chuckled. Oh, Jade, this IS good news! Just not for Mickey. I'll tell him. I'm sure he'll be heartbroken. No worries, mate, I want you to be happy. Bye!" Jade disconnected, feeling considerably better.

That dealt with, Jade decided it was time to get back to her Lawrence family research. She re-read her notes on the meeting with Kevin McInerny and was again struck by the thought that she should be putting something together about what he said at that meeting and what she already knew. She felt that this information wasn't just critical to her investigation, it could be important to her safety. But still the connection just wouldn't come.

Erin's diary told of three generations of murders, most of which were almost certainly the work of three generations of Lawrence family men. She knew that Timothy killed Trevor's wife Marie, then decades later, likely killed his own wife, leaving his son, Ben, without a mother. There was another rash of killings that started in the late 1920's, which could have been the by-that-time elderly Tim, but could have possibly been a young Ben. Then, starting in the late 1950's, and again in the late 1990's two more series. Jade knew that she had uncovered compelling evidence that the Lawrences were behind many of these murders, by her discovery of the Lawrence family crest, the Möbius symbol, on or near several victims, at least one from each of the series since the 1870's murders. And in the case of the more recent killings, Jade had found at least three victims from each series with the Möbius present on or near the body.

Jade also knew that, even though her stalker had been silent these last few days, once she started poking around his business again (and she would, of course), he would again be trying to stop her.

Jade spent a couple hours laying in bed, reading. Then she tried her father's number again. There was still no answer. Restless, and more than a little worried, Jade decided to take a ride over and check on him. When she pulled into her parents' driveway, Jade saw that her father's car was gone and the house was dark. She used her key to get in, then looked around. She saw nothing out of place, and nothing to tell her where her father had gone.

She picked up the phone call called Phyllis. She answered, "Hi Dad, how are you?" Jade corrected her. "Phyllis, it's me. I'm at the house, but dad's not here. His car is gone, too." Phyllis, who was never the first passenger on the worry train, said, "Well, Jade, I guess he's a big boy, and he had things to do. I'd go home and try to reach him again tomorrow, I'll bet he'll be back by then and will give you a very reasonable account of where he was today." Jade was stung by the sarcastic note in Phyllis' voice. Without answering, Jade dumped the phone receiver back in the cradle. Jade decided that, while she was here, she'd get a good look at what was on the bottom of the big blue vase. She went to the kitchen. The vase was gone! Jade couldn't ever remember it being gone before. It was more than a little odd.

Jade walked around the downstairs of the house, looking. There were only so many places a vase that size could be. Jade considered just letting it go. Her father had apparently gotten rid of it, or put it into storage or something. She decided she'd just check upstairs, and if it wasn't there, that would be that. She didn't find the vase upstairs, but what she did find shocked her. Her mother's side of her parents' bedroom was in shambles. Her underclothing was strewn across the floor and on the bed. Her armoire was open and everything in it had been ripped down and thrown in a pile on the floor. Jade couldn't imagine why her father had done this. Or, if it had not been her father, where he was while it was going on. And where he was right now? Jade began to worry that the destruction of her mother's things was somehow related to her father's disappearance.

On a hunch, Jade headed to the upstairs bathroom. There was a loose tile in the bathroom, behind the bathroom door, Jade knew. This was a secret compartment she and her mother used, back when Jade was a young girl, in the midst of her "detective girl" phase. Jade would tuck a secret note behind the tile. A few days later she would find that her note had been replaced with a response. She and her mother played this game for years. Jade always loved the fact that no one knew about this secret note repository. Not Phyllis and not her father. It was something special, just for Jade and Agatha. Jade pulled the loose tile down and there was a piece of folded paper inside! Jade's fingers shook as she pinched the paper and pulled it out. The writing was so messy, she barely recognized it as her mother's.

"Dear Jade,

If you are reading this, then I must have successfully taken my own life. I knew you'd remember our little game. There are a few things I must tell you. You must never tell your father that you know. It is vitally important that you trust me on this. I think he always suspected what I knew, but he never confronted me directly. I know that my decision to keep what I knew to myself was the right decision.

From a very early age, your brother Peter was a difficult child. You father was always strangely indulgent of him, I'm not sure if that was because he felt badly for him, or because he really didn't think anything was seriously wrong. But I always tried harder to keep Peter's more abnormal tendencies in check. Phyllis was always an unemotional, detached child, and she and Peter co-existed fairly easily, as neither cared much for the other, either way. But you, Jade, you were different. You loved your big brother, and you tried very hard to get him to love you back. Sometimes, I'd actually think you were succeeding.

But there was something so badly broken in Peter, you could never really reach him, and he was just human enough to have your efforts cause him pain and regret. The day he set your dress on fire, he took off for the woods and we didn't see him for hours. Your father finally went into the woods and brought him out. Peter was different after that day. Your father became even more tolerant of him after that and when I tried to suggest that something may be wrong with our son, your father was steadfast in his refusal to believe me. Then, when Peter was fifteen, he ran away. Do you remember? We found him three days later, in the woods, dazed and sick. He had blood all over him. What I didn't tell you then was that there was a woman living on the other side of those woods who was killed that week. She wasn't found until days after Peter was found, and luckily the police never made the connection. But I always felt that Peter killed that woman. And I think that may have only been the beginning of what he would later become."

Jade put the toilet seat down and sat heavily. She dropped the note and pulled her legs up, hugging them to her. Now she was beginning to understand the hell her mother was trying to live with, day by day. Alone. Jade remembered very well how indulgent her father had been of Peter, while they were growing up. Jade was suddenly very sad for her mother. And very angry with Peter as well as her father. She picked up the note from the bathroom floor and finished reading it.

"Jade, I told you about the trunk I found in Peter's closet, the one with women's clothing in it. And you remember the Old Port murder, of which Peter was suspected. And you know how cruel and unfeeling Peter has always been. I don't think I need to spell out what I feel in my heart to be true, but I will. I believe that Peter has become a cold-blooded killer. I feel like it was partly my fault. If I could have only taken his deviant behavior more seriously, and put my foot down when your father tried to rationalize away Peter's bad behavior, maybe everything could have been different. I'm sorry to have left you to deal with all of this. In the end, I just wasn't strong enough. I hope you can find it in your heart to forgive me. I love you, darling."

Jade folder the note and put it in her pocket. In a daze, she left for home. She found the right streets and obeyed the traffic laws on autopilot. Half way home, she looked in her rear-view mirror and realized that she had seen the same car behind her, at least three turns back. She was being followed. And the person who was following her wasn't taking any care to not be seen. Jade didn't want to go home while someone was following her. She wasn't sure if the person was Timothy, and if it wasn't and they didn't know where she lived, she didn't want to lead them to her home. Also, she thought, if she drove up to her house and made a mad dash for the front door, she may be caught before she could get into the house. Jade decided to keep driving, and think about how best to keep herself safe.

Instead of going home, Jade drove to the Police Department building on Congress Street. She parked directly in front of the building and fled inside. Just inside the first of the double doors, she stopped, turned around, and watched the street. The car that was following her slowed, the driver obviously having spotted her car, then they drove past very slowly. The car wasn't one she had seen before. It was a burgundy Firebird, maybe a 1995 or 1996. The windows were tinted, and she could only make out a vague shape in the driver's seat. The license plate was partially obscured with mud, probably purposely. Once the car had passed, Jade dashed back out, jumped into her Blazer, pulled an illegal U-turn in the middle of the road (in front of the police station, no less), and headed in the opposite direction. She drove straight to her house, knowing her pursuer would likely turn around and drive past the police station again, to try to spot her, and that may keep them occupied for a precious couple of minutes longer.

At home, she immediately armed her security system. Rummaging through her pockets, she found the note her mother had left behind the bathroom tile for her, and she read it again. Jade remembered that she didn't replace the tile in the bathroom and she wondered what her father would make of it, when and if he noticed it. She wondered if it was her father who destroyed her mother's things, and she wondered at the purpose. For some reason, the vase being gone, her father being missing and the disordered state of her mother's belongings in her parents' bedroom all seemed ominously related. After several minutes, it became clear to Jade that the person in the burgundy Firebird didn't follow her home and she began to relax.

272

Jade felt the need to connect with Diane, to make sure she was okay, to get an update on the possible bloom of romance between she and Brian, and to share with her the strange goings-on involving her father. Jade speed-dialed Diane's number and got voicemail. She left her a message. "Hi, Diane, it's me. I'm sorry I haven't been in touch since the funeral, I just needed some time. I'm starting to feel a little better, and I just wanted to check in with you, see what's going on with you and you-know-who, and tell you about some strange stuff that's going on with me. Call me when you get this message, okay? Love ya." Jade put her cell phone down slowly, lost in thought. Suddenly, she felt that it may have been irresponsible of her to not contact Diane for days, knowing how much danger they both could be in. First her father disappears and now…. Jade realized she was probably jumping to conclusions, but she couldn't shake her uneasiness.

The ringing of the telephone interrupted Jade's reverie. She checked the caller ID, then grabbed the receiver. It was Derrick. "Hey baby, how are you?" Jade smiled at the sound of his voice. "I'm better now. I've had a bit of a strange day." Sounding concerned, Derrick said, "What's up? Are you okay? Please don't tell me you've been playing detective without me?" His voice was teasing but Jade heard a more serious undertone. "No, I mean, well maybe a little. I couldn't reach my dad by phone, so I went over to my parents' house to check on him. Derrick, he wasn't there, and his really big family heirloom vase was gone from the kitchen, and my mother's stuff was completely trashed in their bedroom."

Jade instinctively didn't tell him about the note she had found from her mother. She didn't want Derrick to know anything more about Peter than he already did, and she hadn't yet worked through her mother's admission that she had, in fact, tried to kill herself. She hurriedly continued, "Then, on the way home from my parents', someone in a Firebird followed me. I parked in front of the police station and they drove by, then I rushed home." Derrick answered, "Good thinking, pulling up to the Police Station. But it worries me that someone was following you. Jade, my initial thought about your is that he just needed some time alone. Was his car missing also?"

Jaded told him it was. "He's probably just gone off for a day or two. And the missing vase may be put up in storage somewhere, maybe it reminded him of your mother and he just couldn't look at it anymore. Your mother's stuff being thrown around may have also been a show of grief and anger, on your dad's part, for your mother's 'leaving' him. Jade understood the likelihood in what he was saying, and she gratefully allowed herself to be at least partly convinced. "Yes, I'm sure you are right Derrick, it's probably nothing. I think I'm just freaked because I lost my mother so recently, I'm feeling overprotective of my dad now."

"Jade, you turned on your security system, right?" Jade confirmed that she did. "Okay, make sure your curtains are closed, just in case someone is watching you. I don't want you being any more of a target that necessary." Jade didn't like the sound of that word. Target. But that's exactly what she was. When she wasn't being that other thing. A sitting duck.

Derrick said, "I'm working tonight, so I'll be able to swing by and keep an eye on your house from time to time. I'll be done working at 3:00 A.M. I'll go home after work and crash for a few hours, then I'm coming over. Jade, I want you and Bardo to come over to my house for a few days. I have live-in help there, and my security system is state-of-the-art. Besides, I doubt that your stalker knows about me, or where I live yet. Are you willing to come and stay with me, just for now?" I won't be able to live with myself if something happens to you that I could have prevented." Jade started to refuse his offer, but before he hung up, Derrick extracted a promise from Jade to at least think about it.

Chapter 36

Jade knew it would make sense to get away, and it may actually help by allowing her to get around a little more easily, without worrying as much about being tracked down and followed. She'd need to be very careful when she was driving to Derrick's from her familiar haunts, like her office, where Timothy could pick up her trail. She knew she'd have to keep Diane as safe as she could, also. She wondered what Diane would think of Derrick's house.

Sitting at the kitchen table with a cup of tea, Jade went through her stack of bills and realized some of them were overdue. "Tough week", she thought to herself, forgiving herself for the lapse, and hoping her creditors would too. She reached into her purse for her checkbook, and instead her hand passed over something hard, on the inside of her purse. Puzzled, she took her hand out and looked inside, but didn't see anything odd. She put her hand back in and felt the strange lump again. It was inside the lining of her purse, which had been torn away from the side, then replaced to look undamaged. Jade suddenly felt cold all over. She pulled the ripped lining away and brought the object out.

It looked like a tiny knob, no bigger than the tip of her pinkie finger. She put the object on the kitchen table and put a dish towel over it. She knew, instinctively, that this must be one of the ways that Timothy always seemed to know where she was. It also occurred to her that the transmitter, or whatever it was, was probably put in her purse the night her house was broken into and the diary stolen from her kitchen table, she knew her purse had been sitting on the table also. She recalled the trip to Bangor, and how Brian was attacked in the parking lot and suddenly realized how Timothy had tracked her. And now he also knew about Diane, she realized. God damn it! She thought about where she had been, since the day the diary had been stolen from her house. Suddenly alarmed, she recalled her visit with Kevin DeLayne last week, at Kevin's best friend's house, but then she remembered that she had left her purse at home that day. Thank God! Unfortunately, it was now likely that Timothy knew where Derrick lived now.

Jade's next thought was to call Derrick. Being a police officer, he would know what to do. She dialed his cell number, but her call went directly to voicemail. She left a message, trying to keep the panic she felt out of her voice. The idea of the little electronic spy in her purse made Jade feel exposed. She put her purse in the kitchen broom closet and shut the door firmly. She felt better almost immediately.

She had left Diane a message earlier and now needed more than ever to talk to her. It was unlike her to not call right back. She wanted to jump in her truck and go to Diane's house, to check on her, but knew that she may be followed. If Timothy didn't know where Diane lived yet, she didn't want to lead him there.

To get her mind off her worries, she decided to do some on-line research. She booted up her laptop and connected to the internet. It was definitely time for her to find out everything she could about the most recent members of the Lawrence clan. Specifically, Ben, Daniel and Dillon. Ultimately, she knew her search of Timothy's family may lead to a better understanding of Timothy himself. She felt instinctively that her very life, and that of Diane as well, may depend on her ability to understand this sick excuse for a man, and what drove him.

She would start with the family crest website on which she had stumbled earlier. The home page loaded, much slower than it did on Malcolm's office computer. Jade first started checking the hyperlinks. Even though her laptop was slow, she knew it was safer to stay put, inside her alarmed fortress, and tough it out, just she and her dial-up system.

Jade started her search with Ben, Daniel and Dillon. After several frustrating minutes spent chasing down dead-ends, she finally found an on-line birth and death registry which looked useful. Ben's girlfriend, Alois, Jade learned, was the youngest daughter of the Reynolds family of Falmouth, Maine. It was clear that she had the right person as Alois was exactly the right age, and she was the only woman (or man, for that matter!) with that unusual name listed in the records. In 1935, in the town of Manchester, New Hampshire, twin boys were born to a woman named Alois Reynolds. As further confirmation, there was no father listed, which was relatively rare in those days. The boys' names were Dillon and Daniel. The records indicated that they were put up for adoption, to different homes, at birth, as their mother had died shortly after their birth. Dillon was adopted by a family named McKee, but, within several months, the adoption was rescinded and Dillon was placed in an orphanage. From there, Dillon's trail went cold.

Daniel was a bit easier to trace. Daniel was adopted, and he had apparently stayed with that family. Jade found it interesting that, when Daniel was 18, he divested himself of his adopted name and claimed his birth name, but when he divorced his wife, Lianne, 1979, he made it part of the divorce agreement that neither Lianne nor Timothy, his son, would be permitted to use the Lawrence family name.

At first glance, Jade thought it petty and selfish that Daniel would no longer be willing to share his last name with his former wife and child. Then, she realized that, sometime between 1953 and 1979, Daniel probably found out about the Lawrence family curse. He may have been trying to keep Lianne and Timothy from being part of the Lawrence family, for their own protection. Jade also found documentation, several years after the divorce of his parents, that Timothy Lawry changed his name back to Timothy Lawrence. Jade thought it was likely that, by that time, Timothy knew who and what he was, and thought it appropriate to take back his cursed birthright. Jade then turned her attention back to Dillon.

Jade checked the name of the orphanage in the city directories, but there were no listings. She went back to the family crest website and clicked on the name "Dillon Lawrence" on the genealogy tree she had found before. Scant information came up. Born 1935, raised in Maine, New Hampshire and Great Britain. Alumnus, University of Maine, class of 1960. Jade read that information again, sure that she was mistaken. But she wasn't. Jade realized that this man would have gone to school with her father! She made a mental note to ask her father if he may have known Dillon Lawrence. Of course, assuming she could FIND her father! Jade found no information about when Dillon took the Lawrence name back. She suspected that it had to be between 1953 and 1959, as that the police report documenting the altercation between Dillon and Daniel in the Western Promenade cemetery was dated the late 1950's.

So, both of Ben's sons took the Lawrence family name back, and both of them lived at least part of their adult lives in the same area as Ben Lawrence. Yet Ben didn't know about them until recently. Jade wondered when exactly Daniel found out about Ben and when and if Dillon ever knew about Ben. On the face of it, it seemed strange that there wasn't a Lawrence family reunion long before now.

But, Jade reasoned, if Dillon is a killer, the only other person on Earth who could identify him as such may be his father, Ben. So why seek him out? Unless maybe to kill him. Suddenly, the whole situation felt a bit more complicated. It was also possible that Dillon's twin brother, Daniel had no pressing reason to seek out his father for many years, but then maybe Daniel found out about the family secret and he sought out Ben, his biological father, for answers.

Then Jade made an alarming connection. What if, while she was trying to track down Dillon, he had somehow tracked HER down? It would explain why there were different vehicles following her. Maybe Timothy had help. It would also explain why initially, it didn't seem as if the person who was stalking her meant to kill her, but now that seemed to have changed. Maybe there were *two* stalkers, and the one newest to the game was much more deadly to her. The thought was chilling. She hoped she was wrong.

Jade checked one more on-line resource, linked from the family crest website. The link contained an email address that Jade could use to contact the library in Great Britain where there were more Lawrence family references. Jade requested that they email her back a list of the additional books and reference articles she could consult to learn more about the family.

After taking several pages of notes, Jade logged off the computer. She rubbed her tired eyes and glanced at her watch, amazed to find two hours had passed. As she stood up to stretch, her telephone rang. She realized that the telephone was out of commission while she was on-line and the person who was calling may have been trying to reach her. A spark of hope flared, it may be her father calling. Then she as realized it was well after 9:00 and he likely wouldn't call this late. She checked the caller ID, it was Diane. She grabbed it on the second ring. "Hi, girlfriend." Diane's voice was a welcome sound. "Hey Jade! I'm sorry I didn't get back to you earlier, I was with Brian." The lilting tone in Diane's voice spoke volumes about those two little words, 'with Brian". Jade felt almost maternal satisfaction in seeing Diane happy.

Jade said, "Well, then, I forgive you." Diane laughed, and the bubbly excitement in Diane's voice meant that things must be going well. Diane's next comment confirmed it. "Jade, I can't remember being this happy. We've spent almost every minute together, for the past week, and things just keep getting better. I know he's spent the past couple of years dealing with the death of his step-daughter, then the breakup of his marriage. Now, I think he's ready to move forward, and take back some who he used to be. I'm hoping to be part of that process.

Jade was happy for her friend, but at the moment, more concerned with putting her fully in the picture about what had been happening. "Diane, I'm so happy for you!" Jade's voice turned more serious. "Listen, do you have a few minutes, I need to tell you about something. First, have you had any problems with anyone following your or anything?" Diane said she hadn't but immediately realized something must have happened with Jade. Jade's voice shook with fear and anger. "I found what I think is a transmitter of some kind hidden in the lining of my purse. I think whoever broke into my house a couple of weeks ago didn't just take Erin's diary, I think they put this little device in my purse, too."

Diane immediately understood the implication. "So, where have you been, in the past two weeks, with your purse?" Jade's frustration boiled over. "Just about everywhere! I'm not even sure it's a transmitter. It could be some kind of recording device, or, well, I just don't know!" Diane said, "Well, Christ, I hope it's not a recording device. If it is, then your stalker knows just about everything that we know. And if that's the case, he won't let us live much longer. Not knowing what we know." Diane was scared, Jade could hear it. That's exactly what she was thinking. Diane said, "That's how the asshole was able to track us to Bangor and put a hurt on Brian!" Jade said, "Yeah, that's what I figured too. I tried to call Derrick earlier but couldn't reach him. I'll try again later. I know he's going to want to know about this A.S.A.P. Meanwhile, I have a couple other things to tell you." Diane, ever the smartass, said, "What, having some kind of spy thingy planted in your purse wasn't enough?"

Jade said, "I've been trying to reach my father on the phone for a couple days, but he wasn't calling me back, so I went over there earlier today. He's not there, his vehicle is gone, and it didn't look like he had been there for at least a day or two." Diane said, "He's probably taking a day or two off, getting away by himself to try to make sense of things." Jade said, "That's exactly what Derrick said. But Diane, when I went over there, the saw that the big blue vase was gone. Remember the big blue vase that was always in the kitchen at my parents' house?" Diane confirmed that she did.

"Well, when my mother was hit by the car, and I was with her in the road, she said something like 'ask your father about the vase'. I went over to my parents' house, while my mother was in the hospital, and tried to get a good look at the vase without my dad seeing me. He caught me, and he seemed to panic. He literally shooed me away from it. I found it odd at the time, but knew he was under a lot of stress. So when I went to my parents house earlier today and found my father missing, I thought it would be a good time to take another look at the vase. I went into the kitchen to see it, and it was gone!

Diane spoke up. "Well, is it possible that your dad considers the vase a reminder of your mother, and he put it up somewhere, so that he didn't have to look at it?" Jade heard the note of concern in Diane's voice. "No, I doubt it. The vase was a family heirloom of my father's, and had nothing to do with my mother. I honestly think my dad did something with it to keep me from seeing it." Jade knew she sounded defensive, but couldn't help it.

"That's not all. I went upstairs, thinking perhaps that my dad was upstairs taking a nap" (yeah, probably a DIRT nap, a sly voice in her head taunted), "but I didn't find him. What I DID find were my mother's belongings, thrown all over my parents' bedroom. It looked as if someone were very angry. I thought maybe my father was venting some completely justified rage. But even so, there was just something very 'off' about the way everything was left. I went into the bathroom and looked behind a loose tile my mom and I used to use to pass notes back and forth when I was a little girl, and there was a note in there, from my mother."

Diane's hushed voice said, "Was it an old note, like, from ago, or was it something recent?" Jade pulled the note out and read it to Diane. There was a thoughtful pause over the phone line, then Diane finally said, "Your mother was convinced that Peter was a killer. I'm still not convinced of that. Jade, what you and I know, and what your mother didn't know, is that the person who killed that woman in the Old Port, who your mother apparently believes was killed by Peter, was actually Timothy. I don't know everything that happened when you and Peter were kids, but I know enough to realize that Peter was one seriously messed up young dude. But a murderer? I'm not buying that without a whole lot more proof."

Jade was thankful for Diane's straightforward point of view, and surprised to realize that she shared it. But she had one more thing to tell Diane. "I agree with you. One more thing. When I left my parents' house, I was followed. This time, it was a burgundy-colored Firebird. I didn't go straight home, in case whoever was following me wasn't Timothy and didn't yet know where I lived. Instead, I drove to the police station, parked in front and ran inside. The Firebird drove on. The windows were tinted so I couldn't see the driver. When they turned the corner, I jumped back in my Blazer and rushed home."

Jade told Diane about Derrick's offer to let her stay with him for a few days. Diane was intrigued. "He lives in Falmouth?" "Falmouth Foreside", Jade said dryly. Diane picked up on the sarcasm. "Hey, there's nothing wrong with a guy who's got a little money. If I were you, I'd get my cute little butt over there, and take advantage of this mini-vacation, play house with your man for a few days. Who knows, it may just grow on you. Besides, you need some TLC therapy these days. " Before Jade could even think of a response, Diane said, "Hey, I've got another call on the other line, gotta jet, girl. I'll call you back soon. Love ya."

She suddenly realized that she never got a chance to tell Diane what she found in her on-line search earlier, about the Lawrence family. She picked up her notes and briefly looked them over. There wasn't anything obviously Earth-shaking, but a couple intriguing things did surface and some of it provided confirmation for information she found using other sources.

Jade thought about the current relationship between the three living Lawrence men. Ben had recently found out about Daniel, but likely never knew about Dillon. Ben also knew that Daniel had a son, Timothy, who Ben had already begun to realize was a "bad apple". Jade was beginning to feel as though Daniel may have been one of those apparently rare occurrences, a GOOD Lawrence man. She wasn't sure what kind of man Ben was. Looking at the pattern of murders didn't really help. The killings that occurred in the 1910's and 1920's could have been Tim's (of the Tim and Trevor era), or possibly Ben's. The killings from the late 1950's and up could have been Dillon's. Timothy, she was quite sure, was responsible for the current murders.

Tonight's on-line research was well worth it, but not sleep-promoting. Jade tossed and turned. Sleep, however, continued to evade her. Images of the Lawrence family swirled through Jade's mind. She thought about Erin, and about all the other possible victims of this very unusual family. It had become as possible as not that Jade herself could become another victim. Jade decided then and there to take Derrick up on his offer. In fact, she may even ask him if Diane could come along. That decided, Jade finally drifted into an uneasy sleep.

When she next opened her eyes, the room was almost pitch dark, save for the red glowing numerals on her alarm clock, and the gray light coming in through her bedroom window. Jade's eyes began to drift shut, then she felt a rush of air next to her and her eyes flew open. Someone was standing next to her bed! She froze. This couldn't be happening! She had set the security alarm and the downstairs motion sensors before she went to bed. Be calm!, she told herself. She tried desperately to make out the shadow beside her bed.

Her heart racing, Jade tried to lay very still, hoping the intruder couldn't see that her eyes were open, and, she was sure, looking terrified. The intruder bent slowly toward her, his face moving to within inches of hers. She realized that he could surely see her eyes now, and she shifted her gaze to his face. In her extreme fear, it took her a moment to recognize the face before her. It was her father! She locked eyes with him and saw the sparkle of tears in his eyes, and the wet tracks down his cheeks. He reached out a hand and laid it gently against the side of Jade's face, continuing to look at her. His facial expression belied his gesture. All but his eyes were cast in shadow, but Jade was sure she could see anger in his eyes. And something more. Regret?

Jade opened her mouth to speak, but he put his index finger against her lips, indicating that she must remain silent. A movement beside her father drew her attention. A figure to the side and behind her father, was moving toward them. Suddenly, he was grabbed from behind and pulled back, out of her view. The physical altercation was strangely quiet, and Jade realized that she may be dreaming. She tried unsuccessfully to wake herself. Then she felt cold hands around her neck. The hands tightened, first restricting then completely cutting off her air. She knew she had precious few moments before she would lose consciousness. She used her nails to rake the face of her attacker. He abruptly loosened his hands and recoiled, hissing with pain. Jade sat up, readying herself for another onslaught.

But the stranger had no intention of renewing his attack. Instead he backed away from her, into the shadows. As the figure retreated from her, it turned gossamer. She saw him look down at his hands, his face twisted in horror. The fading eyes glanced her way, for a brief moment, then vanished. It was her father's face, with scratches she knew she had put there. Jade frantically searched every corner of the room. She was alone. Whatever was happening was, thankfully, over. She found it odd that her dream featured her father attacking her, and also attacking himself. She instinctively felt that her subconscious mind was trying to tell her something. Some time later, she drifted back into troubled sleep.

Sunday

Jade woke to a bright and cold Sunday morning. After taking care of her chores, she felt ready to tackle something more substantial. She realized that, day by day, she was coming to grips with the loss of her mother and her brother. Oddly, the feeling made her sad. Since she hadn't heard from her father yet, she called her parents' house again. As she waited for the call to connect, she remembered the dream she had last night. She wondered why her mind would construct a scenario where her father would hurt her. Probably, having someone stalking her, and trying to kill her, would cause that kind of subconscious fallout.

She listened as the line rang through to her parents' house. She knew that her parents used the toll-saver device on their answering machine, which would ring twice when there were messages, four times when there were not. Now, the phone rang four times, indicating that the pending messages had been retrieved. Jade left another message for her father and disconnected, her unease renewed and growing.

Jade sat at the kitchen table, thinking worriedly about where her father could be. She knew she should probably try Phyllis again. But she didn't feel like dealing with Phyllis' condescending indifference right now. If her father didn't call her back by tonight, she supposed she'd have to call Phyllis. She realized how dysfunctional it was to have to be worried completely sick over their dad in order to work up the will to call her sister.

The doorbell broke Jade's reverie. She walked to the front door and pulled the curtain aside to see who it was. Derrick! Jade's heart surged. She opened the door and stood back so he could come in. Instead, he turned and snaked his arms around her, pulling her to him. Holding her, he pushed the door shut and leaned his back against it. His mouth tasted like coffee when he kissed her. Jade purred against his mouth and he broke the kiss, laughing. "That's the kind of welcome a man can learn to get used to!" Jade looked into his eyes, saw the truth in what he said and decided now was the time to tell him she had decided to stay with him for a few days. Before she could form the words, he said, "Have you thought about my offer?" He read her mind! "I would be absolutely thrilled to spend a few days at Chez Zachary. And I appreciate your kind offer, sir!" Derrick grinned. "Well then, pack your bags, baby. Your chariot awaits!"

Jade's suddenly remembered the little electronic gadget she had found in her purse. She didn't know if this further evidence of her troubles may impact his offer of shelter, but she felt the need for full disclosure, in any event. "Derrick, I need to tell you about something. I found a tiny little electronic device in my purse last night. I think it was some kind of tracker. I left a message for you on your cell, but it was pretty late and I know you were working." Derrick looked stricken. He said, "I did drive by your house a few times last night to check on things, but I had my cell phone off and didn't think to check my messages. I'm so sorry! I would have been right over here if I had known about this." Jade was quick to reassure him. "Don't worry about it, I'm a big girl. I'm betting that this thing has been in my purse for several days now. Which is what worries me. I was at your house, Friday night, with this *thing* in my purse. He may already know where you live." Jade looked at the floor, waiting for Derrick's reaction.

When it came, it wasn't at all what she expected. "Shit! This is beyond asinine. Show me, I want to see it." Wordlessly, Jade got her purse out of the kitchen closet, opened it, pulled aside the ripped nylon lining and, without touching it, showed Derrick where it was. He pulled a plastic glove out of his jacket pocket and slipped it on, then gingerly removed the tiny device. He held it up to the light and looked it over thoroughly, then had Jade get him a small plastic zip bag to put it in. "That's definitely a transmitter. It's providing location and movement information to a receiver. Usually these things have a fairly limited range for signal reception. He would probably have to be located within a mile of you in order to pick up the signal. I was afraid that it may also be a sound recorder, but I don't think it is."

Derrick continued. "Now that we've removed the transmitter from your purse, the person who is tracking you may realize that you found it, and that he's potentially being backtracked. I have a good friend who also happens to be an electronics whiz. If it's okay with you, I'm going to run this over to him, right now, hopefully before our perp knows he's been outted, and see if we can track him down before he disconnects the receiver." Jade felt relieved to have a plan, but also worried about the danger. "Definitely that's the way to go. One question, though. Once we locate him, what will we do?" Derrick's expression turned dark. "I won't tell you what I'd like to do to him, and what I'll definitely do to him if he gives me any reason whatsoever." Jade didn't need him to spell that out.

Jade said, "What I'm saying is that, if this guy *is* a Lawrence, he's killed before and wouldn't hesitate to kill again. To keep ourselves from becoming his next victims, I think it would make sense for us to find out who it is but not to do anything with that information for the time being." Derrick looked at Jade, skepticism clearly written on every feature. "Are you telling me that you don't want to take down the guy that's been threatening you? He tried to kill you! It may be him or us, Jade. What *I'm* saying is, if it comes down to that, it'll be him." Jade heard the chill in Derrick's voice. Jade hurried to calm him. "I understand, and I agree with you. But if we can just find out who it was, I don't think we need to confront him right away. If we do, without more than circumstantial evidence of his other crimes, the most punishment he'll get is a slap on the wrist. And confronting him now would only give him more reason to get rid of us. Derrick considered this. "Okay, I get that. You have a point. Let's just find out who and where he is. We can come back later and pick up Bardo and your stuff."

Outside a small, dilapidated house on Danforth Street, Derrick and Jade sat in Derrick's truck. "When I called him, he said it was okay to come right over. Jade, he's a quiet, shy person. He probably won't talk to you directly. He's extremely bright, but also, unfortunately, extremely OCD. He was also diagnosed as mildly Autistic, as a child, so he has unusual ways of relating to others. He's the walking poster boy for "otherly abled". His so called 'disabilities' actually help him focus to a degree that we can't even imagine. He'll get stressed out if you confront him." Intrigued, Jade agreed to follow Derrick's lead and together they crossed the littered yard and knocked at the decrepit front door. Before Derrick's hand left the door knocker, the door swung open.

Standing in the open doorway was one of most handsome men Jade had ever seen. Remembering what Derrick said, she was careful not to stare. She moved slightly behind Derrick and cast her eyes downward. Derrick spoke more softly than Jade had ever heard him. "Hi, Michael, thank you for agreeing to help us." Michael mumbled something inaudible and moved aside for his guests. Sitting at the kitchen table, Michael was all business. "Let's see it." Derrick passed him the plastic bag containing the device and Michael held it up, bag and all, to the light. "Did you fingerprint it?" Derrick told him that he had not. Without comment, Michael pulled a small, flat black case out of a drawer behind him and proceeded to fingerprint the tiny device.

"There's a print here", Michael said quietly. Derrick immediately perked up. Jade, however, realized the print was probably hers. She looked at Derrick. "I touched it when I removed it from my purse, the print may be mine." Michael, continuing to look down at the table, said, "Do you remember which fingers touched it?" Jade held out her right hand, and extended only her index finger and thumb. Michael gently brushed her fingers, then pressed them on to a piece of paper. While Jade washed off the powder, Michael used a magnifying glass to compare the prints. "It's hers", he said, jabbing a finger in Jade's direction. Jade felt absurdly like she had just flunked a test. "I'm sorry, I didn't mean to destroy evidence." Michael finished looking at the device and said, "There weren't any other fingerprints on it anyway, you didn't destroy anything."

After Michael finished his examination of the exterior of the device, he went to work opening it. Within a few minutes, it was open, the inner wiring exposed. Michael said, "Some of these remote trackers have a dead-man switch on them, so if the processor is removed, it trips an alarm to alert the person who planted it that someone is attempting to access the chip. The alarm is often set up with an automatic kill switch so if it's tripped, the connection between this unit and the receiver is automatically severed. I have a tool that will keep the alarm from tripping by keeping the switch depressed even after the processor is removed."

Jade watched Michael intently. Michael apparently knew exactly what he was doing. He gently coaxed the tiny spatulate tool into the space between the processor and the switch underneath. After the tool was placed, he removed the processor. Michael then left the kitchen, taking the processor with him. After a few minutes, Derrick went to check on him. They both came out together within a minute or two. Derrick was holding a piece of paper. "Michael used GPS and Google Earth, and was able to track the coordinates of the receiver to this address." Derrick passed Jade the paper. "It's the address to the Payson-Smith Hall at USM." Jade didn't know of any connection Timothy had with USM, but she immediately recalled a connection between Dillon and USM. Her on-line research last night uncovered the fact that Dillon was apparently a graduate of USM. Jade went very still. Several puzzle pieces snapped into place as she suddenly recalled other connections involving USM. Mrs. Pelletieri had said that she tracked the murder of her daughter to someone she thought was an employee at USM, which used to be called University of Maine at Portland. Mrs. Augerbois' husband told Jade that, the night his wife went missing, she had said she was going out to speak with some kind of shrink or teacher over to the University. DeLayne McInerny, another likely victim, was a criminal justice professor at the University. This, she knew, was the elusive connection she had been searching for since she met with Mr. McInerny. Then Jade recalled another USM connection. Her own father taught there.

The world swam out of focus for a moment as Jade stopped to consider this new information. Derrick watched Jade carefully. "Jade, what is it?" Jade told him about the several ways her investigation intersected with the University. He found it odd, but not necessarily indicative. "This is a small town, much of life here centers around the University." Jade agreed with him, but still felt that five coincidences such as these were not coincidence at all. She suddenly wished she could talk to her dad, to lay out the information she had uncovered and ask him if any of it meant anything to him. Derrick and Jade thanked Michael for his help and they climbed back into the truck.

Jade suddenly remembered something she wanted to talk to Derrick about. "Derrick, did you know that the police department apparently knew about the possible connection between several murders, almost 2 years and at least 3 murders ago?" Jade watched Derrick's face tighten in anger. He shot her an almost hostile look and said, "Where did you hear that?" Jade hastened to explain. "When Diane and I met with Nate Small a couple weeks ago, he said that the police report on his wife's death contained a note that there were other previous, similar deaths. Storm clouds continued to build in Derrick's expression. "I can't imagine that something like that wasn't followed up, Jade. If he's right, it would have resulted in a much larger investigation, and one in which I would likely have been involved, either as a primary or as back up for others who were tagged for the investigative team. Of course, it's possible that a potential connection between victims was investigated and dismissed."

"I'll tell you what. I'll pull the file on the Small murder, and see what I can find out." Jade was thankful for Derrick's open minded response and told him so. Derrick made a quick phone call, speaking in a kind of cop-shorthand, flipped his cell phone closed and looked over at Jade. "I'm having my partner Leo email the Small file to my PPD inbox. When we get to my house later, I can review it." The remainder of their ride to Jade's house was spent in thoughtful silence.

At Jade's house, they quickly gathered up items needed for Jade's stay with Derrick. Derrick took all of Bardo's things, except his favorite toy squeaky bone, with which he absolutely would not part. Derrick pulled out on to the road, Jade following close behind. In Jade's Blazer, Bardo stood on his hind legs, on Jade's lap, squeaky toy dangling all but forgotten in his jaws, and watched as their home slipped from sight. He made little distressed whining sounds, and Jade cuddled him as best she could as she drove.

At Derrick's house, Jade put Bardo down on the kitchen floor, and he immediately got busy sniffing out his temporary new home. Jade's cell phone rang and she rescued it from her purse, flipping it open on the third ring.

"Hey Jade, where you at, girl?" Diane. "Hey PD, I'm at Derrick's house. Bardo and I decided to take him up on his offer and hang out here for a few days. Where are you?" There was a pause, and Jade could hear Diane talking to someone. "Sorry, I was talking to Brian, I'm at his house." Jade immediately felt better knowing Diane was many miles away from here, and probably far removed from any Lawrence family members. She decided not to ask Diane if she wanted to also stay at Derrick's. By the sound of it, she was all set.

Jade quickly told Diane about what she and Derrick had found out about the transmitter, and about the other USM connections. Diane's reaction was much closer to her own than Derrick's had been. "Jesus, that's creepy. It's more than creepy. It's definitely important and it may be the key to this whole thing. So the only connection between the Lawrences and USM is that Dillon may have graduated from there" Jade said, "That's the only connection that I know of, and it isn't Timothy's connection, it's Dillon's. Diane, what I'm afraid of is…" Diane interrupted, as was her habit. "I know! You are worried that, if you can't find some kind of connection between Timothy and USM, it must mean that Dillon is also stalking you." Jade felt reassured that Diane understood.

Derrick was listening to Jade's side of the conversation, a look of worry on his handsome features. She finished her conversation with Diane and flipped her cell phone closed. Derrick took Jade into his arms and looked down into her eyes. "Listen, I didn't mean to make light of the USM connections you found. I agree that it's pretty weird. And like you just told Diane, it could mean that Dillon is now stalking you. I just want you to know how glad I am that you're here. I have the next two days off from work, and I'm going to use the time to help you gather whatever information we can, to nail whoever's after you."

Jade snuggled closer to Derrick, enjoying the warm, solid feel of him. "I want your help, Derrick, but I also need to gather whatever hard evidence I can on the murders. I have a pretty good idea of who committed each of the murders I know about. But I realize that just having a 'pretty good idea' isn't going to cut it. The key to my long-term survival, and potentially that of Diane, may be in getting the Lawrences off the street. Otherwise, I can't imagine they will just decide to leave me alone. I already know too much, and they obviously realize it. So while you are gathering evidence on who's stalking me, you won't mind if I'm trying to solve the murders, will you?"

Jade said this in a partly joking manner, but when Derrick didn't respond, she turned her face up to look at his expression. He looked worried and angry, in about equal measure. "Jade, you're treating this like some kind of game! I know you understand that you are in danger. I'm just not convinced that you understand *how much* danger." Derrick dragged his hand distractedly through his thick silver hair. "I can't protect you if I don't know where you are and what you are doing so keep me in the loop. Capisce?" Jade reluctantly agreed. "But", she said forcefully, "this does NOT mean that you have the right tell me what I can and can't do. *Capisce?*" Derrick agreed, but Jade could see by his expression that he'd likely keep her from doing anything he didn't agree with, by sheer force if need be. Which was fine because Jade had crossed her fingers when she agreed to tell him everything. Fair was fair.

Derrick and Jade put together a simple dinner of steak, salad and red wine. Jade tried unsuccessfully not to overly enjoy the homey feel of preparing a meal with Derrick. She knew she had to face what she was feeling for him, one day soon. But today was not that day. After dinner, Derrick showed Jade his office, and logged into his computer. "Let's see if Leo's on the ball." Jade watched Derrick type, marveling again at how nimble his fingers were, flying confidently around the keyboard. His work email screen began to load and Jade suddenly realized that much of what may be in his inbox could be confidential, so she moved her chair from beside Derrick until she was sitting off to the side. She could see Derrick's face but could not see the computer screen. Derrick looked up and smiled at her. He looked back at his screen and his smile faded, replaced by a quizzical expression. Then, as Jade watched, his face turned stony. Jade watched quietly, hoping that Derrick was reading something completely unrelated to her issues with the Lawrences. Her hope faded when he looked at her and ground out "How did the murder weapon from the Ben Lawrence crime scene end up in your truck, Jade?"

Chapter 37

Jade looked at Derrick, stunned. How could he know about that? Realizing how guilty her face probably looked, she immediately tried to clear her expression of all emotion. Derrick watched her carefully. "Jade, look at this." Derrick turned the screen to face Jade. "I just found this picture in my email mailbox. I recognize the box of squeaky toys you keep in the back of your truck for Bardo. This email is a picture of back compartment of your truck, and the bag contains a wooden table leg." Jade could see that, like the picture she received in the mail, the bag sagged away from the table leg, so that more than half of it was exposed, including the ornately carved portion. Derrick continued, his voice tight with anger, "The reason I know it's from Ben Lawrence's house is that I memorized the carving pattern on it, having had to look through everything in his apartment for it. I need to know, *right now*, how you got this, and where it is now."

Jade stood up and began pacing the length of the room. When she was as far away from Derrick as she could get, she turned to face him. "That picture was also sent to me, but not by email. I found a hard copy of it in my mailbox, the day after Diane and I went to Freeport shopping together. When I saw the picture, I realized that someone had planted something in the back of my truck. I ran out to my truck and retrieved it. I knew it had to be what killed Ben Lawrence. Derrick, I wanted to call you so much. But I knew it was going to be a pretty tough sell to make you believe that I found it in my truck and that I had nothing to do with Ben Lawrence's death."

Jade stopped talking and looked squarely into Derrick's eyes. "I burned it, and the pictures too." She looked away from Derrick's piercing stare and waited for his reaction. He asked an unexpected question. "You said 'pictures'. How many pictures were there and what were the other ones?" Jade thought back. "One was of Diane and I in Freeport. There was one other picture, it was of Ben Lawrence just after he had been killed, but before the drawing on the wall behind him was done." Derrick nodded, obviously thinking. Jade wondered whether he was going to accept her explanation, after all. He said, "Jade, I know you didn't have anything to do with Ben Lawrence's murder. I just wish you hadn't destroyed that evidence! God! That could have contained trace evidence. Do you have any idea what you've done?"

Confused, Jade asked, "How are you so sure I didn't have any part in Ben's murder?" Derrick answered, "Because part of my job was to check out all viable suspects. You were, at one point, a suspect, and I had to verify your whereabouts at the time the crime was committed and I did that, and eliminated you as a suspect." Jade felt immediate relief. "Derrick, I don't know how I feel about you suspecting me of this, even initially. I guess you were just doing your job. I'm thankful now that you did your homework then. And I wish I hadn't destroyed that evidence. I feel like a complete idiot!" Derrick stood and, in four long strides, had folded Jade into his arms. Jade, who needed more reassurance than could be given in a vertical position, took the lead in seeking reassurance of a more horizontal variety.

Two hours later, after lovemaking, a short nap and a long, languorous shower, both Derrick and Jade were back at the computer. This time, Derrick found what he had been looking for earlier. Gavin Leo had emailed him the Small file. Derrick used a de-encryption program, then began paging through the file. Derrick was, Jade knew, looking for any evidence that the police may have connected the several murders that had been happening in the area. Jade also realized that, since there was no indication that the police were even now treating the murders as related, Derrick would also be looking for confirmation that the police had suspected a link between the deaths, then subsequently ruled it out.

Jade sat across from Derrick, watching his eyes scan the computer screen. From where she sat, she couldn't see the screen, but could see his reaction to what he was reading. Derrick stopped scanning, seeming to find something particularly interesting, then told Jade that he found the report that was filed by the investigating officer the day after the Small murder. There was a hand-written note in the margin and Derrick read it out loud. "Mr. Small has repeatedly asked this investigating officer to determine whether the death of his wife is connected to several other murders that have taken place in recent months in this area. See addendum." The note was dated October 21, 2002, the day after the murder.

Derrick watched the blood drain from Jade's face. "What's wrong, Jade?" For a moment, Jade couldn't speak. She very specifically remembered Nate Small telling her that, at the time his wife died, he had no idea that there had been other deaths. He said that when he read the police report, weeks or months later, he discovered from reading the police report that there had been other similar deaths. Nate Small had lied to her. He already knew about the other murders when his wife was killed. He must have thought that Jade would never see the police report. At the time of his wife's death, he obviously mentioned the other murders to try to deflect suspicion from himself. Then he pretended he didn't know about the other murders until well after his wife was killed, when he was talking with Jade. Nate's lie could have been one of opportunity, or it could have been his effort to conceal the fact that he, himself, murdered his wife.

Finally, Derrick's concerned voice pierced Jade's thoughts. "Hey, what is it?"

Jade told him about Nate Small's inconsistent story. Derrick immediately grasped the seriousness of Jade's revelation. "Shit! Either Nate Small is a pathological liar with a persecution complex or he's a murderer!"

Relieved that Derrick didn't think her completely mad, Jade nodded. "Well, we're going to need to do something about that. I'll look through the rest of the reports and documentation to see if anything suggest Nate Small as his wife's killer. I'll look for that addendum. Once I get everything together, I'll talk to the captain, and see if he'll look into it. I know it may not be what you want to hear, but in order to take this case to the next level, we need some kind of evidence. This lie that Small told you is incriminating, but it doesn't prove anything. Meanwhile, I still want to find out whether the other homicides that fit this M.O. were ever investigated as a series." As Derrick was speaking, he was paging through documentation and peering intensely at the screen. His words slowed to a trickle, then stopped. Jade headed to the kitchen to make a pot of coffee. It might be a long night.

At 2:00 A.M. Bardo padded silently into Derrick's office and laid down at his feet. The motion startled Derrick, who was dozing over his keyboard. He logged out of the computer, and headed up to bed. He smiled and quickened his step when he remembered the warm, sexy woman waiting in his bed.

Monday

The next morning, Jade woke to dappled sunlight on the ceiling. Bardo was sitting in the bedroom doorway, anxiously watching her. She slid gently out of bed, extricating herself from beneath Derrick's arm and his leg. Without Derrick's body heat, the room was chilly. She pulled a pair of Derrick's sweat pants on under her nightgown. Downstairs, Jade pulled on a jacket and boots, and clipped on Bardo's collar. After a quick run around the backyard, Jade led Bardo back into the warmth of the kitchen. The smell of hazelnuts met her. Someone had apparently made coffee. "I could get used to this," she sighed, heading for the coffee pot. Since it was full, she was guessing that Derrick didn't yet have a cup. She filled two mugs, added cream and headed upstairs to wake her man.

"I could get used to this." Derrick said from the warmth of the bed. Jade smiled, remembering that she said this very thing, a short time ago. Derrick reached for her.

Half an hour later, pulling the sheet over her naked torso, Jade smiled. "Your coffee's cold." He smiled back. "Worth it."

After breakfast, Jade and Derrick sat at the kitchen table. Jade was curious about what Derrick may have found out last night, looking through the Cathy Small murder file. She knew there were things that Derrick would not be able to tell her. As if Derrick had read her mind, he said, "I found out a couple more interesting things last night about our favorite murder suspect. Want to hear them?" Jade sat forward. "I'd love to." Derrick chuckled. "Yeah, I thought so."

"First of all, there was no misunderstanding about what Nate knew and when he knew it. I spoke with the investigating officer last night." Jade said, "It must have been a pretty late phone call. I'm surprised he didn't cuss you out." Derrick explained, "Ronny works the night shift anyway, so I patched through to his cruiser and had him call me back on my more private land line. He remembered Nate Small right away, and he told me he got a vibe from him.

There was just nothing he could find that pointed in his direction. No motive, in particular." Jade asked, "Not even a nice big life insurance policy?" Derrick answered, "Nope, we checked into that. I told Ronny about your encounter with Mr. Small, and that he told you that he didn't know about the murders until well AFTER his wife was killed. Poor Ronny, I thought he was going to throw a PVC. He remembered specifically that Nate Small kept bringing up the other murders during his interview with the police. Ronny thought it was strange at the time, but he put it down to the shock of the man's wife turning up dead."

"Meanwhile, the last page of the file was the 'addendum' that was referenced on the first page of the report. It was a VICAP report. VICAP is a computer program provided by the FBI and used to track violent crimes and offenders. The database picked up on two other murders, within the three years preceding Cathy Small's death, that were similar enough to the M.O. used by Cathy Small's killer to be grouped together. However, there were seven other deaths that were sufficiently dissimilar to be excluded. The program's algorithm is designed to spot patterns that would indicate a possible serial killer at work. Since there weren't enough deaths and the ones we had weren't sufficiently similar, the database didn't indicate a strong correlation. Now, if there were other murders SINCE Cathy Small's, and if they involved many of the same elements, it's possible that the program will send up a flag suggesting further research. Jade, I know you've been researching the murders. How many did you uncover that were alike enough to be likely the work of the Lawrence killer, in this most recent series?"

Jade was already out of her chair, heading for her duffel bag in the living room. After a quick review of her file, she said, "I had six names on my list so far. Three of them I've researched in enough detail to be confident they fit the pattern." Derrick said, "It's possible that our database has a tolerance that is fairly specific, so there's less likelihood that the program would come up with a false positive, i.e., the computer saying there may be a correlation between two or more deaths when it turns out there's not. That said, I think it's possible for the program to miss a pattern, especially if the details of one or more of the crimes weren't entered into the database. I'm glad to know that we DID check out the possible connection between Cathy Small and other victims, but I also think we'll need to be open to the idea that this could be, and likely is, a serial killer at work, with the possible exception of Cathy Small, who I now believe was likely killed by her husband."

Jade took a moment to digest what Derrick said. She realize that she, also, felt strongly that Nate Small was a murderer. She realized that she and Diane were probably in danger the night they paid their call to him. She also knew that Nate probably agreed to see them because he wanted to see what they may have on him. Apparently, he decided they weren't a threat. Jade shuddered, wondering if there were other times she was in danger recently and just didn't realize it. Something like that could get her killed. She turned frightened eyes up to Derrick. "I just realized how much danger Diane and I may have been in the night we went to Nate Small's house to talk to him."

The color drained from Derrick's face. "You did WHAT?" Jade looked at him uncomprehendingly. "You went to this sick bastard's house? Jesus Christ, Jade! You could have been killed! I thought when you mentioned him earlier he was just one of the telephone calls you made." Derrick's angry concern pushed Jade abruptly into self-defense mode. "How could I have known then what we only suspect about him now? He was the grieving husband of a murdered woman. I took Diane with me when I went to his house. We met for less than half an hour, and were out of there. End of story." Derrick looked only partly mollified. "No, not 'end of story'. I want you to take this as a wake up call. I want you to promise me that you won't meet with anyone else, especially at their house, unless I'm with you." After more discussion, Jade finally agreed, understanding Derrick's need to protect her but also feeling strongly that she needed the freedom follow her instincts, wherever they led. Only Bardo saw Jade's crossed fingers under the table.

Jade realized that Diane should be brought up to speed on Nate Small, just for her own safety. She felt sure that, once he realized that the police would be reopening their investigation, he would likely make the connection to she and Diane. Jade pulled out her cell phone and speed dialed Diane. She didn't answer. Jade left her a detailed message about the inconsistency between Nate Small's statement to them, and his previous statement to the police, regarding when he knew about the previous murders. She told Diane to be careful and to contact her if Nate Small happened to get in touch, as the investigation into the death of his wife would likely be heating up.

Then Jade thought about her father. She checked her cell phone for messages; there were none. She called home to check her answering machine. There was a message! Gripping the phone tightly, Jade retrieved it. It was a hang up call. Jade wished she could at least see the caller ID on that call. Frustrated, she snapped her phone closed. Derrick said, "It wasn't your father, was it?" Jade told him it wasn't. She thought about the note her mother had left her and knew she needed to show it to Derrick, even though her mother revealed her conviction that Peter had done terrible things. With Peter murdered, her mother having apparently taken her own life and her father missing, Jade knew that Derrick, and maybe only Derrick, could help her make sense of these things now.

She pulled the note out of her purse and held it under her hand on the kitchen table. "Derrick, I need to tell you about something else that happened a couple days ago." Derrick looked steadily at Jade, saying nothing. "I told you before that I went to my parents' house to check on my dad. And I told you about my dad's big blue glass vase being missing, and I told you about my mother's stuff being trashed. What I didn't tell you is what I found there that day. On a hunch, I checked the loose tile in the bathroom where my mother and I used to leave little notes for each other, when I was a child. There was a note. Here it is." Jade handed Derrick the note and watched while he unfolded it and read it. After he finished reading it, he looked away for a moment, thinking. Then he refolded it and handed it back to her. He waited expectantly for her to go on, knowing there was more. "The fact that my mother did try to commit suicide, and ultimately succeeded, wasn't a surprise. I saw her face just before she walked out in front of the car, that day. I even tried to tell my father, but he would hear none of it. What bothered me most about that note was what she apparently believed about Peter, and how my father wouldn't, or couldn't, concern himself with her suspicions."

Derrick looked at Jade's troubled face. He said, "I'm so sorry that you had to deal with your mother's suicide alone. You are an amazingly strong person, Jade. I could spend the rest of my life just getting to know all the wonderful things about you." The exact right thing to say, at exactly the right time, Jade thought. She struggled with tears, and held tightly to his hand. He said, "It sounds to me like Peter was a trial, to everyone who lived with him." Jade silently looked at the table. She felt, once again, the loss of his potential, of the life he should have had. The regretful ache of the road not taken. Suddenly, it was all just too much. Emotion slammed through her. She put her head down on her folded arms and wept.

Derrick gave her a few minutes to work through the worst of the tempest. Then he scooted his chair over next to her and gently pulled her into his arms. Her arms snaked around him and her tears dampened his neck. She gradually relaxed against him. He pulled his handkerchief out of his pocket and handed it to her. She blew her nose noisily, causing them both to laugh. "I'm not so strong now, am I?", Jade asked, mockingly. Derrick tightened his arms around her. "Crying or not crying has nothing to do with being strong. You deal directly with everything that comes your way. If it makes you cry, then it does. But you meet it head on, you deal, then you move forward."

A potential problem had occurred to Jade, and, as if to bear out what Derrick was saying, she immediately brought it up. "Derrick, since you've read the note, and you know my mother killed herself, is there anything legally that you, or I, are obligated to do about that?" Derrick thought a moment, then said, "Since we can't verify the authenticity or the authorship of the note, it's likely that it would be considered like 'hearsay' in terms it's weight in jurisprudence. Do you know what kind of life insurance your mother may have had?" Confused about this seeming non-sequitur, Jade said, "She and my father are both insured through the USM faculty group life plan. I remember witnessing a beneficiary designation form for them, a few months ago. Why?"

Derrick said, "Some life insurance policies will not pay benefits, usually just for the first two years, if the insured's death was the result of suicide. But since your dad has worked for USM for many years, the policy that insures him and your mother would be well past the suicide exclusion period if there is one." Jade shot Derrick an impressed look. "I'm just trying to establish whether the situation surrounding your mother's death makes any kind of legal difference. As far as I can see, it doesn't."

Jade wasn't completely placated. "What about the information in the note about

Peter? Is that information anything that you can or should take action on?" Derrick picked up the note and re-read it. "I don't think there's anything about the Old Port murders specific enough to take action. Besides, I think you and I both know who committed most of them. The murder that took place near your childhood home, well that's another thing. There's some specific information in the note about that, and about why your mother thought Peter may have done it. I'll need to check that out. The bottom line, however, is that Peter can't be held accountable now, so if we do determine that he was the likely perpetrator, no charges can be filed now anyway. We'll likely never have a definite answer, since Peter is gone. But I can check into it and find out if anyone was ever convicted, and if so, I can review the evidence against them and decide, based on your mother's additional point of view, whether it is reasonable to assume the right person was convicted."

Jade thought it over and decided that she was agreeable to that course of action. She, too, wanted to find out if there was a chance that Peter could have committed that murder. "I agree that we need to get at the truth about Peter, if we can. Are you allowed to let me know what you find out?" Derrick said, "I can tell you whether someone was convicted, as that's public information. And I can tell you about any investigation I do that specifically involves Peter."

Jade felt much better for having told Derrick about the note. "I'm especially glad to get the fact of my mother's suicide out in the open, Derrick. I didn't realize how that one thing has complicated my ability to deal with everything else. Sharing it with you seems to have taken some of the sting out of it. I'm also glad that my mother's suicide will stay just between her and I. Well, and you."

After lunch, Derrick had errands to run. Jade elected to stay behind and take a bath while he was gone. She spent an indulgent hour in the whirlpool bathtub, reading through her Lawrence file. After her bath, she went downstairs to Derrick's computer. Derrick had a cable broadband internet connection, so it was always on. Jade hit the space bar and the screen sprung to life. She opened an internet icon and checked her home email. There was a response from the British Library. She opened the email message and saw several attached documents and several links listed beneath them. These people were certainly on the ball!

One attachment caught her eye. The file name said "Alois Reynolds". She double-clicked on it and an image loaded almost instantly. All rational thought left her as she stared at the image on the screen in front of her. She was looking at a picture of herself! But she knew, she had never posed for this picture. The woman in the picture appeared to be in her late teens. The photo was black and white, and was obviously taken decades ago. The woman's face was a study in conflicting emotion. In her arms were two swaddled babies. The camera flash reflected clearly the tears on her face, but still she smiled. A sad and proud smile. Jade printed the picture, then found a magnifying glass in the top drawer of Derrick's desk.

Jade was interrupted by a discreet knock on the office door. She felt strangely like an interloper, suddenly, and hoped her "come in" didn't betray it. An elderly gentleman quietly crossed the room and laid a silver tray in front of her. "Mr. Derrick left me specific instructions to provide you with refreshments in his absence." Jade smiled up at the man and asked, "What should I call you?" His smile illuminated the room. "I'm Terrance. Very nice to make your acquaintance, my dear." Terrance walked silently from the room. Jade turned to the tray and was amused to see a cup of hot chocolate and a small bowl of chocolate covered peanuts.

Popping a chocolate treat into her mouth, Jade got back to work. She used the lens to look at the picture in more detail.

The woman was wearing a ring. Jade ran the lens over the ring and the familiar Möbius symbol jumped into sharp relief. An important part of the puzzle clicked neatly into place as she gazed into the face that was, yet wasn't, her own. THIS is why Ben Lawrence reacted the way he did when he saw me, Jade thought. This woman was the love of his life and she was lost to him. How confusing and so very sad for the poor man! Jade wished with all her heart that Ben Lawrence could see this picture. Alois holding his children and, as evidenced by the ring, still obviously in love with him. Jade sat back from the computer screen and considered the picture before her. Alois. She looked impossibly young and fragile. She had always heard that everyone has a twin, somewhere. There was apparently no rule that said the twins had to have lived in the same era. Here was her very own twin, staring back at her from across time.

Jade had a fleeting thought about Erin, and how she lived in fear of Tim. Tim later fathered twins, one of which died, but the other, Ben, whom she herself had met, had loved this courageous young woman and their love had produced these two beautiful children.

Jade closed the picture, then opened the next image. It was a newspaper account of a series of murders that took place in Great Britain, back in the late 1840's. The newspaper, the Edinburg Herald, was dated August 27, 1849. The story was a recap of several homicides that had occurred in and around the town of Edinburg, over the two years prior. A name immediately caught her attention. Lawrence. According to this news report, William Lawrence, who was suspected in at least one of the deaths, had disappeared from town the day before, along with his pregnant wife and two of their servants. Jade realized that this information answered two of her questions. How did the Lawrences of Great Britain end up living in Maine, and why did all the accounts she found show the earliest killings suddenly starting in 1850, as if someone had thrown some kind of murderous switch?

Jade closed the second image and looked at the next one. Another news account, this time of the murder of Louisa Lawrence in 1907. Since it happened in the United States but involved a British family, it received passing mention in the Edinburg Herald. The news report made a point of mentioning that Tim Lawrence's father was William Lawrence, who fled England 57 years prior, after being sought for questioning in a series of murders. There was no mention of whether the police had ever tracked him down and questioned him, after he had fled England. The next several images were additional recapped stories of murders that took place in the United States which involved in some way, a member of the Lawrence family.

Jade next checked the three links she was sent with the emailed images. The first one was a website devoted to uncovering the roots and meanings of family crests. Jade found the Lawrence family crest and clicked on it. The screen immediately filled with the familiar image of the figure-eight Möbius strip. The biographical information under the picture indicated that the Möbius was a mathematical representation which was discovered and publicized in the late 1850's. The meanings varied from "forever" to "change" to "nothing and everything". Since there were no surviving records evidencing the initial adoption of this family crest by the Lawrences, there was no known information about why this symbol was chosen and what, if anything, it meant specifically to the Lawrence family. Jade clicked on the other two hyperlinks in turn, and found genealogy information she already had. Frustrated, she logged off the computer. As she pushed out her chair, she found several of Bardo's toys around her feet. He had apparently brought them to her while she was on the computer, although she had no memory of it. She picked up the toys, damp with doggy-drool, and went to the kitchen in search of Bardo. Through the beautiful bay windows, Jade could see that the sun was just dipping below the horizon.

On the way to the kitchen, her cell phone rang. "Hey Diane, what's up, girl?" There was silence, punctuated by a faint hissing noise. Then she heard Diane's voice, sounding very faint. "Where are we going? You can't just...." Jade heard a sharp slap. "Owww!", said Diane loudly. Diane was in trouble! Jade knew Diane probably managed to get hold of her cell phone and dialed the first speed number, which was hers. Her heart hammering in her chest, Jade listened, hoping for some kind of clue about what was happening.

Thinking quickly, Jade took her cell phone with her to Derrick's landline phone, picked it up and dialed Derrick's cell phone number. He answered on the second ring. Jade spoke softly, "Derrick, I've got Diane on the line, and she's in trouble. I don't think she can talk. Someone is taking her somewhere, by car, by the sound of it. I think she managed to speed-dial me on the sly." Jade's voice cracked and she fought back terror as she waited the short moment it took for Derrick to process her words. "What's Diane's cell number?" Jade gave it to him. She heard him put his cell phone down on the seat and speak briefly into his squad car radio.

He got back on the line with Jade. "My dispatcher is tracing the call right now. We may not be able to pinpoint Diane's exact location, but we should be able to get an approximate fix on her by tracking her phone pinging from cell tower to cell tower. Wait, I've got something. She's in Portland. The cell tower is on

Commercial Street." Jade suddenly knew exactly where Diane had been taken. She gave Derrick the address, 178 Commercial Street. He told her to stay put. Like hell, Jade thought. On the way out the door, Diane's phone connection to Jade was broken.

At the Lawrence house, Jade saw three cruisers parked out in front. The second story windows were illuminated in turn as an officer walked through the house checking each room with his flashlight. Jade parked her Blazer at the end of the block and walked back toward the house. As she approached the house, she saw that the police officer was now on the third floor. Then there were two beams, crisscrossing each other across the third floor rooms. Jade knew that Derrick wouldn't betray her confidence unless he absolutely had to, so she was assuming he would somehow "happen" to find the false panel in the library room, and check it out to make sure Diane wasn't there. The beams went still for several minutes, then both beams disappeared. The two men exited the house through the front door, which she noticed had been forced open. One of the men carried an evidence bag, with something small and fairly heavy in it, which he took directly to his cruiser. With a guilty start, Jade remembered that she had accidentally left her small flashlight upstairs when she was here and had fled so abruptly. She hoped it hadn't just been found.

Jade caught sight of a familiar figure walking toward her. "Jade! I didn't want you to come down here, you knew that! You are staying at my house for the specific purpose of keeping you OUT of harms way. Did it cross your mind that the kidnapper may have let Diane make that call as a way to lure you here?" He looked at Jade's stricken expression, and softened his tone. "I'm sorry, I didn't mean to frighten you. I just worry about you. I know there are just too many variables here to allow me to be sure of your safety. Please, go back to the house and wait for me?" Jade said, "No, I'M sorry. I didn't even think about the fact that this could have been a trap, as well as a kidnapping. I'll go home, but before I do, I want to ask you something. What was it you found in the house? I saw the evidence bag." Jade thought she saw Derrick wince, but it was so fleeting that she couldn't be sure. "It was Diane's cell phone. I checked that secret room in the third floor library. I saw the skeleton. We took a look around the hidden room itself, then I checked the skeleton over. I found the cell phone in the skeleton's apron pocket."

Anger and fear fought for dominance in Jade. "He better not hurt her! Goddamn sick freak bastard!" Jade tried unsuccessfully to rein in her runaway anger. "Damn! Now that we don't have Diane's cell phone, we can't track her. How are we going to figure out where he took her? We can't just wait for him to call. We need to do something now. He could have already killed her. Or he could be getting ready to! Derrick, we have to help her!"

Derrick put an arm around Jade and gently turned her back toward her Blazer. "First we are going to comb this immediate area for evidence of any kind. There's a team on the way specifically to process the skeletal remains. I'm going to get all the information I can on Timothy Lawrence, AKA Steven Lawry. I'll find out what kind of car he drives, and since we already know where he lives, or at least recently lived, I'll send a cruiser by to check that out. Maybe most importantly, I'll find out if he has a cell phone. If he does and if it's on, we can likely track his movements. If Diane is with him, we'll be tracking her too." Jade felt sure that, since Diane's cell phone was placed in Erin's apron pocket, the only person who could have taken her would be Timothy. Or Daniel, she thought suddenly. She had concluded that Daniel must be a good guy, but what if she was wrong? Was she prepared to bet her best friend's life on it? Then of course, there was Dillon. Jade knew he was also probably out there. What a nightmare!

312

Chapter 38

Jade got into her Blazer and headed back to Derrick's house. Her mind was working furiously. Where had he taken her? Jade thought about what Derrick said. The kidnapper may have been laying a trap for her. The cell phone left in the house was just a lure to see if she would come. He may have been waiting somewhere nearby, watching to see if Jade would take the bait. When the police arrived, Jade was sure that, if he were nearby, he'd have fled. To where? She mentally reviewed any locations she knew about which would have significance for Timothy, or for any of the Lawrences. Suddenly she knew. The Promenade! But there were two of them, the Western and the Eastern. Which one? She knew from her research that more than one victim, including her brother Peter, had been found at the Western Promenade. She only recalled one victim found at the Eastern Promenade. So she'd check the Western Promenade first.

She thought fleetingly of calling Derrick, then decided against it. But, in case something happened to her, she wanted Derrick to have someplace to start the search for her. She pulled over on Vaughn Street, pulled out a piece of paper and a pen, and hastily scrawled a note: "Derrick, after you found Diane's cell phone at the Lawrence house, I realized that there were only a couple other places that Diane would have been taken. One was the Western Promenade, one was the Eastern Promenade. As there have been more victims found at the Western Prom, and I know Peter was found there, I think the killer may have a stronger affiliation with that location and I'm going to try there first." After a moment of thought, she added, "I love you." She put the note under her seat, and drove the last few blocks to the Western Promenade.

Jade parked the Blazer off the road, behind a small copse of trees at the entrance to the park on the northern end of the Promenade. The infrequently placed streetlights did little to pierce the inky darkness. She walked up a long, winding hill, staying to the darker shadows cast by the trees. Every several steps, Jade stopped to listen carefully. She knew that in Winter, with the ground frozen and the trees bare, sound travels much longer distances. The night was very quiet. Jade felt sure that she had made the right decision in coming here. She knew that Peter's body had been found here, on the northern slope just feet from where she was standing. Somewhere, she also knew, not far from this very spot, was a monster who had killed countless times, and who would kill again, this time taking her precious friend, unless he could be stopped.

At the top of the hill, Jade saw the lights of Maine Medical Center in the distance, but all around her was fragrant wilderness. Jade stepped out from the shadow of the trees and stood in the middle of the small paved road, listening. One sound gradually began to separate itself from the other night sounds. It was a rhythmic hollow clacking sound. Jade walked forward a few steps. The sound retreated. Jade moved back to her previous position. The sound came back. She walked back toward the cover of the trees. The sound again retreated. She walked slowly to the other side of the road, where, instead of trees, there was a gradual sloping hill leading several stories down to another roadbed below. Jade looked out over the scrub-covered cliff; the sound was coming from there.

Jade walked a few feet down into the scrub, listening intently. Then she spotted a small red box, sitting incongruously among the weeds, several feet to her left. She made her way to it, the volume of the clacking increased. Jade approached carefully, listening and watching around her. The red box was latched from the top. Jade left the box where it was and gingerly slipped the hasp on the top. Inside the box Jade saw a strangely familiar mass of dark hair. Horrified, Jade froze, staring at the hideous contents of the small red box. As she watched, she detected slight, rhythmic movement from within the box, something beneath the hair was moving! Jade abruptly let go of the lid and scrambled backward. Nearly hysterical, Jade watched the box from several feet away. As her mind worked furiously to make sense of what she saw in the box, she realized that her tormentor was likely nearby, watching her reaction.

Instead of approaching the box again, which she was sure would be expected of her, she walked away from it. She looked around at the trees, the road and the scrub-covered slanted terrain on which the box had been placed. After a moment's thought, she headed into the trees directly across the road from the box. She knew her instinct had been right when she heard the furtive sound of someone trying to move quietly in the opposite direction. She picked up her pace, and heard the corresponding quickening in the sounds a few feet in front of her. Empowered by her obvious effect on her prey, Jade dropped all attempts at stealth and hurtled herself through the trees, desperately trying to catch her tormentor.

Almost out of breath, Jade burst through the trees to another road, and saw a dark figure running, much faster than she was, the distance between them lengthening as she watched. She gave up and turned back to the woods. She walked back to the box, catching her breath and trying not to think about what may be in it. On her knees in front of the box, Jade once again heard the clacking sound coming from inside it. With shaking hands, Jade reached out and opened the lid again. Jade reached into the box, her hand tangling in the silky dark hair. Jade clutched a handful of the hair and slowly drew the object

315

upward. Facial features came into view.

Relief flooded her when she realized the head wasn't real. It appeared to be a wax reproduction, and it was eerily lifelike. Jade raised the head to eye level and looked carefully at the face. The source of the clacking sound immediately became apparent. The mouth, ringed with garish red lips, was open. Inside, Jade saw teeth, which were opening and closing. Jade put her finger into the mouth and stilled the teeth. She pulled the mechanism out and examined it. It was a chattering teeth toy that could be purchased at any joke shop, powered by a tiny battery. Jade took a good look at the wax head. It was obviously made to look like Diane, but the resemblance wasn't exact, and wasn't really even that close. The hair, though, was surprisingly lifelike, and gave Jade a chill just touching it. Jade put the head down on the grass and took another look inside the box. There was a neatly folded note. Jade pulled it out and, handling it gingerly to preserve any fingerprints, she read it.

"My Dearest Jade,
Congratulations! Once again you have proved your intelligence and courageousness. I have your friend. She's fine, although a little frightened as I'm sure you can understand. Here is my proposal. I will return your friend to you, in more or less the condition in which I found her. You will drop your investigation into my family and their, shall we say?, - strange proclivities.   In essence, I'm asking for an exchange of Diane's life for mine. You've been more than a worthy adversary. But the time has come to dispense with this ridiculous witch hunt of yours. I think you realize how readily I will hurt your friend. Will you be able to live with yourself if you are responsible for her death? I think not. I know you'll do the right thing. If not, please know that Diane will merely be the appetizer. You, my dear, will be the main course. And if you tell your new man about this, and he involves law enforcement, I

can't be held responsible for what I do.

I understand that it'll do me no good to ask you to turn over all your files. You'll just make copies. What I need from you is your solemn word that you will stop. And your realization that breaking your word will result in the death of someone close to you and subsequently, your own death. I'll call you in a couple of hours. Be waiting. If I can't reach you, you'll have another funeral to attend."

The note was unsigned. Jade knew it must be from Timothy. Or Dillon, or maybe Nate Small, her frightened mind rejoined. Either way, he meant what he said. Jade looked at her watch and realized it was now after midnight. Instead of just waiting for the phone call, Jade decided to spend her time trying to figure out where Timothy was holding Diane. Jade retrieved the box with the wax head in it, and headed back to her truck.

As soon as she got into the truck, she ripped up the note she had written to Derrick. She headed back to Derrick's house, hoping to beat him there. When she arrived, she didn't see Derrick's truck. She left the Blazer in the circular driveway, along with the box and what it contained. Terrance greeted her at the front door. Jade gratefully slipped into the house.

Within fifteen minutes, Derrick arrived. Jade met him at the door. He took one look at her face and knew something else had happened. "Did you hear from the kidnapper?" Jade tried to sound calm and reasonable as she explained, "Well, sort of, I did. After I left you on Commercial Street, I started thinking about where Diane may have been taken. On a hunch, I went to the Western Promenade. I know he's dumped more than one victim there, one of them was my brother."

Jade glanced quickly at Derrick's face, noted the storm clouds he was trying unsuccessfully to hide, and quickly told him what happened. When she was finished, Derrick appeared calmer. He only asked her whether she had touched the note. Jade responded, "I did, but only the very corners, between my nails, and very carefully so I could preserve whatever evidence may be on it." Derrick nodded. "Okay, where is the box now?" Jade told him it was in the Blazer. He put on a pair of latex gloves and headed outside. Within seconds, he was back, the box held between his gloved hands. He had Jade spread two paper towels, side by side, on the kitchen table, and he put the box down on one of them. He opened the lid and gingerly lifted out the wax head. The chattery teeth in the bottom of the box clacked twice, then fell silent.

Derrick held the head up to the light and looked it over carefully. Jade was amazed at how fake it looked, here in the brightly-lit kitchen. She felt a little foolish for being so frightened of it. Derrick, in his usual fashion, picked up her vibe effortlessly. "This is a pretty clumsy attempt at terrorizing, but I can see how, in the dark, and looking a bit like Diane, it would be pretty creepy."

Derrick put the head down on the other paper towel, next to the box. Then he fished the note out from the bottom of the box. He carefully opened the note, read it, and put it back. Jade watched him for a reaction. He put the head back in the box, then turned to Jade. "Please don't take this wrong, but I can't figure out why he didn't just kill Diane outright. There must be a reason he feels she's worth more alive than dead. Unless, and I'm hoping I'm wrong about this, Diane is already dead" Jade answered thoughtfully. "I thought of that, too. All I can figure is that he wants me to know he's serious, but he also wants me to know that he's capable of dealing fairly. It's a really big deal for him, getting me to stop my investigation, and he must realize that, if he killed Diane, that may be the red flag this bull needs to charge. Since I can't deal with the idea of Diane being dead, I'm moving forward on the assumption that she's alive." Derrick smiled at Jade's logic. "That's exactly how you should be thinking."

A little over an hour later, Jade's ringing cell phone, clutched in her hand, woke her abruptly as she dozed on the couch. The caller ID indicated "private caller. It was him! "Hello?" The voice that followed her down into her nightmares every night responded. "Hi Jade, how are you?" Amazingly, the ignorant little bastard was waiting for a response from her! "How do you want me to be?" Derrick, who had also been dozing, came fully awake in the armchair at the sound of Jade's caustic tone. Jade's caller responded to her sarcasm with a chuckle. Jade said, through clenched teeth, "I agree to your terms. If you let Diane go, unharmed, I promise to stop my research into you and your family." The kidnapper responded with a note of ersatz sadness in his tone, "I'm afraid it's a little too late for the 'unharmed' part. She'll be okay, I think. I just had to, well, discipline her." Jade leaped to her feet, outraged. She opened her mouth to let him have it, and the phone was suddenly yanked from her hand.

Derrick put his index finger to his lips in a motion of silence. He held the phone out to one side and gave Jade a cautioning look. Jade took a deep breath, let it out slowly, and nodded. She reached out and took the cell phone back. In a carefully neutral voice, she said, "Is Diane okay? What did you 'have to' do to her?" There was no response, and Jade feared she would lose him if she kept trying. She tried a different tactic, again using Diane's name to try to personalize her to the kidnapper. "Where can I pick her up? Diane must be cold and scared. Please let's get this over with. Tell me where I need to go and I'll go, right now." A contented murmur came over the line, and Jade once again gathered her tattered control around her. "I just love it when you do things my way. See how much easier it is? I dropped Diane off under the

Million Dollar Bridge, on the Portland side. It's a cold night, I'd leave now if I were you."

Jade and Derrick were on the road within moments. Derrick called the station and asked that they try to determine the source telephone number of the call Jade just received on her cell phone, and he also asked that a trap be put on Jade's cell phone, in case he called again. Luckily for Jade, and likely for Diane as well, Derrick's reputation as a first-rate senior detective allowed him to employ police resources with a minimum of explanation.

The million dollar bridge, so named because it was rumored to have cost that much to build, several decades earlier, transected the end of Commercial Street, opposite from the end on which the Lawrence house sat. Jade and Derrick parked Derrick's truck on the side of the road and walked hurriedly the last few hundred feet to the underside of the bridge. They both saw her at the same time. She was laying on the ground, on her side, her back turned to them. She wasn't moving.

Jade started to move toward Diane, terrified about what she may find but knowing she needed to help if she could. Derrick held a staying hand across her, blocking her from walking any closer. "Let me do this. You stay put, okay?" Guilty relief flooded her. She nodded. Derrick approached carefully, using his flashlight to illuminate the area. He covered the last few feet to Diane and knelt down in front of her. He looked at her for a moment, the reached a hand to enclose her wrist. He could see Jade watching anxiously. She had moved closer and was now only a few steps away. Derrick held Diane's wrist between his fingers and waited, his fingertips trying to detect any sign of life.

Jade ran the last few feet and, sobbing, laid her body across Diane's and pulled her into her arms. Diane's limp hand tumbled from Derrick's grasp and fell to her side. Jade put her hands on either side of Diane's head and brought her face even with her own. Diane's face was dirty, scratched and tear-stained. Jade unexpectedly felt movement under her hands. A pulse! Diane was alive! Jade smiled through her tears and looked over at Derrick. "She's alive. I can feel her pulse. It's weak, but it's definitely there!" Derrick moved closer and put his palm close to Diane's slightly parted lips. "She's breathing!" "Oh thank God!", Jade cried.

Derrick quickly checked Diane for any obvious signs of injury. He took off his jacket, then uniform shirt, folded his shirt several times and slipped it around Diane's neck, tying it securely as a makeshift cervical collar. Then he wrapped his coat around Diane. He turned an agonized look on Jade. "I really don't want to move her, but I just don't want him to come back, maybe to finish the job." Jade agreed with Derrick and told him so. Derrick immediately looked more at ease with the decision to move Diane. Jade held Diane's head steady as Derrick lifted Diane slowly into his arms and walked with her back to his truck. He laid her across the backseat .

Chapter 39

At the hospital, Jade and Derrick waited in a pastel-colored, crowded room.

Diane had been taken to emergency exploratory surgery almost an hour ago. Jade looked out a window listlessly as the sky began to lighten. With a jolt, she realized that Brian probably had no idea what happened to Diane. She retrieved her cell phone from her purse and started looking for Brian's number. Then she realized that it would be cruel to wake him up, tell him what happened, and tell him they had no idea how serious Diane's injuries were, or even if she was going to pull through. Jade flipped her cell phone shut and just held it, waiting.

A doctor finally approached them. "Mr. And Mrs. Danner?" Jade said nothing to correct the doctor. "Yes?" The doctor looked at both of them in turn, with a strange expression on his face. Speculation. Jade, suddenly impatient, said, "Is Diane okay? Do you know what happened to her?" The doctor took both of them into a small conference room. He sat down across from them and got right to the point. "Diane has been poisoned. We aren't sure yet what she took or was given. Do either of you know?" Jade and Derrick looked at each other, then back at the doctor. Derrick spoke first. "Doctor, Diane was kidnapped. I'm a police officer and I'm investigating, but unfortunately we have very few leads.

"A couple hours ago, the kidnapper called my girlfriend, Jade, who is Diane's best friend. He told Jade where she could find Diane and we immediately went to get her. We are in the process of having the call traced, but I'm not very hopeful we'll get far with that. What will happen if we are unable to determine what Diane was given? The doctor's expression grew concerned. "Well, unfortunately, there are hundreds of poisons. Some of the antidotes are contraindicated for other poisons, so in order to give Diane the best care, we must find out what she was given." Jade grabbed Derrick's hand, her distress apparent. Jade asked the question to which she most dreaded the answer. "Is there a chance that she could die?" The doctor reached a hand across to cover

Jade's other hand. "It's too early to tell. We don't know yet whether it's reached it's full toxicity yet. We should know more in the next 24 hours."

The doctor excused himself, leaving Derrick and Jade alone in the small room. Jade stifled a sob. This could NOT be happening. This was all her fault! If she hadn't brought Diane into this hellish nightmare, she'd be fine right now. Jade turned haunted eyes to Derrick. She knew he could see exactly where her thoughts were taking her. He put an arm around her. "Try not to worry, I have a feeling your buddy is one strong gal. We'll do whatever we can to help her, and we'll track down the sorry son of a bitch who hurt her. I'll force him to tell me what he gave her. Then maybe he'll have an unfortunate accident." Jade heard the anger in Derrick's voice and turned to face him.

"Derrick, I know how you feel, I feel the same way. Let's not let our anger at Timothy erode any of our usefulness, okay?" She watched Derrick slowly unclench his jaw, then take a deep, cleansing breath. "Yeah, you're right. Let's check on Diane, if they'll let us, then go back to the house for a few hours of sleep. I'm going to take the next few days off. I have a shitload of PTO time coming, I might as well use it." In response, Jade yawned hugely. She knew she was so tired she wouldn't be much use until she got a few hours of sleep. She felt guilty about needing to take time out to crash, but she had no choice. Since she wasn't a doctor, she knew there was nothing she could do for her friend that her caregivers couldn't do better.

Derrick and Jade were only allowed a quick peek into Diane's room. Diane was not conscious, and hardly recognizable amid the wires and tubes. Jade felt a rush of furious determination. She would do whatever was necessary to save Diane, or die trying.

Tuesday

On the drive home, Jade reluctantly pulled out her cell phone and paged through
the incoming calls. When she found Diane's last call to her, from Brian's
house, she felt a little pang, remembering how happy Diane had sounded. She
hit the button to select that number and dial it. Brian answered immediately.
"Jade! Have you seen Diane? I've been calling her since yesterday and I can't
reach her! I'm getting worried." Jade said, "Hi Brian. That's why I'm calling.
There's been a little accident…." Jade quickly told Brian, in broad strokes,
what happened. When she told him that Diane had been poisoned, she heard
Brian's sharp intake of breath and knew how difficult is must be for him to be
hearing this. But Brian had suffered great adversity in his life, and, to his credit,
he immediately started problem-solving. "My best friend used to work at the
Poison Control Center. I'll give him a call and see if he can do anything to help
us figure out what Diane's got on board. Then I'll get some clothes together
and head down there. I should be there by tonight. I have Diane's house key so
I'll stay at her house. Did anyone feed her cat?"

At first, the comment seemed such a non sequitur, Jade wasn't sure she had
heard him right. "Diane has a cat?" Brian answered, sounding impatient,
"Yes, she got her about two weeks ago from the shelter. I'll drop my stuff at
Diane's, feed Baby Girl, then head straight over to the hospital."

At Derrick's house, Jade and Derrick undressed, took a quick shower and
crawled into bed. Derrick set the alarm clock for 3:00 P.M., then took Jade
gently into his arms. When she turned her face to his, her cheeks were wet with
tears. Derrick wiped her eyes and pulled her head against his chest. Jade knew
nothing further until the alarm woke them both. The mid-winter sunlight was
already slanting in the window from low on the horizon. Jade felt a moment of

strange displacement, then her awakening brain registered that she was at Derrick's house. The sun looked odd because it was an hour or two from setting. On the heels of that, Jade remembered Diane. Derrick was gone, but his side of the bed was still warm. Jade threw on jeans and a sweater, took a quick bathroom detour, then headed downstairs. Half way down, the smell of coffee quickened her step.

Derrick was at the stove, preparing scrambled eggs and toast. Jade walked up behind Derrick and slipped her arms around his waist. Jade heard Derrick's voice "MMMMmmm, how you doin', sweetie?" Jade's smile was small, but genuine. "I'm okay. Worried about Diane. I think I'll give Brian a call, see if he's here yet." Derrick served their late-afternoon breakfast while Jade called Brian. When Brian answered the phone, Jade could hear the sounds around him and knew he wasn't just here, in town, he was already at the hospital. "Hey Brian, you made good time. How's Diane?" Jade heard rustling sounds, then footsteps. His voice came over the line much quieter than it had been earlier. "Diane's holding her own. She know's I'm here. She woke up for a few minutes about an hour ago, but she's gone back to sleep now. The doctor said it's the best thing for her right now."

Jade was relieved that Diane's condition wasn't worsening. "That's good. Were you able to talk to your friend about the poison?" Brian said, "I did. He had a textbook that I borrowed from him and showed to Diane's doctor. There's some good information in it about what kinds of chemical changes different substances will cause in the blood. There's got to be something else we can be doing. I feel so useless!" Jade hurried to reassure him. "Listen, Brian, there's only so much any of us can do. You are doing everything you can. Just be there for her. Derrick and I are going to see what we can do to find the bastard who did this to Diane. Will you do me a favor?" Brian's voice had thickened considerably. "Anything, Jade. Name it." Jade was suddenly aware that, contrary to Brian's obliging manner, he actually had every reason to be angry with her. After all, she put Diane in danger by taking Diane into her confidence. She struggled to keep her voice level. "If there's any change in Diane's condition, for better or for worse, would you please call me immediately?" Brian agreed that he would. Jade finished her call with Brian and disconnected, feeling a rush of new purpose.

Derrick and Jade took a few minutes to strategize before heading out. Their first stop was going to be to check in with Michael, who Derrick assured Jade, could hack any database. They would need his services to find out everything about Timothy Lawrence that would help locate him. Derrick would then see if the trace on Jade's cell phone netted anything, and if his detective friend had found any cell phone number on record for Timothy or any combination of his aliases. Then they would check in with Diane to see if there was any further information on the source of her poisoning and how it could be treated. Having a plan, Jade decided, gave a welcome illusion of control over her fate.

At Michael's house, Michael took surprisingly firm control of the conversation. He asked that Derrick and Jade both remember everything they could tell him about Timothy Lawrence a.k.a. Steven Lawry. He explained that anything they told him could be a means to finding him. He took copious notes while they both called out any and all information that came to mind. When Jade was done reciting her knowledge of the Lawrences, Derrick expressed his amazement about the level of detail she had been able to recall. Jade smiled at his surprised expression. When they were done, Michael took a moment to review his two pages of notes, then bent to his task.

Derrick and Jade sat quietly at the kitchen table, watching as Michael's fingers flew over the laptop keyboard. After just a few minutes, he was able to provide a wealth of information. "Mr. Timothy AKA Steven Lawrence is the son of Daniel Lawrence, who is the son of Ben Lawrence, who is the son of Tim Lawrence, who is the son of William Lawrence. I have his last three known addresses here, as well as his cell phone number as it was given on an application for a gun permit two months ago." He copied down the addresses and the cell phone number. Jade and Derrick looked worriedly at each other, obviously thinking the same thing. A gun permit! "I may be able to get more information, but it's going to take more time." Jade and Derrick took the information and thanked Michael for his help. Michael told them he'd call them later with whatever else he found. Derrick and Jade headed out to their next destination, Derrick's office.

Derrick parked his truck in his usual space behind the Police Station and entered through the back door. The office was almost empty. Most detectives spent most of their time in the field, investigating leads, and very little time in the office. At Derrick's desk, Jade saw a stack of pink "While You Were Out" messages on a spindle. His desk was tidy. There was a thick manila envelope sitting at the center of his blotter. He picked it up. The front of the envelope said "Small". Under the envelope, there were several pieces of paper. Derrick picked them up and glanced through them. He took Jade's hand and led her down the hall to another office. He motioned for Jade to sit on the bench outside, and he went in. Jade heard a brief exchange of voices, then he came back out, collected Jade and together they walked out of the building.

Not willing to wait for Derrick to decide when and what to tell her, Jade spoke up. "So, what was that all about?" Derrick glanced at her, then took her cold hand and tucked it into the crook of his arm. "That was the 'Loo. There was a message on my desk to stop in to see him, so I did. He wanted to discuss the

Small case. I told him that I had been working on another case that had a possible connection to the Small case, so I had reviewed the Small file. Leo had already told him that Mr. Small recently told you he knew nothing about the previous deaths until well after his wife died. The 'Loo also reviewed the documentation written by the investigating officer indicating Mr. Small's repeated requests on the day his wife died, that the police check out the previous murders to see if there was a connection to his wife's. The 'Loo agreed that it was odd, and definitely worth of a closer look. So he wanted me to know that it's officially back on the front burner. He's got Gavin Leo working it." Jade squeezed his arm. "I'm so glad. I was ready to believe Cathy Small was another victim of the Lawrence family, but now I think something even worse may have happened to her. What could be worse than being killed by someone you love and trust?"

Back in the truck, Derrick took a closer look at the papers he took from his desk. "These are updates on the cases that have been assigned to me. I do much of the work myself, but I also have officers help with the field work, and the lab to analyze evidence. This is the final report on the vandalism of your truck at the mall. The only thing we were able to find was a video of a black Mercedes parked in front of your truck for a few minutes, at about 4:40 P.M. We couldn't make out a license plate on the car, and we didn't get any clear shots of the person." Jade expected as much. At least her insurance carrier had paid the claim and her truck was fixed.

Derrick moved on to the next report. "This is another case I'm working on, a drug bust." He shuffled the report to the bottom of the stack and took a moment to scan the next report. "This is interesting. It's the blood analysis on the knife we found in the trunk of your mother's car. The report says that there are three contributors for the blood. One of them was Paulina Nielson. The other two were apparently males, and fairly closely related. We don't have either of their DNA profiles in the CODIS database, so all we know is that they have several alleles in common."

Jade thought for a moment. "So, could the two related contributors be Timothy and his father, Daniel?" Derrick looked back down at the report in his hands. "I guess it's possible. This report doesn't indicate what specific relationship may have existed between the contributors, only that there was one." Jade knew instinctively that this was yet another piece of this mysterious puzzle. She needed to figure out how this information fit with what she already knew.

Derrick put the DNA report on the bottom of the stack and looked at the last sheet. His lips turned slightly up at the corners, crinkling his eyes. Good news, apparently. Jade gave him a gentle poke. "Okay, I'll bite. What is it?" He passed her the sheet of paper and she scanned it quickly. "Is this the report from the kidnapper's telephone call last night?" Derrick nodded. "So he was actually calling from a landline?" Derrick nodded again, smiling wider. "At this address?" Derrick said, "Bingo!" Jade whooped with delight. "We've got him! Let's go!"

Derrick put a staying hand on her arm. "Not yet. If we want to get in and check the place out, we're going to need a warrant." Jade's face fell. "Damn. Okay, how can we get a warrant?" Derrick thought about it. "I doubt we can. He hasn't seriously screwed up yet, that we know of." Jade said. "Yeah, that we *know of*. I'll bet he screwed up somewhere, we just have to figure out where." Both of them fell silent for a moment. They both understood all too well that Diane's survival may depend on their ability to get to her abductor, and find out what he gave her.

Jade realized it was going to take too long to figure out what Timothy may have done to incriminate himself and use that knowledge to get a warrant to check his house. In the meantime, Diane languished in the hospital, possibly getting sicker. They needed something else. Jade remembered something she heard recently about the Lawrences and poison. It danced just through her consciousness, just out of reach. She knew eventually it would come to her. But Diane didn't have the luxury of "eventually."

Jade put her head back on the headrest and closed her eyes. She knew that her frustration was beginning to verge on panic, and she wasn't thinking clearly. As she often did in crisis situations, she heard the calm and welcome voice of her mother. "Jade, empty your mind. That's it. Picture yourself standing at the very center of a white room. Now let the information you seek come to you. It wants to. There it is, do you see it?" Jade did see it. And suddenly remembered. It was a telephone conversation she had with Ian, from the Portland Public Library, a couple weeks ago. A Lawrence family member had been accused of poisoning a girlfriend with Thallium. That was it! She felt the solid click as this information fell into place. "Derrick, we need to get to the hospital, I think I know what he gave Diane."

Derrick folded the reports he had been looking at and put them in his coat pocket. "You got it, baby."

As they walked together into the lobby of the hospital, Jade's cell phone rang. It was Brian! "Brian, is Diane okay?" Brian's voice sounded frightened. "She's not doing well. The doctor said that she's going into respiratory failure and the blood tests indicate the beginning of organ failure. If we can't treat the poison soon, the damage will be irreversible." Jade said, "We're here, downstairs, we'll see you in two minutes. I may have some information that well help." A

330

sound, suspiciously like a sob, escaped Brian. He covered it with a cough. "Please hurry." Grimly, Jade ran up the three flights of stairs, Derrick in quick pursuit. Brian had already rounded up the doctor, and both stood next to Diane's bed, watching the door anxiously as Jade burst through it. She wasted no time. "I think he gave her Thallium! Can you test for that?" The doctor reached across the bed to shake hands with Jade, then with Derrick. "I'm Dr. Bolton. We can test for Thallium but the full toxicology for a conclusive confirmation will take time. How sure are you about this?"

Jade glanced down at Diane and was shocked by the difference between last night and this afternoon. Her friend wasn't conscious, and her skin was now pale and waxy, blue veins clearly visible beneath her translucent skin. But most shocking was that her gorgeous mane of thick dark hair was mostly gone, leaving in its place thin clumps of lank hair. Her eyebrows had also thinned, the outer portion of them seeming to have disappeared. Jade knew she would not have recognized Diane if she hadn't known it was her.

Tearing her gaze away from her dear friend, she turned brimming eyes to the doctor. Derrick placed a supportive arm around Jade's waist. Jade said, "I don't think we are going to be able to get confirmation from our sources in time to save Diane. My research into the history of the family of who we think had Diane turned up an incident of reported Thallium poisoning." The doctor frowned at Jade. "This doesn't sound at all definitive. And, if my memory serves, Thallium poisoning will often take several days to manifest outward symptoms. If it's Thallium poisoning, it likely didn't occur in the past 48 hours. If we find that you are right, I would get rid of any food, drink or medication she has had access to, in her house or in anyone else's home where she's been. The large dose she seems to have on board indicates she likely ingested it, and it wasn't something she came into contact with casually. Someone could have added the poison to anything ingestible, and whatever it's in could still be around. A fatal dose is only about a quarter of a teaspoon, and Thallium is odorless, colorless and tasteless.

The doctor continued, "The antidote for Thallium poisoning is very hard on the body. It's a chemical compound called Potassium Ferric Ferrocyanide, or 'Prussian Blue'. The way Thallium poisoning works is that the Thallium molecules slip into spaces reserved specifically for Potassium molecules. Your body doesn't know the difference and your body begins to experience a Potassium deficiency. As you know, without Potassium, the body soon begins to shut down, which is apparently what's happening to your friend. Her symptoms ARE consistent with Thallium poisoning. I suggest that we give her a half-dose of Prussian Blue and put her immediately on hemodialysis, to help take the stress off her kidneys. We can then watch her very carefully for several hours, to see if the progression of the poison through her organs slows. If it does, we can give her the rest of the antidote."

Jade asked the doctor the question she most feared to ask. "If we are wrong about the source of the poison, could Diane die?" The doctor looked gravely at each of them in turn. "If we do nothing, she will likely die." All were in agreement to the doctor's treatment plan. Dr. Bolton asked one last question, "Is there a family member, closer than any of you, who should be consulted?" Jade spoke for all of them. "Doctor, we ARE her family. Her parents were killed in a car accident several years ago, and she was an only child." The doctor nodded and immediately excused himself to arrange Diane's treatment.

Derrick and Jade managed to convince Brian to take a break from Diane's bedside and they headed to a nearby fast food restaurant. At the tiny plastic table, the three of them picked at their food, each refusing to talk about what was plainly the biggest issue on their minds - Diane. After they finished eating, Brian finally addressed the fear they all shared. "What if it's not Thallium, Jade? What will we do then?" Jade covered his hand with one of hers. "We'll know shortly. Let's cross that bridge when, and if, okay?" Brian's face twisted with the effort of not breaking down. "It's the not knowing that's the worst. I can't lose her, too."

Jade realized that Brian had already had so much tragedy and loss in his life, and she suddenly understood what it must have cost him to allow himself to love again. And now this. She felt an almost welcome anger beginning to build. What kind of God destroys lives and hurts good people like this? Some of what she was feeling must have shown on her face as both men were looking at her with sympathetic expressions. She was suddenly angry at them, too. "Stop looking at me with those hangdog expressions, both of you! Damn it! Diane's GOT to be okay. If no one's going to eat, let's head back to the hospital and see if there's any news yet."

The first dose of Prussian Blue had been administered through Diane's I.V. The three of them kept their bedside vigil with Diane until sunset, then Derrick and Jade left Brian, with his promise to call if there was any change in Diane's condition.

Back on the road, Jade watched Derrick intently as he drove. Derrick caught Jade's uncharacteristically somber expression and said, "A penny?" Jade smiled sadly. "I'm just thinking about what the doctor said about the timing of Diane's poisoning. If it was days ago, it could have happened anywhere. How are we going to find out where it came from? I think we both know the *who*, but I'd also like to know the *how* and the *when*." Derrick responded, "I'm not sure if we are going be able to find out any more than we know now, and we don't even know yet if it was Thallium." Jade's face turned stony. "I'm pretty sure it was. It just fits, you know?" Derrick reached over and squeezed Jade's shoulder. "I'd trust your instincts with my life." Which, Jade thought, was exactly what Diane may be doing.

Thankfully, Derrick interrupted her train of thought before it derailed completely into despair. "Jade, where does Diane live, and do you have a key?" Jade gave him Diane's address and told him that she knew where Diane kept the spare key. Derrick turned the truck around and headed in the direction of Diane's house. Puzzled, Jade asked, "Why do you want to go to Diane's house?" Derrick answered, "Because maybe we can do a little checking around and figure out how she was poisoned. Now, do you know when her trash pickup day is, by any chance?" Jade thought a moment. "Yes, actually it's the same day of the week as mine is, Wednesday." Jade realized that tomorrow was Wednesday, which means that, several days of trash should be there.

It would have been much harder to poison Diane's food or drink away from home, Jade reasoned, so it was likely that someone poisoned something she had at home, and evidence may still be there. Even if they didn't find it, Jade would throw out all the food and beverages in Diane's house, just in case. She would replace everything once Diane was back at home. If. Jade swallowed the lump in her throat and turned her tired, tear-filled eyes to watch the road passing by her window.

Chapter 40

334

At Diane's house, Jade disappeared behind the house for a moment, then re-emerged with the spare key in her hand. Jade noted that there was no filled trashcan or trash bag outside, so whatever trash Diane had generated during the week was likely inside the house, in her trash closet. Derrick took the key from Jade's cold fingers and inserted it into the lock. As they opened the door, a mewling little fur ball darted between their legs in a desperate bid for freedom. Jade reached down and grabbed the kitten by the scruff and held it up. It was a long-haired tiger kitten, with huge double front paws! It cried piteously. Jade was immediately smitten. "So, you're Baby Girl. Very nice to meet you, little lady. I'm your Auntie Jade." Snuggling the kitten, Jade followed Derrick into the house.

Jade hit the kitchen light switch and looked around. Nothing was obviously amiss. After a quick walk through the house, Jade and Derrick started looking through Diane's trashcans. Derrick pulled a set of sheer plastic gloves from his inside jacket pocket. Jade used Diane's rubber cleaning gloves from under the sink. Neither the small trash can in Diane's bedroom, nor the one in her bathroom contained any food, beverage or medication containers, so they took the kitchen trashcan outside to the larger trash barrels and started to sort through it, putting the trash into the barrel as they checked it. Halfway through the contents, Jade saw a familiar bag. She remembered that Diane had "borrowed" a bag of chocolate-covered peanuts from her cupboard on the day the two of them went to Freeport together to shop. Diane must have brought them home with her and finished them off, a few days ago, judging from the bag's position halfway down Diane's weekly pile of trash.

Derrick stopped sorting trash and moved closer to Jade as she examined the bag. He took a penlight from his pocket and looked carefully at the crumpled bag. He frowned, and Jade looked from him to the bag, not sure if he was seeing anything that concerned him, or if he was just concentrating intensely. He headed into the house, Jade in close pursuit. In the kitchen, Derrick smoothed the bag out and held it up to the light. Jade could clearly see a tiny hole in the center of the bag, where none should be. Derrick said, "I think it's likely this is what was contained the poison." Jade swayed, and Derrick anchored her to his side with one long arm, steering Jade into a chair. Jade said, "That bag of candy came from my house. Diane wanted something to eat, we were headed out shopping, so she grabbed these from my cupboard on the way out the door. Oh my God, Derrick!" Jade put her head down on her arms and her shoulders shook with her sobs. Derrick pulled Jade to him and turned her face up to his. "You didn't do anything wrong, Jade. The poison must have been meant for you. How could you have known?"

Jade watched an alarmed look cross Derrick's face. "Wait a minute! Did you eat any of these candies?" Jade shook her head no. Derrick hugged her tighter. "Thank God! Okay, now, do you have any more bags of candy at your house?" Jade nodded. "Since your house is on the way, let's get over to your house and grab your other bags of candy. Then we can take this bag over to the hospital and see if there's any residue on or in it. Then I want to process this bag for fingerprints or DNA evidence. After searching several drawers and cupboards, Derrick located a plastic sandwich bag, placed the crumpled candy bag in it, and put it in his pocket.

They decided not to throw out all the food and medications yet, as it was possible the police would need to go through the house later. Jade quickly gathered the cat carrier, with Baby Girl in unhappily residence (after a difficult search-and-rescue mission), a bag of litter and food, and they headed back out on the road.

They made a quick stop at Derrick's house. Jade put the cat-carrier, containing an only slightly frightened Baby Girl, on the floor so that Bardo could sniff her over without being attacked. After a few minutes, Jade put Baby Girl, fresh food and water and portable litter box upstairs in their room, shutting the door. She left Bardo with run of the rest of the house. Derrick and Jade made the anxious ride from his house to hers in near-silence.

At her house, Jade went straight to the overhead cupboard where she kept her candy stash. There was one more bag of chocolate-covered peanuts, which she pointed out to Derrick. Derrick took the candy from the cupboard, with gloved fingers, and carried it to the table, where he examined it under the light. "There it is. See?" He turned the bag toward Jade and she clearly saw another of the tiny holes, in the center of the bag. This time, the bag was full and unopened. Anger and horror were at war inside her. She struggled for control, remembering the night her house was broken into and she thought the doer had just taken the diary. Later, she later realized he must have planted the transmitter in her purse on the table. Now she knew his other, more deadly task. And she suddenly realized why two of the bags of candy were sitting on the counter when she came downstairs, after he had fled that night. He apparently didn't have enough time to stuff them back into the cupboard before he had fled. She turned to another cupboard and withdrew an empty plastic zip lock bag, handing it to Derrick. He squeezed her hand as he took the bag from her, gingerly putting the poisoned candy bag in, and zipping it shut.

"Now, Jade, do you have any more of that candy anywhere?" Jade opened the freezer and pointed to several bags. Derrick took a couple of them out and looked at them closely under the light. "These look fine, they haven't been tampered with. Being in the freezer, I doubt our guy realized you had them. My guess is that he had to get in and get out, and he just poisoned the two bags of candy, which is what he was able to get to quickly. But, just to be on the safe side, I'd feel better if you would toss out everything edible in your house. You'll need to weed things out anyway when you start packing to move in with me." Jade, already feeling a bit overwhelmed, filed that little jewel away for later examination and said nothing.

At the hospital, Jade and Derrick located Dr. Bolton and told him what they found, at Diane's house and at Jade's. He took both the baggie and the larger zip lock bag containing the full bag of apparently poisoned candy, and promised to only handle the insides of the candy bags, and only with gloved hands, leaving whatever evidence may be on the outsides of the bags for Derrick to collect. Derrick and Jade then proceeded to Diane's room. There was a cot, with rumpled blankets and a tiny pillow on it, in the corner of the room. Jade realized that Brian wasn't willing to leave Diane, even to sleep. Brian was sitting on the edge of the bed, holding Diane's hand and talking to her.

Jade felt a little thrill of hope, maybe Diane was awake and talking! Jade walked around to the side of the bed and looked at Diane. She didn't look better. In fact, it seemed to Jade that she actually looked a little worse. The small wisps of hair she had earlier were gone. Diane was now completely bald, except a small part of the inner portion of her eyebrows. Her skin was ashen, her lips colorless. Jade sat on the other side of the bed and took Diane's other hand. "Diane, it's me, Jade. You are going to be okay. I think we figured out what's going on and how to fix it. Just hang in there. I love you, girl." Jade stifled a sob and turned away, still clutching Diane's hand. Brian watched Jade as she struggled for control. In a too-bright voice, Jade spoke to Diane again, this time trying to lighten the mood.

"Hey, guess what? I met Baby Girl. She's a sweetie! I just couldn't leave her at your house, so I packed her up and brought her to Derrick's house, so she'll have company until you are feeling better. Bardo didn't know what to make of her. I put her in our bedroom, she's warm and comfy, laying on the bed like she owns it. Until you get better, Baby Girl will be with me. Okay?" She realized that Diane couldn't answer, but as she studied her face, she realized that Diane's lips were moving, ever so slightly! She was trying to talk! Jade looked wildly at the two men. "Brian, Derrick, do you see that? Diane's trying to talk!" Both men immediately saw it too, and Brian ran out of the room to find a nurse. Jade squeezed Diane's hand. "Don't try to talk, we can tell that you know what's going on. I think you are going to feel a lot better very soon. I think the worst is over." Jade felt Diane's hand move, ever so faintly, in hers and realized that Diane was trying to squeeze her hand back.

The nurse came in, checked Diane's pulse, pupils, and the monitors beside the bed. She smiled at Jade and the men. "It seems our patient is beginning to come around. This is excellent! Her fever is down and her vital signs are stronger. That may mean that whatever has been stressing her body and losing its grip on her. I'll get some blood tests and see if what we think is happening is really happening. It may be too early to tell. If she's improving, we'll give her the rest of the dosage of Prussian Blue." The nurse bustled out, and Derrick moved to Jade's side and wrapped his arms around her shoulders as she sat on the bed with Diane.

"The test results on Diane's blood probably won't be in for hours yet. Let's go and get some sleep while we can and come back early tomorrow morning." Jade looked at her watch and was amazed to discover it was after midnight. "Good idea, I'm exhausted." Jade gave Diane a quick gentle hug, then gave Brian a firmer, longer hug.

When Derrick and Jade got back to Derrick's house, Derrick went directly through the bedroom to the shower. As soon as he opened the bedroom door, however, Baby Girl shot out and down the stairs. Jade, halfway up the stairs, turned and headed back down to oversee the big confrontation between Baby Girl and Bardo. In the kitchen doorway, a bemused Jade watched the two of them circle each other cautiously. Bardo wanted to play. Baby Girl obviously wanted Bardo dead. Since the kitten was too small to hurt Bardo much, and Bardo was obviously too spineless to hurt the kitten, Jade left them alone to work things out and headed back upstairs. The sound of the shower greeted her and she shed her clothing on the way to join Derrick.

An hour later, Jade and Derrick slept contentedly, wrapped in each other's arms. Baby Girl was stretched languidly across Jade's pillow. Bardo was snuggled at the bottom of the bed, between Derrick's feet.

Wednesday

"I did not!" Jade threw Derrick an exasperated look. "You did", Derrick replied with calm conviction. "Well I don't remember it, then!" Jade threw her hands up in surrender and Derrick reached out to take them, pulling Jade's upper body across the table and giving her a quick kiss. The kitchen table was strewn with the remains of their bacon-and-egg breakfast, and a pot of coffee that was almost empty. Derrick smiled teasingly. "When we were at the Lawrence house, and you were getting ready to leave, you said you were going home. And you meant MY home. And your home, too, if you want it to be." Jade, who was stirring her coffee, stopped and looked up at Derrick. "Are you asking me to move in with you?" Derrick smiled and just looked inquiringly at Jade. Jade wished she could feel the confidence in the future that Derrick so obviously felt. Maybe it would rub off on her. One could always hope.

"I think it's too soon to think about making any big changes like that. But that's the direction I'm hoping for." Derrick said, "Okay, that's good enough. For now. But you are going to stay here for another day or two at least, right?" He looked so earnest, so hopeful, that Jade was charmed. It was a wonderful feeling. "I'll tell you what, I'll stay tonight, but tomorrow I need to go home, I mean, my home. I'm going to talk to Malcolm about going back to work Friday, and I have some getting ready to do." Derrick pulled a comically exaggerated sad face and Jade laughed delightedly.

After they cleaned up the kitchen, Derrick and Jade slipped out into crisp, sunny morning for the quick drive to the hospital.

At the hospital, the news was good. They met Brian in the hallway on the way to Diane's room carrying two cups of Dunkin' Donuts coffee. They spotted each other at the same time. "Hi Jade, hey Derrick. Diane's MUCH better this morning. She's awake! She woke up a little after 5:00 this morning. The first thing this said was, "Where's Jade? Is she okay?" Jade smiled, realizing that her worry about Diane was apparently reciprocated. They got to Diane's room and Jade opened the door for Brian. He crossed to Diane's bed and handed her a coffee. Diane, who was propped up on pillows, lit up at the sight of the coffee, and squealed with delight at the sight of Jade. She put her coffee on the stand and held her arms out for Jade, who happily ran into them. Derrick and Brian decided to take a little break and leave the women alone.

"Thank God you are better! I thought we were going to lose you, for a little while there." Diane wiped her eyes and looked at Jade. "Me too! Brian told me that you were able to figure out what poisoned me, and the doctor gave me the antidote. How in God's name did you figure that out?" Jade said, "At first,

I had no idea. I panicked! Then, I remembered information I got from the library about a woman possibly being poisoned by a Lawrence family member, years ago. They used Thallium." Diane was amazed, "That's some kind of detective work, J." Jade looked at Diane, obviously troubled. "Don't be too impressed. It was me that got you into this situation in the first place."

Diane reached out to take Jade's hand. "Honey, listen to me. You are my best friend, remember? The sister I would have chosen if I were lucky enough to have one. If you were in this much danger and you didn't let me help, I'd be furious! So putting me in the picture was an act of self-defense on your part. Got it?" She looked sternly at Jade. Not trusting herself to speak, Jade nodded. Now, tell me what you think of Baby Girl. Isn't she a little princess?" On less troublesome ground now, Jade launched into an account of Baby Girl and Bardo's budding friendship. When the men returned, both women were laughing.

Not wanting to tire her out, Derrick and Jade went in search of the doctor after their brief visit with Diane. Dr. Bolton wasn't on shift, but the on shift doctor led them to the nurse's station and pulled a chart from the wall rack. The chest pocket of his crisp white lab coat bore the name "Dr. Topkis". After a moment looking through the pages on the clipboard, he looked at Jade. "You're Jade?" Jade confirmed she was. "You were right on the money. Diane apparently ingested a potentially lethal dose of Thallium. The candy bags you brought in also tested positive for Thallium, as did the candy that was still in one of the bags. Do you mind if I ask how you knew?" Jade thought she detected a note of suspicion in his voice. That was to be expected, she supposed. If she were in this shoes, she would certainly be asking the same question. "Dr. Topkis, this is Detective Derrick Zachary. He's been working closely with me on a related situation involving Diane Venezia." Derrick shook hands with the doctor, and the doctor turned back to Jade.

Jade started to respond, but Derrick smoothly interceded. "I'm afraid the answer to that question is confidential, as it relates to an ongoing investigation. What I can tell you is that the poison wasn't meant for Diane, it was meant for Jade." The doctor nodded curtly. "I understand. Please also understand my position. Any time injury occurs as a result of poisoning, especially with the use of a highly controlled substance such as Thallium, the law dictates that I must report it to the authorities. I was pending completion of the process so that I would be able to include your explanation. But since you are unwilling to provide that information, I'll need to file the report without it." The doctor's expression clearly communicated his frustration with both of them. Derrick said, "Dr. Topkis, I apologize for the 'cloak and dagger' routine. I just can't jeopardize an ongoing investigation. I hope you understand my position." The doctor looked frostily from one to the other of them. "And, I hope you understand mine. I'm sure you'll be hearing from someone in the Department of Homeland Security." Dr. Topkis turned on his heel and strode away. Derrick and Jade looked at each other, and rolled their eyes in unison as they watched Dr. Topkis' ramrod straight form recede.

As they climbed into Derrick's truck, Derrick's cell phone rang. Derrick answered it, was silent for a moment, then said, "Okay, we're on our way." Jade asked, "On our way where?" Derrick answered, "Michael's. He's apparently found some interesting information about the Lawrences. Jade had forgotten that Michael was continuing his online sleuthing for them. "Since we had a little time, I told him we could head over there now. That's okay, isn't it?" Jade sat back and watched the road. "Absolutely. It's about time we got some helpful intel. Bless Michael's strange little heart." Jade looked over in time to catch Derrick's fleeting expression, which was seemingly part hurt, part bemusement.

At Michael's house, Jade and Derrick sat in kitchen chairs, to each side of Michael, and watched while he once again worked his magic. "This is a chat room posting from a week ago. You don't even want to know the kind of website this was." After a few clicks of his mouse, Michael opened a picture. It was Ben Lawrence's death scene! Derrick said, "This isn't one of the police photos, look at the angle. The person who took this picture would have had to be sitting on the sofa at the back of the room. And look at this! The murder weapon is on the floor in front of Ben's body!" Jade looked closer, and saw the bloody table leg on the floor. She instantly recognized it as the same one that had been planted in the back of her truck.

Jade looked at Ben's limp body, thrown on the floor like an unwanted doll and she felt a surge of anger. To have taken a picture and posted it on the internet! Derrick, too, was affected by the callousness of the killer. "Goddamn it! We have to catch this guy! He's apparently proud of what he's done, and wants to share it. If we can track this photo back to him, it would be a good start." He looked at Michael, and Michael immediately dashed any hope he may have had. "Your guy is good, really good. His online access has been routed through several servers, some of which are overseas. There's no way to track him, and believe me, I've tried." Derrick pushed away from the table, clearly frustrated.

He paced the kitchen restlessly, then stopped and turned to Michael. "You said we wouldn't want to know what website you found this picture on. What was it, Michael?" Michael looked away from Derrick, suddenly uncomfortable. "It was a snuff site. Pretty horrific stuff." Jade asked Michael, "How did you find this?" Michael smiled, seeming pleased with himself. "I reviewed the notes I took about the Lawrences. Then I put in a Boolean search with the words

'Möbius" (and) "Murder'. The person who posted the picture on the site called himself "ShadowOfMöbius". Jade made herself look more carefully at the photo. If this was all Timothy was giving them to go on, she was going to make sure she got every possible clue from it. "Michael, is there a way to increase the resolution on this?" Michael clicked a couple times on the toolbar at the top of the picture and it jumped into sharper relief.

Jade continued to scan every inch of the photo. "Now, can you further enlarge parts of the picture but still keep the resolution?" Michael asked, "What part of the picture do you want to see more clearly?" Jade pointed to an object on the floor, in the corner of the photo, partially cut off but still visible. Michael clicked an item on the toolbar at the top of the screen once again, then rolled the mouse over that section of the photo. The object instantly enlarged. Her suspicion confirmed, Jade looked at Derrick. "How could Ben Lawrence have the same blue vase that my father has?" Derrick took a closer look at the picture. "I don't know, but I do know that the killer must have taken the vase with him because it wasn't there when the police processed the room."

Jade then remembered her mother's words to her, just after she had been hit by the car in front of the funeral home. "Ask your father about the vase." Jade knew that Ben Lawrence's death may have had something to do with the vase. She knew that there must be at least two vases. She last saw her dad's blue vase AFTER Ben Lawrence was killed and Ben's blue vase disappeared from his room. And her father's vase was missing. As was her father.

Jade was shaken from her reverie by Michael's next comment. "There's something else I think you need to see. I was directed to this website when I clicked a link in the Lawrence family information I had previously located in public records. A website came up that Jade instantly recognized. "This is the family crest website I already found, Michael." Jade felt vaguely disappointed. Michael said, "I realize you may have seen this, I remember you mentioning a family crest website. But, I went deeper, and look what else I found." Jade watched Michael's hands fly over the keyboard, and a moment later, a new page appeared, one she hadn't seen. Michael said, "This is an online conversation between Daniel and his twin brother Dillon, dated just over a month ago." Jade leaned closer to the screen and began to read.

Prof12635: I'm not going to warn you again, stay away from me and my family, Daniel.

MobiDan8: Dillon, I know what you've been doing and it needs to stop. My son is looking for you, and if he finds you or your family, you know what will happen. You know there can only be one Möbius at a time and your time is up. My son isn't going to allow you to continue. I told you what our father did to his father, when his father refused to yield to the next generation. I don't blame you for the unspeakable things you have done; I'm not sure you could have prevented becoming who you are. But it's time to step aside. Don't think for a moment I care about you, I care about your family, they will be the innocent victims.

Prof12635: I told you to NEVER call me Dillon. My name is Brandon. What I do, and the fate of my family is of no concern to you.

Jade reached out to hit the page down key, but there were no further entries. Michael and Derrick watched, with matching expressions of puzzlement, as Jade's tears overflowed, rolling down her cheeks. Derrick stood up and moved to the chair next to Jade's. He put an arm around Jade and pulled her closer. Jade stiffened, resisting the comfort he offered, then she slumped against him and let the tears come. When Jade's sobs had subsided to deep, watery sighs,

Derrick spoke. "Jade, if we are going to be able to help, you need to tell us what this information means to you."

Jade looked up at Derrick, her face a study in sorrow. When she spoke, her voice cracked with emotion. "Prof12635 is my father. That's his online screen name. He's a professor at USM, and his home address number is 12635. He's had that email address for years." She fell silent for a moment, while both men considered this. "Don't you see? Daniel and my father have been in contact, and for some reason, Daniel thinks my father is his twin brother Dillon. How could that be true? We know the Lawrences are killers. My dad isn't a Lawrence, and he certainly isn't a killer." Jade's resolve turned to doubt, and she looked at Derrick and whispered, "Is he?"

Jade sat silently, spent. She thought about her father, all the secrets, all the strangeness that seemed to surround her and their family when she was a child. She realized that the reality she was trying so hard to reject may actually answer many of her questions. Michael said, "Jade, I found a picture of Daniel online. Since he thinks your father is his twin brother, and from what you said you found in the police records, Daniel and Dillon were definitely identical, seeing a picture of Daniel may help you determine whether there's any truth to what Daniel is saying. Do you want to see the picture?" Jade thought about this, sensing the import of the decision. If she refused, she may be able to continue to believe in her father. If she agreed and the picture didn't look like her father, she could continue to believe in her father. But, if she looked at the picture and Daniel did look like her father, she knew that would be the proof she really didn't want, that her father was, in fact, Dillon, a Lawrence, and possibly a psychopathic killer. Jade realized that she wouldn't be able to put her fear to rest without conclusive proof, either way. "Yes, please show me the picture."

Chapter 41

She watched, breathlessly, as the screen-sized picture of Daniel swiftly filled the page. Jade looked at the picture, then at Derrick, then back at the picture. The picture was her father. Yet, it was not . The man in the picture looked more tired, a bit sadder. If her father had had a much more difficult, less fulfilling life, this, Jade thought, is what he would look like now. She realized that she must have known, on some level, that things with her father were not what they seemed, because she wasn't as shocked as she probably should have been. Derrick, who had met Jade's father at the hospital, obviously recognized the man in this picture as a relative, and a close one. He said nothing, preferring to let Jade work things out for herself first. After another moment of reflection, Jade spoke.

"Suddenly several things make sense. First, I know now that it was no accident that I was commissioned to do the appraisal on that jewelry case. *I'm* a Lawrence family descendant! Also, the library in England emailed me, among other things, a picture of Alois, the mother of Ben Lawrence's children, and she looked exactly like me! I couldn't get over it at the time, and I remember how upsetting I found it, without really understanding why. Now I know. You remember the blue vase we saw in the picture of Ben Lawrence's room, and my recognition that my father has one just like it? It must be a Lawrence family heirloom set. I also remember seeing a man at the cemetery, at Ben Lawrence's grave, who looked just like my father. He was with a woman, and I was so freaked out about my father being with another woman that I didn't think about it beyond that. It wasn't my father, it was Daniel, Ben's son, paying his respects."

Derrick said, "Jade, this is going to be a difficult question for you to answer, but your safety may depend on your ability to answer it honestly. I know the evidence seems compelling, but do *you* think your father is a killer?"

Jade thought about it carefully before she answered. A series of images shot through her mind. Her mother's note saying that Peter's transgressions seemed to be too much indulged by their father. She also recalled that her mother said Peter may have committed the murder of the woman in her neighborhood when Jade was just a child. She remembered the trunk her mother found in the closet of Peter's room, filled with women's clothing and some of their father's jewelry. She remembered all the times her father was gone for days, and her mother telling Jade, with a voice and expression clearly at odds with her reassuring words, that her father just had a few things he had to do, and he'd be home soon.

Jade also recalled how alarmed her father seemed when she recently showed interest in the big blue vase. How he had rushed to take the vase away from her as she tried to turn it over to see what may have been written on the bottom of it. Then she remembered the dream she had recently, where her father was trying to kill her, his face fully of sorrow and regret as someone who looked exactly like him stood behind him. She realized that several of these puzzle-pieces had been floating through her mind for days, and her subconscious mind may have been working through things more quickly than her conscious mind. One of her dream images could have been her father, Brandon, who his family knew as Dillon, and the other person could have been Daniel. The full force of her realization hit. Her father could be a killer. She had no proof, but she needed to allow for the possibility, given all the evidence and given her own instinctive reasoning.

Jade worked to get control of her feelings. Calmer now, Jade said, "Michael, is there any way to track down my father, or to at least determine the last time he corresponded with anyone over the web using that email address?" Michael responded, "I tried to track him through his ISP but there was no further activity posted under that email address or screen name." Jade then turned to Derrick and answered his question. "I think it's possible that my father IS a Lawrence, and by association, I must be too." Jade shivered involuntarily, then reined in her scattered thoughts and continued. "But I'm not completely ready to accept that my father is or was a mass murderer. Some of what I remember about my father, while I was growing up, may point in that direction. But again, I have no solid evidence of anything. I think I owe my father the benefit of a doubt until I have more information either way. All we have here is Daniel's statements that my father is a killer. I have to tell you, I think it's also possible that Daniel is the killer, instead of my father."

Derrick listened to what Jade had to say, then said, "I think your logic is sound, Jade. I do want you to be cautious around your father, just in case, okay?" Jade's misery was clearly written on her face. "My father is still missing. It's possible, reading this, that he could be dead. If he's not dead, and if I get a chance to confront him, I'm going to." Derrick said, "I do NOT want you confronting him. If you see him, I don't want you to let on that you suspect anything." Jade thought about that. "I'm not sure I can act as though nothing has changed, Derrick. EVERYTHING has changed. And I want and need to get to the bottom of who my father is and what he may have done. My whole life up to this point may have been a lie!" Jade put her head down on the table, wrapping her arms around herself.

The soothing voice of reason, Michael spoke up. "Jade, if your father is not who you thought he was, that has nothing to do with who you are. His possible false life is his problem, not yours. Yes, you've had to pay a price for his deceit, but it's not your fault and does not, and should not, reduce you in any way." Jade turned a watery smile on Michael, pleased that he would step so far out of his comfort zone to try to comfort to her. "You are absolutely right. What my father did or didn't do has nothing to do with me. I'm not going to let this take anything more from me than it already has."

On the way to the truck, Jade's cell phone rang. It was Malcolm. She suddenly realized that they had a lunch date that day. She spent a few minutes chatting with him, then begged off lunch. She agreed to call him over the weekend to set up a new lunch date.

At the hospital, Jade was pleased to see that Diane's condition had improved dramatically. "J, get me the hell out of here?!" Jade looked over at her friend, sitting up, arms crossed, looking charmingly petulant, do-rag and all. Jade smiled at her and said, "Tomorrow afternoon, if all your tests come back okay, the doctor said he'd release you. Tonight, you stay right where you are and get waited on for just a little while longer. I know it's a hell of a sacrifice, but I'm afraid it's not negotiable." Diane further exaggerated her glum expression, then laughed. "I know, I know. I'm just ready to go home, you know?" Jade remembered how close Diane had come to dying, and such a short time ago. Now look at her! Ready to take on the world again! Jade and Derrick said their goodbyes, and they headed back out into the darkening late afternoon.

After a quick stop at Hannaford to pick up dinner supplies, Jade and Derrick headed home. Jade realized with a feeling halfway between pleasure and fear that she had begun to think of Derrick's imposing estate as "home". As soon as they stepped into the door to Derrick's house, Derrick's land line phone started it's crazy ring tone. Derrick checked the caller ID quickly, then took the call. "Hi Michael, forget something?" He listened for a moment, growing still and serious. He thanked Michael for calling then disconnected. Jade said, "What did he forget to tell us?" Jade wasn't surprised to find herself bracing for yet more bad news. Derrick said, "He called to warn me that he got an automated email message from his spy ware program that a Trojan horse had been attached to his internet access ID. Michael ran a diagnostic on it to look at the code prior to nuking it, and realized that the program that was inserted on his computer was designed to track his keystrokes, and to report through a series of switchback IP addresses where he's been and what information he accessed."

Jade immediately grasped the implication. "Timothy, right?" Derrick nodded. "Michael wasn't able to trace the source of the spy ware, but he WAS able to confirm that it was inserted at the exact moment that he entered the website that he found with the message board conversation between Daniel and your father. Michael seems to think that Timothy rigged Daniel's computer with the Trojan Horse source code, probably through an attachment that Timothy would have sent to Daniel. Then, whenever Daniel used the computer, the program would replicate, which, in this case, is exactly what it did."

"Michael wasn't too worried about the damage the program did, but he wanted us to know that Timothy likely knows that we've uncovered his connection to you, and your connection to the Lawrences. Michael told me to tell you to be really careful. This program was extremely sophisticated. He also wanted us to know that he checked out the cell phone number and the addresses for Timothy, and they were all dead ends. He said he'd try a couple more ways to find him, but he doesn't believe he'll be able to."

Jade struggled to shake off her feeling of impending doom. "Well, I guess it's good to get everything out in the open. I'm hoping that, if Timothy knows I'm aware of who he is, maybe we won't have to find him, maybe *he'll* contact *me*. Would he really kill his own cousin, do you think?" Derrick looked disgusted. "Yes, I definitely think he would. I think he probably killed his grandfather, Ben Lawrence, and I hate to say this, but I think it's possible he may have killed your father, Jade." Jade thought about it. She nodded sadly. "Okay, I accept the possibility. We'll have to be vigilant, and hope we can stay a step ahead of him." In the harsh light of the kitchen, Derrick took a good look at Jade's face. She looked pale, and dark circles ringed her sad eyes. Jade turned away from his scrutiny when she caught his troubled expression.

After dinner, Jade and Derrick sat on the couch, cognacs in hand, and talked about the events of the day. Jade spoke about what weighed most heavily on her mind. "I'm still trying to deal with the idea that I'm a Lawrence. Now I know why that jewelry case ended up in my hands. I remember feeling very strangely the first time I held it, when I found the note inside the false bottom. Derrick, I honestly think that some kind of trace ancestral memory, deep inside me, was crying out. Do you think that's strange?"

Derrick took a sip of his drink, then turned to Jade. "To tell you the truth, many of the things that have happened lately defy explanation. Far be it from me to judge you or anyone on the basis of something I can't hope to understand. I believe in you, and I'm going to keep you safe." Jade said, "I'm all for that. But, seriously, I just can't see my father as a murderer. I wish there was some way to prove this thing, one way or the other." Something pulled at Jade's memory then. She caught hold and pulled, and it came to her. "You remember that murder I told you about from my childhood? You know, the one that involved a woman who was killed on the other side of the woods behind my parents' house?"

Derrick immediately brightened. "Oh yes! I think I have information for you about that. Since the detective who was in charge of the case no longer works for the department, I contacted the records department and had the case file pulled. It's all on computer now, so I asked that the information be emailed to me. I saw it in my email mailbox earlier, but I didn't have time to read through it. Let's take a look now." They moved into Derrick's computer room. Derrick hit a button and the computer leapt to life. Within a few seconds, the screen displayed Derrick's email inbox. Derrick used his zip file program and his password to open the records he received that morning.

Jade knew the drill, and she moved her chair so that she couldn't see the screen. Derrick glanced at her, smiled, and turned back to the computer screen. "This is it." Jade's heart sped up as she watched Derrick's face as he read the information. There was definitely something there! She had confirmation a moment later when he said, "I shouldn't be sharing this information with you, since the case was not solved, but since it's been cold so long, I don't see the harm. One of the suspects was your father. Your brother was mentioned, briefly, but he was cleared for two reasons. One, the brutality of the crime, and the strength it would have required were beyond your brother's fifteen-year old's capability. The woman's throat was slashed so deeply she was almost decapitated. Her hands and feet were disarticulated. And there's mention of a symbol, scratched into the dirt at the victim's head. This file is almost 30 years old, and there are no pictures of the symbol, but I think you might recognize the description. 'The symbol is a number eight, and there are smaller symbols inside each of the loops, which cannot be discerned.'"

Chills marched up and down Jade's arms. Somehow, she had known that this murder was going to end up being connected to the Lawrences. Derrick clicked the file closed and pushed back from the computer. "No one was ever convicted of the crime, and there was never even enough evidence to charge anyone. God, I would love to solve this. And also solve all those other murders that you've been looking into. Even if we aren't able to get the proof we need, do you realize how much stronger some of these cases are going to become when we are able to connect them through the Möbius symbol? I don't have much pull, and all of these cases were handled by other detectives and some of them aren't still working for the department. But that doesn't mean I can't poke around on my own. I know you are focused on the Lawrence killer. I want you to know that, although my purpose is a little different, we both want the same thing. Most important of all, I know you aren't going to be safe until we stop this man, and whoever else is also killing."

Jade nodded her agreement, then said, "I think we can do it, Derrick. First, I need to know if my father is one of the Lawrence family killers. Then, I want to find him, dead or alive, I need to know what happened and where he is. I'm starting to feel more strongly now that my father is dead." Jade looked down at her lap, struggling for control of her emotions. She took a deep breath and looked bravely at Derrick's face. She tried for matter-of-fact, but her voice shook. "I think I'm also more than half convinced that my father is, or was, a killer. If he is, I'll need to face the fact that I never really knew him at all. How can I feel so much pain for some who's likely a stranger to me? If he's the man I'm afraid he is, how can I be related to him?" Jade looked back down again, suddenly not able to meet Derrick's eyes.

Derrick put a hand gently to each side of Jade's face and turned her head up to face his. "Listen, honey. In case you haven't figured it out yet, I love you. I'm here for you, and I will be here for you, as long as you want and need me. Just hang in there, and let me help when I can help, okay? I promise, you won't be alone." Jade smiled through her tears and looped an arm around Derrick's neck, pulling him to her for a salty kiss. "You're fabulous, do you know that?" He chuckled and said, "Of course I know that. You are so lucky to have me!" Derrick logged out of his email mailbox. "There wasn't much else in the report. They didn't have any other suspects or leads, the case went cold."

Jade and Derrick spent the rest of the evening watching TV together, then went to bed. Jade drifted off to sleep smiling at the idea that even making dinner and watching TV with Derrick was better than any "date" she'd ever had with anyone else.

Thursday morning brought warm temperatures and rain. Jade loved the rain because it made the snow melt, and she didn't like snow. Or cold, for that matter. Warm and comfortable under Derrick's comforter, Jade lay quietly, listening to Derrick's slow, even breathing. She wondered where her father was, and if he was alive. She looked at the clock beside the bed, and was startled to learn that it was almost 9:00! She was getting much too accustomed to sleeping in these days! She picked up the telephone, and before she would let herself think too much about it, she punched in Phyllis' telephone number. Phyllis' husband, Alex, answered on the second ring. Jade asked for Phyllis, then waited while Alex went to fetch her. She could hear the sound of Phyllis' kids arguing in the background. Phyllis' son was almost nine, and her daughter, just turned six. Both headstrong and intelligent, like their mother. At the moment, Jade thought, they sounded more headstrong than intelligent.

The sound of Jade's voice on the phone had awakened Derrick, and he turned to Jade with raised eyebrows. She cupped the receiver and said, "I just realized that I haven't checked in with Phyllis for awhile, she may have heard from my dad." Derrick nodded, ran a hand through his hair, and headed for the bathroom. Phyllis came on the line as Jade watched Derrick's tight little butt disappear behind the bathroom door.

"Hey Jade, what's up?" Jade reined in her distracted thoughts. "Hi Phyl. Have you heard from Daddy?" Phyllis said, "No, not a word. I do think it's strange, but I also know he's an adult, and he's got a lot to deal with right now. He has the legal right to disappear forever, and there wouldn't be anything you or I could do about it." Jade realized, listening to Phyllis, that Phyllis just didn't get it. "I know you're right, Phyllis, but don't you also think that Daddy has a moral obligation to keep us from worrying unnecessarily? After all, we just lost our brother and our mother, all in a very short period of time." Phyllis appeared to think this through, but her next words confirmed to Jade that Phyllis wasn't considering anyone's point of view but her own.

"Jade, you were always Daddy's Little Girl. You were the baby of the family, and Daddy spoiled you rotten. We both know it. If I'm not as close to him as you are, that's probably why. I think he probably just needed to get away for a little impromptu vacation. I, for one, am not going to 'borrow trouble' by becoming overly concerned before I even have proof that anything is wrong. I would suggest that you figure out a way to rein in that emotional brain of yours and do the same. Now you have a good day, and try to stop worrying!". Phyllis hung up, without giving Jade the opportunity to respond. Par for the course, Jade thought bitterly, replacing the receiver.

Derrick came out of the bathroom and ushered Jade in. Jade took a few minutes to wash up, change into some jeans and a sweater and run a comb through her hair. When she came out of the bathroom, she followed her nose downstairs to the coffee.

Jade sat down at the kitchen table, steaming mug of coffee clutched in one hand. The telephone rang, and Jade laughed once again at the ring tone. The deep male voice saying, "Book 'em Derrick", over and over. As Derrick hurried to answer it, he stuck his tongue out at Jade as he passed her, which earned him the infamous Jade eye-roll. Derrick brought the receiver to Jade and held it out. "It's Diane. She asked if you could please come and get her, now. She knows she isn't supposed to be released until this afternoon but she sounds a little stir crazy. Talk to her!"

Jade grabbed the phone. "Diane, you know you can't leave until your blood tests come back this afternoon. Did the nurse come to draw blood already?" Diane verified that she had. "Well then, all you have to do is wait. Surely you can do that?" Derrick chuckled when he heard, from several feet away, the sound of Diane whimpering. "I know you hate being there. And I know you have things to do. Just don't do anything stupid." There was a pause, then Jade said, "Yes, Baby Girl is just fine. I'll call you at noontime to see if there's any news, okay?" Diane reluctantly agreed to wait. Jade continued. "Stay put, okay?" Diane's response made Jade grin. "Yeah well, takes one to know one. Talk to you later, doll."

Jade hung up the phone, then walked over to Derrick and climbed into his lap. Warm at last! Derrick smiled down at her. "What do you want to do today?" Derrick smiled broadened. "It may not be a good idea to sit on my lap and ask me what I want to do." Jade snuggled a little closer, then started to understand what he meant. She jumped off his lap and sat in the chair next to him, a study in primness. He laughed heartily. "Really!", Jade said in her best elderly spinster voice. Then, she sobered. "You have to go back to work tomorrow, and I'll probably go back to work after this weekend. It would be nice to make some headway on the Lawrences today, if we can." Derrick said, "Definitely, let's make that our priority. After we take a quick ride down to the station. I had a voicemail message on my cell this morning from Leo, he has some information to share with me about the Small case, and I told him I'd stop by this morning."

At the station, Gavin Leo saw Jade and Derrick come in and intercepted them. "Let's talk in here." He motioned to a small interview room and all three entered, Leo shut the door behind them and they all settled around a small rectangular table. Leo looked from Derrick to Jade, questioningly. Derrick said, "Leo, Jade's the person who provided the additional evidence to jump start our investigation. I'd be grateful if you would go ahead and tell what you found out. Don't worry about Jade, she's not here in any official capacity." Jade put a hand up, palm out. "That's right, I'm not here, ignore me." She gave Leo an encouraging smile and he shifted his attention from her to Derrick. "

"The Loo gave the case to my yesterday. I did some nit-picking through all our evidence. You aren't going to believe what I found." Leo sat back, looking smug. Both Jade and Derrick started clamoring for more information, and Leo stood up, laughing and holding both hands up in surrender. "Okay, okay, simmer down, I'll tell you. Derrick, you probably remember from the police report that Nate drove a burgundy Firebird?" Jade suddenly pushed herself away from the table. "What did you say? A burgundy Firebird? Derrick, remember the last time I went to my parent's house, a few days ago, and found that note, the day I realized my dad was missing? I was followed home by a burgundy Firebird!"

The color drained from Derrick's face. "Oh man! I didn't make the connection. I guess something should have clicked after you told me you were followed, when I read the Small report. It had to have been the same car. There just aren't that many burgundy Firebirds around." Leo, who was beginning to look decidedly impatient, interrupted Derrick's self-flagellation. "Hey, okay if I finish or what?" Derrick pulled Jade closer to him and nodded.

Leo continued, "Okay, good. Anyway, we pulled the plate numbers for Mr. Small's car and ran them. He had several outstanding parking tickets as well as a serious moving violation for which he has not paid the fines. So we impounded his car, as was within our legal right. In securing the vehicle for transport, we found an illegal substance sitting on the front passenger seat, in plain sight, which gave us authorization to search the vehicle, which of course, we did. In the trunk, we found a hard copy of a book that Nate Small has written and apparently intends to publish.

"But, get this, the manuscript, which is all about the murder of his wife, contains a reference to our holdback." He spotted Jade's confused expression. "A holdback is some element of the crime that the police keep from the public, including the family. It's often done to weed out the kooks from the legitimate witnesses and suspects. I can't tell you the specifics, but I can tell you that no one but the police and the killer would have known this. It's not in the police report that was provided to him, I checked. Since Nate Small definitely isn't police, well…." Jade and Derrick sat in stunned silence. Jade recovered first, pounding her fist on the table. "I knew it! As soon as I met that guy, I KNEW there was something wrong with him. Please tell me you picked him up and he's in jail at this very moment?"

Leo nodded. "You bet he is, and madder than a wet hen. Can you imagine the unbelievable arrogance of the man, to use the police holdback in the book he wrote, then to pursue having it published? Does he think the police don't read books? Shit, the guy's a friggin' idiot!" Derrick said, "Well I feel better having him put away. Maybe now that he's safely locked up, that's one less reason for Jade to be afraid." Jade said, "Now, if we can only take care of that other, slightly more serious matter…" Derrick said, "We will, you just watch." Leo looked from one to the other of them, obviously curious. He cleared his throat and said, "Well, I just wanted to let you know that this is one cold case that's been solved. And we have your lady here to thank for that."

Chapter 42

On the road, Jade pulled out her cell phone and called home to check her messages. There were two "hang ups", then, the third message that at first appeared to be just another hang up, but a male voice suddenly spoke, one that Jade instantly recognized. "Hey cousin, it's me." There was a long pause, punctuated by muffled laughter. Jade waited in silence for Timothy to continue speaking. "Well, you know everything now. Okay, actually, you know ALMOST everything. There are a couple details I know you haven't tumbled to quite yet." Derrick, watching Jade's face, realized who must have left this message. "Jade, it's Timothy, isn't it?" Jade nodded, continuing to listen. Derrick's face tightened as he drove them into the back of a parking lot and stopped the truck. Timothy was laughing again. After a moment, he made a final, chilling statement. "You dad says hi... from Hell!" The sound of his laughter was cut off abruptly as Timothy disconnected.

Derrick said, "What did he say?" Jade stared straight ahead, and Derrick's alarm clearly showed on her face. Jade didn't even hear him! "Jade, honey, are you okay?" Jade slowly turned to face Derrick. As the sunlight hit her face, he could see the sparkle of tears. Her voice, when she answered, sounded strangely detached and emotionless, as if all feeling had been wrung from her. "Derrick, I think he killed my father." Derrick sat for a moment, then he asked, "Did he say that?" Jade answered, still speaking in that not-quite-there voice, "He said that my father said hi, from Hell." Derrick pulled Jade closer, and felt her body shivering. "Don't give up on your father, yet, okay? Timothy could very well be trying to mess with you. He may know your father is missing, if he's been stalking him, but he may not have any more idea than you have where your father is and whether he's okay. He took a chance and he hit a nerve, that's all."

Jade knew Derrick was right. She wanted to find out where her dad was, find out if he was a killer and if so, get him, and any of the other Lawrences who were killers off the street. Derrick was apparently thinking along similar lines. He said, "Jade, I know there are several things we need to get done here. Do you have any idea what you want to do first?" Jade answered, "It's almost creepy how you do that." Derrick looked puzzled. "Do what?" "Say what I'm thinking." Derrick chuckled. "Oh, well, I'm extremely psychic, you know." Jade filled him in on her priorities, and mentioned that he should already have intuited them, being psychic and all.

They pulled back on to the road, and Derrick said, "I've got an idea. You said your first priority would be to find your dad. I think we should check the caller ID on your home phone, to see if there was a number associated with that call from Timothy ." Jade said, "His previous calls have all been listed as 'private caller'. Derrick answered, "I still think it's worth a look. He could have gotten sloppy, or maybe he decided he didn't care if you knew the number from which he called." "Or," Jade said, "he could be letting me track him, baiting me to come after him."

362

At Jade's house, she headed straight for the caller ID box and tabbed through the entries. She was amazed to discover that Derrick was absolutely right. There WAS a number associated with Timothy's call. And it was a number she immediately recognized as her parents' number. Shit! This was NOT looking good for her dad! "Derrick, we need to go to my parents' house, Timothy made that call from there." Without a word, Derrick scooped his keys off the kitchen table and headed out the door, Jade in close pursuit.

In the truck, Derrick immediately pulled Jade closer after he navigated them on to the highway. "You're shaking." Jade burrowed closer, worrying about what she would find at her parents' house. Derrick, reading the direction of her thoughts, said, "What was the time and date on the call from Timothy, did you notice?" Jade said, "It was 7:45 this morning." Derrick was quiet for a moment, then he said, "Somehow, Timothy was involved with that Trojan Horse program on Michael's computer. It's the only way he could have known, for sure, that you now know who he is." Jade agreed. Somehow, realizing that Timothy was behind something so technologically advanced and insidious didn't make her feel any better at all.

At Jade's parents' house, everything seemed in order, at least from the outside. Jade retrieved the spare key and unlocked the door. As she grasped the doorknob to enter the house, Derrick gently moved Jade to the side, held a finger to his lips in a gesture of silence, then quietly moved ahead of her through the open doorway. They went room to room, silent and searching. Everything looked as it had the day Jade had been here looking for her father, with the exception, inexplicably, of things being more tidy.

She went upstairs, to show Derrick the condition of her parent's bedroom, remembering the mess someone had made of it. She stopped just inside the doorway. The room was pristine! Jade hoped it meant her father had been here, at least for long enough to clean up. Derrick looked at Jade, puzzled. "I thought you told me that this room was trashed?" Jade said, "I did, I mean, it was." Derricked walked out of the bedroom and down the hallway to the stairs, Jade trailing uncertainly.

"Well, since you've spent so much more time here than I have, do me a favor and look around carefully, tell me if anything seems out of place." Jade spent the next few minutes walking through the house, looking at the placement of furniture, appliances and bric-a-brac. There was nothing obviously out of place, and she told Derrick so. "Okay, then I'd say it was likely that your father came back, straightened up, then left again. If it had been someone else, someone who didn't know where things belong, you would have noticed that things weren't put in their usual places." Jade smiled at him. "Pretty clever, aren't you?" Derrick said, "Do you have a pen and a piece of paper? I'm going to leave a note for either your dad or Timothy, whoever shows up here first." Derrick sat down at the kitchen table and started writing. When he was done writing, Jade read the note.

Please call us at 555-0981. We know about what's been happening. We need to talk, and soon. Before things go any further. Please don't make us hunt you down.

Jade smiled, understanding instantly what Derrick was up to. "You wrote this note to apply to either my dad *or* Timothy. And you worded it to make it sound like we are in control, to try to put whomever reads this off their A game. Excellent! Jade propped the note up against the lazy Susan on the kitchen table, facing the front door, so it would be spotted immediately by anyone entering the house.

Driving home, Jade called the hospital to see if Diane's blood tests had come back yet. Diane was even more impatient than she had been earlier that day. "Jade, I swear to God, if you don't come and get me out of here right this very minute, I'm going to take a nurse hostage and use her to bargain my way out!" Jade grinned, knowing Diane probably wouldn't do it, but that she had likely worked out all the details in her head by now. "Diane, you know you can't leave until the doctor clears you. Have the blood tests come back yet?" There was a sullen silence, then Diane said, "No, but I just sent Brian to find the doctor again, so we can find out what the hold up is." Jade thought, poor Brian. "Okay, I'll tell you what. Derrick and I are in the truck, headed back to his house. If the doctor clears you, call me on my cell and we can be there in fifteen minutes." Diane reluctantly agreed, then with a dour "Ciao", disconnected.

Derrick said, "Well she's certainly got her panties in a twist!" Jade chuckled. "She may call right back, and if she does, we'll need to zip right over to the hospital and relieve them of her." Derrick said, "I'm all over it." Before Jade could put her cell phone back in her purse, it started to ring. "That's got to be her." Jade flipped the phone open and was greeted by the sound of Diane's voice, whooping and yelling. "Well, I guess you've been liberated!" With Brian happily singing in the background, Diane confirmed that she was, in fact, free to move about the city. Jade said the words Diane was waiting to hear. "Get dressed and pack your shit, I'm on my way."

At the hospital, Jade and Derrick saw Diane and Brian waiting in the reception area just inside the hospital doors. Diane stood up, hurried over to Jade and embraced her. When they drew apart, Brian stood up and crossed to where Jade was. He looked from Jade to Derrick. "Dr. Bolton wants a word with you both,

before we leave. We'll wait for you here." Diane said, "Hurry up! I want out!"
Jade and Derrick turned as one and walked to the elevator.

On the floor where Diane's room had been, Jade approached the nurses' station
and requested the duty nurse page Dr. Bolton. Within moments, Dr. Bolton
appeared. "Thank you both for your time." He turned and strode briskly into an
empty patient room across the corridor, Jade and Derrick close behind. The
doctor closed the door most of the way, then turned to face Jade. "Let me start
by saying that Diane is going to be fine. I don't want you to worry
unnecessarily. But I do feel the need to speak frankly about something. I think
it's possible that Diane might be somewhat, well, delusional." He looked from
Jade to Derrick, noted the identical expressions of confusion, and continued.
"She's tried very hard to keep to herself the circumstances surrounding her
brush with death, but she's said a few very strange things, and I was a bit
concerned about her."

Jade felt herself flush and willed the guilty color out of her cheeks. She said,
"Dr. Bolton, I'm not sure how much of what's happening you know about, but I
can tell you that Diane is NOT delusional. She almost died because she ate
poisoned candy that was intended for me. She was kidnapped by the man who
has been stalking me, in an effort to get me to stop investigating his family."
Dr. Bolton looked thoughtfully at Jade for a moment, then said, "That would
explain why she's so jumpy. I only hope you can get this investigation of yours
concluded rather quickly, before anything else happens to your friend." Jade
looked at the floor, stung by the doctor's censure. Derrick squeezed her hand
and said, "Dr. Bolton, we appreciate everything you've done for Diane. But I
have to also speak frankly. I resent the implication that Jade or I in any way
caused Diane's misfortune, simply by virtue of knowing her."

366

The doctor held both hands up, palms out. "Whoa, wait just a second. I didn't mean that the way you took it. I'm worried about Diane, that's all." He looked at Jade. "Jade, Diane would walk through fire for you, you know that, right?" Jade nodded. "Well, if there's any way to get her out of harm's way, just until you get this situation figured out, it would really be so much better for her." Jade immediately saw the logic in that. "Okay, Dr. Bolton, I agree with you. I'll talk to Diane and Brian, and see how we can keep her safer going forward." Dr. Bolton looked immediately relieved. "I'm so glad." Jade thanked the doctor for his concern and Derrick apologized for initially misunderstanding his caring message.

Downstairs, Brian and Diane were sitting in the lobby, wrapped in each other's arms. Jade saw with amusement that Diane had removed her do-rag and was proudly sporting her shiny white pate. Brian, on the other hand, had Diane's pink flowered bandanna on *his* head. Jade elbowed Derrick. "What a couple of goobers." Derrick nodded his agreement. Diane spotted Jade, then looked at Brian, said something, then walked down the corridor to meet Jade halfway. "Can I talk to you for a second?" Derrick understandingly walked away toward Brian. Diane spoke softly. "Jade, listen, Brian and I have been talking about where I need to go from here. What I mean is, and no offense intended, but I don't feel safe around here anymore."

Jade nodded encouragingly, and Diane immediately looked relieved. "I don't want to leave you holding the bag or anything, but I definitely can't stick around here. Brian asked me to move in with him, at least until things calm down. What do you think of the idea?" Jade looked at her friend's hopeful expression and realized how important her answer was. "I think it's an excellent idea. I don't think it'll be much longer before things are resolved, but in the meantime, I'd feel better knowing you were safe." Diane threw her arms around Jade, squeezing her almost painfully. "I knew you'd understand. You aren't upset with me, are you? I don't want you to think I'm bailing on you." Jade pulled back and looked into Diane's face. "Not only do I not think you are bailing, I was actually going to suggest you make yourself scarce around here, just for awhile." Arms around each other's waists, Jade and Diane walked back to their men.

Later, at Derrick's house, Jade stretched out beside Derrick on his king-sized bed and luxuriated in the warmth radiating from him. "Diane said she'd call me in a couple days, as soon as she gets settled in with Brian." Derrick, already more than half asleep, managed a sound resembling agreement. Jade smiled at the sound and let herself drift for a long languid moment. As she slid into sleep, she felt Derrick's warm hand on her back. "I love you", he whispered sleepily in her ear.

Friday morning brought torrential pre-Spring rains. Jade awakened to Derrick's face, inches from hers, a bemused expression on his face as he watched her sleep. "You snore, did you know that?" She sat up, which caused the sheet to slip down her naked torso. Derrick's eyes moved downward, his face unable to suppress an interested grin as she snatched the sheet back up. "I do NOT snore." Jade sauntered off to the bathroom, ignoring Derrick's snickering behind her.

At the breakfast table, Jade munched happily on Derrick's peanut butter toast as he poured coffee for them. "What would you like to do today?", Derrick asked. Jade said, "Let's find my dad, prove he's not a murderer, then find Timothy and rip his…" Derrick interrupted her, "Do you have any idea how we are going to go about all this?" Jade answered, "No, you didn't say I needed to work out all the details, you just wanted to know what I'd like to do. That's it." Derrick opened his mouth to reply and was silenced by a voice saying "Book 'em Derrick". Jade laughed, as Derrick crossed to the phone, glanced at the caller ID and answered it with a cautious "Hello?" Jade heard only Derrick's clipped responses. "Okay, we'll be there." Silence from Derrick, then, "Yes, that's fine."

Derrick dropped the receiver back into the cradle without saying goodbye, then turned to Jade and said. "That was Timothy. He wants us to meet him at the mall, in an hour. He said he'd be right where you were waiting for him before. He also said he has information about your father." Jade said, "You obviously think we should go. What will stop him from killing us right there?" Derrick responded, "If he tries anything violent toward us in a public place like that, he's much more prone to be caught. I don't think he's willing to take that chance. I think he just wants to gloat. But he may give us important information. My initial reaction is to meet with him myself, but I know he won't tell me jack without you. Are you up for this?" Jade nodded. "Definitely. I agree with you. We need to do this."

Derrick went upstairs for a moment, then returned with a gun in his hand. Jade heard a click, and the magazine fell into his hand. He checked it, then expertly rammed it home again. "Jade, I have another gun, just a small .22, I want you to put it in your purse, just in case. Derrick strode purposefully to the computer room, opened the desk drawer and took out a small gun case. He checked it over, then passed it to her. The metallic smell of the gun made her feel immediately nauseous. She knew how to shoot, but had never aimed a gun at a living person. The idea that she may have to do that very thing was overwhelming. "Derrick, I don't know if I can do this." Jade looked at Derrick pleadingly.

Derrick stood in front of her, gazing down at her with a decidedly displeased look. "Jade, listen, I honestly don't think you'll need to use this, but if, for some reason, I get into trouble, I need to know that you have my back. Could you shoot someone if they were going to kill me?" Jade nodded unhappily. "That's all I ask, that you be my backup plan if I need one. I also worry that we could get separated somehow, and I won't be able to protect you." Jade watched Derrick strap on a shoulder holster and skillfully seat his gun. He pulled his jacket on and helped Jade on with hers.

As they intended, they were at the mall almost a half hour early. They drove around the parking lot, checking for the black Mercedes or the white Cadillac, but found nothing. Inside, Jade and Derrick walked through the mall and sat where Jade had sat, weeks ago, when Timothy was trying to get Erin's diary from her. Both of them watched the thinning crowd, but only Jade knew what Timothy looked like.

When he approached them, they were both caught unaware. "Hi Jade, it's nice to see you again." Jade whirled around, standing abruptly to face Timothy. Her chair started to fall back and Derrick reached behind her and neatly caught it. He stood up beside Jade, and faced him. Derrick's voice was colder than Jade had ever heard it. "You said you had information about Jade's father. Let's hear it."

Timothy, ignoring Derrick's confrontational and unfriendly demeanor, sat down at their table, leaned back in his chair and eyed both of them speculatively. "There are some things I want you to know, Jade. Before we get started, Derrick, take the tape recorder out of your pocket, put it on the table and turn it off." Stunned, Derrick did as he was told. Jade couldn't keep the surprise out of her expression. Timothy laughed. "Didn't even know about that, did you

Jade? He's a wily one. If it were me, that's what I'd be doing. Let's get started."

"Jade, I know you have questions, and I'm going to tell you a little story, which will likely answer many of them. First of all, I didn't kill your brother. Dillon did, I mean, your father did. Yes, I killed Paulina Nielson, and Peter was getting much too close to having enough proof to get me put away. He actually broke into my apartment, went though my stuff and took some things from me, things that I wouldn't have wanted anyone to see." Jade remembered the papers her mother found in Peter's room, about all the murders in the Old Port. Timothy continued, "I started stalking Peter, hoping to get the opportunity to take him out. I planted the knife in your parents' VW and kept an eye on Peter.

"As you know, my father, Daniel, knows about my secret vocation, and that knowledge was a fairly recent thing. Oh, he knew years ago about the family secret, but he didn't know what I had become, until just a few years ago. I always knew that I had these strange tendencies, which I indulged, of necessity, but kept carefully hidden from the world. In any event, I started to notice my father in places where he shouldn't be, and realized he was following me. So, turn about being fair play, I broke into his house and went through his belongings. I couldn't believe what he had been keeping from me! No wonder I do what I do! Finally, I understood everything. It's not my fault that I kill people, it's a genetic malfunction.

"A malfunction, which, strangely enough, Daniel didn't appear to have inherited. But what I found led me to believe he not only knew about me, but that he also knew that his twin brother, Dillon, had also inherited the family curse." Timothy looked from Jade to Derrick, checking their reaction. Nodding his approval at their stricken expressions, he continued. "My father had notes about your father, Jade. Notes that went back to the 1960's. Apparently, your daddy has been a very naughty boy." Jade struggled to remain impassive, not wanting to give Timothy any further satisfaction. "I took the notes, read them, then put them back where I found them. I don't know if Daniel even knows I saw them. I know he knows about me and my habits, but we never talked about it."

Timothy continued. "Then I made a mistake. I knew Peter was also a Lawrence, and I wondered if what had consumed most of the Lawrence men had also consumed him. I approached him, told him about his father. I admit a big part of why I did that was to get a reaction out of him. Of course, he didn't believe me. Accused me of killing the people your father had killed, Jade, and of trying to pin those deaths on him. I could tell from Peter's reaction that part of what he was feeling was denial, that things must have happened to him when he was younger. Things that gave him a clue about who, and what, his father was. He's your father, too, Jade. So I decided to push him a little bit. I told him about Daniel's notes, how my father had put together solid proof of Dillon's complicity in the murder of that woman in the woods behind your house, when Peter was a teenager.

"I gotta tell you, Jade, this struck a chord with Peter, it was obvious to me that he already knew something about it. Then Peter must have gone home and confronted Dillon, because that was the last time I saw or heard from Peter. I came to Peter's birthday party, the day after I saw Peter last, and knew, when he didn't show up, Dillon must have silenced him." Jade's face had lost all color. Derrick put a steadying arm around her and she leaned into him. Timothy watched this exchange with something akin to disgust on his face. Derrick, obviously worried about Jade's emotional condition, said, "Okay, whether or not what you've said is true, this doesn't tell us where Jade's father is now.

That's why we're here. Do you know?" Timothy smirked at him. "Of course I know. Daniel killed him." Jade suddenly stood, reached across the table and grabbed Timothy by the shirt.

"You tell me where my father is, right now! I'm sick of your lies and your bullshit, Timothy." Derrick looked around and saw that they were attracting attention. "Jade, for God's sake, let go and sit down!" Derrick gently pulled Jade's hands away from Timothy's shirtfront, and guided her back into her seat. Timothy's expression hadn't changed. His eyes burned into Jade's, and he said, "Jade, I don't know why Daniel would have killed your father. I only know that he did. I've found nothing to indicate that my father actually inherited the family gene, but I guess I could be wrong. The reason I know Dillon is dead is that I was waiting at my father's house one night about a week or so ago. He came home late, covered in blood. He didn't want to talk about what had happened. It was obvious to me that he wasn't hurt, that the blood was someone else's. I didn't talk to him that night, about that or anything else. A couple days later, I saw him driving Dillon's white Cadillac."

Jade interrupted him, "My father drives Lexus." Timothy's expression was one of pity, and triumph. "The car he drives as Brandon is a Lexus. The car he drives as Dillon is a white 1966 Caddy. Jade, don't you remember that car, when you were growing up? He used it as the family car until the early 1970's. Then, I would imagine, he probably started to feel that his distinctive car could become his downfall. He put the car in storage for a few years, then he started driving it again, but never around his family."

A distant memory came to Jade then. She, her brother Peter and their parents, going to the Saco Drive-In in the Cadillac. Getting ice cream cones at Red's, her father warning her not to get any on the seats. For some reason, she had completely forgotten about the Caddy, until now. She suddenly recalled the day she went to the cell phone store and how she had seen the Cadillac in the parking lot, when she got there, but when she looked a few moments later it was gone. Later, she had reviewed the pictures of the Caddy she had taken with her new camera phone and spotted USM stickers on the windshield. Now she knew why her father, who was supposed to be at the hospital with her mother, wasn't there and showed up a few minutes after she did. He had been following her. Then Jade remembered something more incriminating. There were several victims' families who related information about seeing a car matching this description in the vicinity of where victims were taken or killed. Jade immediately put this together with the information she had which seemed to point back to the USM campus or surrounding area as being a place the murderer worked or lived. Everything was pointing to the fact that her father was a serial killer.

And here, across the table from her, was another serial killer. Jade took a moment to begin to assimilate the information, then turned her anger on Timothy. "God damn you and your whole fucked up family, my father included. If what you say is true, why didn't you just kill your father? Or me, for that matter? Both of us know who and what you are, and we could help rob you of your precious freedom to kill, at any time. Don't tell me you suddenly grew a conscience?" Faced with Jade's anger, Timothy turned defensive. "Don't imagine I didn't think of that. I actually did try, if you recall. I laced your favorite candy with Thallium, remember? Unfortunately for your friend, I must say. Is she dead yet, by the way?" Jade clenched her fists to keep from pummeling Timothy. "That's none of your business."

Unconcerned, Timothy continued. "Having both you and my father out of the picture would solve a lot of problems for me. Unfortunately, my father was smart enough to protect himself before I could take action. If he turns up dead, I'm guaranteed to go to prison for a very long time. You see, he's arranged with someone close to him to check in with them at regular intervals and if he doesn't, information will be automatically mailed to the police about me. That's the reason Daniel hasn't just winked out of existence. My reason for sparing you, Jade, is a bit more complex. First of all is your resourcefulness. You've been careful, and you've been lucky. I've also enjoyed watching you play Nancy Drew, and I've been amazed and delighted at your abilities. You've been more than a worthy adversary and I can't say that I've tried extremely hard to get you out of the way. Yet anyway. At first, I wasn't sure what you may have on me and if you had some kind of 'dead man switch' set up, like my father does. Now that I've been in your house and through your stuff, and I've had the opportunity to go through your computer, I'm reasonably sure that your death won't spring some kind of booby trap on me, all bets are off. It's also highly likely, now that we've had this meeting, that you won't live long enough to construct any kind of trap. More than anything else, I just wanted to tell you that and see your face when you realized it."

Jade ignored the threat, but something else occurred to her. "I know you've been in my house, at least twice, but what do you mean, you've been through my computer?" Timothy's grin lit his face from within, and Jade understood that she was looking on the countenance of pure, insane evil. He answered her question with one of his own. "You mean you didn't realize that the email you got from the British Library was actually from me? Oh dear, that's rich! Who do you suppose sponsors the family crest website you visited, on which you left your question? I saw your question and just had to take a personal interest. After all, you're family! Of course, I inserted a virus into one of the attachment files I sent you and immediately had access to your computer. I also got into Derrick's computer, since you used his computer to check your email, Jade."

Derrick's arm around Jade went tense and she moved back against it in warning. Timothy looked insolently at Derrick. "And of course, I got into Michael's computer, too, but only for a moment then his spyware detector caught the Trojan Horse and deleted it. But that's okay, I've seen enough now to know that I have nothing to fear from you, Jade."

Jade and Derrick sat silently, gazing with disbelief at Timothy. Timothy looked back at them with an air of defiance. Finally Jade broke the tense silence. "So, you are telling me that your father killed my father?" Timothy nodded, thought for a moment, then shrugged. "I'm not positive, I didn't see him do it. But I saw blood all over him, and he's now driving your dad's Cadillac. Have you seen your dad in the past week or so?" Jade shook her head. "No, I haven't. I do think he's dead. But if you are asking me to believe that it was Daniel, and not you that killed him, I'm not prepared to do that." Timothy's smirk was back. "Believe what you will, being a Lawrence, you will anyway. But does it really matter who killed your father? Dead is dead, isn't it? The man was vermin."

Jade stood abruptly, turned away and started to run, Timothy's laughter following her. At the end of the corridor, she turned the corner, then stopped, leaning against the wall for support, struggling not to start screaming in frustration. She knew, if she gave in to it, she may not be able to stop. Derrick came around the corner, spotted Jade and pulled her into his arms. "If what Timothy said about your father is true, I'm so sorry you had to hear it that way. The man is an animal." Jade nodded against Derrick's shoulder. "C'mon baby, let's go home." Derrick gently guided Jade in the direction of the truck. "What about Timothy? Is he still sitting there?" Derrick answered, "I don't give a shit, he's not my priority right now." Jade tightened her arm around Derrick's waist as they pushed through the doors, exiting the mall

Chapter 43

In the truck, Jade thought about what Timothy had said. Amid all the bluster and arrogant rambling, Jade now understood two things. One, that her father was, in fact, likely dead, and that if he was, then either Timothy or Daniel had killed him. And two, she was now in more danger than ever. Actually, she realized, she had become clear on one more thing. Peter, in spite of all his issues, was not a killer. Jade had an idea that he was born with the Lawrence family killer gene, but he had somehow fought it, for all of his short life. At the end, Peter was getting too close to the truth about their family, and that cost him his life. There was no way to tell, yet, whether Timothy, Daniel or even their father had killed Peter. Jade wondered if the same knowledge that Peter had, which was now in her hands, would also cost her her life.

At Derrick's house, Jade sat quietly on the couch, thinking. Close to midnight, Derrick took Jade's hand and pulled her from the couch, toward the stairs. "Time to get some sleep, Jade. Things will seem better tomorrow." Jade looked back at him as she climbed the stairs to his bedroom. "What if things don't seem better?" Derrick had no answer, and Jade didn't really expect one. Jade tossed and turned, and finally, just before 3:00 A.M., she slept.

Jade came awake less than two hours later. She instantly knew that something was wrong. Something had awakened her, some abrupt sound that didn't belong. Her internal radar was suddenly red-lining. She looked over at Derrick. He was asleep, but didn't look as if his sleep was restful. His face wore a distraught expression, and his body language clearly spoke of the stress going on inside him. Jade reached over and gently nudged him. His eyes flew open and immediately fixed on her. "Derrick, I think something's wrong. Something woke me up."

Derrick reached for her and pulled her down into the warm circle of his arms. She settled her head on his chest, eyes wide in the dark, listening. What eventually came to her was not a sound. Rather, it was a distressing scent. Smoke! Jade recognized the smell instantly and jumped out of bed, awakening Derrick. He sat up and looked around. Then he also smelled it. "What the hell is that?" He quickly climbed out of bed, pulled on his jeans and went to the top of the stairs. Jade pulled on a robe and followed him. At the top of the stairs, they could both smell the smoke more clearly. Jade saw an orange glow coming from the downstairs hallway. They both moved down the stairs, Derrick a few steps ahead. He reached the downstairs landing and grabbed their coats and Jade's purse from the closet.

He turned to Jade and threw her coat up to her. She put her coat on, and pulled her purse over her head, like a mail bag. Derrick steered her back up the stairs. "The downstairs looks like it's fully engulfed, we can't go that way. Luckily, there's more than one way to get out." Jade suddenly realized that Derrick was shouting, then she realized why. The fire had started up the stairs toward them. At top of the stairs, Derrick moved past Jade, taking the lead. He grabbed her hand and led her past the bedroom and down to the end of the hallway. Jade heard distant barking. Bardo! She called him, and the barking abruptly stopped.

She heard his tiny claws clacking across the floor, and suddenly he was at her feet. She bent to pick him up, but he darted through Derrick's bedroom and to the bathroom door. He barked once, sharply, and was answered by a tiny mewling cry. Jade dashed to the bathroom door and threw it open. Baby Girl cowered in the corner, obviously terrified. Jade scooped her up and put her in the oversized pocket of her bathrobe. "Good dog, Bardo!" She grabbed Bardo and headed back to the hallway. Derrick led Jade to the end of the hallway. Jade watched Derrick grab a small hook, at chest level, on the back wall. Derrick pulled, and a door came away from the wall! Derrick yanked the door fully open, and pushed Jade through it.

Jade glanced back and saw with horror that the flames were now at the top of the stairs and starting down the hallway toward them. Jade's view of the flames was mercifully cut off when Derrick pulled the door shut behind them. She felt Derrick's hands groping over the wall behind her and a moment later watery light filled the small space. Jade looked around and saw the source. It was a battery-operated tap light. Jade saw that they were on a large landing, and that there were stairs leading down. Derrick pulled Jade down the stairs, across another smaller landing, and down another set of stairs. Jade could still smell the smoke, but could now also smell something else. A musty smell. They were in a daylight basement. Derrick crossed the stone floor to the corner of the room. He reached toward the wall, and Jade watched as he grasped a handle, turned it, and pushed. Jade realized there were small double doors, likely leading outside. They didn't budge. Derrick tried again, using his legs as pistons. The doors moved slightly, but held. Jade put Bardo down on the floor, then quickly ran a hand over her robe pocket, making sure Baby Girl was still there.

She ran to Derrick and added her strength to his. Still the doors didn't give. Jade suddenly became aware of a change in the light level. She looked back to the stairs leading up into the house and saw smoke and flames pouring down into their cellar area. Jade saw Derrick grab a cement block from the floor and use that to smash the doors. They bent, buckled, but stubbornly held. The smoke had reached Jade and she realized she likely had only moments left before she was overcome. She scanned the walls of the basement and saw a tiny vent window at ceiling level, several feet away. Under the window, she saw a rake standing against the wall. Grabbing the rake, she aimed it at the window and smashed it. Cold, clean air rushed in, buying them precious time.

Derrick continued to batter the doors, without success. A sound penetrated Jade's panicked awareness and she grabbed Derrick's arm in mid-swing. "Listen, do you hear that?" Derrick froze, listening intently. It was the screech of metal giving way. Then they both saw the dented doors above them start to move. A rectangle of cold, starlit sky opened up above and expanded as they watched. Jade grabbed Bardo and checked her pocket for Baby Girl, then Derrick pulled her out through the doorway. Jade heard a loud creak, then watched as the first floor of the house collapsed into the cellar, smoke billowing out around them. Across the backyard, Jade saw a shadow move swiftly into the trees. She only saw it for a moment, and had almost convinced herself that she imagined it, when Derrick said, looking in the same direction as she was, "Did you see that?" Jade could see that Derrick wanted to give chase, but realized the figure had too much of a lead. He looked around, and his gaze fell on a two-by-four, sitting beside the open cellar doors. He closed the cellar doors and put the board through the door handles. They fit perfectly, right down to the notches in the board caused by their struggles to dislodge it.

He looked at Jade and said, "He isn't the person who started the fire, he saved us." Jade looked at the board, then at Derrick, shivering. "Someone meant for us to die in that fire, and someone else apparently decided not to allow it." Derrick nodded. "If I had to guess, I'd say it was Timothy who started the fire and Daniel who saved us." Now that Jade was safe, she realized how angry she was. "I can't believe he actually burned your house down!" Jade furiously

380

glanced behind Derrick at the house, which was now fully engulfed. She could hear the fire truck sirens in the distance, becoming louder. Her glance fell back on Derrick's face. "I'm so sorry this had to happen. You've done nothing except try to protect me. Now I've cost you your home. I promise you, Timothy's going down. Before either of us lose anything else."

Derrick put an arm around Jade's slight, shaking form. "I'm so relieved that we are both okay, I don't think I've even begun to process the rest. What I do know is this. I love you, and everything else is a distant second to that." Jade threw her arms around him, hugging him to her tightly. "I love you, too." Jade's tears overflowed, and she struggled to stop the spiraling despair that threatened to engulf her. Derrick stood up, pulled Jade to her feet, and picked up Bardo. Derrick, Jade, Bardo and Baby Girl gave a wide berth to the burning house as they made their way to the front of the property to meet the arriving fire trucks.

A fireman jumped off the truck and headed for Derrick and Jade as soon as the truck had stopped. "There's no one else in the house", Derrick told him quickly. The fireman looked at the house, then at Jade and Derrick. His badge listed his name as Fenderson. "Unfortunately, the house is going to be a total loss." Derrick nodded sadly. "Yeah, I figured." Jade watched the fireman's face, realizing that something he saw on the front of the house had caught his attention. Jade saw the fireman's puzzled expression give way to suspicion. He walked a few paces closer to the house and studied the first floor windows for another moment. He turned back to Derrick and said, "Before anything else happens, do you happen to have the key to your truck? If you do, you may want to move it, just in case the fire spreads in that direction." Derrick immediately turned toward his truck. I do have a spare key, in a magnetic case in the wheel well. Thanks!"

When Derrick came back, the fireman said to him, "Is there any reason for you to believe this was arson?" Derrick and Jade looked at each other, a look that was obviously caught by the fireman. "Yes, we do believe it was arson." Derrick joined the fireman and they stood together for a time, watching the activity around them. Another fire truck had pulled up behind the first, and men were streaming around both trucks, setting up hoses. Derrick looked a silent question to Jade. She nodded, and Derrick led the fireman across the street, out of the path of most of the activity. Jade crossed slowly to the men, watching the house as it continued to crumble under the weight of the fire.

The fireman, Fenderson, motioned to another fireman, apparently his second-in-command, and the man immediately stepped up to take over coordinating the activities of the others. "Sir, I'm hoping you'll be willing to explain what's going on here. But, if you've got something to say that could help us in our investigation, I'm going to have to ask you to hold off until our investigator gets here to take your statement." Derrick nodded slowly, then said, "It's not what you think, I didn't do this, and Jade didn't do it either." Andy Fenderson held up a hand, staying Derrick's explanation. "Just wait, okay?" Derrick sat down on the curb, and Jade came over to sit with him. Jade pulled her robe lapel into her lap and checked her pocket for Baby Girl. She was snuggled up, warm and sleepy. Bardo sat quietly at their feet, watching the fire intently. Jade watched the orange glow illuminate the distressed expression on Derrick's face. Jade understood only too well that responsibility for the destruction of this beautiful old house fell squarely on her shoulders. Her's and her stalker's. The weight of her guilt threatened to crush her. She wanted to comfort Derrick, but she wasn't sure how he was feeling about her, right at the moment.

She tentatively put a hand on Derrick's back and he instantly responded, reaching around to pull her into his arms. Jade's relief was immense. Derrick said, "Don't worry. You and I are both safe. Terrance was out for the night. We even got the animals out. The house and everything in it is just 'stuff'. I've never been overly materialistic, and the house and all the contents are fully insured. It's a shame, but that's all it is, and I'm over it. If something had happened to YOU, now THAT would have been a guaranteed death sentence for our Lawrence family psycho." Jade agreed with him, but couldn't for the life of her think of anything to say. She felt raw, angry and relieved, all at once.

A red car pulled up behind the fire engines. Jade saw the words "Fire Investigator" inscribed along the side of the car. Derrick said, "Do you want to put the animals in my truck? It's cold out, and they've had quite a shock already tonight. I have a feeling we'll be here for a while." Jade picked up Bardo and headed down the street. Derrick waited for her to return, then together they approached the fire investigator.

"Hi, I'm Ray Brown." The investigator held out a hand and Derrick shook it. "Andy Fenderson tells me you have information about the fire?" Derrick said, "I can give you the name of the person who set it. Getting proof to nail the bastard is going to be your problem." Ray Brown nodded solemnly, encouraging Derrick to continue. Instead, Jade spoke up. "Mr. Brown, the arsonist's name is Timothy Lawrence. He's also using the name Steven Lawry." Jade gave him Timothy's last known address and telephone number, from memory. Ray Brown wrote everything down, then looked up at Jade. "Why do you think it was him?" Jade said, "Because he's been stalking me for weeks, and Derrick and I met with him, at the mall yesterday. I guess we were trying to get to some kind of resolution. Instead, he let us know, in no uncertain terms, that there was no reason for him to continue to spare my life."

As Jade said these words, she realized how over-the-top they sounded. She rushed to try to explain, hoping he wouldn't decide she was crazy until he had listened to her story.

After her explanation, the fire investigator said, "I'll tell you what we need to do now. I'll contact the police and have a detective assigned to this case." He started to continue, but Derrick interrupted. "Mr. Brown, I mean, Ray, I'm actually a police detective." Ray looked from him to Jade and back. "Be that as it may, it's an obvious conflict of interest to have you file the report on the arson fire at your house. See what I'm sayin'?" Derrick nodded, and Ray continued. "Since this is obviously a police matter, I'll complete my investigation, then we'll get a report filed, so you can use it to file your insurance claim. Jade, whatever information you have on this Timothy Lawrence, you'll need to give it to the police. I know you said you have more research to do, but, if this person is as dangerous as he seems, this all needs to be on the record, as soon as we can get it there."

Jade, Derrick and Bardo and Baby Girl ("the kids", Jade had jokingly started to call them) drove to Jade's house. When they arrived, there was a note on the front door. Jade reached for it, but Derrick caught her hand in mid-reach. "Let me. Just in case it's anything we'd want to collect evidence from later." Derrick pulled a latex glove from the inner pocket of his coat, and put it on. He gingerly retrieved the note from the door and carefully unfolded it. He read aloud. "'Jade, by the time you read this, you'll already be in danger again. You need to get what you can carry and get out, go somewhere you've never been. Timothy will realize, once the news airs, that his attempt to kill you failed. He'll try again, and soon.'" Derrick turned the note over, then back again. "It's not signed, but I'm pretty sure it must be from Daniel." Jade nodded her agreement, then said, "He's right. Let's get what we need and go." Together, they rounded up some basic necessities and within ten minutes, they were all back on the road.

Jade realized how strange it was that the man who had apparently killed her father, at least according to Timothy, was now trying to protect them. Putting that puzzle aside for now, she turned to Derrick. "Do you know where we are going?" Derricks grim expression lightened slightly. "As a matter of fact, I do. There's nothing more confusing to a hunter than when his prey hides in plain sight. Let's check into the Marriot. What do you say?" Derrick waggled his eyebrows suggestively, and was rewarded with a grin. Jade said, "Excellent idea. I could use a little pampering right about now."

At the hotel, they checked in, and took their meager belongings to their room. Bardo and Baby Girl happily roamed around the room. Jade took a shower while Derrick went out for food. Half an hour later, all four of them sat down to pizza. A cell phone rang, and both Derrick and Jade started hunting. Derrick didn't have his cell phone, but Jade found hers at the bottom of her purse. It stopped ringing abruptly just as she held it up in triumph. She gave it a minute, then checked for a message. She was surprised to find that she had apparently missed more than one call! There was a message from Diane, 9:30 P.M. last night. "Hey J, just checking in. I'm in Bangor with Brian. Things are wonderful, and I feel so much better! I didn't want you worrying about me. So return the favor and call me back, girl!" Jade smiled and stored the message, she'd call Diane back later. For now, she had other messages to check.

The next message came in at 5:40 A.M. The associated telephone number said "private caller" and the message was a short clip of white noise followed by a click. Jade knew instinctively that it had to be Timothy. He was either letting her know he realized she was still alive, or he was checking to see if she might pick up the phone, confirming his suspicion that the fire hadn't killed her. Derrick asked, "Who was it?" Jade answered, "It was Timothy, I think." Derrick nodded. "Very likely. Think how disappointed he must be, for surely he knows by now that you are alive and safely stashed." He gave Jade a smug look. She laughed at him, then turned her attention to the last message on her cell phone.

The message had been left just moments ago. The number said, "unavailable". Jade put it on speaker phone. "Jade, I need to talk to you. I can't leave you in the dark about what's been happening any more, it's just not safe for you not to know everything I can tell you. I know you don't trust me, and I don't blame you. After what happened with your father…I promise to explain everything to you when I see you. And see you I must and as quickly as possible. Please meet me at your parents' house, this evening at 7:00. I'll be there waiting for you. I'm so sorry about everything. Please be there, I promise not to hurt you, and I promise to tell you whatever you want to know, if I can. If you call the police, I won't be there."

Jade flipped the cell phone closed, her mind already weighing the risks and benefits of meeting Daniel as he had pleaded that she do. Derrick said, "Jade, this is your call. If you decide you need confront him about your father, I'll do everything I can to make this as safe a meeting for us as possible. Jade's voice, when she answered, was filled with steely resolve. "Definitely we need to meet with him. Whether my father was a killer or not, he was my father and this man apparently took his life. In our civilized world, it would have been fitting to work within the law, and gather the information necessary to put my father behind bars for life, just like I've been trying to do with Timothy. Instead, Daniel apparently just took him out, without the benefit of judge or jury. He needs to be held accountable for that. Besides that, I also have questions for

Daniel. Mostly I want to know how involved he is in all this Lawrence family bullshit. I need to find out whether to include him in my efforts to gather evidence implicating the Lawrences for their crimes, or whether Daniel may actually be able to help me to bring down his son. Let's do it."

At 6:20 P.M., Jade and Derrick arrived at her parents' house. They parked Derrick's truck several houses down the street and walked around the block to approach the house from the back. The house was dark, and there were no vehicles parked in the driveway. The back door was unlocked. Derrick put his warm hand over hers before she could turn the push the door open. "Let me go in first, okay?" Jade nodded silently. Derrick entered the kitchen, fast and low, his Glock in hand.

Chapter 44

At the kitchen table, sitting quietly in the dark, was Daniel. Derrick held the gun on Daniel as Jade carefully sidled into the kitchen. Daniel held both hands up, in a gesture of surrender. Jade was immediately struck by how very much this man resembled her father. Instead of making her feel uneasy, his resemblance to her father, here in her parents' kitchen, somehow comforted her. Daniel had the same beautiful gold-flecked hazel eyes her father had. Jade remembered how, when she first met Ben Lawrence, he had reminded her of her father. Now she understood why. The loss of her father once again threatened to swamp her. She grimly held on, waiting for the worst of the pain to pass. In another moment, she was able to think rationally again. Daniel had been watching her, and Jade saw sympathy in his expression.

When Daniel spoke, Jade realized, with something like relief, that he sounded nothing like her father. "Jade, it's wonderful to finally make your acquaintance, in person. Your father was very proud of you." Jade responded, "'Was'? Is it true that you killed him? That's what Timothy told us yesterday. But that was before he burned Derrick's house down and tried to kill us, so I'm not sure now how to believe." Daniel sat quietly, looking down at his hands, listening to Jade. Then he looked directly into her eyes. "I think your father is dead. I can't be positive but it's very likely. And yes, it was my doing. Before I explain that, is it okay if I tell you what I need to tell you, in order? I've been waiting a very long time and what I tell you about your dad won't make sense to you unless you hear it all. Okay?"

Jade nodded, feeling numb. Derrick stood next to Daniel, his gun still pointing more or less in Daniel's direction. Daniel sat back in the chair and eyed the gun speculatively. "Derrick, if it makes you feel safer to point that thing at me the whole time we're here, knock yourself out. But I promise you that I mean you and Jade no harm." Derrick lowered the gun, but kept it in his hand, at the ready. "That's a little better. Thanks."

Daniel looked back at Jade, and she saw a flash of something completely unexpected. Regret. She met Daniel's sad expression with a challenging glare. "Okay, you want to explain, then do it. If what you tell me doesn't completely change my mind about you, I'm calling the police. Got it?" To her surprise, Daniel said, "That's fine."

Daniel sat forward and reached for one of Jade's hands. She pulled back from the table as if he had slapped her. "I'm sorry, I just feel so badly about everything that's happened, much worse than I thought I would. I want to make up for everything you've been through. None of this has been your fault." Jade nodded, but kept her distance. "I understand that you don't trust me. I wouldn't trust me either! Let me start by saying that I've done everything I could to keep you from seeing me, either a picture or in person. My voice doesn't sound like your father's, but I sure do look like him. The reason I've laid low is that, if you knew about me, and my connection to the Lawrences, then SAW me, you'd know I was part of your family and you, mine. That knowledge could have gotten you killed, by more than one person. I was trying to protect you, Jade, by staying out of your sight.

"I heard you went to the library, early on, to research the Lawrence family." He looked the question at Jade, and she nodded. "Did you see the book about Southern Maine Homicides from 1840 to 1968?" Jade nodded again. "Then you must have noticed the missing pages. I had already been to the library, days before you, and saw a picture in that book that you could not have been allowed to see. It was a police artist composite sketch of a serial killer on the loose in the late 1960's. And it was your father. I knew the sketch was good enough that you'd recognize him. I also found copies of several newspaper accounts of murders in Portland in the mid 1960's, and several of the newspaper photos managed to catch your father, in the crowd. I couldn't let you find those pictures, put things together, and discover the truth about your father, not like that. That knowledge would have eventually cost you your life. Then, when I found out that Timothy was trying to date you, I called my father, Ben. I tried to stay out of it, but by then I had realized that Timothy may know who you are, and if that were so, you weren't safe. Ben's attempt to help me, and you, cost him his life.

"I'm sure you realize now that it was me you saw, that day at the cemetery." Jade nodded thoughtfully. Daniel continued, "I left you two voice mail messages, Jade, trying to get you to stop looking into my family, and the curse.

I would never have hurt you. I only meant to scare you, to get you to stop. But it didn't work. I followed Timothy to the mall yesterday and watched him meet with the two of you. I wasn't close enough to hear what he said, but I didn't have to. He was taunting you. Later, when he left his apartment, I knew he was up to no good and I followed him. At Derrick's house, I watched him throw a Molotov cocktail through the living room window. He had apparently looked the house over and realized he could set the fire at the bottom of the staircase, trapping you upstairs. I don't think he counted on there being a set of service stairs at the back of the house. He was watching the house as it burned, from the woods. Then he saw the storm doors leading from the cellar. He put a two-by-four through the door handles so you wouldn't be able to open it. Then he heard the two of you in the cellar, trying to get out, and I saw him standing on the cellar doors, laughing. When he heard the fire trucks approaching he walked away into the woods. I immediately came out of hiding and pulled the wooden plank out of the door handles for you, then I fled.

Jade's expression had become progressively more puzzled as she listened to Daniel's incredible story. "Why did you save us?" Jade couldn't keep the anger out of her voice. "You apparently didn't have the same hesitation when it came to killing my father." Daniel raised a hand to still Jade. "I'm getting to that. Before we go there, I want to tell you the story of my family. Some of this you may know, some of it you may have guessed. But it's important that you understand." Jade sat quietly, watching Daniel's face as he organized his thoughts. She found herself feeling sorry for him, then was angry with herself for feeling sorry for the man who killed her father. Finally, Daniel spoke again.

"Jade, I want you to know that I'm not a serial killer. I would have been easier if I had been. I've spent the last several years of my life trying to understand what made several other members of my family take the tragic path they took.

This is a story that I've never told anyone." Daniel looked at Jade, his eyes full of compassion. "I have to warn you, once you know the truth, there's no going back." Jade nodded.

"The part of this history that would most concern you is the part that involves our family members who turned out, well, badly." Jade found his euphemism strangely touching. He continued, "My earliest memories are of being in a loving family. I always knew that I was adopted, and that my mother had died soon after giving birth to me. I understood that she was very young, and she did what was best for me. It never caused me to feel unloved, and my adopted parents were wonderful. I was always an exemplary child, getting good marks in school, taking care of others, and working hard at everything I did. But I was plagued with strange, violent dreams, from the time I started puberty. And sometimes, for no reason at all, I would think about hurting someone, and the thought was always accompanied by a strange, compelling thrill. I understood instinctively that this was wrong, and dangerous and I worked hard to keep my impulses firmly in check. After several years, the impulses began to fade. But the violent dreams remained.

"Some days, I'd feel disconnected and foggy all day, from jolting awake repeatedly, from my horrible nightmares the night before. By the time I turned eighteen, I understood that there was something very wrong with me, but that I had somehow, incredibly, learned to control it. Others found me frightening to be around, I knew. I said inappropriate things, and was always moody and unpleasant. At the time, I didn't care. I was just trying to get through each day." Jade's thoughts turned to Peter, and the demons he had fought his whole life. Suddenly she understood much more about her brother. Tears sprang to her eyes when she realized that much of what she had thought, and feared, about Peter was both true and completely misunderstood. She now saw her brother for the noble and tragic person he was. He, like Daniel, fought his demons, and for the most part, successfully. And Peter had the added disadvantage of being raised in a family with someone who had given in to the family curse. Stepping back from her newly found sympathy for Peter, she realized that, somewhere in the past few days, she had begun to accept what her father was. There was sadness in the realization, but also liberation born of enlightenment.

Daniel continued. "Call it what you will, an ancestral memory of some kind, or the desperation of a young man trying to figure out what was wrong with him, but I started trying to find my birth family. After all, there had to be a reason I was given up for adoption, and maybe it was connected to my odd character. In the early 1950's, I contacted the local library and they put me in touch with a service that helped adopted children locate their birth families. After several dead ends, I was finally given one very important clue to my identity. I found the orphanage from which I had been adopted. In their records there was a picture of my mother, holding TWO babies. The date on the back of the photo confirmed that one of the babies was likely me. Jade, you may or may not have seen a picture of my mother. If you have, you know you are a dead ringer." Jade answered. "I think I've seen the picture. At first I thought it was a picture of me." Daniel smiled. "The resemblance is truly amazing. I'm so glad, in spite of everything, that my mother so obviously lives on in you."

Daniel sat quietly for a moment, seeming to drink in the beauty of Jade's face. "The picture gave me two very important facts. One was the fact that I was a twin. I began to wonder if my twin was having as hard a time as I was, trying to control his impulses. The second fact I got from the picture had to do with the ring my mother was wearing." Jade nodded, "Yes, it was the Lawrence family crest ring, with the Möbius on it." Daniel looked at her, obviously impressed. "You really HAVE done your homework!" He reached a hand across the table and lightly patted Jade's hand. She looked down and saw, on his pinkie, the ring. Daniel's gaze followed hers. "Did you find out where the Möbius symbol came from? I mean, in terms of why the Lawrences started using it as a family crest and as their kill signature?" Jade answered, "No, I didn't find out, but I did try pretty hard as it was something I badly wanted to know."

Daniel said, "Do you remember hearing about William Lawrence? He was Tim and Trevor's father, who immigrated from Great Britain after he became a suspect in a series of murders there, in the late 1840's. In the late 1850's the Möbius symbol rose to popularity in scientific communities, then it caught on with the general population. The meaning, while esoterically scientific, morphed for the mainstream as "forever". William, in his dotage by then, had always prided himself on being knowledgeable about all things scientific. He saw this symbol and immediately associated it with his twisted yearning to live forever. By now, he knew he would obviously not be living forever. But the last two of his victims were engraved with the symbol. He must have told Tim, his 'bad seed' son, before he died and maybe provided him with the newly minted family crest, because there are records of several of Tim's victims also carrying this symbol. It has apparently been passed down through the generations, in a way that I do not know, as I was not raised as a Lawrence.

"Most of the information I found about the Lawrence family came from the very library in which you found the secret room, Jade. I found several old books in the house, when I first talked with Ben. When he realized I was his son, he started dropping sly little clues about the family birthright, it was disgusting, actually. I think he was trying to find out how much I knew about it, and if I was 'one of them'. But he gave me access to the house, and the books were there. So I rescued them." He looked at Jade and Derrick, as if asking for their approval. He seemed satisfied with what he saw in their faces, and he continued speaking. "I started researching the ring, with the Möbius on it, as that was my only solid clue. You see, the names of my parents were sealed in the adoption records. Back then, they could not be disclosed. I tried everything I could to get the names of my parents. I even tried to break in to the orphanage. But the place was a fortress and I just didn't have that kind of criminal instinct.

"I had more luck with my investigation of the ring, specifically of the character itself. A jeweler friend of mine told me that it was very common, in the mid 1850's, for families to adopt a family crest, and have jewelry made, most often rings, which contained their family crest. Back then, written correspondence was very much in vogue. The family crest ring would often be dipped into melted wax and affixed to the bottom of a letter, so the reader would have confirmation that the letter was from a member of that family. When I discovered the family that was attached to that particular crest, I was horrified. I was torn between dropping my quest and turning my back on my family, or throwing myself headlong into the task and seeing what could be done to understand, and to possibly halt, the progression of the family's twisted legacy. Realizing the enormity of what I had discovered, I also knew that I was one of them in name, and potentially in nature as well. As penance for who I was and from whence I came, I took the Lawrence name, my own cursed birthright, back, and I swore to change the course of history from that day forward.

"You see, I felt responsible for what had come before. Men with my blood coursing through their veins had killed countless people, and I knew it." Daniel looked down at his lap, a pained expression crossing his face as he struggled to control his emotions. After a moment, he continued, his voice hoarse. "The first member of my family I found was my father, Ben Lawrence, as I've told you. After I read everything I could get my hands on about him, and about the Lawrences, I really had little desire to approach him directly. I suddenly

394

understood that my family "curse" had, in some ways, infected me. Finally I had an answer for why I was different, and why my mind went places that no sane person should go. Since I had read up on all the suspicions about the Lawrence family, through newspaper accounts going back almost 100 years, and knowing my own strange attraction to violence, I knew instinctively that most of what I read about my ancestors was, unfortunately, true. And there was probably much more that wasn't known, or wasn't captured in recorded history.

"What I did find managed to convince me that my father, Ben, had not escaped the family curse." Jade could not hide her dismay. Derrick said, "What's wrong?" Jade looked at Derrick, then at Daniel. "I knew Ben. He was a sweet old man! I remember feeling horrified when I upset him, the one time I went to see him in person." Daniel grinned and said, "I'll just bet you upset him. He must have thought you were the ghost of his precious Alois." Jade nodded. "I didn't know it at the time, but that must have been exactly what he thought. I felt so guilty for having offended him. What made you conclude that he was a murderer?"

Daniel looked sharply at Jade, but not without sympathy. "I found indisputable evidence of several murders that took place after his father, Timothy, died, but before Dillon was old enough to have started killing. You know about the Möbius being found at many of the murder scenes, even more recent ones, right?" Jade nodded. "Three of the murders I found between Timothy's death and Dillon's pre-adolescent years had the Möbius found at the scene. They were Ben's work. There's no question. I also remember Ben's not-so-subtle attempts to find out whether the killing legacy had been passed to me." Daniel let Jade take a moment to internalize this information, then he continued.

"Near the end of the 1950's, I met the woman who would become my wife,

Lianne. I had decided that I didn't want children and I made sure she knew it, before we were married. But of course, 'man plans and God laughs'. Shortly after we were married, Lianne announced that she was expecting. I know my reaction was not what she had hoped. At around that time, I finally managed to locate my twin brother, Dillon. I followed him for several days. While I didn't see anything to indicate he had become a killer, I did see that he acted strangely, and I guess I did know, on some level. One night while I was following him, I saw him go into a cemetery. He was walking from grave stone to grave stone, talking to himself. Gloating, actually. It sickened me. I decided to confront him. It was a disaster. We got into a shoving match. I told him that I was his brother, and I knew from his stricken expression that he could clearly see our uncanny resemblance. The police showed up and broke us up. After that, I only watched Dillon from a distance.

"My research uncovered Dillon's sad history. He was adopted, after I was, his name was changed to Brandon Danner, then he was later abandoned. He went back to the orphanage, keeping his adopted name, in spite of what had to be unpleasant associations. The scant records I found indicated he had violent tendencies from an early age. When he turned eighteen, he struck out on his own. Soon after that, people close to him started dying.

"Jade, you've discovered several examples of your father's handiwork. I'm sure you know that your father killed someone he worked with at USM? Did you know that he also parked his Caddy there, so Agatha wouldn't see that he still had it?" Jade did know about DeLayne McInerny, who worked at USM and had turned up dead, a Möbius present at the scene. She also knew that Mrs. Pelletieri had tracked the potential killer of her daughter to the University, and she remembered that the receiver for the GPS tracking device she found in her purse was located at the University. She also knew that another of the victims from the 1960's had told her husband she was going to meet a "shrink" or some such, at the University, then she had disappeared.

Jade thought about who and what her father was and she felt shame. Suddenly she realized what made Daniel take his name back, and what drove him to dedicate his life to tracking down his relatives and investigating how they had chosen to live their lives, hoping for the courage and opportunity to change the future. Daniel watched the play of unpleasant emotions on Jade's face, then softly told her, "I know how you must be feeling, please believe me I do. If there was any other way, any way to spare you this ordeal, I'd do it. I protected you for as long as I could, but now, for your own safety, you have to know. Part of the reason I didn't tell you all this sooner was that, if your father found out that you knew about him, he'd have killed you."

Jade's disbelief was clearly written on her face, in spite of her newfound resolve to believe in her father's guilt. This was different. Kill *her*? There's just no way! Daniel shattered this illusion quickly and mercilessly with his next statement. "He killed Peter." Jade jumped from her chair and started to reach across the table to slap Daniel. Daniel grabbed her arm in one steely hand and used it to push her back into her seat. Derrick stood ready, but didn't react. Yet. Daniel said, "Peter had found out about Timothy, after he was accused of one of the Old Port murders and started looking into it to try to vindicate himself. He even broke into Timothy's apartment, which is where he found most of the evidence against him. Peter must have known that, since he had obtained the information against Timothy illegally, it couldn't legally be used to exonerate himself or to implicate Timothy. So he decided to confront Timothy. Big mistake.

"Mind you, I found out about this after the fact. Timothy never could keep his mouth shut. He told later what happened. The day before the party your parents threw for Peter's birthday, Peter confronted Timothy. I don't think Peter realized until then that he was actually related to Timothy. But Timothy told him everything. Peter was shocked, I'm sure, most especially to find out his father was a murderer. Timothy also knew that Peter had a troubled childhood, and he apparently taunted Peter for not being man enough to step up and fulfill his family legacy. Timothy then tried to kill Peter, but Peter got away. I found out the rest of the story from you father, Jade. Peter escaped Timothy then went home and confronted your father. Apparently there was some issue with a big trunk that was stored in Peter's room, which was Dillon's trophy stash, from his previous killings, and Peter confronted your father about this, and about a murder that had taken place in the woods behind your house, many years ago. Apparently what happened was that Peter had watched your father leave the house, and he tried to follow.

"He got turned around in the woods and by the time he came out , he was on the other side of the woods. He stumbled on to a dead woman. She had only just been killed. Peter tried to revive her, getting blood all over himself, but it was too late. The shock drove him into a catatonic state for hours, and when he finally made his way home, I think he knew, in some part of his brain, that your father had killed the woman. But your father was never caught, and Peter was aware that there were people who thought *he* was the guilty one.

"As I said, the night Peter was killed, he confronted your father, who was home alone at the time. They talked, then they argued, then Dillon realized Peter wasn't going to keep his mouth shut, that he had to kill him. He dragged the body out to the woods. The night of the party, Dillon and Timothy, who was going by 'Steven' at the time, took a walk in the woods, do you remember?" Jade did remember, and said so, through a descending fog of horror. "They loaded Peter's body into the back of Steven's truck, under a tarp. When 'Steven' left that night, he took the body with him and dropped it at the Promenade later." Jade recalled that cold night, standing in front of Steven's truck, held tightly in his arms, thinking that this could be the beginning of something really good. Suddenly, everything started to spin.

Jade stood unsteadily and walked to the bathroom, Derrick following her progress with concerned eyes. They heard the unmistakable sound of Jade being sick, then water running. Jade came out of the bathroom within a few minutes, pale but composed. She turned haunted eyes to Daniel and said, "Go on. I need to hear all of it." Derrick stood behind Jade's chair and put his hands on her shoulders. She covered Derrick's hands with her own, and looked resolutely at Daniel. He looked at Jade's drawn expression, and he seemed reluctant to do further damage to her. After a moment of indecision, he continued. "Now you understand why I had to tell you. Your father killed Peter, as soon as he found out Peter knew about him. The same thing could have happened to you." Daniel once again seemed to be debating with himself about how much to say. Jade's disbelieving expression decided him.

"In fact, your father already planned to kill you once. That's why he disappeared." Jade thought a moment, then said, "The last time he was in touch with me, he said he wanted me to meet him at this house, the following night. I missed that meeting, because I didn't get his voice mail message in time. I remember thinking at the time how strange his message sounded. His voice sounded like his, but there was something very off about that message." Daniel nodded, "That's when it was going to happen. Your father and Timothy had been in touch several times since Peter's death. Timothy was keeping your father informed about your activities. Then Timothy and your father decided the time had come to take care of you. From what Timothy told me, he and

Dillon were going to make you a joint project. I didn't know that you didn't get the message until after the meeting was supposed to have taken place. I went over to your parents' house that afternoon, after Timothy told me what they were planning to do.

"I found your father going through your mother's things, throwing things around, apparently in a major snit over something. He was surprised to see me, not having seen me in person for several years. I sat down on the bed and watched him, trying to talk to him about what he was planning to do later. I was there when he left you the voicemail message on your cell phone that afternoon. I knew then that I would have to kill him, in order to stop him from hurting you. I didn't want him to realize my plan to stop him, so I changed the subject. I asked him what he was looking for in the bedroom. His answer confirmed that he was every bit as cold-blooded as I thought he was." The look he turned on Jade was strangely apologetic. "He told me that he realized when your mother was in the hospital that she wasn't as 'out of it' as she was pretending to be. When he confronted her, they argued, and she said something to him that made him think she knew about him. Jade, he panicked. He suffocated her. Apparently, he turned off her machines, used a pillow to stop her breathing, then plugged the machines back in and hurried out of the hospital. When they called him on his cell, he told me, he was sitting in his car in the parking garage. He called you, then waited a few minutes, then headed back into the hospital."

To Jade, this was one revelation too many. Daniel watching Derrick murmur soothingly to Jade for a moment. Jade stood unsteadily and again walked in the direction of the bathroom. After a few minutes, she came out and sat down again. It was obvious that she had been crying. To Daniel, she said, "How can I believe that my father killed my brother AND my mother?" How can I continue to exist in a world that permits such things to happen? And how can someone I've known and loved my whole life be capable of such evil?" Daniel nodded in sympathy, then said, "I agree with you. Your father was more brutal than anyone realized. I could do nothing about him killing Peter, or your mother, but I was going to be damned if I was going to let him hurt you, too." Derrick looked at Daniel with new respect and Jade immediately understood why. Instead of going the way of the rest of the Lawrence family, Daniel not only resisted the siren song of the family legacy, he had made it his life's work to try to understand what had happened, then to stop the killing. Jade said, "Daniel, tell me what you did to my father."

Daniel roughly wiped tears from his cheeks. "I killed him. Actually, I hurt him badly enough to know he could not survive, and I was hurt in the process." Daniel pulled up his shirt and Jade saw a pink, partially healed slash, across his abdomen. Daniel continued, "We both had knives. He slashed at me and I stepped back, quick enough to save my life, but not quick enough to avoid his blade. As he cut me, I extended my knife and cut him. He wasn't expecting it, and he didn't have time to step back. By the time he looked down, his guts were dangling on to the floor. His blood seemed to be instantly everywhere. But when I looked down at myself, at the gaping hole in my belly, I realized that at least some of that blood was mine. The copper smell was nauseating. I remember watching Dillon slide down the wall, clutching his stomach, then I must have lost consciousness.

"When I came to, Dillon was gone. I could see by the sickening trail of blood that he had somehow managed to drag himself out the door. He must have thought I was dead, or maybe he didn't have the energy to finish me off. I followed the trail outside, down the stairs, across the patio and into the dirt perimeter that led into the woods. I realized that, as he dragged his wounded body across the ground, he likely got dirt and all manner of contamination inside his wound, never mind the intestines I saw in a loop on the floor in front of him as I fell to the floor. Jade, no one could have survived that. I did check the woods, briefly, but I didn't find any other blood trail and I didn't find Dillon. He very likely crawled away to die. I cleaned up the blood, and put everything away as best I could remember. You see, I had been in your parents' house several times in the past, checking on Dillon to find out anything I could about whether he was a "good guy" or a "bad guy".

Jade dragged her downcast gaze back to Daniel, tears blurring his face. She couldn't take the intensity of his stare and she quickly looked back down again. "Daniel, I'm not even sure I believe what you are telling me." Daniel's expression immediately turned alarmed, he leaned forward, and reached out, pushing Jade's chin gently up so she was again looking into his eyes. "Jade, for your own safety, you MUST believe what I'm telling you. I'll provide you with all the proof you need. To doubt any part of what has happened and what is happening now could cost your life." The obvious concern on Daniel's face convinced her, more than anything else he could have said. Jade knew, believe or not, if there was anything else Daniel needed to tell her, this was going to be her one and only chance to hear him out. "Alright, I'll suspend disbelief, you go ahead and finish your story."

Daniel, still looking a bit uneasy, did as Jade requested. But mercifully, he had left the subject of her immediate family alone for the moment. Jade suddenly realized that, as of this moment, if she believed what Daniel was telling her, she HAD no immediate family left. Except Phyllis. If you'd want to call her that, she thought ruefully. Daniel said, "In 1962, my son was born, and I watched him so very carefully. There was nothing alarming in his behavior at first. Then, at about age 11, he started having nightmares. Still, I hoped it was a phase and had nothing to do with the other. Lianne still did not know about my family history. I had continued my research without involving her. In hindsight, I wish I had told her. When Timothy was 17, I found a book about my family. A sort of 'unauthorized biography'. The book provided information about several deaths within the Lawrence family, that had occurred at the hands of other family members and confirmed information I already had from my research years earlier.

"By this time, I realized that I had, at the very least, a twin brother and father who were both still alive. After that, I feared for the safety of my own little family. By this time, Timothy's behavior had deteriorated to the point that I could no longer tell myself he wouldn't someday give in to his urges, if, in fact, he had not already done so. I sent he and his mother away, and I convinced them to change their names. My son, Timothy Lawrence became Steven Lawry. I hoped it would be enough to keep them safe. I also hoped that Timothy would, in time, grow away from his roots and avoid the family curse altogether. Later, I found out that Timothy had already been taken into the Lawrence family fold and had been actively killing for two years."

Derrick caught Jade's reflexive expression of horror, and put an arm around her shoulders. Daniel's sympathetic expression indicated that he understood how his words affected Jade. He continued, his voice more gentle. "With the loss of my family, I threw myself into continuing my surveillance of my birth father, as well as my twin brother. As I said before, the one time I had approached Dillon, he rejected me, utterly, in spite of the fact that I was clearly related to him. I had never approached my father at all until fairly recently. Now, in addition to watching my brother and father, I knew I had to look into my own son. Soon after he turned 18, he changed his name back. I worried about the other Lawrence men finding him, but I needed have worried. Timothy had been doing research of his own. By the time I was able to get a handle on what kind of man he had become, it was obvious that he was lost to all that was good. What's more, he knew about the Lawrence family curse.

"The fault for that may be partly mine. In Timothy's apartment, I found some of my research notes, from years ago. Apparently Timothy had become curious about our family long before I thought he would. From what I've been able to work out since then, when his mother and I broke up housekeeping and I insisted they change their names to protect them, it was already too late. I spent the next several years following what Ben, then Dillon, then Timothy were doing. God help me, I should have killed all of them. But how would I have been different from them, if I had done that?" Daniel looked pleadingly at Jade. She had no answer, and fortunately, Daniel understood that. Instead, he decided to once again change direction.

"You know about the Lawrence house on Commercial Street, Jade, because I saw you there once. The night you found the trap door in the third floor library." Jade nodded, remembering the eerie feeling she had that someone was there, in the darkness. Daniel easily followed her thoughts. "Yes, that was me, sitting in the shadows watching you. I remember when you disappeared behind the wall panel, then came back out, you must have sensed that I was there. You said something, then you ran, like all the hounds of hell were after you! You left your flashlight, you know." Jade said, "I know. I figured that out later. Did you know about the diary?" Daniel shook his head. "No, I didn't. But Timothy did, later, when he broke into your house and stole the notes you were taking as you read the diary." Jade looked puzzled. "But how did Peter know about me at all?"

Daniel said, "He already knew about Peter, and he was keeping you on his radar, too. Remember it was before that, at the party, that Peter met you as

Steven." Jade thought back and realized he was right. Peter already did know her, at least slightly, before she broke into the Lawrence home and stole the diary. Jade asked, "If you were there, but you didn't know about the diary, did you know about the panel, and what else was behind it?" Daniel said, "Now I know. After you left that day I checked it out. There was a skeleton in servant clothes. Did you ever find out who she was? Was that diary hers?" Jade nodded. "I believe her name was Erin, and yes, I also believe the diary was hers. She was a servant girl in the Lawrence household in the late 1800's."

Daniel's eyes betrayed an important connection he had just made. "I remember reading, in the course of my research, about Tim and Trevor and Marie, and their servant, Erin. No, I didn't realize the false wall was there, in the Lawrence house. And I certainly didn't know about Erin being there." Jade asked, "So, what were you doing there, the night I showed up?" Daniel said, "I had been there several times in the past, Ben told me to feel free to use the house if I wanted to. I couldn't bring myself to sleep there, but I did go there, from time to time, just to think."

Daniel's face looked drawn and exhausted. Whoever said confession was good for the soul forgot to say how much work it was, Jade thought. Derrick moved around the kitchen soundlessly, putting tap water in Dixie cups for each of them. He sat back down at the table and said, by way of explanation, "I think we all could use a little water. I don't dare to use the glasses in the house or the spring water in the refrigerator, but the tap water should be okay, it's city water." All three of them sipped their water for a moment. Daniel, having recovered slightly, had one last thing on his mind. "Jade, it was me who sent you the jewelry case for appraisal. I was the 'family representative'. I didn't know until later, when Timothy broke into your house and took the diary notes, that there was a note inside the case, directing you to the diary, which you, amazingly enough, managed to actually find!" Jade smiled slightly at Daniel's praise, then said, "I can't understand what you hoped to accomplish by sending me the case in the first place."

Daniel said, "Ah! 'Therein lies the rub'! I knew you already, by reputation, and, unfortunately, by tracking down Dillon and his offspring. This was my way to begin to break the ice with you. I knew I couldn't approach you directly, your shock at seeing a face so similar to your father's may have caused you to bolt, then you likely would have mentioned it to your father. If he had any inkling that you knew about him and his 'activities', I didn't think he'd have had any qualm with killing you. I had to find a way to make you curious. Once you had the case, I knew it was likely that you'd research the Lawrence family. I also knew there were major issues with the family that you would definitely uncover, being as thorough a researcher as you are. Once you knew about the family, my plan was to very slowly, and very carefully, bring you into the picture. I didn't want to endanger you, but I knew that you NOT knowing could be just as dangerous for you.

"What I didn't count on, which was very good, was the diary, and how far that went to get you up to speed. What I also didn't count on, which was bad, was how very dangerous both your father and Timothy would be, putting you in much more danger than I had planned. Daniel smiled, somewhat brokenly, and reached out to cover Jade's hand. She didn't pull back this time. "Daniel, thank you for doing everything you could do, even risking your own life, to try to keep me safe. I feel badly for the things I've endured, but I feel even worse for everything you've had to go through. Maybe now, things can be different. I've gathered a great deal of evidence against Timothy. Now that Ben's dead, and my father's dead…" Jade found herself unexpectedly choking up at the mention of her father, then she swallowed the pain and continued, "…if we can get Timothy off the streets, maybe we can all go back to living a normal life."

Daniel's sudden smile lit his haggard face from within. "Now THAT sounds like a plan! In the next day or two, let's get everything we have together, and go to the police. I'm sure, if we show them the evidence we both have on Timothy, they'll start an investigation of their own. Once they do that, Timothy is as good as locked up! Jade, I need to believe that there can be life for me after this. Please tell me, after all this is over, that you'll stay in touch with me? You are all the family I have left now, and I'd be honored to be "Uncle Dan". Daniel's eyes suddenly glazed, and he abruptly fell silent. Jade opened her mouth to call his name and Derrick suddenly pushed her to the floor. What was happening!? From under the table, Jade saw the lower half of Daniels' body, sitting in the chair. She watched in horror as a dark stain began to spread in the crotch of his jeans. Daniel's body suddenly lurched to the left and Jade heard the sickening crack of his lifeless head hitting the wall. One arm dangled below the level of the table. The hand was twitching. Derrick, gun already drawn, motioned with it for Jade to stay put.

Derrick crept around the table and left its shelter next to the kitchen wall. Jade saw his feet as he retreated down the hallway, against the wall, stopping to listen with every step. When he was out of view, Jade became aware of a stealthy sound coming from the opposite direction. She turned her head and stared directly into the barrel of a silenced pistol. Timothy, crouched next to the kitchen table, was looking at her with a bemused expression. "Well, cousin! How've you been? How's the family? Dead? Oh dear, forgive me. That's gotta suck, huh?" He smiled at her then, and there was no longer anything even remotely attractive about him, she thought. Jade opened her mouth to scream and Timothy put his index finger to his lips, motioning for silence. He waggled the gun at her meaningfully. Jade's mouth closed with an audible snap. He grabbed her by the hair and dragged her out from under the table. Poking the gun painfully into her ribs, he prodded her to the front door. Timothy pulled Jade into his arms, protecting himself with her body and holding the gun to her temple as they crossed the driveway and shuffled awkwardly down to the street.

It was fully dark now, and there were no lights coming from the front of her parents' house, or any other house close by. Jade knew she would have to help herself, at least for the moment. Trying to ignore the gun at her head, she kicked Timothy's knee sharply, earning a loud exclamation from Timothy, and the white-hot pain of the gun smashing into the side of her head. The world turned filmy for several precious moments, then Jade's wounded head began to clear. Timothy again swore at her, cruelly yanking her body against his, to stabilize her. Through teeth gritted in pain, he said, "Cut the shit, bitch. I'm getting out of here, with or without you. If I have to leave you, it'll be with a bullet in your head."

Timothy dragged Jade down the street, opened the passenger side door on his black Mercedes and threw Jade inside. He pushed her over to the driver's side and climbed into the passenger seat. He immediately reached across Jade and locked the doors and windows. He jammed the gun viciously into Jade's ribcage, out of view of any passersby. "Start the car and drive away. Slowly. Jade did as she was instructed. She knew he wouldn't kill her while she was driving as the car would likely crash, hurting or killing him in the process. Then she thought about that. She realized she was literally in the driver's seat. She could decide to kill Timothy right now. It would only cost her own life to take him out of the equation, here and now. Jade's foot stomped the accelerator.

Chapter 45

As Jade struggled to control the car long enough to get up to a lethal speed, she caught movement at the corner of her eye. Looking right and left as she drove, she saw it again. There was something moving in the rear view! She fastened her eyes on the road, keeping close watch on the mirror. There it was again! In the back seat, behind Timothy, sat Derrick, his gun pointed at the back of Timothy's head. Thank God! Jade realized that Derrick couldn't just shoot Timothy without taking the chance that Timothy would then shoot her reflexively. She realized that Derrick would want her to make a grab for Timothy's gun and get it pointed away from her for the moment he needed to shoot Timothy. She decided to abandon her plan to kill the both of them with speed. This sounded like a much better plan. She turned the car on to a dark, abandoned straightaway, then she gave a faint nod, hoping Derrick would catch the signal that she was about to move. She took both hands off the steering wheel and grabbed Timothy's gun. She saw a momentary expression of surprise on Timothy's face, then he pulled the trigger and the window behind her head was instantly replaced by whistling wind. Derrick put his gun directly against the back of Timothy's head.

Timothy's surprised expression changed to one, strangely enough, of relief, then with a loud boom, Timothy's face lost all expression. He slumped in Jade's direction and she screamed, involuntarily, but grabbed the steering wheel and guided the car to the shoulder. She slammed the gearshift into Park and jumped out of the car. Timothy's body dropped on to the seat where she had been. Derrick got out of the car and ran to Jade, pulling her into his arms. "Good job, baby. Excellent job. I thought I was going to lose you!" Jade stood for a moment, looking over Derrick's shoulder at Timothy's body. Finally, this was over. Really and completely over. "Derrick, I love you…I'm so sorry…Thank you so much!" Overwhelmed by a strange mixture of sorrow, horror, regret and relief, Jade wrapped Derrick in her arms and was comforted by the warmth of his return embrace. "Goodbye, Daniel, Thank you", she whispered into the night wind.

Epilogue:

Six months later

The night sky was tossed with diamond stars. Jade lay quietly in bed, Derrick's warm leg possessively draped across her. She drifted on a soft wave of sleep. A faint sound jarred her to wakefulness. Around her, the room had changed while she slept. Her logical mind realized the room didn't change, she had been transported here in sleep. A small, beautiful woman approached the side of her bed. She leaned down and placed a warm, soft hand on Jade's cheek. She smiled down into Jade's eyes. Even before she spoke, Jade knew who she was. "Erin", she breathed sleepily. Erin's smile broadened. "Yes, Jade, it's me. Thank you for everything you've done and all that you had to sacrifice to do it. I'm so glad that, in the end, a Lawrence woman DID find my diary, just as I intended. You did everything I could have asked. Trevor and his sweet Marie now rest easily, because the truth is finally known." Jade's sleeping mind watched with undeniable satisfaction as Erin gradually faded back into the sands of time.

September, 2006

"You're going to be late for school, Alex. You've got to get up, right now!" Listening intently for a moment, Phyllis started up the stairs. "Alex! It's your first day of high school!". Inside Alex's room, there was the sound of blankets shifting, then bare feet padding across the floor. The door was suddenly flung open in Phyllis' face. "Back off, mom! I'm up! Jesus-friggin'-Christ!" Alex slammed the door in his mother's shocked face and began to whistle tunelessly as he turned away from the door and headed for his bathroom for a long, hot shower. Bemused, Alex watched as the blood caked on his feet turned pink in the water and disappeared into the drain. He faintly heard a telephone ringing. As he toweled off, he looked through the bathroom window into the back yard. Just inside the line of trees, and only visible from his elevated vantage point, was a patch of newly turned earth. Alex turned to the mirror and smiled into his own gold-flecked hazel eyes, remembering his magnificent evening. His reverie was shattered by his mother's grating voice shrieking at him from downstairs. "Alex, have you seen Beth Danforth? Her mother's been searching for her all night."

THE END

411

71497731R00226

Made in the USA
Lexington, KY
21 November 2017